PASSION DENIED

"Come sit down, Raegan," Chase said, "we must talk."

Raegan reluctantly took a seat across from him, an angry defiance in her eyes. "I don't know what we could talk about. You made yourself perfectly clear last night. I got your message clear enough, and you can bet I'll never come near your bed again."

"I wish you wouldn't take that attitude about what I said last night," Chase said in a low, regretful voice. "Surely you can see it wasn't right, you bein' —"

With a dark, scathing look Raegan finished his sentence. "Anne's daughter! That's a poor excuse and you know it. Why don't you be honest and admit that you found me lacking as your bed partner, that I fell short of what you're used to."

"That's not true. I have never before found such complete satisfaction as I did with you last night."

Other *Leisure Books* by Norah Hess

DEVIL IN SPURS
HAWKE'S PRIDE
KENTUCKY BRIDE

Mountain Rose

NORAH HESS

LEISURE BOOKS  NEW YORK CITY

A LEISURE BOOK®

March 1993

Published by

Dorchester Publishing Co., Inc.
276 Fifth Avenue
New York, NY 10001

Printed in the United States of America.

To Sissy, my first born

Mountain Rose

Chapter One

1868 Idaho/Oregon

In mid-March the weather changed in Idaho. The wind came from the south, bringing a warm rain. After two days of steadily falling rain, the winter snow was gone.

Red-headed Raegan O'Keefe, her feet crunching on the stones and gravel, left the foothills and followed a rough trail that wound up the mountain. In a few minutes, she came to a large boulder that over looked Minersville in all its squalor.

How many times had she come here? she asked herself as she climbed to the boulder's flat top and sat down. Dozens of times, she knew, drawing up her knees and wrapping her arms around them. Her vision blurred with uncontrollable tears as she gazed unseeing at the clear blue sky through a break in the tall spruce.

She knuckled the wetness from her eyes. There were facts that had to be faced. Her mother was dying and she could do nothing about it. For over a year now, death had beckoned Anne O'Keefe, and soon she would go to meet it. The slow consumption that had eaten away at her lungs for several years was winning the battle.

"Oh, Papa," the grieving girl cried out to her father, now dead two years, "couldn't you see that dragging her from one gold field to another, living under terrible conditions, was killing her?"

Raegan promptly put the accusing thought from her mind as she remembered her father—big and splendid, his throaty laughter, his deep love for his wife and daughter. She shook her head sadly. William O'Keefe's unquenchable belief that at any time he would make a rich strike had blinded him to everything else. The day he was shot and killed by claim-jumpers, he left his small family nearly destitute.

She patted the rough head of her pet, who scrambled up beside her and nudged her leg for attention. "What is to become of us, Lobo?" she asked the big wolf. The animal licked her hand as though in sympathy.

Raegan raised her slim, work-roughened hand to massage the knotted muscles at the back of her neck. Mama had said once that if Raegan were ever be left alone, she should go live with her grandparents, or with her Uncle Chase. But she didn't know Mama's relatives, had never seen them. These grandparents—would they want her? They must be up in age now and might not like like the idea of having a young person thrust upon them.

She picked up a brittle stick, unconsciously breaking it into small pieces. As for her Uncle Chase, she doubted she would like him, or that he would be very fond of her. He and Papa hadn't gotten along. Papa had said once that Chase Donlin was as ornery a cuss as he'd ever seen.

But Mama had shaken her head, claiming that Chase wasn't mean-tempered at all. He was only a teenager when Papa had known him and had acted the way he had because he resented the man who was taking his big sister away from him.

"I'm sure he's grown into a fine young man," she'd added. "He's probably married by now and has a nice family."

Papa had snorted and teased, "I doubt there's a woman in those hills who would take him on as a husband." Mama had smilingly ruffled his hair and the subject was dropped.

"And that's all I know about this uncle, Lobo. He's bad-tempered and may be married. And—oh yes, it was mentioned once that he trapped for a living." Raegan put an arm around the animal's thick, rough neck. "What if he, or his wife, doesn't want us?"

Raegan dropped her head to her knees, tears gathering in her eyes and spilling down her cheeks. An uncertain future lay ahead of her. Was she strong enough to meet and conquer it?

Back in the two-room shack Raegan had called home for the past two and half years, her mother was composing a letter. Frail and looking much older than her thirty-six years, Anne O'Keefe sat propped up in bed, her thin fingers clutching the stub of a pencil, moving it slowly across the paper. Her usual neat letters were almost a scrawl this early spring day.

It was a time-consuming and arduous chore, writing this message to a family she hadn't seen in twenty years. She paused often, gripped with spasms of coughing that wracked her rail-thin body. Then, after spitting the blood-streaked phlegm into a rag she kept tucked under her pillow, she had to rest before forcing herself to continue the letter.

She was coughing up her life's blood and she knew it. It was imperative that she get this missive off to brother Chase as soon as possible. She must not die and leave her lovely Raegan alone in this rough mining town.

After another bout of coughing, a tear slipped down her gaunt cheek as her fingers played with the frayed edge of the blanket lying across her waist. "Oh, William." She sighed. "Why did you have to go away and leave us?"

Anne had grieved deeply at the loss of her husband, not once blaming him for dragging his family all over Idaho, ever searching for that elusive gold strike he'd always been so sure of making one day. She did not let herself remember her parents' warning that life would be hard with the big, laughing man. Nor had she blamed him that he had left his family with empty pockets and a nearly bare larder. He had been a good and faithful husband with never a harsh word to her, and she had loved him dearly.

But even as she had grieved, Anne knew that somehow she must provide a living for herself and her daughter. Pride would not allow her to return to those who had warned her against William, to let them know that their predictions had come true. Not that they would remind her that they had been right. Mama and Papa Donlin weren't like that. But in their hearts they would think it, and she would do anything to protect her daughter from the fact that William had allowed their prophesy to come true.

A week after her husband had been laid to rest, when very little food remained in the shack, Anne made a descision. She hung a sign on the shack's outside wall, advertising that she would do the miners' washing for a reasonable fee. O'Keefe had made many friends in the mining community, and these rough men readily brought his widow their mud-crusted clothing to be laundered.

For two years, she and Raegan had bent over great tubs of hot, soapy water, scrubbing all sizes of masculine garb, thus managing to keep body and soul together.

Then Anne's persistent cough had finally sent her to the old doctor, whose office was upstairs over a saloon. After carefully listening to her lungs for several minutes, he gently told her what she had suspected. She had consumption in its last stages.

Her health had deteriorated rapidly after that until there came a morning two months ago when she didn't have the strength to get out of bed. As she grew weaker and weaker, she swallowed her pride for her daughter's sake and now sat writing to brother Chase. He would come for Raegan, she knew, and take her to her grandparents.

The loud crashing of some animal in the chaparral below brought Raegan out of her pensive mood. She should be getting back down the mountain. She had left the old Indian woman, Mahalla, with her mother, and though she was as adept as Raegan when it came to helping Mama when one of her coughing spells came on, Mahalla was not strong enough to climb the mountain to look for her should Mama's condition worsen.

Raegan left the spot she often came to for solace and, with Lobo at her heels, began to retrace her steps. What would become of this old woman of the Shoshoni tribe after . . . after Mama was gone? There was no one who would take care of her, give her food and shelter. She had outlived her husband, and her only son had been killed in a battle with another tribe. Sadly, and to Raegan's irate disbelief, Mahalla's son-in-law had refused to take his wife's mother into their home.

Her eyes sparked angrily as she remembered finding the white-haired woman up in the mountains six months ago. She had been lying under a ledge, curled up, waiting to die. What a slow trip it had been, getting the old soul down off the mountain. Mahalla, weak from hunger and stiff of joints, could not climb up on the mare, and she could not walk alone. Raegan had been forced to half carry the thin little body into Minersville.

But what a blessing it had been, the old Indian's coming into the O'Keefe's lives. Through nourishing food and plenty of rest, Mahalla soon regained her health and much of her strength. With her great knowledge of herbs and barks, she had concocted a syrup that had, at first, helped Raegan's mother. And when the day came that Anne could no longer leave her bed, their new friend had tended to her needs, leaving Raegan free to launder the clothing she found stacked on the rickety porch each morning.

It was not unusual for Raegan to find other things on the porch as well—a haunch of venison or a couple of skinned rabbits wrapped up in a piece of paper. And at least twice a week there would be a string of fish joining the game.

Raegan wondered about the fish. She knew that none of the miners would take time from their diggings to stand and wait patiently for a fish to bite at a lure thrown into the water. On the other hand, it would be a simple matter to bring down a deer or rabbit that ventured too close to where they panned for gold.

She had a sneaky suspicion that the fish came from Mahalla's two teenage grandsons. The grandmother spoke fondly of them, and Raegan was sure the affection was returned. Had those boys been grown men, she doubted their grandmother would now be living with two white women.

Raegan entered the single winding street of Minersville, walking through ankle-deep dust and soil. In the daylight hours, the hurriedly thrown-together town was almost ghostly, she thought, returning a greeting from an occasional woman leaning in the doorway of her shack, answering that there was no change in her mother's condition. There was no one on the street, and all was quiet around the store that carried almost anything a miner and his family might want. Inside the long building was also a place where letters could be dropped off by men passing through. Mail was a hit-or-miss affair, and sometimes letters sent by relatives never reached their destination. Consequently, the residents of the shack and tent settlement didn't receive much mail. It didn't really matter to them, though. Most had left their real names behind and couldn't have been reached had anyone cared to do so.

It was equally silent inside the saloon and brothel situated at the opposite end of the street. Her lips twisted wryly. The "girls" were sleeping a no doubt richly deserved sleep. But once darkness fell and the men left their diggings, the women would be busy. After a couple drinks of raw whiskey at the saloon and a fast bite to eat at the Chinaman's Diner, the men would head for the pleasure house. There would follow drunken singing and laughter until the wee hours of the morning. Much gold dust would be left in the greedy hands of the whores.

Thank goodness their racket was far enough away not to bother Mama, Raegan thought, coming to her shack and stepping inside. She stood in the room that served as kitchen and living room, her eyes skimming over the walls, frowning at the wide cracks where the sun shone through.

The two-room house had been made from unseasoned green lumber, and as the hot Idaho sun dried it, the boards had warped and pulled apart from each other. Raegan shivered, remembering how the cold winter wind had whistled through the boards, bringing drifting snow in with it. Papa had nailed tarpaulin over the worst parts, but a person was never completely warm until summer came.

And summer was almost as bad. The place heated up like an oven, and bugs and flies entered at will—even snakes occasionally. Raegan's gaze drifted to the old woman dropping a handful of potatoes into a pot of simmering stew.

"How is she?" she queried softly.

"She finish letter. Now wait for you to take to store," Mahalla answered as she stirred a long-handled spoon through the meat and potatoes. "It tire her, the writing. She rest now."

Raegan moved quietly across the bare floor and peaked into her mother's room. The sun shone through the small window over the bed, bathing Anne O'Keefe's thin, ravaged face with its light. The fever-bright eyes were open. When they fell on Raegan, the pale lips parted in a smile. She lifted a wasted hand and beckoned Raegan forward.

Raegan hurried to sit on the edge of the bed and take the bony hand into hers. As she gently rubbed it, trying to impart some of her own warmth into the icy one, Anne spoke carefully, in order not to start coughing again.

"Your walk has put roses into your cheeks, honey." Raegan smiled at her and gently smoothed the white-streaked hair from Anne's forehead. "I was lying here wondering if the wildflowers are blooming yet."

Tears threatened to choke Raegan. Mama so loved the wildflowers of Idaho, their brightness and beauty in a wild, harsh land. She gulped back a sob. There had been so little beauty in Mama's life. One did not find such in rough mining towns.

Over the constriction in her throat, Raegan managed to say, "There are no blossoms yet, but I saw quite a few buds ready to burst into bloom any day now. I'll pick you a bouquet then."

Anne did not express her regret aloud that she would never again see a flower bloom, but for a flickering second her eyes spoke the thought. She said instead, "I've finished my letter to brother Chase. Maybe before supper you will take it to the store. I pray someone will soon come through on their way to Oregon."

"Uncle Chase is not really your brother, is he, Mama?" Raegan asked.

Anne smiled fondly as she recalled the gangly youth who had challenged William that day twenty years ago, arguing hotly that a shiftless drifter wasn't good enough for his sister.

"By blood, no, he is not," she answered. "But in my heart he has always been my true brother."

"Do you feel like talking about him?" Raegan smiled down at the pale face animated with memories of a very young Chase Donlin.

"Yes, I think I would," Anne answered, then was silent a moment, gathering her thoughts of long ago. She began speaking finally, in sad fondness. "Three months before my tenth birthday my father died of scarlet fever. He was a wonderful husband and father, and Mama and I missed him terribly. As I look back, I realize that he spoiled Mama a bit, for she was quite helpless without him. When, six months later, Chase's father began courting her, she was ready to be looked after again."

Anne paused, staring thoughtfully at the ceiling. "I don't think Mama loved John Donlin when she married him, but in a short time I'm sure she did. She had to have, to stay with him in an environment entirely new to her. You see, your grandmother had always been a town person, leading a pampered life somewhere in Utah. I forget the name of the town."

She smiled ruefully. "That way of life came to a stop when her new husband moved us from our townhouse to his cabin in the wilderness of Oregon. Other than Indians, I don't believe there were any other inhabitants within ten miles of us. My stepfather was, and still is, I guess, a trapper. He made his living that way, and a good one it was, although you'd never know it from his sparsely furnished home. Of course Mama soon took care of that," she added with a little laugh.

"Papa Donlin adored her, and when she let it be known that she wasn't happy with the sturdy, hand-crafted furniture in the large cabin, he took her to San Francisco and let her buy whatever she wanted. The chosen pieces were shipped up the coast to Oregon, then delivered to us by mule-drawn wagons."

Anne paused again, a gentleness coming into her eyes. "I'll never forget the first time I saw Chase. He was six years old—a shy, wild little boy with a dirty face and unbrushed hair hanging to his shoulders. His mother had died at his birth, and he had been mostly raised by an old Indian woman who kept house for him and his father.

"My, how he stared at Mama and me. In all probability, we were the first white women he'd ever seen. At any rate, Mama's sweet smile and soft, coaxing voice soon brought him from behind the old woman's skirt and to her side. I remember him sitting on her lap, peering across at me with his big dark eyes. I was a bit jealous of him at first, but before I knew it he had crept into my heart and I had acknowledged him as my little brother."

Anne closed her eyes, and after a minute, thinking that her mother had fallen asleep, Raegan started to rise. She sat back down when Anne spoke again.

"I've often wondered over the years what kind of man Chase grew into. I'm sure he's handsome. He was a handsome little boy and teenager. I fear, though, that like all the men who trap for a living, he may be hard and rough-like. It can hardly be helped, living in such harsh country."

She gave Raegan's hand a weak squeeze. "He'd be gentle with you because you're my daughter, if for no other reason. And your grandparents will love you dearly."

With a tired sigh, the ill woman drifted off to sleep and missed the tears that sprang into her daughter's eyes. She didn't realize how her last remark had unintentionally stated clearly that before long that daughter would be with the family she had left so many years ago.

Spring had also arrived in Oregon, and the trees were beginning to sprout pale green leaves that shimmered in the bright March sun. As Chase Donlin rode along a winding, rocky trail, a warm-scented wind swept down from the surrounding hills, making him breathe deeply. He shrugged out of his buckskin jacket and folded it over the pommel of the saddle. It was good to feel the heat of the sun on his body again. The past winter had been a long, cold one.

And lonesome too, he added to himself, swaying easily to the stallion's gait. He'd only seen Liza three times in all those snow-filled months.

His hard, handsome face stirred with an amused grin. The Widow Jenkins hadn't liked that at all. That lady did like her loving.

Chase leaned over and patted the black stallion's proud arching neck. "I hope she's well rested up, Sampson," he said, "for I can give her all the time she wants today."

He rode on, tall in the saddle, wide-shouldered and narrow-hipped. He was a man who was a law unto himself, seeking no fights, but avoiding none. He was much like the wilderness he laid his traps in. Calm, ruthless when need be, terrible when his anger was roused, he was fast with his fists, a good shot, and deadly with the

Bowie knife shoved into the top of his knee-length moccasins.

In short, he was a man not to fool with, as some had found out. Trappers in the region said of him that though he was an honest man, he was the meanest cuss in the woods. When Chase Donlin was in a rage, they said, a sane man would walk a wide circle around him.

Unaware of all that was thought and said about him, Chase had gone his own way, helping his neighbors in need, but otherwise having little to do with them. His one friend, who lived with him off and on, was a half-breed named Jamie Hart. He, too, was adept with the knife, and they made a formidable pair to come up against in a fight. Consequently, they were seldom bothered.

Chase glanced up at the sun approaching its zenith and lifted his mount into a gallop. "We're never gonna get to Liza's if we keep lazin' along like this, Sampson."

An hour later, the rocky trail brought him out of the forest of pine and into a grassy swale where a small cabin sat in its center. Liza's small dog began a shrill barking as Chase approached the building, making the stallion shake his head and snort in annoyance.

"Is your mistress still in bed?" He spoke to the yipping dog. "Usually she's half way across the yard by now."

He wondered suddenly if the widow was all right. She had to hear this damn dog carrying on.

The cabin door burst open then, and a curvaceous dark-haired woman bolted from the cabin, running toward him. He pulled Sampson to a plunging halt.

"There you are, Liza." Chase smiled down at the attractive face lifted to him. "I was beginning to think something had happened to you." He was ready to dismount and grab the widow into his arms, then paused. For the first time he saw the man leaning indolently in the doorway.

Calvin Long. Chase's lips curled slightly. Liza must be in a hard way to take this one in her bed. Knowing the woman's randy nature, he had suspected for some time that she took her pleasure from other men when he wasn't available, but to wallow around with lazy, no account Calvin Long?

The man lived in a run-down shack way back in the hills, along with an Indian and a half-dozen undernourished half-breed children. Not only was the man shiftless, he was a thief as well. He stole the animals caught in other men's traplines, and anything else he could lay his hands on.

Chase remained in the saddle. Although he didn't care how many men Liza slept with, he had no intention of climbing between blankets that still held another man's warmth and scent.

"Since you have company, Liza," he said coolly, keeping his seat, "I'll visit you another time."

"Oh, Chase, honey." Liza caressed a palm up and down his buckskin-clad thigh, afraid there was some tell-tale evidence that she had just spent two lusty hours in bed with the man lounging in the shadows. "Calvin was just leaving. He was kind enough to deliver my monthly supplies."

I'll just bet he was, Chase thought as Liza lowered her lids to hide the anxiety in her eyes.

She had been widowed for three years and desperately wanted a new husband, not only to appease her physical needs, but to support her as well. What money her dead husband had left her was fast dwindling away. She had, a long time ago, decided that Chase Donlin would be that man.

When she saw Chase run his eyes over Calvin, she, too, ran a fast searching glance over the man's stocky body. A small frown creased her forehead. The two top buttons of his fly were undone. Had Chase noticed also?

Chase had, as well as the look of spent passion in the man's slitted eyes. Giving Liza's visitor a pointed look, he said as he lifted the reins, "I'll be on my way, Liza. I just stopped by to see how you were doin'."

As the stunned woman stared at him openmouthed, he wheeled Sampson and galloped back in the direction he had come.

Chase chuckled as he rode out of sight and slowed his mount to a comfortable lope. He knew Liza had marriage on her mind. She had hinted at it often enough. But it was a hint he chose to ignore. Marriage was not for him—especially not to a woman like the widow. Hell, every day that he was out running his trap line, he'd have to worry that she was entertaining some man in his absence.

Be that as it may, Chase thought ruefully, his present condition still exisited. He badly needed a woman. He toyed with two thoughts. There was Rosie and her three whores upstairs in the only saloon in the small village of Big Pine.

Then there was the long-standing offer of choosing himself an Indian maid from a neighboring village, an offer made by Chief Wise Man, leader of a Paiute tribe, for saving his life once. He had never taken the old man up on his proffered generosity.

One morning three years ago, he had come upon the aging Paiute chief cornered by a hungry bear. A couple of shots into the air had frightened the animal, and the shaken old man who had looked death in the face had, from that moment, been Chase's firm friend. Whenever Chase came across him, he was urged to visit his village and choose himself a woman.

When Chase came to a forking of the trail he drew rein, still not having made up his mind between the whores and an Indian girl. The path on the right would take him to Chief Wise Man's camp. He wondered if they were still there or had moved to a different location now that it had warmed up. The Northern Paiutes moved often to hunt, setting up their camp around lakes and marshes, for they were fishermen as well.

I'll never know sitting here, he thought, and lifting the reins, he urged the mount onto the Indian trail. A pretty little redskin might be just what he needed to wile away the summer months.

Although many of the trappers had moved Indian women into their cabins, Chase never had. He didn't want any woman, red or white, underfoot all the time.

In a short time his destination appeared around a bend in the trail. He pulled the stallion up beneath the screen of a low-sweeping spruce and ran his glance over the camp. They were still there. There was a cookfire in front of each cone-shaped house constructed of brush. Children ran and played while women and young girls busied themselves with a variety of work. He grinned when his eyes fell on the old men sitting around a large separate fire, smoking their clay pipes, no doubt boasting of past glories. He saw no evidence of younger braves, nor had he expected to. They were out hunting.

Chase let his gaze drift over the young women and teenage girls. There were a couple of real beauties among them. A throbbing set up in his loins. Either of them could be his for the asking.

Still, he hesitated. What if neither one wanted to go away with a white stranger? They might not want to leave their people, might have an Indian sweetheart. It was not his nature to impose his will on another person, especially a woman. She came to him willingly or not at all.

Chase sat a while longer, still debating. Then, with some regret, he turned Sampson around and headed back toward the trail that would take him to Big Pine. It looked like it would be one of Rosie's girls. He needed to replenish a few supplies anyway. He would wait awhile, then go visit Liza again. He felt sure that the next time he came riding in, he would find her alone. The widow wouldn't take a chance on displeasing him again.

Chapter Two

The sun was traveling toward the western horizon when Chase approached the rude frontier village and drew up in front of a long, weather-beaten building. The sign over its door proclaimed it to be Hank's Saloon and Jake's Grocery.

Hank and Jake were brothers and owned the building jointly. Jake was married and the father of several children. Hank was a bachelor, having the use of Rosie or one of her girls when the whim hit him. According to the girls, that fancy hit him quite often. They didn't complain, though. He took no part of the money they charged their customers, and though he was a lusty fellow in bed, he was no worse than most.

When Chase stepped into the dim interior of the saloon, amusement sparked his eyes. One of the whores had just stepped through the door of

Hanks's living quarters, he right behind her.

"Hi there, Donlin," he called, unashamedly buttoning up his twill trousers. "You been here long?" He gave the skinny whore a light swat on the rear and laughed. "Ole Nellie here was slow gettin' the job done today. I don't think she likes her work anymore."

"That bein' the case, then, I'll take one who does." Chase grinned at Hank as the heavy-set man came around behind the long bar. "Which one is rested up, do you think?"

"Rosie, I reckon. She's been in her room all day." Hank poured them each a glass of whiskey. "The snow gone and all, ain't you gonna be visitin' the widow?"

"I just come from her place," Chase said after taking a long swallow from his glass. "She had company."

"Calvin Long, I'll wager." Hank looked at Chase for confirmation.

Chase looked up in surprise. "Why do you say that?"

"Joe Smith's trapline runs back of the widow's cabin. He's seen Long visitin' her all winter." After a pause, he added, "He's seen that Indian wife of his follerin' him too. Ole Liza had better be careful. One of two things could happen to her—maybe both."

"What are you talkin' about, Hank?"

"Well, that squaw of Long's could put a knife in her back, or he could put a baby in her belly. He puts one in his wife every winter. I'd say he's very careless with his seed."

Chase nodded agreement thoughtfully. What

Hank said was true. Liza could very well end up with a belly full, then claim the child was his. "I think I've made my last visit to Widow Jenkins," he said.

He drained his glass and turned from the bar. "I think I'll go wake Rosie up now."

Chase climbed the rickety stairs, the steps worn smooth from the countless feet that had trod them. He stopped in front of the first door leading off the narrow hallway and pushed it open.

Five minutes later he was back downstairs, throughly disgusted. Rosie had complained that she wasn't feeling well enough to bed him, and he believed her. She wasn't the sort to turn away a customer otherwise.

He was debating having another whiskey when a single mournful wolf howl drifted in from the hills. Night was not too far off, and Chase wanted to get home before dark overtook him. Those varmints up there were hungry, and Sampson would look very tasty to them.

Chase stepped through the door that separated the two businesses and was greeted with a warm smile. Mabel West stood behind the rough plank counter, a youngster riding her hip. She was a pleasant woman, one who had lost most of her attractiveness from birthing a baby every year. She was a good woman and a hard worker, well liked by everyone.

"What can I do for you today, Chase?" She continued to smile as she hoisted the child further up on her hip.

Chase ruffled her clinging son's hair. He liked children, and the only thing he regretted in not having a wife was that he would never have a son. Pa had always been onto him that if he didn't produce a son, the Donlin name would die with him.

He pushed the thought away and turned his attention back to Mabel. "I ran out of flour this mornin'," he said, "and you'd better throw in some lard and salt pork."

Mabel placed the child on the floor and quickly gathered up the items and shoved them into a fustian sack. As she totted up the bill, the little boy whined and dragged at her skirt.

"He's cuttin' a new tooth," Mabel explained her son's behavior as she took Chase's money. "Usually he's the best behaved of all my youngins'. Takes after his Pa, I guess." She smiled fondly at the mention of her husband.

Chase kept his opinion of her husband to himself. Although a decent man, Jake West was as lazy as Calvin Long. As he picked up the bag of supplies, he noted that Mabel was expecting again. Ole Jake wasn't lazy in bed, he thought with amusement.

He wished Mabel good-day and turned to leave. "Wait a minute," she exclaimed, "I almost forgot. A stranger passin' by today dropped off a letter for you."

Surprise widened Chase's eyes. "I can't think of anyone who would be writin' to me."

"Well, it has your name on it. Chase Donlin, Big Pine, Oregon." Mabel handed him the envelope.

Chase recognized the handwriting at once, and his hard features softened with pleasure. "It's from my sister, Anne," he said huskily. While

Mabel waited expectingly, he turned and hurried from the store. He swung onto Sampson's back and sent him racing along the two-mile trail to his cabin. As he pressed the mount on, eager to get home and read what Anne had to say after so many years, his mind went back to the days of their youth.

Ever since he could remember, he had loved and adored his big sister, He would gladly have laid down his life for her had it ever been necessary. He only vaguely remembered the years before Anne and her mother had come to live with him and Pa. It was as though his existence had begun with their arrival. His little bare feet had followed his new sister everywhere as they explored the forests, climbed hills looking for wildflowers, and played with the Indian children from the same tribe he had almost visited this afternoon.

Then Anne had grown into a young lady, sweet and gentle like her mother. She was lovely, with her long black hair and warm brown eyes. The family was always tripping over some young trapper come to court her.

But he hadn't tripped over anyone, he remembered humorously. He had been off somewhere pouting.

None of the callers had impressed Anne until one day William O'Keefe stopped by the cabin to water his horse. He was a big, stocky man with dark red hair and laughing green eyes. He was heading northwest, he'd said, going to make his fortune looking for gold.

Chase had seen the immediate attraction between his sister and the stranger and he had been hit with a frightful thought. Was this the man she would choose? The man who would take her away from him?

His fear became reality. Two weeks later, against their parents' wishes, and despite his own angry attack on William O'Keefe, Anne married the big, friendly Irishman. As the newlyweds had ridden off, Anne, her face glowing with happiness, had called back that she would write as soon as they were settled somewhere.

The first couple of years she had written, always from a different town. But even though O'Keefe couldn't seem to settle down in one spot, Anne's happiness came through in her letters.

But finally messages from her had stopped, and the family hadn't known all these years whether she was dead or alive. They had questioned every stranger who came through from Idaho, but no one had ever heard of William O'Keefe. They fought the idea that she and her husband had fallen prey to Indians, but couldn't think of any other reason that would keep Anne from writing to them.

Chase sighed softly. In the interim, his mother Molly had died one winter from pneumonia, and two years ago Pa had been caught in a blizzard, lost his way home, and frozen to death before he was found. How sad this news would make Anne. For the first time, there was a return address on her letter. He would be able to write her, even go visit her.

Sampson lunged up a small knoll, and his own cabin and outbuildings stood before Chase. He paid no attention to the sturdy, but weather-beaten with the years buildings. They had been there since he could remember and he took them for granted, as he did the green hills and valleys he trapped and hunted. Besides, right now nothing could distract his mind from the letter in his shirt pocket.

He rode past the long, rambling cabin and on to the barn, where he dismounted. He opened a large, heavy door and led the stallion inside. He unsaddled him, then climbed to the loft and pitched down fragrant hay for the animal to eat.

Back down on the barn floor again, he picked up his supplies and hurried to the cabin. It was damp inside, so he took ten minutes to build a fire, and another five minutes to start a pot of coffee to brewing. The sun dropped behind the treeline, throwing the cabin into darkness. He struck a sulpher stick on the underneath of the table, swearing under his breath that he had forgotten to buy kerosene for the lamps.

Pulling a chair up to where he took his meals, he shoved aside a dirty plate and cup and sat down. He took the envelope from his pocket and opened it. He pulled the candle closer, then spread his sister's letter on the cleared spot.

Minersville, Idaho
March 16

Dear brother Chase,

How long it's been since I've written to you. I am so ashamed for worrying you and Mama and Papa Donlin. But the years pass by, William and I always on the move. I guess I became too embarrassed to let you know of our gyspy-like life.

But I want you to know right off, Chase, that I'm not complaining. I have always been happy with William. Happy until two years ago, when he was shot and killed by two men trying to take his digs away from him. I didn't think I could bear it the day we laid him in the ground. But for my little girl's sake, I knew I had to carry on.

It is because of her, Chase, that I write you this letter. I am dying of lung fever and cannot rest for worrying about leaving her alone in this rough mining town. I beg of you to please come and get her and take her to our parents. Her name is Raegan, and she is sweet and lovely. I know you will love her as you did me.

Your loving sister,
Anne

Chase crushed the single sheet of paper in his fist. His Anne was dying. He stared unseeing at the disorder of the kitchen—mud tracked on the floor, ashes spilling out of the fireplace onto the hearth. There were rusty traps and broken pieces of bridles and reins tossed into one corner, a pile of soiled clothes in another. His wet eyes didn't see the cobwebs in the rafters that had been gathering there since Molly had passed away. He saw only the beautiful young girl riding off with her new husband, happy and in love.

And what had that love brought her! Chase jerked to his feet and braced his hands on the mantel, staring down into the leaping flames of the fire. Nothing! It had brought her nothing but slow deterioration of her health and the birth of a little girl—a little girl that he must raise now. It hadn't entered his mind that he would not do so.

"I must start for this mining town as soon as possible," he said to the empty room. "As soon as I have a bite to eat."

As Chase gathered his gear and enough food for at least two days, a full moon rose, lighting the cabin almost as if it as if it were day. *Good,* he thought. *I can get in at least three hours traveling before the moon sets.*

Within half an hour Chase had eaten and was closing the cabin door behind him. He hurried to the barn to saddle Sampson.

Although Anne O'Keefe tried desperately to hang onto life, to see her brother once more, to know that her daughter would be taken care of, she was declining rapidly. Raegan and Mahalla spooned cough syrup and different broths between her pale lips, but she only coughed more often, spit up more blood.

The day the wildflowers burst into bloom, and the day Chase Donlin received his letter, Anne Donlin quietly stopped breathing. With a low cry, Raegan, who had not left her mother's side for two days, hugged the emaciated body to her breast and felt a cold hollowness in the area of her heart.

"Oh, Mama." Tears slid down her cheeks. "You didn't get to see the wildflowers bloom."

In a haze of unreality, Raegan felt Mahalla take her mother from her and lay the thin body back on the pillows. Then, putting one foot in front of the other, as though in a dream, she allowed the old woman to lead her into the main room. Mahalla gently pushed her into a rocker, then went back to her mother.

Mama hadn't gotten to see Uncle Chase either, Raegan remembered as she rocked slowly. It had been two weeks since she dropped the letter off at the post. Had he received it yet? Had he received it and didn't care to come see his sister? Didn't he want to be bothered with her daughter?

There came the sound of sloshing water as Mahalla bathed her mother's body, preparing it for burial. Raegan clapped her hands over her ears to shut out the sound and didn't remove them until the old Indian joined her in front of the fire.

"It is done," she said gently, "Come and see how peaceful Anne look."

And it was true, Raegan saw when she gazed down on the pale, serene face, "She is happy now," Mahalla said beside her, "with your father. Do not grieve for her, Raegan."

"I know I shouldn't, Mahalla," Raegan whispered brokenly, "but I don't know how I can bear it without her."

"You will." The old woman took her arm and led her away. "You are strong. Your mother will always be in your heart, but in time she will become a beautiful memory."

Raegan had just sat back down in the rocker when the miners began to arrive. They stood on the small stoop, unshaven but with faces scrubbed clean and misshappen hats clutched in red, chapped hands. The roughest men among them had a deep respect for O'Keefe's gentle widow and they had come to pay their last respects.

Mahalla opened the door and motioned them in. They trooped into the bedroom, single file, to view the laid-out deceased. In a few minutes they were coming out, some of the older men patting Raegan on the head or gently squeezing her shoulder in silent sympathy. But the younger miners, too aware of her beauty and too shy to speak, quietly walked past her with quick side-long looks.

Big, burly Tim O'Shannon, the last to leave, squatted down beside Raegan's chair. "Lass," he said gently, "the men are makin' a fine pine box for your mother, and some of the others are preparing her a place beside your father. We have a newcomer at the digs called Skinny Ike. He was once a preacher and he'd be pleased to hold services for Anne Donlin."

Raegan nodded her head when the big man added, "William told me once that your mother never took his Catholic religion."

O'Shannon stood up and Raegan grabbed his hand. "Thank you for everything, Tim, and tell the others how much I appreciate their thoughtfulness—all the things they've done for me and Mama since Papa died. I don't know what we'd have done without the help of you all."

The miner shuffled his feet awkwardly, then said huskily, "It's the least we could do for Donlin's woman and young lass."

"Nevertheless, I am deeply grateful." Raegan paused, then said through trembling lips, "Tell Skinny Ike that . . . day after tomorrow . . . around three o'clock will be. . . ."

"I'll do it, Lass," Tim broke in, saving her from saying what was so obviously hard for her.

The stallion was tired and he limped, but Chase plodded on. He had ridden hard the last two days, with only a few hours rest at night.

Chase leaned forward and patted Sampson's arched neck, shiny with sweat. "Just a little farther, fellow," he said. "We should be comin' to Minersville shortly. That is, if that old Paiute didn't lie to me."

He might have, out of pure orneriness, Chase thought ruefully as he guided Sampson across a dry wash, the animal sliding as dirt crumbled under his great hoofs. The red men played such tricks on the pale faces sometimes, and though these mischievous little acts were aggravating, they did not raise too much animosity in Chase. After all, the white men were invading their territory.

Another twenty minutes passed before Chase pulled rein and stared down at the sprawling town of Minersville. Oh, Anne, he thought sadly, has such squalor as this miserable place been your way of life all these years? He wondered which of the shacks was hers, and lifting the reins, he urged the stallion down the slight incline.

He stopped the first person he saw, a youngster whose bare feet kicked up spurts of dust as he ambled along. "Where's Anne O'Keefe's place, sprout?" He smiled down at the tow-headed boy around eight years old.

"The last house at the end of the street." A grimy finger pointed. "You won't find Miz Donlin there though." A spasm of cold apprehension moved through Chase. He knew before the boy spoke again what he would add. "She's bein' buried today. Everybody is at the funeral." Again the dirty finger pointed, only in the opposite direction. "See? If you strain your eyes you can see em' there by that big pine tree."

"Thanks, lad," Chase choked out, his voice shaken. He nudged Sampson with a heel and trotted toward the group of people gathered a half mile away.

As he drew near them, he could see the raw earth of a newly dug grave beside one which had been there for some time. He sucked in his breath and blinked his eyes against the wetness that gathered in them when he saw a pine coffin being lowered into the ground.

He had almost killed his horse getting here but hadn't arrived in time to once more look upon Anne's dear face. He pulled the mount to a walk, stopping a few yards from the gathering. He did not want to interrupt the man who stood at the head of the grave reading from a tattered bible clasped in work-worn hands.

As the man's voice droned on, and the hot sun bore down on the tops of his thighs, Chase's eyes scanned the group of mostly men, looking for his little neice. After a thorough search, he knew she wasn't there. In fact, there were no children at all.

A quick interest leapt into Chase's eyes as they fell on the slender body of a young woman sobbing into a handkerchief. A slight wind toyed with her dark red hair, tossing its curly, shoulder-length tresses into shimmering silk. She lifted her head after a moment, and he stared. Never had he seen a face so lovely, never had his heart beat so fast. He had dreamed of such a woman but had never expected to see one.

"Don't go gettin' your hopes up of takin' that one to bed," he growled to himself. "She's bound to belong to some man. A beauty like that wouldn't be unattached."

He looked over the rough, bewhiskered miners and thought what a waste it would be if she were married to one of them. There was not a man there who would appreciate her loveliness. His eyes scorched over the exquisite body clearly outlined by the well-worn material of her dress. Nor would they take the time to coax and caress those curves into a mindless response.

A wry smile twisted the corners of his chisled lips. He had never before taken another man's wife to bed, but he knew that given half a chance, he would take this one. "And probably never give her back," he whispered.

Chase stopped his day-dreaming and put the young woman from his mind as he heard the scraping sound of gravel. The services were over and Anne's grave was being filled in. He looked away, unable to watch the dirt being thrown onto the pine box. When, after a while, it grew quiet, he turned back to see the miners walking away, followed by a few women. The red-haired one remained beside the grave, an old Indian woman standing close beside her.

She must have been awfully close to Anne, he thought, watching the slender shoulders shake as the young woman continued to sob into her handkerchief.

Finally the old woman led her away and Chase rode the stallion in closer. He dismounted and went to hunker down beside the mound of gravel and red clay, noticing a large bouquet of wildflowers, already wilting in the heat, placed at the head of the grave.

He knelt there a long time, recalling a young, laughing woman, a sister who had meant everything to him. "Rest in peace, dear Anne," he whispered. "I will take the best of care of your little girl. I will love her as I loved you."

Chase stood up slowly, stiff from the long hours in the saddle. He would go find little Raegan and take her away from this hell-hole as soon as possible.

As he rode back toward town he could hear the clink of pickaxes biting into the hard, gravely soil of Idaho. Evidently the miners had gone straight from the gravesite to their diggings. He guessed it was remarkable that those gold-fevered men had even stopped long enough to attend his sister's funeral.

Chase's thoughts were on his sister, wondering about the twenty years he hadn't seen or heard from her, when he came to the end of the dusty street and her shack stood in front of him. He reined Sampson in and gazed at the rough-plank, hurriedly knocked-together building. He tried to imagine his delicate sister living under such conditions.

Sighing, he started to dismount, then sat back down, his right hand snatching at the Colt in its holster. The largest wolf he'd ever seen came bounding around the corner of the shack, its hackles raised and its long fangs exposed in a snarl.

Chase was taking aim at the great chest when a sharply spoken warning froze his hand. "Shoot that animal and you're a dead man."

Chase stared at the barrel of a rifle trained on his heart. When he lifted his eyes to see who held it, they widened a fraction. The little beauty from the cemetary! He gazed at her boldly, his heavy-lidded eyes sliding over breasts that thrust proudly against the material of the bodice covering them.

When the woman shifted indignantly on her feet, he lifted his eyes to her face. Green eyes glared at him furiously. He smiled at her lazily and drawled, "Where I come from we shoot animals that attack us."

"Lobo won't attack you if you stay right where you are."

Chase's gaze dropped to the animal standing protectively beside the girl. "Have it your own way." He shrugged. "I'm lookin' for my little niece. I was told this is the shack that belonged to my sister, Anne Donlin."

Raegan gasped softly. A mixture of excitement

and uncertainty swept over her. Uncle Chase? Could this handsome, though hard-faced man be as nice as Mama had described him? The way his eyes had stripped the clothes off her moments ago, she would have said he was a womanizer of the worst kind. Maybe he'd pull those hungry eyes back in his head when he learned who he was thinking such erotic thoughts about.

She let the rifle butt drop to the floor. "I'm afraid that little niece is me, Uncle Chase." She grinned up at him roguishly.

Confusion, embarrassment, and even a hint of disappointment swept across Chase's face. He could forget what he had in mind doing to her. "You're little Raegan?" He finally asked in incredulous tones.

"That's right." Raegan sent him such a dazzling smile that he blinked. "It's Mama's fault you were misled. She always refered to me as her little girl even after I had my eighteenth birthday."

It was an altogether different look Chase bent on the young woman now. This was his sister's daughter, his niece. Forcing the carnal thoughts from his mind, he studied the beautiful face, looking for some resemblance to her mother. He could see none. There was none of Anne's gentleness on the vibrant face. She was her father's daughter—dark green eyes and dark red hair. Later there might be William's sunniness in her eyes, but right now they were shadowed with grief.

He suddenly had to look away from her. To his shame, he was still attracted to Anne's daughter—attracted as he had never been to any other woman. How in the world was he going to live with her and keep his hands off her?

Dammit, I'll have to. He made himself turn and smile at her. "If I dismount now, niece, do you think you can keep Lobo from taking a chunk out of me?"

Raegan nodded. "Give me a moment to tell him that you won't hurt me." She bent over the wolf, and taking his large head in both hands, she looked steadily and silently into his eyes. After a moment the animal relaxed, gave a wag of his tail, and Raegan released him.

Incredible, Chase thought. She communicated with the animal through her eyes.

"You can get down now, Uncle Chase."

Although Chase knew he would have to remind himself many times that this was Anne's daughter, he still didn't want Raegan calling him uncle. "Just plain Chase will do," he grunted as he slid from the saddle.

Raegan's white teeth flashed in a humorous smile. "All right, Plain Chase." She pushed the door wider, thinking that she had never seen a man less plain. "Won't you come in and I'll make us some supper."

She did have her father's teasing nature, Chase thought, being careful not to step on her pet following close at her heels. He still didn't trust the beast. Raegan was crazy to think a wolf could be tamed.

Yet, he allowed, stepping over the threshold, there seemed to be a bit of wildness in Raegan also, and maybe in her case it was possible.

The moment Chase stepped into the combination kitchen and living quarters he felt Anne's love in the room. He saw it also in the little ways she had managed to make the rudely constructed house into a home. There were brightly stitched samplers on the rough walls, some bearskin rugs on the floor, one spread in front of a small fire-place. He thought of the huge fieldstone hearth back in his own cabin and wondered how much heat this crudely fashioned one could put out. Not nearly enough, he'd wager.

His eyes took in the few pieces of furniture—a table with two benches, a long narrow one against a wall with a mirror hanging above it. There were two chairs, one a rocker, and a narrow bed in one corner. All were made by an unskilled hand, but somehow he sensed the love that William O'Keefe had put into each piece.

Chase's attention was caught by the old Indian woman coming out of what he imagined was a bedroom. "This is Mahalla." Raegan stepped quickly to the woman's side and placed an arm around her skinny shoulders. "She helped me nurse Mama. I don't know what I would have done without her."

Chase offered his hand to the elderly woman and said gravely, "I am deeply grateful for your care of my sister, Mahalla. If ever I can return your kindness I would be pleased to do so."

"That may come sooner than you think," Raegan said softly for his ears alone as she left the old woman's side. "She has no place to go," she continued, taking three plates from an open shelf beside the window. She looked up at Chase, a plea in her eyes. "We'll have to take her with us."

Chase frowned. "Raegan, she'll never be able to make such a long trip," he half whispered.

"She is stronger than she looks," Raegan came back stubbornly. "I will not leave her behind to starve to death." When her green eyes flashed dangerously, Chase threw up his hands in surrender.

As he sat down in the straight-backed chair, he wondered how many times he would bow to her dictates. She was a strong-willed little scrap, and he feared he would be like a piece of soft dough in her hands.

He watched her swing a covered pot off the flames. Some kind of stew, he thought as a mouth-watering aroma wafted into the room when she lifted the lid to peer inside. He studied her fire-flushed face, noting her haunted look, the purple shadows beneath the heavily fringed eyes. She was quietly suffering, he knew, had suffered a long time with the knowledge that she was losing her mother.

Raegan felt Chase's gaze upon her and glanced up at his lean brown face. Her attention caught and held on his sensuous mouth. What would it be like, she wondered, to have it pressed against her own?

Flushing a deep red and not liking the turn her thoughts had taken, Raegan lifted the pot off the crane and, carrying it to the table, said gruffly, "Supper is ready if you are."

"I'm plenty ready." Chase smiled and sat down on one of the benches.

As Raegan heaped his plate with chunks of meat flavored with the wild herbs Mahalla had gathered from the meadow, she said, "It's rabbit stew. The miners have been keeping us supplied with game." She sat down across from Chase, next to Mahalla, and passed Chase a basket of sourdough biscuits. "They've been very kind to me and Mama since Papa was killed. All the miners liked Papa."

"Why didn't Anne write to me as soon as she lost William?" Chase asked. "She must have known that I'd have come to fetch her home."

"She was too proud." Resentment crept into Raegan's voice. "She knew that you and my grandparents didn't approve of Papa, and she didn't want you to know that he hadn't been able to keep his promise of riches."

There was a stiff silence for a moment before Chase broke it. "We didn't dislike William, Raegan. No one could. Had he not fallen in love with my sister and taken her away, he and I could have become the best of friends. But we knew he was too easy goin', too much a dreamer to ever give Anne a great deal of security."

Raegan was silent for a minute, thoughtful as she chewed a piece of meat. "In a way you were right to think that," she said finally. "Papa wasn't a very serious-minded man, but in his way he tried very hard to improve our way of life. He loved Mama dearly, and it troubled him that he could give her so little."

Chase looked into the suspiciously wet eyes and laid his hand on the small one lying on the table. "The important thing, Raegan," he said softly, "is that your mother and father were happy together.

Happiness is very scarce in a lot of people's lives."

Raegan looked back at him, gratitude in her eyes. "Thank you, Chase. I feel the same way. It's not what—" She paused as a rap sounded on the door. "I hope that's not another dumb miner come to offer me marriage," she complained, rising from the table.

Chase watched the sway of her gently rounded hips as she walked across the floor to the door. He could understand why this little beauty would receive many offers of marriage. There wasn't a man alive who wouldn't give his soul to take her to bed every night.

Including yourself, a jeering voice whispered inside him.

No! he silently denied the truth of the words. *She looks on me as her uncle, and that is what I'll be to her. Nothing more.*

Lobo at her heels, Raegan opened the door a crack, then with a wide smile swung the door wider. "Mahalla," she cried, "I think your two grandsons are here."

The old woman jumped to her feet, knocking over the bench in her hurry to greet the two boys while Raegan grabbed the wolf by the ruff of his neck.

All three Indians talked at once in their native tongue. With a wide smile on her face, Raegan picked up the bench, then sat down on it. "It would appear," she told Chase, "that news of Mama's death reached Mahalla's village and her daughter has worn her husband down. He is allowing his mother-in-law to make her home with them. He had refused previously."

Chase smiled his relief. "Thank God. I've been racking my brain how to get her to my place in Oregon."

Raegan stole a glance at the hard, raw masculinity of Chase and thought, *You would have done it somehow.*

Quite a bit of bustling went on then as the old woman darted around gathering up her few possessions and Raegan began clearing the shelves of food for Mahalla to take with her.

"You'd better hold back some of that," Chase advised as she was about to add a bag of coffee and a slab of salt pork to the growing stacks of staples on the table. "We'll need some for our trip back to Oregon. I used up my grub on the trail here."

"Yes. You keep, Raegan," Mahalla instructed. "You give me plenty already."

"I just wish it could be more, dear friend." Raegan affectionately hugged Mahalla. "There were times when, without your support, I don't know if I could have carried on."

"No, Raegan, you would not have given in to your grief. You have your mother's inner strength." She took Raegan's chin and gazed into her eyes. "Do your grieving, then start a new life in this place called Oregon."

She slid bright, wise eyes to Chase. "Find yourself a good man and have lots of babies."

Raegan blushed and Chase frowned into his coffee. Did the old woman's side-long look mean that she had him in mind to sire those babies? Did she know that he really wasn't Raegan's uncle, that there was no blood tie?

The three were saying goodbye then, leaving Raegan and Chase alone, gazing at each other. "So," Chase broke the awkward silence that had descended. "There's been young men wantin' to marry you?" He tried to bring a teasing note to his tone, but failed. There was an undertone of resentment instead.

Raegan, however, hadn't seemed to notice it as she laughingly answered, "Old ones too. Damn fools—what would I want with any of those grubby individuals?" Bitterness crept into her next words. "Hacking away at the same spot of ground, breaking their backs to find that vein of gold that would make them rich." After a long sigh, she added, "And sometimes not even finding enough dust to buy rations."

Chase knew she was thinking of her father, but he said nothing as he sipped his coffee. When he saw that she had brought herself back to the present, he said, "Raegan, there is something I must tell you." When she raised an inquiring eyebrow, he continued, "Your grandparents have passed away."

"Oh, no," Raegan exclaimed, genuine remorse in the two words. "I had so looked forward to knowing them. Mama talked about them all the time. I know I would have loved them."

"And they would have loved their granddaughter," Chase said softly. Then, to break the melancholy that was about to descend on the shack, he teased, "Do you think you can bear livin' with a grubby old bachelor?"

Raegan's soft throaty laughter swept over Chase, settling in his loins. Even so small a thing as her laughter made him want to take her to bed. If he had a brain in his head, he would make other arragements for the girl.

"You're not old and you're far from being grubby, Chase Donlin, and you know it." Raegan rapped his knuckles with her spoon. "You could stand a shave, though. You look like a grizzly bear." Her eyes ran over his high, wide cheekbones and forceful chin. He was the handsomest man she'd ever seen, even with the stubble on his chin.

As Chase grinned and rubbed his hand over his bristly face, she said seriously, "I'd like it just fine, living with you in your Oregon Territory. You don't know how tired I get, always pulling up and moving on. To settle in one place will be heavenly for me."

Heaven for you, but hell for me, Chase mused silently before saying, "You look dead beat. Why don't you go to bed and get some rest. I'd like to get an early start in the morning."

"Yes, I think I will." Raegan stood up and began gathering up the dirty dishes. "It's been a draining few days."

"Leave the dishes." Chase rose and took the plates from her. "I'll tidy up, and if you show me what you want to take with you, I'll pack it up."

Raegan glanced around the room and gave a rueful laugh. "As you can see, there's not much worth taking. Only Mama's pictures and the two bearskins. Papa shot them, and I'd like to keep them."

"And don't forget your blankets," Chase reminded her. "We'll be campin' out a couple nights and the evenins' still get cold."

"Yes, I'll roll them up in the morning." Raegan grinned up at Chase. "I'll need them tonight. It gets cold in here too." The wolf whined at her feet, and when she opened the door he shot away into the darkness.

"Aren't you afraid he won't come back?" Chase looked surprised.

"He'll come back. I let him out every night around this time. He has to eat too."

"Don't you feed him table scraps?"

"Certainly not." Raegan looked scandalized. "That would be insulting to him. He must hunt his own food."

Chase allowed that made sense. A wild animal should catch his own food. He changed the subject. "Is there a place around here where I could purchase you a mount?"

"Oh, I have a horse." Raegan looked up from unlacing her shoes. "A pretty little mare. I call her Beauty. Papa bought her for me the year before he was killed. He'd found a good-sized nugget, and he spent it all on Mama and me for Christmas."

Chase mentally shook his head. That sounded like something the irresponsible O'Keefe would do. Let tomorrow take care of itself, never mind that the money could have gone toward weatherproofing this shack a little. It must have been damn cold in here in the winter.

"Well." Raegan stood up. "I'll see you in the morning then."

"Yes. Sleep well, Raegan."

Chase kept his eyes firmly on clearing the table

as he heard the rustle of Raegan's clothing being removed, then the straw mattress crackling as she climbed into bed. But in his mind he could see the slender perfection of her body, the proud jutting breasts and softly flaring hips.

Suddenly he had to get out of the shack, away from that body curled under the covers.

He stood outside on the stoop, gazing up at the star-studded sky. "God, Anne," he whispered, "what torture you've set up for me."

Chapter Three

The next morning, just at sunrise, Chase opened the door and almost tripped over Lobo stretched out on the rickety porch. "Is this where you sleep every night, fellow?" He wondered if he dared pat the large head.

Deciding it was best not to risk losing a hand, he stepped around the long, lean shape and walked to the side of the shack to answer nature's call.

He'd have to clear out the necessary when they got home, Chase thought as he relaced his buckskins. The narrow little building had been used for storage since Molly had passed away.

He paused outside the door, watching the mining town come alive with the slapping and banging of doors as the miners went off to work, pick axe over one shoulder, nugget pan in hand. Some were jovial, talking and laughing with each other, looking forward to that big strike that might happen today. Others trudged along, silent and morose, shoulders slumped, beaten by the lure of gold, but unable to stop searching for it.

Chase shook his head in pity for these men gripped by a fever that made them forget everything else—family, health, the small enjoyments of life. This striving for gold had killed Willian O'Keefe and his sister Anne.

Lobo followed Chase back inside the shack and sat nearby as he hunkered down before the fireplace and, brushing aside the ashes, coaxed the red coals below into flames with small pieces of kindling.

Raegan had awakened at the sound of the latch being lifted, and she now lay in the warm nest of blankets watching Chase at his task. His face seen in profile seemed almost ruthless, but handsome nevertheless.

Her gaze traveled to his bare shoulders and back. His muscles rippled and bulged as he lifted a log and carefully laid it on the flames. She was shamefully aware of her nipples hardening.

"What's wrong with you, Raegan O'Keefe?" she whispered fiercely to herself. "That's Mama's brother. You have no right to be affected by him like that."

"But you forget," a small inward voice reminded her, "that he is not really your mother's brother. You need not feel shame."

Even knowing this, Raegan blushed a deep red when Chase suddenly called her name. "Are you awake? The sun is up and we should get goin' pretty soon."

"I'm awake," Raegan answered. Sitting up, she swung her feet to the floor and flinched when her bare feet touched the coldness of the rough pine-board flooring. She missed the warm softness of the bearskin that had always lain beside her bed. As she hurried to the fire, she saw the tightly rolled skins lying beside the door where Chase had placed them.

Raegan held her hands out to the warmth of the flames, unaware that their brightness outlined her body clearly through the thin, worn material of her nightgown. His loins knotting, Chase hurriedly turned his head away.

"I'll put a pot of coffee to brew and make us a bite to eat while you're gettin' dressed," he said thickly, hoping that she wasn't always so careless of her attire in front of him. He didn't need added enticements to fire his blood. It was already at a slow simmer.

As the room filled with the aroma of steaming coffee and frying meat, Raegan stood uncertainly, her dress and underclothes clutched in her hand. How was she going to get dressed with Chase only a few feet away? She couldn't bring herself to enter Mama's room for privacy. Old memories would be revived, and she was still too heart-sick to deal with them.

Chase glanced up from the frying pan and hastily got to his feet as he realized Raegan's dilemma. "I'll go saddle the mounts now, if you'll keep an eye on the salt pork."

Raegan nodded, sighing her relief when he walked outside. Mama had described her parents' home as being large. Maybe for the first time in her life, she would have the privacy of her own room at the Donlin house.

Chase returned as she was lacing up her shoes. A short time later he announced that breakfast was ready.

The meal was quickly eaten and the coffee drunk. "Well, Raegan, shall we hit the trail?" Chase stood up, adjusting the broad-bladed Bowie knife in its sheath.

Raegan rose, her eyes becoming damp as they moved over the familar room for the last time. Her gaze lingered a moment on her mother's closed bedroom door and she wished with all her heart and soul that it would open and that the gentle, smiling woman would walk through it.

But that would never happen again, she knew, and taking her rifle from over the mantle, she turned to Chase with a wobbly smile and said, "Let's go."

Outside, before mounting, Raegan shoved the rifle into her saddle scabbard. "Do you know how to use that thing, or is it just for show?" Chase teased.

Raegan threw him an indignant look as she gracefully swung onto the little mare's back. "Papa taught me how to handle firearms when I was ten years old. A female has to know how to protect herself in a rough miners' camp."

"You'll need that same know-how where I'm takin' you, Raegan," Chase informed her. "Man is at his crudest in the wilds of Oregon. Most have forgotten any niceties their mothers might have taught them."

"What about Indians?" Raegan picked up the reins, and with a nudge of her heel the mare followed the stallion as Chase led off. "Are they civil, or are they still fighting the whites in that region?"

"Some are friendly, some are not."

"You sound as if you like the red man." Raegan said.

"I've got nothin' against him. If he leaves me alone, I don't bother him. I'm on good terms with a Paiute chief near my place. I trust him more than I do most white men."

The morning was clear and cool with a sharp, dry tang in the air. Its briskness made the horses want to run, and in accord Raegan and Chase left off talking and put the horses into a long, swinging canter, Lobo easily keeping up with them.

With each mile that took Raegan farther away from the shabby shack, the two lonely graves beneath the lone pine, her spirits drooped more. A lump formed often in her throat, and the trail was blurred by her tears.

Chase glanced at her once, then quickly looked away from her drooping shoulders and tear-stained face. He had heard her sobbing in bed last night but hadn't dared go comfort her. If once he took her in his arms, God knew how it would end. The one imperative was that he must keep his hands off her. He suffered by just brushing up against her, or catching a scent of her hair that smelled like roses.

By the time the sun had moved overhead, they had entered country unfamilar to Raegan. It was a softer, greener place than she was used to. Her poignant memories faded somewhat as she gazed around at the wild, beautiful area. She was able to smile and say thank-you when Chase pulled the stallion to a walk and handed her a strip of pemmican.

"Are you tired?" he asked. "Would you rather dismount while we eat?"

Raegan shook her head. "I'm fine. I'd just as soon keep riding."

Admiration flashed in Chase's eyes. For all her delicate look, she was a sturdy little piece. "You're gonna fit into my country right well, Raegan." He smiled at her.

"I hope so." She returned his smile, swaying easily in the saddle. "Do you have many close neighbors? Women, I mean."

"There's a few. Not close by like maybe you're used to. The closest one is a couple miles from my place. They're mostly trappers' wives, a rough, hardy lot but good of heart. I think you'll like them." His smile widened. "They'll like *you*."

Raegan returned his smile, looking forward to meeting these women he described. She and Mama hadn't mingled with the women who followed the men from one gold field to another. There had been few wives among them, and the others were not of the highest caliber in regard to morality. Consequently, she had never known the friendship of a young woman her age.

Meantime, Chase had remembered Liza Jenkins. That one wouldn't like Reagan one bit. Up until now she'd enjoyed the distinction of being the most attractive woman in the Oregon hills.

Once everyone saw Raegan, Liza's title would disappear like the mists when the sun hit them. Raegan was not only pretty, she was beautiful. And sweet-natured also.

There wasn't much sweetness in the widow's nature, Chase mused. She was selfish and grasping, interested only in herself. She tried to hide it, but she wasn't altogether successful, not where the women were concerned. The women in and around Big Pine saw through her. They suspected her flirty ways with men, especially with their own men, and the widow wasn't very well liked.

When they had consumed the pemmican, they urged the horses back into a canter. It was close to sunset when the Idaho border was left behind and they entered Oregon country. A short time after that they sighted a wide, muddy river. "The North Platte," Chase explained. Raegan held the mare back when they came to its banks and Chase, without pausing, rode the stallion into the water. She knew she was expected to follow him and, a little apprehensive, she urged Beauty after him.

The mare neared the center of the stream and Raegan flinched as she felt the cold water moving up her legs. She hurriedly yanked her dress up above her knees, then clutched the reins tightly as she felt Beauty swimming. Her eyes anxiously sought the other shore.

Finally Beauty's hooves hit bottom again, and soon the mounts were leaving the river, water streaming down their legs. "We'll make camp here." Chase swung to the ground and stripped the saddle off Sampson. Raegan did the same for Beauty, then spent some time admiring the area, awestruck by the beauty and grandeur of the graceful, towering pines and spruce.

Then, her shoes squashing water, she walked over and stood beside Chase's hunkered figure. While she had gazed enthralled at their camp-site he had gathered a pile of dry tree limbs and now had a cheerful fire started.

He glanced up at her and frowned. "You'd better get those wet shoes and stockings off and prop them beside the fire to dry."

"I could have taken them off before I crossed, had you told me the river was so deep in the middle," Raegan spoke disgruntedly as she sat down on a flat rock and struggled with stubborn wet laces.

"You're right," Chase agreed ruefully, glancing down at his wet moccasins and buckskin pants legs. "I didn't think about your leather shoes and dress tail." His lips lifted in a grin. "I'm not used to ridin' with ladies."

"You're forgiven." Raegan grinned back, then unselfconsciously pulled her dress up past her knees and rolled a water-soaked stocking down over her shapely leg and off her narrow foot. She continued to talk as she bared the other leg.

Chase didn't hear a word she said. His eyes and attention were glued to the white flesh, the glimpse of the thigh he'd seen, the long length of leg and neatly turned ankle.

When she looked up at him questioningly, he tore his gaze away, realizing that she had asked him something. "Sorry, Raegan, but I didn't catch what you were sayin'. I was thinkin' about startin' supper," he lied.

Raegan pulled up her knees and tucked her skirt around her toes. "I asked if you'd please bring me a pair of dry stockings from my saddlebag. My feet are freezing."

"Right away." Chase jumped to his feet, thankful for the excuse to walk away from her. Otherwise he might have hunkered there indefinitely, ogling her legs. And, he told himself firmly, he would stay away while she donned the dry hose.

Soon the fire was crackling, blue smoke curling from it and disappearing into the tree tops. Raegan sighed with the comfort of dry feet and the warmth of the fire as she watched Chase bent to the task of cleaning the rabbit they would have for supper. To her amazement, he had shot its head off from the back of his mount.

Lobo came and threw himself down beside Raegan and laid his big head in her lap. She idly scratched his rough ears as she gazed into the flames, her thoughts back at the rude little shack in Minersville and of the mother and father no longer there.

When Chase handed her a tin plate full of crispy roasted meat, she forced her memories away and smiled her thanks. They both laughed when Lobo jumped up and bounded off through the forest.

As Raegan and Chase consumed their meal, night came on. An owl hooted high in a pine, and a small pack of coyotes came and squatted on their haunches just inside the shadows.

Raegan looked at Chase with alarm filled eyes. "Don't be frightened," he said soothingly. "They'll not come any closer. The fire will keep them back."

"What about while we're sleeping and the fire goes out?"

"It won't go out. I'll add wood every hour or so."

"What makes you sure you'll wake up in time?"

"Don't worry about it." Chase bit into a rabbit leg. "I'm used to doin' it. Relax and finish your supper. They won't stay long anyhow. They're just curious. They'll scoot when Lobo returns."

Raegan's appetite was pleasantly sated when Chase handed her a cup of steaming coffee. They sat a moment in comfortable silence, sipping the strong brew and thinking their own thoughts. Raegan mused on the turn her life had taken, and Chase wondered how he was going to keep his hands off Anne's daughter, wondering how it would all end.

The wind stilled, and suddenly the coyotes were gone. There was only the thump of hobbled hoofs heard in the darkness surrounding the camp.

Raegan's lids began to droop, and with an amused twist of his lips, Chase stood up and moved to the gear propped against the two saddles. He dragged out the bedrolls and spread them close to the fire, only a foot or so apart. He grinned at Raegan, who watched him sleepily, and motioned her to crawl inside one. She did so, pulling the top blanket up around her shoulders.

She knew no more until the rising sun striking her in the face awakened her.

* * *

The country grew more rugged the farther Raegan and Chase traveled. They crossed series of ridges and steep hills; the trees grew taller, and the air had a keen, invigorating edge. The trail they followed wound along the North Platte, and in the early dawn they saw deer trooping out of the forest and going down to the stream to drink. Raegan also caught glimpses of coyotes slinking through the trees and saw on the surface of the river wide circles made by feeding fish. This was all new to her and she was fascinated by it.

She broke a long silence between her and Chase. "Do we cross the river again at any point?"

Chase shook his head. "No, and to my knowledge no white man has ever gone into the wilderness on the other side. That is Tillamook land. Anyone tryin' to hunt or trap those woods is gonna be killed by Indians."

Raegan peered across the wide stream at the thick, dark forest and shivered. "Do *they* ever cross to this side?"

"I don't think so. No one has ever seen them if they have. It's like an unspoken agreement between us."

They drifted back into silence then, not speaking until an hour later when they came upon a spring trickling from under a large boulder. Chase reined in the stallion and slid to the ground. "We'll give the mounts a drink and let them rest a spell. It's tiring for them, climbin' up and down the hills."

Beauty and Sampson were led to the cold, fresh water, the stallion snorting and sidling as Lobo too lapped up water only a few feet away. Sampson, unlike the mare who had known the wolf since a cub, had not completely accepted the wild animal.

Raegan called Lobo to her side, and with her hand on his head, steered him the yard or so to where the spring formed a pool before disappearing into a fern-choked ravine. She waited until he had quenched his thirst, then knelt to drink also.

As Raegan cupped the water to her face, she heard the crackling of brush, then dull thumps on the needle-strewn ground. She jumped to her feet when she heard the sharp crack of a hoof on stone. She glanced nervously over her shoulder for Chase, but he was nowhere in sight. When she turned her head back, a frisson of fear shimmered down her back.

A spavined horse, no longer young, limped out of the forest, an obese bearded man on its back. His pig-like eyes widened when he saw her standing beside the pool, to all apperances alone. A sharp bend in the trail hid his view of the mounts, and Lobo had wandered off.

"What have we here?" The unkempt beard stirred around his lips as he heaved himself out of the saddle. "You lookin' for a man, little purty?" He took a step toward Raegan and she shrank from the ugly light in his eyes.

Where was Chase? her mind was screaming in panic when, like a gray ghost, Lobo sprang in front of her. He stood on braced feet, his teeth bared, a warning growl issuing from his throat. The man took a startled step backward, gasping, "What the hell!"

"You'll think it's hell," Raegan warned. "If you don't get back on your mount and ride out of here, he'll tear your throat out."

"I'd rather mount you, Missy," fat lips jeered as grimy fat fingers jerked a gun from the waistband beneath a bulging stomach. The pistol was cocked and aimed at Lobo's chest. "A dead wolf ain't gonna do me no harm. You'd better call him off."

Raegan felt a cold, sinking sensation in her heart. If Lobo thought she was in danger, he would pay no attention to any order she gave him. Death was only seconds away from her beloved pet.

I can out-run him, she was thinking frantically, then suddenly Chase was there, advancing on the man, his cold eyes staring out of a hard, still face.

"You're a long way from home, Roscoe," he said quietly, but warningly. "What brings you this far south?"

"If it's any of your business, Donlin, I came to get me a squaw."

"Why come this far when there's plenty—" Chase broke off in mid-sentence, an unbelivable thought hitting him. "You crazy bastard, you weren't stupid enough to cross the river and steal a Tillamook woman, I hope."

The fat lips twisted in a smirk. "I didn't have to cross the river. Only had to ride my horse into the middle of it and grab one who was takin' herself a bath."

Chase uttered a string of oaths before he asked, "Where is she? Did you kill her after you finished with her?"

"Naw, this one is young and good lookin'. She's still tight and gives me a good ride." His beefy hands reached for the rope tied to the saddlehorn, the other end dragging on the ground and reaching out of sight. He gave it a hard jerk and yelled, "Get out here, you red bitch!"

He grinned wolfishly. "She's a mean one. I have to slap her around to get her to do what I want." His hand went to the crotch of his dirty pants. "She bit me once. I had to work her over that time."

"I'll bet that bothered you a lot." Chase sent the repulsive man a contemptuous look.

Roscoe's brutality to women was well known in the area. Even the whores in Big Pine wouldn't have anything to do with him because he was so cruel in using them. That left the hapless Indian women who were forced to satisfy his sexual perversions. Two stories circulated in the village about him—one, that he had beaten to death at least two women while in a drunken rage, and also that he would use an Indian lad if he came across one alone in the woods.

As Raegan stared at the man, appalled, he gave the rope another hard tug, and with a sharp cry of pain, a young Indian woman stumbled forward, the other end of the rope tied around her neck.

Raegan gasped and cried out at the sight of the woman's face. One eye was almost swollen shut, and her lip was split, a trickle of dried blood showing at the corner of her mouth.

"Oh, Chase," Raegan began, meaning to implore him to take the woman away from the vile man, but Chase gripped her arm warningly and she grew quiet and waited.

Chase kept his eyes steadily on Roscoe's face, as the brute took in Raegan's horrified reaction. Like most weak men, Roscoe was crafty, and Chase knew he'd have to move carefully if he was to overpower him and rescue the woman.

He wished for the colt he had lifted from its holster before kneeling down to drink from the spring. Just as Chase was going to try reasoning with him, Roscoe gave the rope another yank. His big hand lashed out, catching the unprepared woman across the mouth. She let out a cry as she was knocked to the ground. As she struggled to her knees and Roscoe took his eyes away from Chase a moment to lay a heavy hand on her head, Chase made his move.

His lean body dove at the fat man, his hard fist ready to lash out at his bearded chin. Then, just as quickly, he dug in his heels, coming to an abrupt stop only feet away from the cringing woman and her abuser.

Roscoe held a gun at her head.

"Take one more step," he said, "and I'll blow her brains out."

Chase knew the bestial man would do exactly as he threatened. To his backward way of thinking, an Indian woman was no more than an animal, an animal to be killed if it suited his purpose. As he tried reasoning with him, he knew he was wasting his breath, but nevertheless he had to try.

"Why don't you turn her loose, Roscoe?" he cajoled, fighting to keep the anger out of his voice. "She's just another squaw. You can find plenty of them on this side of the river."

When Roscoe's beady eyes only stared back at him, the gun still pressed at the terrified Tillamook woman's head, Chase tried another tack, one that might put fear in the man.

"You're gonna bring the whole Tillamook nation down on the settlement, and when that happens the men will strip every piece of skin off your fat body."

For a moment, dark apprehension flickered in Roscoe's eyes and Chase dared to hope that his words had made him think rationally. But the next moment Roscoe was saying cunningly, "Dead women don't tell no tales. You give me any more trouble and she's a dead woman. You think about that before you go yappin' about me havin' her.

"Now," he added with a leering grin, "take your purty little gal and ride the hell away from here. I got me an itch."

"This is gonna be the sorriest day of your life, Roscoe," Chase said before walking back to Raegan and taking her by the arm. "Come on," he rasped, "Let's go." He pulled her along with him, walking so fast she had to run to keep up with him. He hurried her onto the mare's back, grabbed his colt and swung into the saddle, frustration beating at his brain.

"Don't look back, Raegan," he ordered, giving the mare a hard swat on the rump, sending her into a hard gallop.

"I wish you could have killed him," Raegan yelled furiously over the noise of the pounding hooves, helpless tears running down her cheeks. "I wish you could have shot him right between his mean little eyes."

When they were out of sight of the pair back on the trail, Chase slowed Sampson to a walk. "I've never wanted to shoot a man as badly as I did that one back there," he said tightly. "but as cruel as it may sound, maybe it's better I didn't have my colt on me. When the Tillamook men come lookin' for the woman it's best all the way round that they find her with the guilty man. Otherwise they're gonna kill every white man they come across. There are a lot of good, decent men livin' in these woods, and they don't deserve to die because of one man's despicable act."

"Do you really think they'll come after her?" Raegan looked nervously over her shoulder as if afraid the Tillamooks were already following them.

"Oh, they'll come. I don't know when, but an Indian never forgets a wrong and never fails to get even."

"I hope they don't wait too long," Raegan said. "The poor woman won't live long with the treatment that man will hand out to her."

"She might if she doesn't have to take his abuse too long. Indian women are very strong in both body and mind. She might even manage to kill him some night while he's sleeping."

"Oh I hope so." Raegan spoke so vehemently that Chase grinned.

No more was said between them as once again the mounts were lifted into a mile-eating gait.

When the sky became overcast, Chase urged Sampson into a full gallop, Raegan hard on his heels. After about a mile he slowed to a walk, his gaze searching the forest as though looking for something in particular.

"Ah, here it is," he said finally, nodding at a dim path leading off through the trees. "It's just a hairline of a trail, but we can follow it. It will take us to a fur post where we can spend the night." He glanced up at the sky where black clouds tumbled and rolled threateningly. "I hope we make it before the rain arrives."

Chase turned the stallion onto the path and Raegan followed him as closely as possible, dodging the branches that swung back and slapped at her face as Chase's broad shoulders thrust through the overlapping branches of spruce and pine.

It was close to sunset when they entered a clearing. Chase looked over his shoulder and frowned. Through the gloom of approaching twilight, a falling sheet of rain was coming toward them.

"Make that mare run, Raegan," he called, giving his mount a thump of his heel. "The post is just beyond that line of trees. Maybe we can out-run the rain."

Chapter Four

Big plops of rain were peppering Chase's and Raegan's head and shoulders as the two horses thundered up to a long, barracks-like building of unpeeled logs. "There's a shed of sorts in the back where we can stable the mounts," Chase called over his shoulder as he turned the stallion toward the rear of the post.

By the time Chase opened the door to the lean-to and led Sampson inside, the rain was coming down in earnest. Raegan dipped her head to avoid banging it against the top of the door frame as she urged Beauty to follow behind the stallion. There were three other horses already in occupancy and Chase tethered Sampson in a far corner away from them.

"He'll fight the others," he explained to Raegan who looked up questioningly from snubbing the mare next to a small pinto.

Tufts of hay hung from a half-loft and Chase forked down some for the mare and stallion. He and Raegan stood ready to go then, but before they made a dash through the rain to the dry warmth of the post, Chase cautioned, "Raegan, whatever I say or do in there, play along with me. All right?"

Raegan gave him a puzzled look, but with a nod of her head agreed that she would. Then Lobo shoved his nose in her hand and she exclaimed, "What about Lobo? Someone inside might shoot him."

"That is a poser." Chase ran slim fingers through his wet hair. "I'm so used to him now I forget that he's a wolf."

"I'll stay out here with him." Raegan turned to walk back into the dark interior of the small, drafty room.

"You can't do that!" Chase caught her arm. "You'd catch your death out here under this leaky roof."

"Well I'm not going to take a chance on him being killed. Can you think of anything else?"

"Maybe." Chase looked thoughtful. "Does he know the feel of a rope around his neck?"

"Yes." Raegan nodded. "Ever since he was little. Papa braided him a leather collar with a lead rope attached to it. We kept him tied to a tree out in the yard until he was grown and could take care of himself."

"Do you have it with you?" When Raegan nodded that she did, Chase added, "Put it on him and keep him beside you until I can get us a room. We'll put him in there then."

"You're sure no one will harm him in the meantime?" Raegan looked doubtful.

Chase patted the Bowie at his waist. "No one will lift a finger against him."

"Well, all right," Raegan agreed, though reluctantly, and went to her gear to fetch the collar and leather rope. She was saddened as she rummaged around for it, remembering her father fashioning the leash in the evenings as the wolf cub scampered around the shack. Those were such happy times, she and Mama and Papa together.

Lobo looked askance at his old leather ring, but stood quietly, allowing Raegan to fasten it around his thick muscular throat. When she picked up the lead rope and moved to the door, he walked at her heels. Raegan gave Chase a strained smile and said, "We're ready."

"Let's go then." He smiled back at her, and grasping her arm, they sprinted through the pelting rain.

The raucous din inside the dimly lit tavern room faded to silence when Chase opened the door and pushed Raegan ahead of him. The men stared at her water-soaked beauty, the wet dress clinging to her body, molding all her curves. It took a full minute before their gaze moved to the wolf standing protectively at her side, his ruff raised. There came a dark muttering and uneasy hands hovered over knives and guns.

"Hey, Donlin," a tall, bone-thin trapper called out, "What the hell you doin', bringin' a damn wolf in here?"

"Don't fret about it, Tom," Chase said quietly. "He's my wife's pet." His hand dropped to the hilt of his own knife. "If no one comes near her, he won't bother you."

Raegan almost gasped aloud. Chase was passing her off as his wife? She remembered in time what he had advised her and wiped the surprise off her face. If he said they were married, he had a good reason for doing so. And looking at the scurvy lot here, she had a good idea what it was.

Voices picked up, but not as boisterously as before, as the customers kept a wary eye on the wolf and a leering, appreciative one on Raegan.

"So, Donlin, you went and got yourself hitched, did you?" A big, bearded trapper rumbled as Chase guided Raegan among the tables. "I never thought to see the day a woman could put a halter around your neck, no matter how purty she might be."

When Chase made no response, another man entered the teasing banter. "How's the widder Jenkins gonna feel about you tiein' the knot with another woman, do you reckon? The story goes she had in mind that she'd be the female movin' into the Donlin cabin."

The man was set to continue, but a threatening look from Chase snapped his mouth shut. He, along with the others who had left the bar and gathered in a wide circle around Chase and Raegan, knew of Chase Donlin's ability with the Bowie shoved into his knee-length moccasin. Too many times they had seen the broad blade draw blood with deadly accuracy.

A wide path opened up for Chase as he steered Raegan toward the bar running the length of the room. None cared to get too close to the wolf that stalked alongside his mistress, his lips pulled back in a silent snarl.

Raegan felt the men's hungry eyes following her and felt that the walk to the spirit-stained bar was the longest one she'd ever taken.

"Johnson," Chase said to the genial-faced man who operated the post, "I'd like you to meet Raegan."

A big hand reached across the bar. "I'm right proud to meet you, Raegan." When, with a friendly smile curving her lips, Raegan laid her small hand in his, he added, "You're sure gonna brighten up these hills, little lady." He glanced down at Lobo. "And that wolf of yours is gonna scare the pants off a lot of people."

Johnson gave Chase a worried look. "What are you gonna do with him, Donlin? He's makin' my customers nervous as the dickens."

"We'd like one of your better rooms for the night, and we'll put him in there."

John nodded with a sigh of relief. "I'll give you the one Mr. Hayes from the Hudson's Bay fur company uses when he comes up here to check out how everthing is goin'. It's got a bolt on it so you won't have to worry about anyone bustin' in on you when you're in the middle of somethin' important." His eyes twinkled teasingly, causing Raegan to blush a bright red.

Chase ignored the sly innuendo, sorry that in this case his lie had caused Raegan to be embarrassed. "I'll just settle Raegan at that table over there in that corner," he said shortly, "and after I've put the wolf away, maybe you can bring us something to eat."

"I sure can." Johnson grinned, unaware that Chase was perturbed with him. "My wife cooked up a big pot of beef stew today. I'll have her fetch you some as soon as you're settled." He jerked a thumb over his shoulder. "The room is back of the bar. More quiet than upstairs. It gets pretty noisy up there sometimes, if you catch my meanin'."

Chase nodded that he knew what the big, well-meaning man was talking about, then led Raegan to a rudely constructed table and seated her on a three-legged stool. Then, taking Lobo's rope from her nervous fingers, he said softly, "Don't feel frightened. That lot over there may eat you up with their eyes, but no one will dare lay a finger on who they think is Donlin's woman."

A weak smile curved Raegan's lips. She wished that she was as sure of that as he was. She knew that every pair of eyes in the room was still upon her. Would those wild trappers be willing to just look after Chase left the room?

Chase gave her shoulder a reassuring squeeze and led Lobo away, leaving her sitting with downcast eyes, waiting to see if any man *did* dare approach her. When several minutes passed and the area around her table remained empty, she raised her head and surreptiously ran her eyes over the roughest-looking bunch of men she'd ever seen. They were worse than the miners she had known in the many mining camps she had lived in.

Of course, she had known the miners, Raegan remembered. She had learned that behind their rough-looking visages were often tender hearts. Look how nice they had been to her and Mama after Papa was killed—never a disrespectful look nor word, supplementing their diet with fresh game.

Perhaps, she thought, these men were the same. Maybe in time, as she got to know them better, she would see them in a different light also. After all, Chase was a trapper, and though he didn't have the face of an angel, his every act and word toward her had been that of a gentleman.

Raegan ignored the sneaky inner voice that suddenly accused her, "You'd like it better if he wasn't such a gentleman," and transferred her gaze to the women who moved from table to table, coaxing men to come upstairs with them. She had known already that they were prostitutes from their heavily painted faces and stained satin dresses.

She felt a stirring of pity for these women whose youth was gone, used up by drink and the demands of their profession. They had probably migrated here to the wilderness when they were no longer able to compete with their younger sisters in the big cities.

Raegan's face flamed red, and she stared down at the table when one of the women was pulled into a drunken trappers' lap, a shrill laugh escaping her red painted lips when he thrust a hand down the front of her dress.

She was wishing Chase would hurry back when the heavy post door banged open with such force that it slammed back against the wall. The heavy bulk of a man stood in the opening, the wind blowing the rain in behind him.

"Shut the door, you dumb lout!" Sid Johnson shouted at the man who made the hair stand up on Raegan's arms.

She stared at the newcomer—the man she and Chase had come across on the trail—thankful that she sat in the shadows. Uneasiness gripped her nevertheless when, with a loud oath, Roscoe slammed the door shut and plowed his way to the bar, shouldering his way between two patrons standing there.

"Hey, you big tub of lard, who in the hell do you think you're shovin'?" the younger of the pair growled, his hand going to a knife at his waist.

When Roscoe made no response, only stepped back and moved to the far end of the bar, Raegan realized the man was a coward, brave only when it came to brow-beating a helpless woman. She remembered the Indian woman he had abducted from her tribe, her face battered at his hands, and wished that the man had struck Roscoe instead of yelling at him.

Where was the Tillamook woman? she wondered. Had that monster at least found her a pile of hay to lie in, or had he even bothered to give her shelter in the stables? What if she was outside somewhere, huddled in the rain?

Raegan was debating going to look for the Tillamook woman when Chase arrived at the table, an Indian woman following him carrying a tray of food in her hands. As she placed steaming bowls of stew in front of her and Chase, he said, "Raegan, this is Ruthie Johnson, Sid's wife."

Raegan hid her surprise and stood up to shake the hand held out to her. The woman, who looked to be approaching her fortieth birthday, was quietly attractive with a proudly-held head. That she was loved and cherished by the big man behind the bar was evident in the serenity of her features.

Ruthie Johnson smiled, showing white, even teeth. "A name given to me by Sid. He cannot prounce my birth name."

Raegan and Chase chuckled at her remark, and she placed a pot of coffee on the table and turned to leave. "Do you have time to have a cup of coffee with us?" Raegan smilingly asked.

A pleased flush moved over Ruthie's high cheeks. "Well, maybe for a short time. Unless in the next minute a hungry drunk demands food." She laughed. "I'll have to get back to the kitchen then."

As she poured the fragrant coffee into the cups she had brought along, Chase looked at Raegan's pale face. "Something has upset you," he said. "What?"

Raegan looked meaningfully toward the end of the bar. "That awful Rosecoe man came in while you were gone."

Anger darkened Chase's face. "Did he say or do anything to you?"

Raegan grabbed his arm as he started to lunge to his feet. "No, Chase, he didn't see me."

Chase eased back down on the stool. "Is the Tillamook woman with him?"

"I don't know. She didn't come in with him. Do you suppose the poor woman is dead?"

Chase shook his head. "She's probably tied up in the woods or a cave somewhere."

Although Raegan and Chase had barely spoken above a whisper, Ruthie's keen ears heard every word. With alarm in her eyes and uneasiness in her voice, she exclaimed in low tones, "Did that fool Roscoe steal a Tillamook woman?"

Chase nodded soberly. "I'm afraid he did. Raegan and I ran into them a few miles back. From the looks of her, he's been abusin' her somethin' awful."

"But, Chase, why didn't you—"

"Why didn't I kill him, take the woman from him?" Chase interrupted Ruthie before she could finish her question. "There wasn't a thing I could do because he held a gun to her head, threatened to kill her.

"And not only that, he said if I told anyone he had her, he'd kill her so she couldn't talk and point the finger at him."

Ruthie stared down at her clasped hands. "We've lived in peace with the Tillamook until now, but once they decide someone from this side took their woman they'll cross that river in a hurry."

"And a lot of good people will be killed because of that crazy man's action," Chase muttered.

"We can only pray that the Tillamooks find the woman alive so that she can point a finger at him," Ruthie said and lapsed into troubled silence.

Raegan pushed her bowl of stew away, her appetite gone. Where was the poor woman? Was she dead or alive? Was she lying out there in the cold and rain shivering from pain like some wounded animal? Oh, how she wished she could sic Lobo on the horrible Roscoe, let the wolf tear the fat flesh off his bones.

Chase nudged her clenched fist lying on the table and coaxed, "If you'll eat your supper, I'll go outside later and look for the woman."

"And I'll go with you," Ruthie said. "I'll bring along some food and my medicine bag just in case we find her."

Chase gave the fat man at the end of the bar a glaring look, thinking of all the things he'd like to do to him. Then, as though out of the air, another thought hit him.

His friends and neighbors had a right to know of the trouble that loomed over them, for once Roscoe tired of the Indian woman, he would pass her on to some other man for a price. And he in ignorance of where she came from, would pay the consequences when her men came looking for her.

Chase raked his fingers agitatedly through his hair, then drummed them thoughtfully on the table. When should he tell the men? Right now, or wait and see if he found the woman first? For all he knew, she could be lying dead where he had first seen her. Roscoe might have become frightened and killed her as soon as he and Raegan were out of sight.

He'd not say anything just yet, he decided. He'd look for the woman first.

Ruthie rose and began gathering up the dirty dishes. Chase came back to the moment when she said, "Settle Raegan in your room and meet me out back in about ten minutes."

Chase looked at Raegan, his lips quirking in amusement. She was half asleep, her eyes blinking, her head nodding. He wasn't surprised. She'd had a tiring day considering the long distance they'd covered and the horror of seeing Roscoe abuse the Tillamook woman. It had been plain by her indignant anger that she had never seen a woman abused before. He guessed that he could at least thank William O'Keefe for protecting his women from the brutality of some men.

Regretably, Chase hadn't been able to do the same for Raegan. In this untamed land of rough men, she would see the baser side of men more than once.

He rose and assisted Raegan to her feet. "Come on," he said, "There's a big feather bed waiting for you."

As he steered her toward the door left of the bar, whiskey-rough voices called out ribald advice to him. But it was all good-natured teasing, and Chase took no offense. The most drunken one of them knew that he would draw his knife on the one who spoke or showed disrespect for his "wife."

The room Chase ushered Raegan into was small, but neat and clean. It was sparsely furnished, a cheerfully burning fire and the bed taking up most of the space. But there was room for a small table with a cloudy mirror hanging over it.

Raegan stood in front of the looking glass, shaking her head ruefully as she gazed at her tangled hair and rumpled dress. "I'm a beautiful sight, aren't I, Lobo?" She leaned over and patted the big, rough head that nudged her leg for attention.

You are indeed, Chase thought broodingly, watching her reflection in the mirror, the red curls framing her delicately carved face, the full red lips and dark green eyes the color of wet firs. His eyes drifted down to where her wet bodice clung lovingly to her full breasts, the chill-hardened nipples easily discernible. God, but he'd like to undo those buttons and free one to his hungry mouth!

He felt the beginning of an arousal, and his eyes were drawn to the bed. The men in the other room expected him to share that bed with her tonight, to make love to her. And Lord, he'd give ten years of his life if she wasn't Anne's daughter and he could do just that. To feel those long legs wrapped around his waist as he moved in and out of her would be like entering heaven.

He pushed the impossible from his mind and wondered suddenly what she had thought when he introduced her as his wife. Had she resented it?

He nervously cleared his throat and said, "Raegan, I hope you didn't mind my claiming you as my wife out there. If I hadn't pretended we were married, I might have had to fight every man-jack of them for you."

Raegan, standing with her back to the fire now, her hands held back to its warmth, wondered why she wouldn't have been just as safe if he had simply said that she was his niece. But maybe it hadn't occured to him. He had probably made the decision in a hurry.

She shrugged her shoulders and answered off-handedly, "Of course not. You only did what you thought best."

The tension eased out of Chase. "I'm glad you weren't offended," he said huskily.

"Not at all," Raegan shook her head. "However, I have been wondering how we'll get out of the charade. Are you likely to run into these men again? Where we're going, will you introduce me as your wife?"

For a minute Chase was dumb-struck. He hadn't thought that far ahead. The truth was, he ran into the trappers all the time. They came across each other often when running their trap lines, not to mention that they all brought their furs to this post.

He ran his fingers through his hair. "I don't know, Raegan," he answered honestly. "It seemed the right thing to do at the time, but I guess I didn't think ahead. The fact is, I see those men all the time." His eyes searched her face. "Do you have an opinion on the matter?"

Raegan bewilderingly found herself wishing that Chase's lie was the truth. She quickly told herself not to be a fool. So what if for the first time in her life she was drawn to a man, a man whose touch or look brought sensations to her she didn't understand? That didn't mean that she loved him, did it? When she wed, she wanted it to be like her mother and father's marriage had been. Total love on both sides.

And Chase hadn't shown the least sign of being attracted to her in a romantic way. To him she was Anne's daughter, a legacy of the stepsister he had adored. Still . . .

She carefully schooled her expression and said, "Why don't we just go along with the deception until a solution comes along. Papa used to say that things have a way of working out."

Chase was ashamed of the elated relief Raegan's words brought him. For a while at least, there would be no young men hanging around the cabin trying to court her, eventually taking her away from him as William O'Keefe had done with Anne.

But the lie couldn't go on forever, he told himself, bending to lay a log on the fire. Raegan was a young, healthy woman who deserved a husband and children. She would, one day, fall in love and he would lose her.

A knot formed in the pit of his stomach. Could he bear it? Yes, he thought determindedly, watching Raegan digging around in her cloth bag of clothes, I'll have to. He blinked and stared when Raegan unself-consciously stepped out of her damp dress, and in her bloomers and camisole spread it over the foot of the bed.

"There," she said, smoothing out wrinkles in the material, "it will be dry by morning." She smiled over her shoulder at him. "Make sure you do the same with your clothes before retiring." She glanced at his bedroll tossed in a corner. "Shall I unroll it and put it in front of the fire to dry for you?"

Chase let go of the breath he'd been holding. He had thought for a moment she imagined he would be sharing the bed with her. And that would certainly have been out of the question. There was no way on God's green earth that he could have kept himself from seducing her once he lay beside her. "Then bear the shame of it the next morning," his conscience nagged him.

He managed to say, "Thank you, Raegan, that's a good idea," knowing that he wouldn't be coming back to this room tonight. Even sleeping in the same room with her would be too hard to bear. "Well, he said, "Ruthie is probably waitin' for me, so I'd better get goin'."

"Good night then, if I'm asleep when you return."

Oh, you'll be asleep, Chase thought wryly as he ordered, "Make sure you put my colt under your pillow when you retire."

"That won't be necessary." Raegan smiled, patting the wolf's head. "Lobo is all the protection I need." She scratched his pointed ears. "Poor fellow, I hope he's not too hungry."

"That's right. He's usually out huntin' at this hour, isn't he?"

"Yes, but he'll be all right until morning. We'll be leaving early, won't we?" The look on her face made Chase's lips twitch. She was very nervous around his rough friends.

"Just as soon as it's daylight," he assured her.

He opened the door to go join Ruthie, then stopped short when Raegan asked, "Who is the widow Jenkins?"

So, she hadn't missed that remark tossed at him about Liza. And what should he answer? He couldn't tell her that the widow took care of his baser needs. She might not understand how it was with a man, about his need for sexual release.

But hell, he wasn't going to pretend that he was courting Liza either. Finally he said, "She's just a woman who lives in our community."

"Oh. No one special . . . to you?"

"Not in the least." His tone assured Raegan that he spoke the truth.

But why should I care whether or not the woman means anything to him? she chided herself. *It's none of my affair if he's courting her.* She stripped away the rest of her clothes and pulled her nightgown over her head. But as she climbed into bed and snuggled into the feather mattress, she admitted that it would bother her very much to know that Chase was involved romantically with a woman.

The rain had slowed to a drizzle when Chase joined Ruthie at the back of the post. "I guess I'm a little late," he apologized. "I had to settle Raegan in."

A tiny smile quirked the corners of Ruthie's lips. "Yes," she agreed, a bit of her amusement evident in her voice, "young brides usually take a bit of settling."

Chase sent the Indian woman a searching look, not sure whether he was being teased or not. But if he understood Ruthie's tone correctly, she was way off in what she was thinking. If he had really been doing what she guessed, it would take him all night.

Ignoring Ruthie's remark, he took the lantern from her and she bent over to pick up a paper-wrapped package and a small leather bag. "I hope we find the poor woman in the stables and not out in the rain somewhere," she said, following the path the lantern lit as Chase walked ahead.

"I just hope that we find her," Chase said, then swore as he slid in a patch of mud.

Drunken laughter from the post drifted on the damp air as he pushed open the sagging door of the slant-roofed shed. When he and Ruthie had slipped inside, he held the lantern high, moving it slowly to search out the corners. Other than the horses in the small, smelly room, they saw nothing else. There was not a sound save that of grinding teeth on hay and the occasional stamp of a hoof.

"Well," Chase said, disappointment in his voice, "She's not in here. Do you want to stay here where it's dry while I go poke around in the woods?"

"No, I'll go with you. I don't like it much in here."

Halfway to the door Chase stopped suddenly, grabbing Ruthie's arm, holding her still beside him. He held the lantern to shoulder height and pointed upward. As Ruthie looked up, a sifting of chaff settled on her face. She looked at Chase and nodded.

"Let's go," Chase said, and led the way up the ladder. At first they saw nothing but piles of hay in the loft, then Chase caught sight of a moccasined foot. "There she is," he said and went forward.

Ruthie gasped and Chase swore when they looked down on the Tillamook woman. The rope was still around her neck, and Roscoe had snubbed it tight to the roof's supporting post. It held her head at an awkward angle, causing her battered face to scrape against the post's rough bark.

"Oh, you poor soul." Ruthie went down on her knees beside the woman. When Chase would have knelt to cut her free of the rope, deep-seated fear flared in her blackened eyes.

"He won't hurt you," Ruthie soothed the woman in her native tongue, "he's here to help you." She picked up the paper-wrapped package she had laid beside her and, unfolding it, revealed a thick beef sandwich. "Give me your knife, Chase, so I can cut this damn rope."

The sharp blade slashed through the tightly drawn knot, and with a sigh of relief the woman straightened into an upright position. Ruthie held the meat and bread out to her. "Eat this, then I'll treat your poor face."

It was clear the woman didn't understand Ruthie's tongue, but the fact that she was female and had the same dusky skin as her own, calmed the woman a bit. She still kept a wary eye on Chase, however, and every time he moved, she cringed.

"Chase," Ruthie said, "why don't you go stand back out of sight? Understandably, she's scared to death of white men."

Chase nodded and moved away. From his leaning stance in a dark corner he watched the Indian woman's teeth tear into the food Ruthie had brought her. It was a safe bet that she hadn't eaten since Roscoe abducted her.

Why was it, he asked himself, that such evil lived in some men? Were they born that way, or had life done it to them? He supposed the harsh life on the Western frontier could turn a weak-charactered man mean.

Half an hour had passed by the time the Tillamook woman finished eating and Ruthie had done what she could for her cuts and bruises.

"What now, Chase?" Ruthie asked, sitting back on her heels. "Should we take her back across the river while we have the chance?"

"It would be awfully risky to do that," Chase answered. "By now her people will have missed her and will be combin' the woods and river. If they should find her with us, they'd kill us before we could open our mouths to explain why we have her."

"I know you're right, but it seems sinful to leave her with that man."

"I understand your feelins', Ruthie, but there's a whole lot of people who will be in danger if this isn't handled carefully. It's very important that when the Tillamook men find her, she's with Roscoe, and she'll explain to them that only he is responsible for stealin' her away.

"I guess it comes down to her life against many of our own."

Ruthie knew Chase was right and reluctantly picked up the rope. "I guess I'd better tie her back up then. She might try to make it back to her village and be attacked by a cat or a pack of wolves."

"Just tie her hands to the post, with enough slack in the rope so she can lie down."

"And you think Roscoe is going to leave it that way?" Ruthie snorted scornfully.

"He will, because he's not comin' back here tonight."

"Oh? How do you know that?" Ruthie finished tying the rope to the post.

"I'm gonna keep buyin' the bastard whiskey until he passes out." The woman had lain down and wearily stretched out her bruised body. "Pile some hay over and around her, then let's get back to the post before Roscoe decides to come back."

When a short time later they splashed through mud and puddles of water, the lantern lighting their way, Ruthie worried out loud, "I hope her people find her soon. She won't live long in Roscoe's hands."

"An Indian man demands strength and endurance from his women. I'm sure she'll survive Roscoe's brutality somehow."

Ruthie pushed open the back door of the post and they stepped inside.

"When will you tell the others what Roscoe's done?" Ruthie put her leather bag in a cabinet.

"First thing in the mornin'." His hand on the latch that separated the kitchen from the barroom, Chase paused. "Has my friend Jamie been around, Ruthie?"

Ruthie shook her head and smiled sympathetically. "I haven't seen him, Chase. Has he disappeared again?"

"Yeah." Chase nodded his head soberly. "Somethin' or somebody set him off." He lifted the latch. "He'll be back when he gets whatever it was out of his system. Maybe in a week or so."

Chase stepped inside the big room smelling of spirits and stood at the end of the bar. "Raegan all settled in?" Sid Johnson put a bottle of whiskey and a glass before him.

"Yeah." Chase nodded. "Listen, Sid, I want you to do me a favor."

"Sure. Just name it, friend."

"Keep Roscoe's glass filled with whiskey until he falls into a drunken stupor. I'll settle up with you when he passes out."

Sid looked at him quizzically. "You're gonna treat that bastard to free drinks? How come? There ain't a man in this room who'd buy him a glass of water if it would save his life."

"I have my reasons," Chase said grimly, "and it has nothin' to do with friendship. Ruthie will explain it to you later."

"Okay, if that's what you want." Sid took a bottle from the shelf behind him. "I'll start him on the path to oblivion right now."

Sid walked down the bar and Chase poured himself a glass of whiskey from the bottle his friend had left beside him on the bar. As he sipped the fiery liquid, his thoughts turned to Jamie Hart—Jamie, half breed, wild and reckless: with an angelic smile.

Jamie had became a part of his life five years ago. The young man, around twenty-one years old, had beyond a doubt saved Chase's life. He could remember the time.

Mists were still hanging in the valleys that morning when he saddled Sampson and rode to a meadow a few miles away, hoping to bag a deer. The animals' favorite time to browse was in the early daylight hours.

He had barely secreted himself in the dark shadows of a wide spruce when six head of them trooped out of the brush and began daintily snipping at the tall, lush grass. He tightened his knees around the stallion's belly, signaling him not to move. He pulled his rifle from its sheath, brought the butt to his shoulder and carefully took aim at a yearling.

Chase never pulled the trigger. For suddenly he was surrounded by a pack of wolves. He thought there were at least eight as he fought to stay on Sampson's back, the stallion whinnying his terror as the hungry animals snarled and snapped at his legs, trying to pull him down.

Before Chase knew it, as if it was happening to someone else, he was flying through the air. He landed hard on the ground as his mount went thundering down the valley, the empty stirrups slapping him in the belly. Chase put his hand to his holster and groaned. The gun wasn't there. Looking frantically around, he spied it lying at the feet of a large, snarling wolf.

As he watched the night prowlers circling him, coming ever closer, he thought of his helplessness with blind, black rage. He was going to die. His throat would be torn out by those snarling, hungry beasts.

"At least I'll go out fighting," he muttered grimly, reaching for the Bowie shoved into the top of his moccasins.

He was on his feet, the knife gripped in his hand, his eyes unwavering on the battle-scared leader, when the sharp crack of a rifle split the air.

With startled yips and yelps the wolves scattered, disappearing into the forest.

Chase wiped the cold perspiration off his forehead and looked up at a young man who sat with arms crossed on the pommel of his saddle, his eyes creased in a lazy smile.

"You came damn near bein' their breakfast, didn't you, hoss?"

"I've never come closer to bein' eaten." Chase grinned. He lifted his hands and watched them tremble. "I was just minutes away from meetin' my Maker and it scared me witless, I don't mind tellin' you. Ain't no way my sin-filled soul is ready to meet Him."

The young man laughed and slid gracefully out of the saddle. "Jamie Hart," he said, offering his hand.

"Right pleased to meet you, Jamie Hart." Chase gave the slim hand a firm shake. "Chase Donlin."

"I've heard of you." The half-breed studied Chase's face. "It's said that you're a mean cuss, fast as lightnin' with either gun or knife."

"Well I wasn't very fast with either one today," Chase grunted, walking over to retrieve his gun. Shoving it into its holster, he said, "My cabin is in the next valley—come have breakfast with me."

"What about your mount? Should I go run him down?"

"Naw. Let him come to us." Chase stuck a finger and thumb into his mouth and blew a loud whistle. It hadn't stopped echoing through the hills when Sampson came galloping up to them.

"He's a fine-lookin' animal." Jamie admired the black stallion. "I'll bet he can run like the wind."

"He's fast," Chase admitted, swinging into the saddle. "But you let me down today, didn't you boy?" He gave the sweating, arching neck an affectionate pat.

"A pack of hungry wolves would make any animal panic." Jamie made excuses for the stallion as he turned his mount and followed Sampson.

"They sure as hell scared me." Chase laughed.

Later, as Chase fried a couple of steaks and a skillet of sliced potatoes, Jamie told him a bit about himself.

"I've floated around a lot," he began. "I've been a cowpuncher, a bronco rider, prospected for gold, and for a short time I rode shotgun for a coach."

"That's a lot of different jobs for a man so young," Chase observed, dishing up the meat and raw fries. "Weren't any of them to your likin'?"

Jamie was silent for a moment, staring down at his plate. Then, shrugging indifferently, he answered, "I liked breakin' horses." He looked up at Chase. "I was never kept on very long."

"How come? Are you lazy?"

Jamie shook his head. "You see, I've always had to walk a narrow path. My Indian mother on one side, my Irish father on the other." He made an attempt at light laughter. "I don't know if it's the Pauite in me that people don't like, or the Irish."

Chase went along with the amused note. He grinned and said, "No doubt it's the Irish."

Jamie laughed, recognizing the name Donlin as being Irish.

How it came about, Chase never fully understood, but Jamie stayed on with him. Five years now, celebrating his twenty-sixth birthday last week. They trapped together in the winter, hunted in the summer, caroused together in between. Jamie had became the younger brother he had always wished for.

And though he was seemingly content with his life in the Oregon wilderness, Jamie was often restless. The other trappers in the area had taken an immediate liking to the carefree young man, accepting him as one of them. But the wives, although they too were fond of the handsome Jamie, would not allow him to court their daughters. And though he pretended he didn't care, even joked about it, Chase knew better. Jamie hurt like hell, being judged by his Indian blood.

Chase sighed and tilted the bottle over his glass again. When life with the whites became too much for his friend, he disappeared for a while.

The ignorance of some people, he thought glumly.

Chase looked down the bar at Roscoe. He had a glazed look in his eyes, and his movements were awkward and unsure. One more slug of whiskey and he should be stretched out on the floor, dead to the world.

Chase transferred his gaze to the four men playing poker at a table lit by a hanging lantern. He downed his drink, swung away from the bar, and joined them. Pitting his wits against the gamblers would make the night go faster and keep his brain sharp, so he could keep an eye on the fat man.

A couple of the players ragged him about leaving his new bride to sleep alone, but when he didn't rise to their ribbing, the cards were dealt and the game went on.

The black of night was just giving away to the gray of approaching dawn when the game broke up. The cards were gathered into a stack and left in the center of the table for whoever wanted to use them next. There were no new decks passed out every night at the post. If anyone was caught trying to mark cards, he was barred from ever playing there again.

Consequently, new cards appeared when the old ones became dog-eared in such a way that everyone knew who had what by the certain way the corners were worn down.

There came the scraping sound of chairs being pushed back and complaining voices. "I lost everything but my name," one trapper gripped, while another grouched, "You was mighty lucky tonight, Donlin. Thanks for leavin' me my back teeth."

"You're welcome, Ike." Chase stood and stretched. "I didn't want you to have to gum your breakfast."

The good-natured grousing went on a few minutes more, then the trappers prepared to go to their individual homes.

From the corner of his eye Chase saw Roscoe stir, then sit up from the spot on the floor where he had snored all night. "Hold on a minute, men," he called, striding over to the fat man and hauling him to his feet. "Roscoe wants to tell you somethin'. He wants to let you in on his latest dirty adventure."

The trappers stared at Roscoe expectantly, but he remained silent as he struggled to free himself of the iron fingers grasping his arm. "Go on, you bastard," Chase ordered coldly. "Tell them of the danger your action will bring down on them and their families."

The trappers, having drunk or played cards all night, were in a sullen mood with aching heads and burning, bloodshot eyes. All were anxious to get home, eat, and go to bed. Their tempers grew short when Roscoe still wouldn't speak.

"Spit it out, you tub of lard," one man growled. "What did you do that's got Donlin all riled up?"

When Roscoe only continued to look down at the floor, his mouth working wordlessly, someone yelled, "Look at him, he's scared witless." He took a step toward Roscoe. "Have you been foolin' round with some youngin', you bastard?"

"You'd better tell them, Chase." Sid Johnson came from behind the bar. "You ain't gonna get a word out of him."

Tightening his grip on the fleshy arm, Chase bit out, "He's got a Tillamook woman tied up in the stables."

For a moment, stunned silence filled the room as the trappers stared at Roscoe in disbelief. Then one man found his voice. "You worthless piece of dog dung, you fat bastard! Damn your miserable hide, bringin' the wrath of the Tillamook down on innocent people. Only you would do somethin' like that!"

The dark muttering that had started grew to a roar as one by one, the trappers started to close in on the cowering man. Their intent to beat him to death was clear in their rage-spitting eyes.

Chase hurried to stand in front of the sagging man. Holding up his hands for attention, he spoke loudly to be heard over the bloodthirsty men. "Men, stop and think for a minute. Killin' him is the worse thing you can do."

"How so, Donlin?" a man demanded as they all came to a halt. "If ever a man needed killin', it's him. He's jeopardized our famlies—all of Big Pine is in danger. Them Tillamooks are gonna swarm into this valley, killin' every man, woman, and child they come across."

"Not necessarily," Chase reasoned. "Oh, they'll come lookin' for her all right, but don't it stand to reason that they'll want to find the woman first? That the man they find her with might be the only one who gets killed?"

It quietened down in the room and Chase saw that his words were being turned over in the trappers' minds. He held his breath, hoping they would realize the sense of them. Finally the one called Ike spoke.

"Could be you're right, Donlin, but we want him and the woman away from here, clear out of the region, and right now."

"Of course, that goes without sayin'," Chase agreed. "Also"—he turned on Roscoe—"If you have in mind to take the woman out in the woods and kill her, give it another thought. I'm gonna have one of Chief Wise Man's braves track you, keep an eye on you and the woman. If she turns up dead, you'll follow her in short order."

He grasped Roscoe by the collar. "Do you understand what I said? You're a marked man."

Roscoe nodded sullenly, and when someone held the door open, Chase shoved him through it, calling, "And don't stop for any *pleasurin'* "

Chapter Five

Loud curses, mingled with the sound of tramping feet across a wooden floor awakened Raegan. She heard a door slam, then it grew quiet in the barroom with only a low murmur of voices. Had there been a fight? she wondered. And where was Chase?

She sat up in bed and looked at his empty bedroll. It hadn't been slept in. It was exactly the way she had spread it out last night. Where had he slept?

She wouldn't let herself finish the thought that crept into her mind.

Raegan got out of bed and padded over to the window that looked out over the area around the post. "Oh no," she cried. Roscoe and the Tillamook woman were leaving—he riding and she limping stolidly behind him, her face expressionless, hiding whatever pain she might be feeling.

Poor soul, Raegan thought, then turned around when the door opened. "Well, I see you're up." Chase smiled at her, then looked quickly away. The thin nightgown didn't hide any more than it had last night. "As soon as you get dressed, we'll have a bite of breakfast and leave," he finished huskily, bending over his blankets and rolling them up.

Raegan was tempted to ask him where he had slept last night, but knowing that it was none of her business, she hurried to take her undergarments from the back of the chair where they had dried overnight.

"I saw that dreadful Roscoe leaving," she said. "From the noise I heard, it sounded like the men chased him away."

"They did." Chase nodded.

"And the woman? Did you and Ruthie find her last night?"

"Yes. She was in the stable tied to a post. Ruthie fed her and tended to her bruises. You'll be happy to know that she had a full night free of Roscoe's attention."

"How did you manage that?" Raegan looked her surprise.

Chase grinned. "I had Sid feed him whiskey until he passed out."

Raegan giggled and stuck one slender foot into her mid-thigh bloomers. "That was mighty enterprising of you. I'll bet . . ." The door slammed and she became aware that she was now speaking to herself. Chase had bolted at the first sight of the trim ankle and calf disappearing into the white lace-trimmed undergarment.

Her lips curled in amusement as she finished pulling on the bloomers and tying them around her waist. She must remember to practice more decorum from now on. She had never had to bother about dressing and undressing before. There had only been Mama and Papa, and later the old squaw, to see her.

By the time Raegan finished dressing she had come to the conclusion that there were a lot of things she must learn. She was beginning to realize that up until now she had led a very protected life. Mama and Papa had shielded her from a lot of ugliness, had kept her somewhat naive as to how the world truly was sometimes.

When Raegan walked into the barroom, she found it empty except for Chase, Ruthie, and Sid. The three sat around a table, platters of steaming food in its center.

Chase smiled at her and Ruthie said, "Good morning, Raegan, did you have a good night's sleep?"

Raegan laughed as she sat down in a chair across from Chase. "I don't know if I slept, or I died for several hours. I don't think I even moved."

"Well, Chase, it's plain your little bride didn't need your presence to lull her to sleep," Sid teased.

Ruthie saw both Raegan's and Chase's faces flame red, and she slapped Sid playfully on the hand. "Hush up, you randy ruffian." She handed Raegan a platter of eggs and ham. "Eat hardy, Raegan. You have a fifteen-mile ride ahead of you."

"Where in the world did you get eggs and pork?" Raegan gaped, wide-eyed. "It's been over two years since I've eaten either one."

"I buy them from Aggie Stevens, one of the trapper wives. When she came here to the hills, she brought along two dozen hens and one rooster, plus a boar and a sow. That was seven year ago. Today she has over two hundred chickens, and every fall after it frosts, Ike, her husband, butchers a half dozen hogs. Aggie keeps people supplied with eggs and pork for miles around."

Raegan looked hopefully at Chase. "Will we . . . ?"

"There's a good supply at the cabin right now," Chase interrupted with a wide grin. "I picked up a couple dozen eggs along with a side of bacon a day before I got your mother's letter. I'll get a ham from Aggie too."

"Good." Raegan grinned back and dug into her breakfast.

Shortly, she and Chase were astride their mounts, taking leave of the Johnsons. "Come visit soon," Ruthie called as they rode away.

"I will," Raegan assured the first friend she'd made in Oregon. "I want you to teach me how to make that tasty stew I had for supper last night."

"Sid and Ruthie are good people," Chase said as they rode along, Lobo running ahead of them.

"They certainly are," Raegan agreed. "Do the women of Big Pine associate with Ruthie?"

"Most do. Of course, like everywhere else, you find a few ignorant, biased people." Like Liza

Jenkins, he thought silently.

"It's their loss then, not getting to know her," Raegan remarked.

Although spring had come to the hills and valleys, the mountain tops were still snow-capped, and when the wind blew down from them, as it did now, it was definitely chilly.

Raegan pulled her jacket collar up around her ears and nodded agreement when Chase grinned at her action and said, "Kinda brisk this morning, huh?"

No more was spoken between them for the next hour. Raegan was occupied with her surroundings, marveling at the towering firs and a sky so blue it made your eyes hurt to look at it. She was going to be happy in this country, she knew it.

Chase's thoughts ran along the usual line. How was he going to keep his hands off Raegan? Never in his thirty-two years had he wanted a woman so badly. It was going to be pure hell living with her, pretending that he had only avuncular feelings for her.

Suddenly, their silent musings were broken with a nerve-shattering jolt. From high on a distant hill came the scream of a panther. Raegan's whole scalp prickled, and Beauty tossed her head nervously.

"Them big cats sound just like a woman screamin', don't they?" Chase remarked, tightening his grip on the snorting stallion.

"It's a scary sound." Raegan shivered.

"A panther is somethin' to be scared of," Chase said. "Because of them, and many other varmints that range the hills, don't ever go into the forest alone, Raegan. There are stories of men who have gone into those thick woods and never returned. It's still debated whether they were killed by Indians or animals, or become lost and starved to death.

"I thinks it's best if you . . ." Chase broke off, and grasping Beauty by the bridle bit, he pulled the two mounts behind a tall thicket of bushes.

"What is it?" Raegan asked in a low voice, alerted to the frown on Chase's face that it was imperative not to make a noise.

Chase swung out of the saddle and motioned Raegan to do the same. "I just heard the slap of a paddle on the river below us. I want to see if it's friend or foe." He carefully parted the bushes so that they had a view of the Platte flowing along.

They hadn't long to wait. Within minutes, at the bend in the river, a canoe came into sight, sliding smoothly and silently through the water. While they watched with held breaths, another followed, and then another, until six in a row slid past them.

"Tillamooks?" Raegan asked in a whisper, her hand unconsciously gripping Chase's arm.

"Yes. It appears they have begun looking for the woman." Chase grabbed her chin, forcing her to look at him. "Raegan, promise me that you will never go far from the cabin alone."

She nodded, unable to speak. She had never before stood so close to Chase, never felt his hands on her bare flesh. She had the urge to move closer, to melt against him, to feel his arms go round her, his lips cover hers. When she saw an answering flare in his eyes, she leaned closer to him.

She blinked when Chase snatched his hand away and said brusquely, "We'd better get goin'."

Raegan cringed inside as she climbed back on Beauty. Had Chase read what must have shown in her eyes? Was he disgusted with her? Did he think she was a loose woman?

She'd never be able to look him in the face again, she wailed silently, lifting the reins and setting Beauty to walk behind Sampson.

Chase's mind was filled with uneasy thoughts also. Raegan's desire had wafted from her body in waves, meeting and mingling with his own. He had found himself weakening in his determination that there would never be carnal knowledge between them. When she leaned toward him, her soft lips parted, it had been the hardest thing he'd ever done in his life not to grab her in his arms and hungrily devour her red lips.

But he had listened to the inner voice that warned him, "You must not lose control. You must be the strong one. It's up to you to walk away."

But now, as they rode along, Raegan trailing behind him, Chase knew that she was embarrassed, probably had hurt feelings. He pulled Sampson in, and when Raegan came abreast of him, he said with his usual friendly smile, "Over that next hill is your new home."

Relief washed over Raegan. Chase hadn't noticed her wanton behavior back there after all. A wide smile stretched her lips. "I can't wait to see it," she cried, and gave Beauty a jab of her heel that sent the little mare racing away.

Chase laughed and sent the stallion galloping after her, praying that he would never be tempted by her again. His will power was only so strong. Another time might be his undoing.

The mounts lunged up a small hill, then at a slower pace descended the backside of it. And there, at the bottom of the hill, drowsing in the warm afternoon sun was a long, L-shaped cabin. Chase reined in his mount, bringing both horses to a halt so that Raegan could get a slower, more rounded view of everything.

Raegan's gaze moved over the building of peeled logs, frowning at its neglected state. Where were the flower beds Mama had described so glowingly, the rose bush that climbed up the chimney walls? There was nothing in the yard except tall weeds that grew right up to the wide porch stretching the width of the cabin.

She ran her glance over several out-buildings set some distance from the log house, the largest being a barn. There was no deterioration in any of the structures, however, including the cabin. It was the weedy growth, the dead flower beds, the negligence of the entire area that made one think at first glance that it was an abandoned homestead. She imagined that such things were of small importance to a man. After all, Grandmother Molly had been dead for many years.

"Well, what do you think?" Chase probbed after Raegan's long, silent scrunity.

"It's much like Mama described it," Raegan answered after a hesitant moment. "She talked about her home a lot. Especially the last months, when she was bed-ridden." She paused, then added, "I was wondering, though, what happened to the flower beds she spoke of, and the big rose bush that covered the chimney in red blossoms in the spring?"

A small frown etched Chase's forehead, as though he had noticed for the first time the absence of the things she mentioned.

"Pa tended the yard after Molly passed away, but I'm afraid I didn't do the same after his passin'. Actually, I guess I didn't even notice how the weeds were takin' over. I'll get the sickle after them tomorrow."

He lifted the reins and they moved out, arriving at the cabin in a short time. When the mounts were tethered to a hitching post, the mare a safe distance from the stallion, Raegan followed Chase along a beaten path bordered with waist-high weeds. Here and there she saw a flower struggling for its share of sun and air.

I'll help you tomorrow, she thought, then stepped through the door Chase held open for her.

She stood just inside a large room for a moment, peering into the gloom of drawn drapes. Stale air greeted her, as of a room long shut up. When Chase tramped across the floor and pulled aside the covering on the two windows, her sweeping glance took in the accummulated dust and grime. Her eyes lingered a moment on the dead flies caught in cobwebs formed in the corners of the glass panes, then dropped to the floor where sand and grit had somehow blown into the room and now lay in small drifts.

To complete the dismal look of what she knew was the parlor, although she had never been in one, the furniture was shrouded with sheets and blankets. The one piece of beauty she could see was the fieldstone fireplace built into an outside wall.

Raegan started when Chase spoke close behind her. "This room has been shut up the past couple years. In fact, all the rooms except for the kitchen and one bedroom have been closed off."

When Raegan only stared at him, wondering how anyone could willingly live in just two rooms, he added defensively, "It didn't seem reasonable to keep the whole place open."

"Well," Raegan said sharply, "I've lived in two rooms all my life and I hated it. I hope you won't mind if I open up all the rooms."

"Of course not," Chase assured her hastily. "This is your home, Raegan. You do whatever you want to with it." He surveyed the room slowly, a look of long-ago memories coming into his eyes. "I'd like it fine to see the place lookin' like it used to again. Pa tried, but somehow the warmth that Mother Molly always brought to it was missin'. I'm thinkin' that you'll have her same knack for makin' this place a home again."

Raegan heard the sadness in his voice and remembered her mother saying how fond the little boy Chase had been of his new mama. "I shall do my best, Chase," she said softly. "And now," she said briskly, "Shall we go to the kitchen?"

Almost with reluctance, Chase walked to a door in the center of an inside wall and, opening it, said, "Right this way, madam."

Raegan giggled at his teasing tone and words and followed him down a hall where two doors on either side stood closed. Bedrooms, she imagined, then walked through one at the end of the passageway when Chase held it open for her.

She barely suppressed a cry of dismay. Never had she seen anything like this kitchen. The sun shining through the uncurtained kitchen windows threw into relief the dirt and disorder, missing not one piece of debris scattered about. It shone on rusty, broken traps, pieces of broken bits and bridles, a heap of dirty clothes kicked into a corner, and a table and dry-sink stacked high with dirty dishes, pots, and skillets.

But glory of glories, in one corner sat a big, black cooking range. It was grimed over with grease, along with food that had spilled from pots and pans and baked onto its surface.

Nevertheless, it was beautiful in Raegan's eyes. She had never cooked on one before. This pleasant surprise didn't take away her disgust of the filthy kitchen, however.

She swung angrily on Chase, her green eyes spitting fire. "This is a regular boar's nest! How can you live like this?"

Dumbfounded at her verbal attack, Chase could only stare at Raegan for a moment. Then, slowly, he saw the deplorable state of the kitchen through her eyes. Would she understand, he wondered, that during the winter months he worked from first dawn to early night running his traplines? And that was only the first part of his day. After lugging home his catch, they had to be skinned, then stretched over special boards sized according to how big the pelt was. Would she sympathize that sometimes he was so tired that he almost fell asleep while eating a hurriedly prepared meal? Would she believe him if he explained that once his traps were put away for the season, he always scrubbed out the kitchen, polished the stove, and kept it that way until the cold weather arrived again?

Before he could say all this to Raegan, she sighed and said, "A fire must be built and water brought in to heat. I doubt if there's a clean plate, pot, or skillet to be found."

Chase knew she was right about that, but she was wrong about water having to be lugged into the house. He walked over to the dry-sink and moved dirty dishes around until a small, red hand pump was revealed. It eased his embarrassment a bit to say, "You've got all the water you'll need right here."

He worked the handle up and down a few times and water gushed forth, hitting a big pot and splashing onto the floor. It wet the dry, caked dirt beside the sink, turning it back into the mud it had been when it was tracked into the kitchen.

But Raegan didn't care. The floor could be scrubbed. The important thing was that there was water right here in the house. She couldn't believe how fortunate she was. There would be no more hauling pails of water to scrub and clean with, no more trips to a creek to do dirty laundry. She had often wished for such a convenience, but had never dreamed that such luxury would ever be hers.

She lifted shining eyes to Chase as she took off her jacket and rolled up her sleeves. "If you'll make me a fire, I'll start some water to heating."

"Yes, ma'am." Chase saluted her smartly, the gesture losing some of its smartness when his moccasined heels didn't make the appropriate click. He and Raegan shared their laughter.

"Were you ever in the Army, Chase?" Raegan asked, sorting the dishes from the cooking utensils and placing them in a big dishpan while he started a fire in the range.

"No, I've never been in the regular Army, though I was a scout for little over a year during the worst of the Indian uprising. I don't think I could go along with all the rules and regulations the army puts such importance on."

He looked at Raegan and grinned. "I like to go my own way, I guess."

Raegan studied the strong face turned to her, the clear eyes, straight nose, and square jaw. Yes, she thought, you are a law unto yourself, Chase Donlin—making up your own rules, biding by no one else's.

From the corner of her eye, she saw steam rising from the large tea kettle spout and was thankful for the excuse to pull her eyes away from the disturbing ones that were suddenly locked with hers.

She forced herself to look away, to mutter, "The water's hot. I'd better start on these dishes so I can begin supper."

"Yes," Chase answered curtly, turning quickly away from her, forcing back the desire to kiss her soft lips. "There's soap in the cabinet below the sink," he managed to say as he walked toward the door. "I'll go tend to the horses now."

Raegan made no response, afraid that her voice might reveal how her pulse was racing. She bent down and rummaged through an assortment of items, searching for the soap. She spotted it at last, and her trembling fingers gripped the dried and cracked yellow bar. She straightened up, shaking her head as she dropped it into the pan of water. From its dry, shrunken condition, it hadn't been used in a long time.

She worked up a suds in the hot water, then washed only enough dishes, cups, and flatware to use for supper. She then washed a pot and skillet to cook the food in. While they drained, she attacked the long table, scrubbing away ground-in grease and food spills with a brush she'd also found under the sink. She set the table, then went to find Chase. There was nothing but staples in the larder, and she had no idea where he kept his meat.

Chase curried the stallion and mare, then turned Sampson into the corral off the side of the barn, all the time making sure he didn't think about Raegan.

As he leaned his elbows on the corral's top rail, the warmth of the sun faded and twilight shadowed the land. There was no sound, no wind, no movement. Nevertheless, as he stared into the gathering dusk, he kept his ears attuned for the scuffing sound of moccasined feet, the soft thud of unshod horses.

The Tillamooks were on the prowl and he must be ever alert. He had a responsibility now, one very dear to his heart. The thought of Raegan being taken by the angry Tillamooks, raped and mistreated, was more than his mind could stand thinking about.

The snort and tramp of a horse brought Chase back to the present, his hand dropping to his colt as he spun around. He dropped his hand and smiled widely when a masculine voice drawled, "You're gettin' careless, hoss. Like you're so fond of tellin' me, a careless man don't last long in the wild Oregon hills."

"It's about time you're showin' your face around here, Jamie Hart." Chase watched the slim, lithe half-breed swing gracefully from the roan. "Where in the hell have you been?"

"Oh, here and there and no place in particular." The young man uncinched the saddle and lifted it off the horse's back. "Spent some time with my mother's people—my grandmother. Helped her get her garden in."

Jamie swung open the corral gate and shooed his mount through it. "She's agin' fast, Chase." There was regret in his voice. "I'll miss her when she's gone. Her wise counsel always puts strength back into me when I go to her, sick of life, tired of tryin' to see a future for myself."

He came and stood beside Chase, his elbows next to the one man he could call friend. As he stared off into the twilight, Chase said, "Jamie, did you ever give any thought to makin' a life with your mother's people—marry a nice Indian girl, raise a family?"

Jamie gave a harsh laugh. "The Indians look on me much as the white man does. Like the pale-face don't like the Indian blood in me, the red man don't like the white blood runnin' through my veins. And like the white man not wanting me to marry his daughter, neither does the Indian want me marryin' his either."

Chase knew this was true and had no rebuttal to Jamie's claim. To lighten the gloomy atmosphere Jamie's observations had caused to settle round them, Chase laughingly slapped him on his back and said, "Well, we'll just have to find you an orphan, won't we? One who doesn't have a father to object to your marryin' her."

"Now that's a thought." Jamie joined Chase's levity, pulling himself out of his dark thoughts.

The two men stood in companionable silence for a while, then Jamie said, "Comin' in, I'm sure I saw some Tillamook braves skulking around in the forest a few miles back. Do you suppose they're finally goin' to rise up against us?"

"I'm afraid they are," Chase said soberly, then related what had happened in Jamie's absence.

"That stupid bastard," Jamie swore. "He's gonna get us all killed."

Chase started to agree, then stopped when a feminine voice called, "Chase, where are you?"

Jamie sent Chase a questioning look. "Have you moved a woman in with us, friend?" He grinned.

"She's off bounds to you, *friend*." Chase tried to speak in a joking tone, but there was still a soft warning in the words. "She's not just a woman, she's my woman."

As soon as the words left his mouth Chase wanted to call them back. He could tell Jamie the truth about Raegan. Their secret would be safe with him. Why hadn't he explained that Raegan was his niece, but that circumstances had forced him to claim her as his wife and now he didn't know how to correct the deception? That deep down, he didn't want to? That he couldn't bear the thought of the bachelor trappers coming around to court her?

But while he considered telling his friend all, Raegan walked through the dusk to join them.

Chase felt Jamie's startled reaction, and from the corners of his eyes saw the young man's gleaming appreciation in the gaze he swept over Raegan. A slow smile curved his lips and he held a hand out to her. "My friends call me Jamie."

Her eyes twinkling back at the handsome young man, she laid her hand in his and said, "My friends call me Raegan."

"Where'd you find a beauty like this, Chase?" Jamie continued to hold Raegan's hand. "She's not from around here. I know every woman in these hills."

"I'm from Idaho," Raegan answered before Chase could, gently freeing her hand.

"Any more like her there in Idaho?" Jamie teased, then grinned when Raegan blushed.

"I couldn't tell you." Chase grinned too. "As soon as I saw Raegan, I didn't look at another woman."

"Will you two stop it?" Raegan spoke in confusion, the male eyes looking at her so intently making her nervous.

"I'm sorry, Raegan," Chase said gently, "don't pay any attention to us. We're just a couple lamebrains. Did you want something?"

"I wanted to ask what you want for supper. I can't find any meat."

"The perishables are in the cellar beneath the kitchen." Jamie answered instead of Chase. Chase frowned as his friend took Raegan's arm and started walking toward the cabin, asking softly, "Could we have steak for supper? I haven't had beef in ages."

Chase stared after the couple, his face like a black thunder cloud. What in the hell did Jamie think he was doing? It hadn't been said right out, but hadn't he hinted strong enough that he and Raegan were married? The man knew women inside and out—surely he could tell that Raegan wasn't the sort who just moved in with a man.

He stalked after them, wondering how and when his and Raegan's deception would end.

He walked into the kitchen and saw that the trap door was laid back and that Raegan and Jamie were in the cellar. He heard them talking and laughing, and his jealously grew. Slowly then his clenched fist uncurled. "Stop it right now, mister," he hissed to himself. "You have no right to be jealous. The sooner you realize that, the better off you'll be."

But the feeling persisted, growing as Raegan's and Jamie's heads appeared above the floor, Jamie's hand on Raegan's elbow, guiding her up the shallow steps. Chase came to the firm decision that he'd keep an eye on that young man. He'd never seen him so taken with a woman.

Words he had spoken to Jamie came back to haunt him. "We'll just have to find you an orphan. One who doesn't have a father to object to you marryin' her."

Well, by god, *he'd* object. He'd object stronger than any father would. And not because Jamie was a half-breed, either.

Chase lowered his lids, hiding his dark thoughts as the pair stepped onto the floor and Jamie lowered the trap door. But Raegan knew by his stiff stance that something had displeased him.

But what? she asked herself. What could have happened in the short distance between the corral and the cabin?

She decided that whatever bothered him couldn't have anything to do with her or Jamie. She laid the steaks that Jamie had sliced off a haunch of beef on the table, and Jamie dumped the potatoes held in the crook of his arm down beside them. Two rolled onto the floor and, laughing, he and Raegan chased after them, bumping heads in the process.

When Raegan stood up, a potato clutched in her hand, her face flushed from laughter and activity, her eyes fell on Chase and the amusement died in her eyes. He wasn't laughing. In fact his face was dark with anger and disapproval.

In confusion, she started to peel the potatoes. Didn't he want her to be friendly toward Jamie? Surely he must. Jamie was his best friend. Jamie had told her in the cellar that he had lived with Chase.

She must get the pair of them out of the kitchen, she thought. Chase was making her nervous with his cold eyes and stiff jaw. She turned her head and looked at both of them. "I can use more wood," she said.

Neither man moved, then Chase said gruffly, "Come on, Jamie, let's cut some wood." Jamie grinned in amusement, then followed his black-browed friend outside.

Raegan heaved a sigh of relief when the pair left the kitchen. A short time later there came the sound of an axe cutting into wood. Somewhat relaxed now, she started the sliced potatoes to frying, then set the big cast-iron skillet on the stove to heat. She hurriedly washed another plate, knife and fork, then set the table.

The frying pan was hot by now, and after putting a small amount of lard to melt in it, Raegan laid the steaks on top. She picked up the coffee pot and frowned at the splattered grease on its surface. She didn't have time to scrub it, but the men would expect a cup of coffee to finish off the meal.

Surprisingly, when she lifted off the lid to pump water into the pot, she found its inside sparkling clean. Well, she thought, Chase is not a complete sloth.

She was turning the steaks when Chase entered, his arms full of short split logs. When he dropped them into the woodbox behind the stove, she smiled at him and said, "You and Jamie can wash up now. Supper will be ready in five minutes."

Chase looked at the scrubbed table, the plates placed neatly, the flatware beside them. He frowned at the two candles burning in the table's center. "I'm sorry you've had to cook by candlelight," he apologized. "I forgot to buy kerosene for the lamps. Make out a list of anything you need from the village store and add it on."

Raegan nodded. "There are a few things I see you're out of."

As Chase went out the door to call Jamie, Raegan turned back to the stove, wondering what she was going to do about bread for tomorrow's meals. She had never baked bread before, not even biscuits. Mama had always seen to the baking, and when she became ill, she had taught Mahalla how to do it.

I don't even know how to work the oven, she despaired. Actually, she didn't know a lot about cooking—only how to make stew and fry meat.

Supper was a jolly, laughing affair—for Jamie and Raegan anyway. They bounced bantering remarks back and forth at each other, thoroughly enjoying themselves. They had at first tried to draw Chase into their nonsensical exchange, but he only grunted or answered in gruff monosyllables, and they finally gave up bothering with him and continued to tease each other.

Chase grew quieter and quieter, his brow growing darker as the gay chatter went on around him. Damn Jamie, he thought and clamped his jaws together. *He's deliberately baitin' me, tryin' to get a rise out of me.*

And doing a fine job of it too. His inner voice seemed to laugh at him also.

Finally, the longest meal Chase had ever sat through was over. The meat and potatoes had been eaten, the coffee drunk. When Jamie said in a forlorn voice, "I'd better get my bedroll and find a pile of hay in the barn," Chase was ready to agree whole-heartedly.

But Raegan spoke before he could open his mouth. "Sleep in the barn!" she said scandalized. "Nonsense. This is your home. You'll sleep in your old room as usual."

"Well, I don't know about that," Jamie drawled, his eyes twinkling. "Me and Chase bunked together. I'm afraid it would be a little crowded—three of us in the bed."

In his aggravation with Raegan, Chase was tempted to let her handle Jamie's remark on her own. But with one look at her flustered face, he softened. He scowled at Jamie when he stood up. When the young man dropped his eyes to his plate, realizing he had pushed his friend too far, Chase looked down at Raegan.

"Come with me, and I'll show you where the bed linens are kept—I'll even help you make up a bed for my ignorant friend with the runaway tongue."

"Come on, Chase," Jamie protested, "you know I was only funnin' Raegan. I wouldn't . . ." He spoke to an empty room. Chase had ushered Raegan out of the kitchen and closed the door behind them.

He's jealous as hell of me, Jamie thought, mischief sparkling in his eyes. This coming summer promised to be a very amusing one. Ole Chase was going to be like a raging buffalo all season. He'd see to it.

"How many bedrooms are there?" Raegan asked as she and Chase walked down the hall.

"There are four, although Molly used one for her sewing room," Chase answered, stopping in front of a tall cabinet near the end of the hall. "There's a loom in there also. She used to weave beautiful rugs on it. I took them off the floors and stored them away in one of the sheds. I'll bring them in tomorrow. You'll most likely want to put them in the bedrooms."

Chase swung open the double doors of what Raegan discovered was a linen closet. She was amazed at the stack of sheets, pillow cases, quilts and bedspreads. She and Mama had gotten by with one set for each bed. Each week they were washed and dried and put back on the bed. And they had never had any quilts—only itchy army-issue blankets.

On the lower shelf was what Raegan imagined were tablecloths and runners for dressers and such. Mama had talked about how her mother would embroider such items in the winter evenings as they sat before the fire.

She looked down at her rough, chapped hands, her worn dress, and wondered what her lady grandmother would think of her only granddaughter if she could see her.

She pushed the useless thought from her mind and returned to the present. The linens were yellowed from disuse, she saw as she took down four sheets and four pillowcases, but they were clean and smelled of dried rose petals. She loaded the articles into Chase's arms, then added two quilts from the top shelf.

"We'll put Jamie in the room next to mine," Chase said, motioning her to open a door on the right side of the hall, "and you can have the one opposite mine. It's the biggest and nicest. It used to be your grandparents' room."

Again stale air greeted Raegan as she stepped inside the large room. When Chase lit a candle on a small bedside table, she walked over to the window and raised the sash. Cool, fresh air floated in, brisk from the hills. She took a deep breath, then set about making up the bed. As she shook out a sheet, Chase moved to the other side of the bed and, catching its edge he tucked the sheet neatly under the feather mattress that lay on top of a straw tick.

"Jamie believes we're married, doesn't he?" Raegan asked, unfolding a top sheet.

"I think he does . . . for the time bein' at least. He's sharp, though. I don't know how long we can fool him."

"Maybe I'd better wait a while before making up my own bed then," Raegan said thoughtfully. "After he's retired."

"A good idea," Chase agreed, and no more was said as cases were pulled over feather pillows and a quilt smoothed over the bed.

Jamie was backed into a corner, a helpless look in his staring eyes when Raegan and Chase returned to the kitchen. "Lobo! No!" Raegan sprang to the side of the snarling wolf. "Friend, Lobo! He's a friend." She grabbed the raised ruff.

"What's wrong, friend?" Chase couldn't help doing a little teasing of his own now, get back a bit of what he'd been put through. "Are you afraid of our pet?"

"Pet, hell," Jamie's voice quavered a bit. "That's a damn wolf. Came walkin' in like he belongs here."

"He does, Jamie," Raegan said quietly. "He's my pet wolf. Keep your voice down, and I'll explain to him that you won't harm me."

Jamie looked dubious, but didn't move a muscle, barely breathed as Raegan knelt beside the big animal and gazed into his eyes. After a moment Lobo's tongue came out and licked her cheek, then he stalked over beside the table and flopped down on the floor.

"Whew!" Jamie exclaimed, rubbing the back of his hand across his sweating forehead. I thought for a minute there that I was a goner. I was so scared, I lost my voice. I couldn't even yell for help." He slid a wary glance at Lobo, who now lay with his great head between his paws "Are you sure he's tame?"

"He's tame enough," Raegan answered, beginning to gather up the dirty dishes. "It would be unkind to take all the wildness out of him. I only allow a few select people to know him. If I let him think that everyone is his friend, he'd be no more than a pet dog."

"I guess," Jamie agreed reluctantly, wondering why Raegan couldn't be satisfied with owning a dog. He looked at Chase. "I'm gonna look in on my mount before turnin' in. Comin' with me?"

"Yeah." Chase nodded, pulling a sack of tobacco from his shirt pocket as he followed Jamie out the door. A few moments later the aromatic smell of burning tobacco drifted through the open kitchen door.

Raegan sniffed deeply, a memory of her father coming to mind. He, too, always rolled a cigarette after his meals. "Don't think of Papa," she whispered, "Put aside your memories for now, concentrate on what's at hand. Like making some order out of this mess called a kitchen."

The mellow boom of the clock in the parlor struck eleven times as Raegan snuffed out two of the candles on the kitchen table. She picked up the third burning one and lighted her way down the hall to the bedroom alloted to her.

Chase and Jamie had long since retired, Chase saying a gruff good-night as they passed through the kitchen, Jamie lingering a moment to ask if he could help in shoveling out the dirt, and did she need more wood brought in?

She had smilingly shook her head to both questions, thanking him for his offer. "I work best alone," she'd added.

And work, she had. Raegan stretched her aching back. She had heated numerous kettles of water, washed dishes and cooking utensils until her fingers were wrinkled from their long submersion in hot soapy water.

Then the broom got a work-out after she had cleared the corners of rubbish and carried piles of soiled clothing out onto the back porch. Her last act was to scrub the floor.

But she was aware of a sensation of satisfaction as she paused mid-way down the hall to open the doors to the linen closet. By the wavering light of the candle flame she took out two sheets, two pillowcases, and a quilt.

The candle, now only a stub, burned out just as she stepped inside her grandparents' room. Half asleep on her feet, she made up the big bed by the moonlight filtering through the open window. She undressed down to her mid-thigh bloomers and camisole, then climbed into bed, sighing her pleasure in the cool breeze coming through the window. Chase must have opened it to clear the air, she thought muzzily.

She fell asleep to the sound of a lonesome wolf yowling at the moon.

Chapter Six

The sun striking her across the face awakened Raegan the next morning. She was disoriented for a moment, having slept so soundly. She blinked at a large dresser directly opposite the bed, not at first glance recognizing her own image, her tousled curls hanging over one eye.

Everything came back to her then, and she was clearly cognizant of her surroundings, even though she hadn't fully seen the room last night. The aroma of freshly brewed coffee wafted under the crack of the closed door and she gave a horrified gasp when she smelled bacon.

"My clean kitchen!" She visualized splattered grease all over the stove she had scrubbed and polished until her arms ached. "And probably all over the floor," she muttered, scooting out of bed and grimacing as she pulled yesterday's dirty dress over her head. She had no idea where

Chase had put her bag of clothing.

Then, as she combed her fingers through her hair, she saw the carpet bag leaning against the dresser. When had he put it there? Had it been in the room last night and she hadn't seen it in the darkness, or had he brought it while she slept?

She knew the answer when she saw steam rising from the big porcelain pitcher sitting on a long, narrow table beneath the window. Chase had been here, and not too long ago, judging by the hot water.

Moving across the room to the pitcher, she looked down into its matching basin. An oblong bar of pink, scented soap lay inside it, a wash cloth and soft towel beside it. She smoothed a finger over the painted flowers on the water receptacle, which had been filled to the top. She remembered sadly the old chipped gray one she and Mama had shared. It could only be filled part way, the top six inches having a deep crack through which the water seeped out.

"I told you not to think back, Raegan O'Keefe," she ordered herself, blinking back the tears that gathered in her eyes.

She filled the basin with water, undressed, then opened the bag. There were few clothes inside it, and it only took a moment to bring out fresh underclothing and a checked gingham dress. The soap was sweet-scented and lathered luxuriously as she rubbed it over the wet wash cloth. It felt like warm cream sliding over her breasts and down her flat stomach. And suddenly, without warning, she imagined that it was Chase's palm caressing her bare skin. She closed her eyes in growing ecstasy.

The angry squawk of a crow outside her window startled Raegan back to reality. "What's wrong with you?" She glared at her reflection in the glass panes, then began to scrub her skin briskly. "Chase Donlin has no interest in you that way, you simpleton. How many times must I tell you that?"

She hurriedly dried off her body, then after she had dressed, she dragged a brush through her shoulder-length curls. "Set your sights on Jamie," she ordered, laying the brush down. "Maybe he's interested in you."

As she left the room and walked down the hall, however, she knew that although Jamie was handsome and would be a wonderful companion, she could never love him in a romantic way.

Raegan walked into the kitchen with dread. What kind of mess would she find? She stood in the doorway, a slow smile spreading over her face. She had worried needlessly. Everything was spotless, just as she had left it last night.

She walked over to the table where a plate, cup, and flatware had been set out and picked up the note folded inside the cup. "Raegan," she read out loud, "your breakfast is keeping warm in the oven. Jamie and I have gone hunting. Won't be gone long. Have your list ready by the time we get back, and don't go far from the cabin without Lobo. Remember the Tillamooks. Chase."

Raegan smiled, thinking how very thoughtful Chase was to have made her breakfast. She took the bacon and eggs from the oven and consumed it in record time. She had been starved. As she sipped at a cup of coffee, a little too strong for her taste, she began jotting down her grocery list on the pad of paper Chase had left on the table, along with the pencil.

Soap headed the list. There was only a sliver left of the bar she'd started out with yesterday. She had noted, while inspecting the contents of the pantry, that the sugar container was nearly empty, and she hadn't found any molasses. Pancakes was her favorite breakfast meal. When she could think of nothing else, she wrote kerosene in her neat hand.

Her coffee finished, Raegan rose, picking up the pad and pencil. She walked to the dry sink and pulled open the drawer built into one side of the maplewood cabinet. She had seen the pad of paper lying there yesterday when she was looking for a dish towel. As she started to place the pad back in its proper place, her attention was caught by a flat, age-worn book. Across the front of the thin volume was printed in bold letters, *Personal Recipes of Molly Donlin*. Her eyes alight, Raegan picked the book up and carried it to the table. She poured herself another cup of coffee, then opened the book.

As if in answer to a prayer, the first page was labled "Light Bread." She quickly scanned the page for the ingredients she would need to try her hand at making bread. One large potato, two cups warm water, three level teaspoons sugar, salt and flour, and a cake of yeast. Yeast? Had she seen any in the pantry?

Raegan chewed thoughtfully on a thumb nail for a moment, then stood up and opened the door to the long pantry. She sorted through the staples kept on the shelves, wondering if she should be looking for a tin box or a paper bag. She was about to give up when she spotted a small wrapped package about a half inch thick and two inches long. Could this be it? she wondered, turning the small container over in her fingers.

She grinned when the word "yeast" seemed to jump out at her. Carrying it carefully, much as a miner would a gold nugget, she laid it on the table. She went back to the pantry then and picked through a sack of potatoes until she found one the size of Chase's fist, which was a big one.

She cut a finger slightly on the sharp knife in her hurry to peel the potato and put it on the stove to boil. The recipe had said to cook and mash the vegetable.

When it began to simmer, Raegan amassed all the other essential items according to her grandmother's instructions, then measured them into a bowl. Twenty minutes later, the potatoes were cooked and mashed and added to the first step to making a loaf of bread. After stirring the mixture throughly together, she put it near the warmth of the sun shinning through the window, a warm place in which to rise.

She stood with one knee resting on her chair seat, scanning the rest of the recipe. After the mixture had risen, she read, flour was to be added until a firm dough was formed. Then it was left to rise again, and then at that time the round ball was to be kneaded and shaped into loaves, about an hour altogether. At last, after it had risen yet again, the loaves were ready to go into the oven.

Raegan shook her head. This bread-making took a long time—although, she reminded herself, she'd probably have enough to last a week.

While the future bread went through its first transformation, Raegan went to Jamie's room, made up his bed, swept the floor, and dusted the small table beside the bed and the tall chest of drawers.

She moved on to Chase's room next. She stood in the doorway, his own personal odor—outdoors, tobacco, and clean flesh—swept over her. He always smelled the same, never sweaty like most men—at least not that rancid unwashed smell that nearly choked a person.

Her gaze swept slowly around the room. It was larger than Jamie's, almost as large as her grandparents' room. She still couldn't refer to it as her room. It was clearly meant for a husband and wife, with the large bed, the big dresser, the wardrobe that could easily accommodate two people's clothing.

She moved into the room and timidly approached the bed, its sheet and blanket tossed part way to the floor. It seemed that Chase was a restless sleeper. She stretched a hand out to the indentation on one pillow. A warm glow grew in her lower body, knowing that his head had lain there last night.

When Raegan caught herself stroking the hollowed-out spot, she jerked her hand away, hissing, "Raegan O'Keefe, stop it this minute!" She set her mind on making the bed, telling herself it was no different from the one next door.

The dust flew as she swept the floor, concentrating on the corners filled with several months of built-up dust and lint balls. When the sweeping was finished, she started dusting. Her determination that she would treat this room like any other flagged at bit when she came to Chase's dresser. It was as though a part of him lay on its smooth surface. She stood for a long moment gazing at his razor and shaving mug, the comb and brush, a few brown hairs clinging to the bristles.

The mellow bonging of the parlor clock brought Raegan out of her preoccupation with Chase's personal effects. She quickly finished dusting and breathed a sigh of relief when she left the room, closing the door behind her. She hurried down the hall. It was time she formed the dough into loaves.

And bake them in what? she wondered, walking into the kitchen. Were there special pans for them? Mama's bread had never been this complicated. She just stirred it up, then baked it in a big heavy iron pot whose three legs squatted over a bed of red coals.

She opened a cupboard and rummaged through a miscellany of pots and pans and discovered away back in a corner a stack of six narrow, long pans about six inches tall. Her lips tilted in a happy grin. They could only be used for one thing. Baking bread.

Raegan was carefully positioning the last loaf into a greased pan when Chase and Jamie returned home. She looked up and smiled a greeting when Chase darkened the doorway. She received a curt nod in return. Jamie saw the bewildered, hurt look that shot into her eyes. *Chase, you damn ignoramus,* he thought and gave the curl that hung down Raegan's back a teasing tug. "Good mornin', pretty lady," he said softly. "I see you're hard at work."

Raegan gave him a warm smile. After Chase's curt acknowledgement, she was gratified that at least Jamie was his usual sunny self.

"This is my first attempt at making bread," she explained, then motioned to the open recipe book. "I found my . . . Chase's mother's cookbook," she hurriedly corrected the words that would have made Jamie curious, suspicious of the relationship between her and Chase. "I hope I've followed all the directions correctly," she rushed on.

"The loaves look all right." Chase walked over to the table and looked down at them. "You have to let them rise again before bakin' them, don't you?"

Raegan's heart gave a small leap. Chase sounded friendly. He hadn't been displeased with her. "That's what your mother has written here." She traced a finger across the sentence put down in Molly Donlin's fine hand.

She glanced up at Chase with a worried frown. "I don't know how hot to make the oven though. It says here to bake in a hot oven."

"If I remember correctly." Chase leaned over her shoulder, reading the recipe, "Mother Molly kept a good fire goin' in the stove."

Jamie leaned against the dry sink, his arms folded across his chest. Why was Chase so stiff around her? he wondered. Why didn't he ever touch her? At night, in bed, did he take her like he would a whore? A couple of thrusts of his hips, then roll off her? Surely not. What man could? If ever there was a body that could entice a man to caress it, to linger over it, it was Raegan Donlin's.

None of Jamie's thoughts showed on his face when Chase moved away from Raegan and said, "Let's go dress down that deer you shot."

Outside, the gutted deer's hind legs were bound together and hauled a few feet off the ground, the rope tied to a tree. Jamie drew his razor-sharp knife from its sheath and started making strategic cuts on the suspended animal. As he pulled the skin off the hind legs, he looked up at Chase.

"Friend," he said, "I don't understand you. You're more affectionate with the whores at the village than you are with your wife, not to mention widow Jenkins. If Raegan were mine, I wouldn't be able to keep my hands off her."

Chase gave him a look that said he was treading on dangerous ground. "How I treat Raegan is no affair of yours, Jamie. And as for keepin' your hands off her, I notice that though she's not your wife, you never miss an opportunity to touch her."

"Just bein' friendly." Jamie shrugged off Chase's remark. He hadn't missed the warning note in the hard voice, however. He laughed inside. By god, his friend was jealous. The big oaf was crazy about his beautiful wife and didn't know how to show it.

In his misconception, there was born in mischievous Jamie the desire to rile the big man, to push him until he lost that control that he was usually in firm control of. If he thought he was about to lose Raegan to another man, maybe he'd shed his awe of her and show her the love and attention that she clearly craved from him.

An hour later, when the deer was fully dressed and cut into steaks and small pieces for stew, Chase and Jamie carried it into the kitchen. Chase wrapped the individual cuts in brown grocery paper, and when he carried an armfull down to the cellar, Jamie went looking for Raegan.

As he walked down the hall, his moccasined feet making no sound, he could hear Raegan softly singing and followed the low notes to the door opposite Chase's.

He stopped in the open doorway, his eyes widening in surprise. Raegan was just smoothing a bedspread over the big four-poster. "*This* is her room!" he exclaimed to himself, not the one across the hall where her husband slept. Stunned, his eyes skimmed over the room, noting the brush and comb on the dresser, hair ribbons, a small lacquered box, and a faded tintype of a man and woman. His eyes swung to wardrobe whose door had been left ajar. Three dresses and a jacket hung inside. There was no doubt about it, Raegan slept in this room.

Jamie slowly backed out into the hall and slipped back down it. Raegan would be embarrassed to know he had discovered her secret. As he stamped through the kitchen he gave Chase a black look that made the trapper wonder what made him look so angry. Had he taken liberties with Raegan? Had she slapped his face for it?

He, too, walked down the hall, also drawn by her soft singing. He stopped in the doorway, almost barking, "Did Jamie just leave you?"

Raegan gave a startled jump and turned from the window she was cleaning. She shook her head, wondering at Chase's black look. "No." She shook her head. "I haven't seen him since the two of you went outside to skin the deer. Why?"

"It's not important," Chase answered shortly, feeling foolish. Turning on his heel, he left Raegan staring after him.

Chase strode through the kitchen and on out to the back porch. He could see Jamie leaning on the top corral pole, staring off down the valley. He had seen his friend do this many times. It usually followed that in a day or so he would disappear for a time.

As he stepped off the porch and walked toward the handsome half-breed, he found himself wishing, for the first time since knowing him, that his young friend would leave. He was much too attracted to Raegan, and she enjoyed his company too much.

Chase made sure his footsteps were loud enough for Jamie to hear as he approached him. Everyone was uneasy these days, what with the Tillamooks wandering around, looking for the woman. Jamie was almost as swift and deadly with his knife as Chase was with his. If he should appear suddenly at the young man's side, the knife at the slim waist could be drawn and plunged into his heart before Jamie realized whom he had stabbed.

When Jamie turned his head and gave him a brooding look, Chase leaned against the corral beside him. "Are you plannin' on some more 'woods runnin', Jamie?" he asked after several moments of silence passed between them.

Chase started when Jamie's head snapped around and he bit out, "Why doesn't Raegan share your bed, Chase? She's too fine a woman to be treated like an unpaid whore, visitin' her only when you need relief."

In the black rage that came over him, Chase wasn't aware that his fist had lashed out, catching Jamie on the jaw. He stared in gaping surprise at his friend stretched out on the ground.

His anger still raged. His eyes fierce, he stood over the fallen man, his words striking him like the snap of a whip. "Don't ever mention Raegan's name with whore in the same breath. The relationship between us is our own business." He turned and stalked away, angrier than Jamie had ever seen him. He fingered his jaw, watching Chase disappear into the barn, more confused than ever. But one thing he was still sure of was that Chase Donlin was crazy about his wife. He rose to his feet and dusted off the seat of his pants, his lips firmed in determination. The plan he had formed earlier was unchanged. He intended to make his stubborn friend admit he loved Raegan. He would make up to the lovely young woman until Chase was blind with jealousy.

Back in the cabin, Raegan fired up the stove, and with fingers mentally crossed, slid the first three loaves of bread into the oven. The recipe was very vague about how long to bake them. Grandmother Molly had only written to test it for doneness. Did that mean half an hour, an hour?

She decided she would check the loaves every half hour and went into the parlor to check the time. Goodness, she thought, it was almost one o'clock. Where had the time gone? She heard Chase call to her from the kitchen and hurried to see what he wanted.

"I'm goin' to the village now," he said when she stood beside him. He lifted his eyes from the white slip of paper she'd left on the table. "Your list is pretty small. Are you sure you've listed everything you need?"

"No, as a matter of fact I haven't." She took the list from him and picked up the pencil still lying on the table. "I need some more yeast, and I used a lot of flour making the bread." She wrote the two items down then mused out loud, "In Grandmother's cookbook, I saw how to make corn cakes, so I'll need some corn meal and baking powder." She used the pencil again. "And there's a recipe for ginger bread and dried apple cake. That means baking soda, ginger, cinnamon, raisins, and dried apples."

The pencil flew across the sheet of paper and Chase grinned good-humoredly when a minute or so later she handed over the sheet of paper, the list tripled in length now. "I can't wait to eat that dried apple cake." His grin widened as he folded the paper and slipped it in his shirt pocket.

Raegan heard the teasing note in his voice and her heart fluttered. It reminded her of how things had been between them when they first met. "Did Grandmother make it often?" she inquired shyly.

"Yes, she did." A softness came into Chase's eyes. "Pa was awfully fond of it."

"And Grandmother was fond of Grandfather." Raegan's eyes twinkled up at him, anxious to keep him talking.

"That she was," he answered as he walked toward the door. He paused before stepping outside. "Jamie is around somewhere, so don't be nervous, thinkin' you're bein' left alone."

"What do you want for supper?" Raegan followed him onto the porch, reluctant to see him leave.

"It doesn't matter." Chase swung onto Sampson's back. "When I took the venison down to the cellar, I saw a piece of ham I'd forgotten I had. If you're hungry for pork, cook that up."

He gave Sampson a nudge with his heel, then held him back to say, "Mother Molly always stuck a clean broom straw in the bread to see if it was done. If the straw comes out dry, the bread is baked through."

Raegan watched him ride away, sighing. But it was a happy sigh. Chase was definitely like his old self, friendly and teasing. She stepped back into the kitchen and took a peek at the bread. It was forming a crust and smelled delicious. Now for a look at the parlor. She smiled in anticipation.

Her first action when entering the big family room was to pull off all the furniture coverings and carry them to the back porch. "I'm getting quite a wash built up out here," she muttered, then reminded herself that it was nothing compared to the piles of filthy miner's clothes she used to scrub.

She hurried back to the parlor, anxious to have a good look at the room her mother had so often described in glowing terms.

Raegan stood in awe for several seconds, her moving eyes missing nothing. Never had she seen or dreamed of such beauty, such warmth, in a house. How had this come about in the Oregon wilderness? She recalled then her mother telling how Grandfather Donlin had shipped the furniture from San Francisco, then had it hauled in wagons to the cabin.

She wandered around the room, running her fingers over the shiny surface of a table flanking a dark blue, damask-covered sofa, noting that the two windows were hung with matching drapes. She gazed in wonder at a desk with slender, straight legs—Chase could have told her it was a Hepplewhite, that all the fine pieces of furniture were Hepplewhite, that his step-mother had loved the design, and that her favorites were a center drop-leaf table and the two chairs with heart-shaped backs.

Raegan spotted a bookcase with glass doors and hurried over to it. There were five shelves, each one crammed tightly with books. What pleasure she would have on cold winter evenings curled up with a book in front of the huge fireplace.

She ran her eyes over the walls, lingering on the landscape paintings with their wide, scrolled frames. She walked over to one oil and ran a finger over it. Mama had told her about this one—a little blond girl holding a white, fluffy kitten. It had been her favorite, she had said. Looking at and touching the same picture as her mother had so many years ago, gave Raegan an inner peace. She told herself that when she missed her mother so dreadfully it seemed unbearable, she would come to this picture and draw comfort from it.

She moved to a tall, narrow mirror on the wall with pewter candle holders attached to each side of it. Smoothing back a curl that had escaped its ribbon, she said to her image, "I am so fortunate to live in such a lovely home. I hope that you know, Mama, I am here where you knew such love and happiness." The odor of baking bread drifted to her and she hurried from the room.

In the kitchen she opened the oven door and gave a happy cry. The loaves of bread were a golden light brown. They looked and smelled done, but to be on the safe side she would test them. She broke a straw off the broom leaning in a corner, washed and dried it, then stuck it into one of the loaves. It came out dry.

She grabbed two hot pads and carefully removed the pans from the oven to the table. Then, just as carefully, she placed the other three mounds of dough side by side on the rack.

The kitchen was smothering hot from the fire going so long in the stove, and Raegan stepped outside to catch a cooling breeze. She wandered around the cabin, wading through tall growth, clicking her tongue in disgust at the healthy growth of weeds choking out the flowers that struggled for life in their beds. Perhaps, she thought, while she did the wash tomorrow Chase and Jamie would cut the grass—or should she say weeds? And the following day, she planned, she would set to work attempting to bring back to life the half-dead flower beds.

Raegan paused on her return to the kitchen to look down at the barn area. She didn't see Jamie about and wondered where he had gotten off to. She hoped he hadn't gone off on one of the trips he so often took, according to Chase and Ruthie. In the short time she had known him, she had become very fond of the gentle, laughing young man.

She was thinking how she would miss his tall tales that made her laugh and the way he teased her and tormented Chase, when Jamie came walking from behind one of the out-buildings. He saw her and waved. With smiling relief, she waved back. She hadn't realized until now that she had been a little anxious about being alone. Even at this moment, Tillamook braves could be watching the cabin, watching the people around it.

How was the Tillamook woman faring? she wondered. Had Roscoe's brutality killed her yet? She didn't know whether to wish that it had or that it hadn't. If the poor woman was dead, the evil man could no longer inflict pain on her, yet if she still lived, there was always the hope that eventually she would get back to her people.

One thing Raegan was sure of—she hoped the Indians found Roscoe soon. She hoped that they would make his death a long and extremely painful one. Never had she felt such hatred for any person.

While the last batch of bread baked, Raegan lit a candle and descended the narrow steps to the cellar. She set the candle holder on a flat rock positioned in the middle of a shallow stream about a foot wide. She dipped her fingers into the flowing water, then jerked them back. It was icy cold. To be so freezing cold it had to come from a spring.

"My step-grandfather was a very clever man," she said with respect, "to build his cabin over such a stream. Meat and other perishables would remain fresh down here for weeks, and some of the hardier vegetables would probably last from one season to the next."

There grew inside Raegan the desire to have a garden. She would start it tomorrow. No, she corrected herself, first the flower beds. To her, having beauty in her life was almost as important as having food. Beauty had been so lacking in the mining towns and camps where she had spent most of her life. Day after tomorrow, she would coax the two men into spading up the garden patch back of the cabin.

She had noted neat rows laid out in the fenced-in plot, the remains of dried-up vegetables buried beneath a growth of weeds. There were also three fruit trees just coming into bloom. Apples and peaches, she hoped. She remembered also seeing gnarled vines covering an arbor. They had to be grape vines.

Raegan sighed happily. A long busy summer lay ahead. Maybe she could even make some jelly. Most likely there was a recipe for it in Grandmother Molly's cookbook.

She had no difficulty finding the ham butt. It sat on a shelf built along one wall. She counted several slabs of bacon and salt pork lying beside it. She sniffed the cloth-wrapped meat and nodded her satisfaction. She could tell from its aroma that it had been sugar-cured.

Holding the meat in the crook of her arm, she picked up the candle and climbed the steps to the kitchen.

She knew her second batch of bread was done by the mouth-watering aroma seeping through the oven door. The parlor clock struck four and she became busy starting supper.

The sun was a great red ball nearing the tree-line, as Raegan stood at the stove frying thick slabs of ham and glancing often at the window, watching for Chase to appear. She had just finished setting the table when she saw Sampson descending the hill from the direction of the village. Her heart beat excitedly, and her eyes never wavered from the big man sitting tall in the saddle.

"Stop it!" Her small fist struck at her heart. "Do you want him to hear you beating like a crazy thing?"

She composed her face and tried to dim the glow in her eyes. Chase must never know how she felt about him. He would scorn her if he knew that his mere presence sent her pulses to racing.

A short time later, she heard Chase and Jamie splattering water while they washed up on the back porch. She went to the door to say that supper was ready, but held back the words. An old woman, astride an old mule, was coming down the same trail Chase had just traversed.

"Granny Pearson." Chase called when the aging mount clumped into the yard and stopped on its own accord. Smiling affectionately, he dried his hands and hurried to help the white-haired woman to dismount.

Her back was badly bent, Raegan noted, and the thin fingers that clutched Chase's arm were knotted and twisted with rheumatism. Nevertheless, she was quite spry as she proved by the brisk way she walked to the porch.

She paused before stepping up on it when she saw Raegan standing in the doorway.

Her piercing blue eyes studied Raegan's face for a moment, then she said in a voice cracked with age, "You remind me of someone, girl. Who could it be, do you reckon?"

Raegan started to say that she looked like her father, and had the old woman known William O'Keefe? She caught herself in time, and glancing at Chase saw that he had been holding his breath, afraid of what she might blurt out.

She smiled down at the old woman called Granny Pearson and answered, "I wouldn't know, ma'am. I only arrived here yesterday. I'm from Idaho."

Granny shook her head in thought. "You sure do look familar." After a short pause, she asked abruptly, "Are you livin' with this scamp, Chase Donlin?"

"Shame on you, Granny," Chase laughingly chastised her when he saw Raegan blush at her sharp question. "Raegan is my wife." He took hold of her arm and helped her up the two steps to the porch.

"Your wife?" The old woman jerked to a stop, "You don't say." Again she turned her eyes on Raegan. When Raegan stirred nervously from the over-long study of her features, she received a toothless smile.

"You sure picked a purty one. Yes, might purty," she said, making Raegan blush again. "Thank God you had enough sense not to get hooked by that man-chasin' Liza Jenkins."

Before Chase, his ears red, could claim there was never any danger of his getting hooked by the widow, Granny spotted Jamie standing off to one side, watching her with amusement. Her face grew gentle. "How are you, boy?"

Jamie grinned good-humoredly. This old, kind-hearted harridan had called him "boy" ever since he met her five years ago. Well, not always. Sometimes she called him Jamie—when she was displeased with him, like the times he took off without telling anyone.

"I'm in fine shape, Granny," he answered. "And how are you gettin' along?"

"Fine, just fine. My old bones act up sometimes, but it's to be expected at my age, I reckon." She turned sharp eyes back to Chase. "You keep an eye on that one, Donlin. You know the slick way he has with wimmen."

Chase lowered his lids, hiding from the shrewd old woman that already he was worried about the same thing. Making his tone light, he said, "Come on into the cabin, you mischief-makin' ol witch." He urged her spare frame through the door as Raegan stepped back. "You're just in time for supper."

"Well I must say it smells good, and I am hungry. Ain't eaten since early this mornin'," Granny said, removing her heavy shawl and handing it to Jamie.

"Why is that?" Chase seated her at the table.

"That Henry Jones came knockin' at my door just at sunrise, complainin' that Meg was tryin' to birth her baby and was havin' a hard time of it, and would I come help her."

"I didn't know his wife was expectin' again," Chase said absently, his attention on Raegan and the graceful way she moved as she put supper on the table.

"That poor woman is expectin' every time she turns around. And unlike her first husband, who gave her four children, none of Henry's git lives or comes to full term." The old woman's eyes burned fiercely. "It's cause he won't leave her alone, always wantin' his pleasurin'."

"So this one died too," Jamie said softly.

"And God's blessing it did." Granny sighed. "Its scrawny little body was all misshapen. And even if it had lived, it wouldn't have been right in the head. I could see it in the little thing's wide, flat face. And you know somethin' else—Henry would like to be pleasurin' them two stepdaughters of his too. I saw the lustful way he looked at them all the time his wife was tryin' to bring his youngin' into the world. It wouldn't matter a snap of his fingers that them two girls are his stepdaughters."

No one had noticed Raegan's white face, the horror in her green eyes at the scorching denunciation of Henry Jones. Jamie finally noted her aghast expression and reached over to cover the fingers tightly gripping her fork. "Ah, Raegan," he said softly, "you've never heard of such men, have you?"

Raegan shook her head. "It's hard to believe that a man could act so dastardly."

"It doesn't happen often." Chase frowned at Jamie's hand still lying on Raegan's. "But there are a few two-legged animals like Jones."

"Why does his wife put up with such treatment?" Raegan's eyes flashed green fire.

"Meg?" Granny shook her head. "That poor thing had the spirit tramped out of her a long time ago. As far as brutality is concerned, her first husband was worse in a way than Henry is."

"I never knew her first husband very well," Chase said. "He died shortly after they moved here."

"I knew him, knew him well." Granny's eyes snapped. "He was a mean one. Me and Joe was in the same wagon train with him and Meg what brung us to Oregon. Meg and their four youngins' did all the work—makin' camp, hitchin' and unhitchin' their bony old mules. All he did was drive and spend half the night playin' cards."

"What happened to him?" Jamie asked after Granny's long tirade.

"He drowned in the Platte," Chase answered. "It was in flood and his boat got caught in a swift current and overturned. Meg said he couldn't swim."

"Yeah, the old river got him." Granny nodded her white head in satisfaction. "And we was all happy for Meg. Finally she was rid of that lazy no-account, we all said. Said her and the kids could make it, seein' as how they done all the work anyhow. Then along comes Henry Jones, sweet-talkin' her, actin' real nice. And Meg, poor thing, never havin' anyone say nice things to her for so long, she believed his deceitfulness. She didn't learn until after she married him that he was just as lazy as her first husband, and on top of that he was as randy as a ruttin' buffalo."

When Granny opened her mouth to continue, Chase urged a bowl of potatoes on her. "Better start eatin', Granny, food's gettin' cold."

Everyone settled down to the meal then, with nothing said except, "Please pass the bread," or the potatoes, or the ham. Mid-way in the meal Granny looked at Raegan and said, "You're a right good cook, child. This bread is as light as a feather."

Pleasure shone in Raegan's eyes at the praise. "Thank you, ma'am. I found the recipe in my—in Chase's mother's cookbook." She silently berated herself. Again she had almost given away her and Chase's secret. She hurried to speak of something else.

"Why did the man Jones call on you to deliver his wife's baby, Granny? Do you live near them?"

"No I don't. No closer than any of his other neighbors."

"Granny is a midwife, Raegan," Chase explained. She's helped most of the young ones around here into the world."

"Oh." Raegan smiled at Granny, interest in her eyes. "That must make you very proud."

"Mostly it does. Course I feel bad when they don't make it, like today. It hurts turrible, hearin' a mother cryin', seein' the father chokin' on his tears, afraid to let them fall for some asinine reason." She paused a moment, then added thoughtfully, "Men are strange animals."

Chase and Jamie bit their lips not to roar with laughter, and Raegan was hard put to keep a straight face. Granny's words had been said matter-of-factly, as though they were gospel.

"Were you married a long time, Granny?" Raegan asked, frowning a warning at Chase and Jamie.

"Oh my yes. Me and my Thomas was married fifty-two years. He was a trapper," Granny said proudly. "A bear attacked him one early spring day a couple years back. A day don't go by that I don't think about him." The sadness in the aged voice chased away the mirth in the men's eyes and it grew quiet around the table as everyone tended to eating supper.

Twilight had descended by the time the meal was consumed, and Raegan lit candles to drink their coffee by. She hoped there was kerosene in the fustian bag Chase had dropped onto the porch earlier. When she returned the coffee pot to the stove and sat back down, Granny's keen eyes fastened on Chase.

"So," she began, "I take it you met this little gal in Idaho. Have you been keepin' her a secret all this time? Is that why you've never married any of the wimmen that chase you all the time?"

"You sure are full of questions tonight, Granny." Chase looked a little annoyed. "But no, I never knew Raegan before."

"You're sayin' then that you took to her right off?"

Chase was aware that Jamie was watching him and was waiting for his answer also. From the corners of his eyes he saw Raegan's hands go still on her coffee cup. He squirmed inwardly. How was he to answer his aged, prying neighbor? Her remark "took to her right away" meant in the old woman's mind that he must have fallen in love with Raegan the first time he saw her. How could he answer that he had lusted for her on first sight and that, to his shame, he still did?

Finally, he said teasingly to Granny, "I married her, didn't I?"

Chase felt Jamie's heated glower on his face. He stole a look at Raegan, but she was staring into her cup, her long lashes hiding what she was thinking. He slowly heaved a relieved sigh when the old woman set her empty cup down and rose stiffly from the table.

"Me and my old mule best be gettin' home," she said. "He's probably hungry too." She gave Raegan one of her toothless smiles. "Thank ye kindly for supper. You must come visit me someday."

"I would like that very much," Raegan said, rising also. "Maybe you would tell me about some of the babies you've ushered into the world."

Granny cocked her white head and gave Raegan's features a close scrutiny. "You sure are a purty little thing, and Chase is lucky to have found you."

Jamie took her by the arm and turned her toward the door. "If you're finished flappin' your lips, I'll see you home." He winked at Chase. "I'm told there are some bad injuns' roamin' the woods these days."

That the old woman had noted his tongue-in-cheek reference to those whose blood he shared was evident as she answered smoothly, "Yes, Jamie, I heard tell them heathens is skulkin' round."

Chase snorted his mirth and Raegan couldn't help giggling. Jamie grinned, and draping his arm across the bony shoulders, he guided Granny to the door. "I ought to let them slice off a piece of that sour tongue of yours," he growled affectionately as he led her onto the porch.

Chase and Raegan following behind them, laughed loudly when Jamie received a jab of a sharp elbow in the ribs, making him yell. "Hey, you old shrew," he growled, "that hurt. I feel like I've been stabbed with a knife."

"Then learn to keep a respectful tongue in your mouth, Jamie Hart."

"What did I say?" Jamie asked innocently, boosting the slight body onto the mule.

Granny ignored his question, and lifting a hand to Raegan and Chase, she prodded her mount to follow Jamie to the barn. A few minutes later, Raegan and Chase watched their dim shapes ride down the valley.

"Do they always rag each other like that?" Raegan asked, laughter still in her voice.

"Always." Chase answered. "They both enjoy it. But there's a deep affection between them. Jamie has great respect for Mrs. Tilda Pearson."

The long yowl of a wolf drifted down from a distant hill, and Lobo, sitting at Raegan's feet, pointed his nose at the moon creeping over the trees and answered the challenge. When he loped off into the darkness, Chase stepped off the porch and walked toward the corral, and with a sigh, Raegan returned to the kitchen. Tears glimmered in her eyes when a few minutes later she heard Chase ride away, headed for the village.

Chapter Seven

Raegan stood up and stretched, then with dirt-grimed fingers massaged the small of her back. A hot breeze blew against her, flattening her skirt against her thighs and drying the perspiration on her body. She brought her hands in front of her and studied them. They were full of scratches—some shallow, barely breaking the skin, others gouged deep into the flesh.

She and Jamie had been working for the past hour on the neglected rosebeds in the chimney corner. Jamie was pruning the briars, claiming that he knew how to do it correctly from helping Granny Pearson with hers. Since she knew nothing about such things, she had crawled along behind him, rooting out the weeds and grass that threatened to choke the life from the bushes that had, according to Mama, bloomed profusely under Molly Donlin's care.

Jamie squinted over his shoulder at Raegan and teased, "Hey, are you gettin' lazy on me? Is a little weed-pullin' too much for you?"

"No, I'm not *gettin'* lazy on you." Raegan gave his sweat-wet hair a sharp tug, then dropped back down on her knees. "I was just getting a few kinks out of my back."

"You shouldn't be out in the sun workin' like this," Jamie said, serious now as she picked up the hand spade and attacked a thick-stemmed weed. "Me and Chase can take care of the weeds."

"Well, I don't see him around, do you?" Raegan answered sharply, bitterly. "Anyway, I like doing it. I enjoy getting my fingers in the soil, it feels alive somehow. Maybe I inherited my father's love of mining."

Jamie sat back on his heels, enjoying his view of Raegan's face as she concentrated on digging out the last root of a stubborn piece of bunch grass. He had never seen a woman so lovely. How could Chase treat her so indifferently?

"Damn him," he swore silently. "It's pure stubborness. Jealously is eatin' him alive, and still he won't let Raegan know how deeply he cares for her. Hell, sometimes when he thinks no one will notice, the way he looks at her isn't even decent, the hunger in his eyes."

Jamie shook his head and turned back to the rose bush. As soon as he and Raegan had started grubbing around in the yard, Chase had stalked off to the barn, his back rigid with disapproval.

For the first time since knowing the big man, Jamie had wanted to go after Chase, swing him around and plant his fist in the handsome face.

Raegan didn't deserve the treatment she was receiving from him. His coolness hurt her deeply. He could see it in her eyes, in the droop of her soft lips.

Unknown to Raegan and Jamie, Chase sat a few yards from them, half concealed beneath a pine. He ground his teeth together when Raegan laughed, peals of husky mirth issuing from her lips. He watched the pair jealously, feeling shut out of the companionship Raegan and Jamie shared. He felt like an onlooker, wishing, but not daring to enter the warm circle. For if he should lay a hand on Raegan's shoulder the way Jamie had just done, it wouldn't stop at that. He would be unable to keep from pulling her into his arms and crushing her red lips with his own.

A long sigh escaped him as he stared up at the clear blue sky. He knew it was said of him that Chase Donlin was a law unto himself, letting no man stand in the way of what he wanted. Ironically, in this instance, he stood in his own way—he and his conscience.

As he had a dozen times over the past two weeks, he ignored the small voice that nagged, "She is not a blood relation. It is not shameful that you hunger for her." He didn't bother to argue back as he usually did, "She is still Anne's daughter."

As if his inner voice had read his mind, it taunted, "If that's the way you truly feel about it, why do you sit here pouting? Why don't you get yourself down there and act like the uncle you insist you are. Pitch in and help your *niece* pull those weeds."

"All right, I will," Chase muttered and stood up.

He was within a yard of the pair scrabbling in the dirt when a feminine voice hailed him. He turned around and groaned under his breath. Liza Jenkins was riding toward him, and from the sullen pout on her face, the widow was out to make trouble.

Suddenly, he was sorry he had ever known the woman. He had never come close to loving her, and come to think about it, he didn't even like her. She was a grasping, unfeeling female, her only appeal being her lustiness in bed. But out of politeness, he raised a hand to help the rather plump woman to dismount, saying cooly. "How are you, Liza?"

"I'm just fine," she answered and Chase had to quickly raise both hands to catch her as she threw herself from the saddle. As she clung to him, pressing her lush curves into his lean body, Chase glanced at Jamie and Raegan, a guilty flush spreading over his face when he found them staring at him and Liza.

When he saw the wounded look in Raegan's eyes, the condemning one in Jamie's, he quickly put Liza away from him. Angered that she had deliberately put him in this compromising position, he glared at her, bitting out, "That was quite unnecessary, Liza. And what are you doin' ridin' alone? You know the woods are full of Tillamooks these days."

Liza ignored his criticism and latched onto his last sentence. "You'll just have to see me safely home then, won't you?" She smiled coyly at him as they walked across the yard to where Raegan and Jamie worked.

"Bitch!" Chase muttered under his breath. "That's what you planned all along." He wondered if he could talk Jamie into escorting her home. Jamie didn't like Liza, never had, but not to have Raegan shamed, he might do it.

"I want you to meet my wife." Chase grabbed Liza's elbow when she would have walked past Raegan and Jamie and gone straight to the cabin. Liza gave him a reproachful look. "Yes, I heard you had taken a wife. Almost a child, it's said."

"I don't know who told you that lie," Chase said, laughing. "Raegan is hardly a child, as you will see. She's well past eighteen. I remember you tellin' me once that you were sixteen when you got married."

Liza deigned not to answer the truth of Chase's charge as they came to a halt in front of Jamie and Raegan. A brooding hostility clouded her pale brown eyes when Raegan stood up, waiting expectantly.

"Liza, meet Raegan, my wife," Chase said stiffly. "Raegan, this is Liza Jenkins, a neighbor."

Liza shot Chase a sullen look, not liking at all to be classified merely as a neighbor. She paid no attention to Raegan who, having had good manners drummed in to her, held out a hand.

When her offer of a handshake was ignored, Raegan's whole being became alert. This woman was her enemy. She mistakenly thought that her man had been stolen from her by his "wife." Well, she hadn't stolen him yet, but Raegan O'Keefe was going to do everything in her power to make it come true.

Although she wanted to fasten her hands in the rude woman's hair and pull out a handful, she fought the desire. An act like that would only make Chase angry and would bind him to the widow all the more. She must be very careful how she struck back.

Forcing a sham sweetness to her smile, she said, "I've heard so much about you, Mrs. Jenkins. I understand that you and my husband have been friends for a long time." Her smile widened. "So that makes you my friend too." She looped an arm in Chase's. "I'd hoped you were nearer my age, though. I don't imagine we have much in common." She looked at Jamie and said innocently, "But Jamie assures me there are several young girls in the neighborhood, so I guess I won't lack for female companions."

A mottled red spread over Liza's face. She knew that she had been deliberately and successfuly paid back for her own unbecoming behavior. Her anger turned to rage when she heard Jamie snicker. Already piqued that he hadn't risen at her arrival, but had gone on with his work, silently announcing that she wasn't worth the trouble to acknowledge her presence, she turned her ire on him.

"I see you still have no manners, breed," she said scathingly.

Jamie squinted up at her and answered just as scathingly, "My manners are about the same as yours, whore."

Both women gasped. But where Raegan stood

rooted to the spot, Liza took a step toward Jamie, the riding whip in her hand raised to strike him in the face.

Jamie shot to his feet and, grabbing her wrist, glared at Chase and warned, "You'd better step in, Chase, before I break the bitch's arm."

With a muttered curse, Chase twisted the quirt out of Liza's hand.

"Did you hear what he called me?" Liza cried, squeezing tears out of her outraged eyes.

"I heard. I also heard you start the name-callin'," Chase spoke sharply, flinging the short whip into the brush.

"You always take up for that—him," Liza said tearfully. "A person would think that after all we've—" She stopped, pretending embarrassment at what she had almost said.

She fooled no one. When that fact became clear to her, Liza tossed her head and said sweetly, "I'm parched, Chase. Ain't you gonna ask me in for a glass of water?"

Raegan and Jamie had returned to their labors, and Raegan didn't see the trapped look on Chase's face—a look that said he wished Liza Jenkins a thousand miles away. In her imagination she saw him eager to get his lover inside the cabin, away from her and Jamie.

When an embarrassing amount of time had gone by, Chase cleared his throat and said thinly, "Of course." He turned to Raegan and Jamie, and jerking his head toward the cabin, said, "Come on."

Both shook their head in unison. "I'm not thirsty," Jamie declined. He looked at Raegan.

"Are you?" She shook her head and they continued with the flower bed.

Chase's face was as dark as a thunder cloud as he stamped toward the cabin, a gleeful Liza trying to keep up with him. There was no way he'd be able to talk Jamie into escorting Liza home now, he swore under his breath. And stuck in the cabin alone with her, he'd have his work cut out convincing the lusty widow that he wasn't going to take her to bed.

And what was Raegan thinking? he wondered helplessly. He couldn't just say out of the blue, "Look, Raegan, I'm not gonna bed the bitch."

He had the strong urge not to let Liza enter the cabin. He would bring her a glass of water, then tell her to be on her way. He mentally shook his head then. In all conscience, he couldn't do that. The foolish woman could be attacked by a Tillamook brave.

With an inward sigh, he stepped aside, allowing Liza to proceed him into the kitchen.

"That bitch," Jamie grated when Liza closed the door that had been standing open all morning. "I knew she'd be around, tryin' to make trouble."

Raegan kept her head down, pretending her whole concentration was on the weeds she dug at blindly through her tears. When Jamie finally ceased calling Liza every unfavorable name he could think of, she swallowed a lump in her throat and asked, "Have she and Chase been—you know, close?"

Jamie laughed contemptuously. "No closer than half the men in and around the village have. She doesn't know it, but she's referred to as the Lusty Widow. She's had half the married men and most of the single ones findin' their way to her door."

"Does that include you?" Raegan tried to tease above the ache in her heart.

"Nope, not me. That's why she hates me so. She tried coaxing me into her bed once, and I bluntly refused her. I can't make love to a woman unless I at least like her. Liza Jenkins, I definitely don't like."

"Then she's not . . . Chase doesn't . . ."

"Chase doesn't give a snap of his finger for her," Jamie interrupted her stuttering question. "But that's not to say ole Liza feels the same way about him. Even though she lies with most any man who comes along, it's Chase she wants permanently. Be wise to her, Raegan, she won't fight fair."

When Raegan made no answer, Jamie glanced at her suffering face and stood up. "Come on," he said, offering his hand for an assist up. "Let's go visit Aggie Stevens. It's time you met some of your *nice* neighbors."

"But, Jamie." Raegan brushed at the dirt clinging to her skirt. "I couldn't go like this."

"Sure you can. We'll probably find Aggie grubbin' in the dirt too."

"I should at least wash my hands." Raegan looked at the cabin, chewing at her bottom lip.

Jamie sensed that she didn't want to go inside the cabin. "Go wash up at the horse trough," he said gently, "while I go saddle up the mounts."

Raegan scrubbed the dirt off her hands, then wet her handkerchief and wiped her face. She smoothed back her hair, refusing to look toward the cabin, blocking from her mind what might be going on inside. When Jamie arrived with her mount and his roan, she managed to smile brightly at him.

"That's my girl," he said, helping her to mount. He swung onto the roan, and together they raced across the meadow, their gay laughter floating back to the man who waited impatiently for his unwanted guest to finish the glass of water he knew she hadn't wanted in the first place.

Damn you, Jamie Hart. Chase's fists clenched. And damn you, Liza Jenkins.

Jamie and Raegan crested a hill and pulled their mounts into a walk as they descended it. Below nestled a sturdy, well-kept cabin, a barn, and several long, low sheds. "Those are Aggies's chicken houses," Jamie explained when he saw Raegan looking curiously at the unusual-looking buildings. "Behind each one is a tight pen with a wire stretched over it. Without that protection the varmints around here would soon put an end to her flock."

When there came to them a continuous clucking and squawking of hens and the crowing of roosters, Jamie growled, "If I had to listen to that racket all day, I'd put an end to them myself."

Raegan laughed. "I imagine one gets used to it. Aggie probably doesn't even hear it."

"Yeah," Jamie agreed. "Especially when you know that each time a hen cackles she's laid an egg. Ike was braggin' that Aggie made more from her eggs and chickens last year than he did trappin'. He was right proud of his wife, but a little put out too. He figures runnin' a trap-line is ten times harder and colder than feedin' a bunch of chickens twice a day and gatherin' their eggs."

"That may be, but look how much stronger he must be than his wife," Raegan pointed out.

"You women always stick together, don't you?" Jamie pretended to be aggravated, but the quirking of his lips gave him away.

"We have to, otherwise you men would walk all over us." Raegan shaded her eyes with a hand. "Is that Aggie? The woman who just stepped out of one of the sheds with a basket on her arm?"

Jamie nodded and grinned. "She's been gathering her white gold. Eggs," he explained when Raegan raised an eyebrow.

The short, plumpish woman spotted them right off and, smoothing her graying hair back from her face, waved and called out, "Hey, Jamie!" She walked briskly to meet them.

Raegan and Jamie slid from their saddles, and her bright brown eyes crinkled at the corners as the motherly-looking woman smiled at Raegan. "You'd be Chase's wife." She held out a work-worn hand.

Raegan's smile weakened a bit as she returned the gesture with a warm grip of her fingers. Like Ruthie Johnson, Sid's Indian wife, Aggie Stevens was a nice woman and she hated lying to her. She evaded acknowledging that status by saying, "Chase has spoke often of you. My name is Raegan."

"What about me?" Jamie demanded as the women shook hands. "I speak of Aggie too. Didn't

I tell you that she makes the best pies in the area?"

Raegan looked thoughtful for a moment, then her green eyes sparkling impishly, she said soberly, "I'm sorry, Jamie, but I can't recall you saying that."

Jamie pretended an injured look and, laughing, Aggie said, "Come on in. I just might have an apple pie to go with our coffee." Raegan and Jamie followed her into a spotlessly clean kitchen, and at her invitation sat down at a table beneath a window. Aggie set her half-filled basket of eggs on a small table, then asked as she washed her hands, "Why didn't Chase come with you?"

Raegan and Jamie spoke together. As Raegan said, "He went to the store for supplies," Jamie explained that he had gone hunting.

"Well, which is it?" Aggie looked curiously at the red-faced pair as she took cups and plates from a cupboard.

"I thought he went huntin'," Jamie mumbled. Neither he nor Raegan looked at Aggie, and she finally shrugged her shoulders. Evidently, Chase trusted his new wife with the handsome rascal Jamie.

The coffee had been poured and forks were cutting into slices of flaky pie when two teenaged girls burst into the room, their faces red from the argument they were engaged in. They saw Jamie, and all else was forgotten.

Ignoring Raegan, they cried with shining eyes, "Jamie, when did you get back? We missed you," the oldest girl said.

"A few days back, Mary." Jamie gave her a lazy smile, making the young lady blush with pleasure.

"But we haven't seen you around," Mary said, reproach in her voice.

"I've been busy, helpin' Chase and his new wife get settled in." He motioned toward Raegan.

"Oh." The girls turned their heads and finally looked at Raegan. Their eyes widened at her good looks, then, remembering their manners they smiled shyly at her and Mary said, "We heard that Chase had finally taken a wife. We were sure surprised about it. Everyone had given up on him ever settlin' down and becoming a family man."

The younger girl giggled. "Most of the girls in these parts were very disappointed when they heard he'd gone off and got married."

"That will do, Angeline." Aggie frowned at her daughter. When both girls would have taken a seat at the table, scrimmaging a bit to sit next to Jamie, she said curtly, "You two go on about your chores."

It looked for a minute that Mary might give her mother an argument, but after a threatening look from Aggie, she nodded her head. But there was a sullen pout to her lips as she mumbled her good-byes and left the kitchen, Angeline following reluctantly behind her.

Raegan was disappointed that the girls were sent away. Especially Mary. She liked the girl's sunny disposition and would have liked to know her better. Raegan's parents had moved so often, she'd never had the time to make a friend of anyone her own age.

She glanced at Jamie and wondered at the dry amusement twisting his lips. Then Aggie started talking about her garden and she turned her attention to her hostess.

"The soil is gettin' awful dry," Aggie was complaining. "If it don't rain soon, half the seeds I planted will shrivel up and die. All our hard work will be for nothin'."

"Oh I hope not," Raegan exclaimed. "Chase and Jamie promised they'd spade up our garden patch. I can't wait to plant seeds. It will be my first attempt at trying to grow things." She sighed. "I sure hope it rains."

"Do you have your seed already?" Aggie urged another piece of pie onto the willing Jamie.

Raegan nodded. "Yes. I found some in tins underneath the sink."

"Don't use them, Raegan, you'll be wastin' your time. There's no tellin' how old they are. They might be some that Chase's mother saved. I'll give you some of what I gathered from last year's crops."

"That's very nice of you, Aggie." Raegan's face lit up. She had a sense of being accepted, a part of the people who populated the Oregon hills. Granny Pearson had seemed to like her, and so did Ruthie Johnson. The widow Jenkins face flashed before her. That one didn't like her. But that was all right. She didn't like the widow either.

Jamie and Raegan visited with Aggie another twenty minutes or so, then Raegan announced it was time she and Jamie were getting home. "I have to start thinking about supper."

"I'll get you the seeds." Aggie rose from the table. She dragged a box from under her dry-sink and sorted through several cloth bags of seeds. When Raegan said goodbye to the genial woman, she carried away a future growth of corn, peas, turnips, cabbage, pumpkins, and squash. She hugged the seeds to her breast as her father would have, had they been nuggets of gold.

But she and Jamie were barely out of sight of the Stevens' home when the excitement died out of her eyes. Would the widow Jenkins still be at the cabin, or had she left, taking Chase with her? She sighed and forced the bothersome thought from her mind. After all, it was none of her affair if Chase went home with the woman. And certainly he would feel no guilt about it if he did. It wouldn't enter his mind that she, Raegan O'Keefe, would be tormented, thinking of him and Liza together, for to him she was only his niece.

Turning her head to Jamie who rode alongside her, Raegan said, "Mary Stevens is a very pretty young woman."

"Yes, Mary is pretty, and a nice girl too."

"She likes you, you know."

A dry look of amusement came over Jamie's face. "Maybe, for all the good it will do her."

"Oh?" Raegan raised a brow at Jamie. "Doesn't she appeal to you?"

"That's neither here nor there." Jamie's lips twisted in a bitter half smile. "Didn't you notice how fast Aggie shooed the girls out of the kitchen?"

"Well yes, but they had chores to do."

"No." Jamie shook his head. "She didn't want them around me."

"You must be mistaken. Aggie likes you, I could tell."

"Yes, I believe that she does, but that's not to say she'd let me court her daughter."

"Are you sure about that, Jamie?" Raegan protested.

"Dead sure. As you get to know the rest of your neighbors, pay attention to how the mamas watch their daughters when I'm around."

Raegan wanted to express her sympathy to the handsome young man with the bitter look on his face, but she knew he wouldn't want it. Jamie Hart was a very proud man, and that he had revealed as much as he had was a compliment to her.

She contented herself with saying, "They are very foolish women then. You would make a wonderful husband, Jamie Hart."

Jamie's only answer was "Maybe" as he kicked the roan into a gallop.

When Raegan and Jamie arrived at the cabin, Raegan sensed immediately that the building was empty. There was only Lobo sitting on the porch to greet her. Her heart beat painfully. Over two hours had passed since she and Jamie had ridden off to visit Aggie. As she swung to the ground, she wouldn't let herself think about what was keeping Chase at the widow's place for so long.

When Jamie suggested, "Chase must have

decided to do some huntin'," she made no response. She couldn't, her throat was too choked with unshed tears. Jamie watched her enter the cabin, wishing that he could get his hands on Chase Donlin.

"Damn the bitch!" Chase wheeled the stallion and sent him sprinting away from Liza's cabin. He had begun to think that he would never get away from her. Back at his place, she had dallied around, sipping on three glasses of water, dragging out the time until almost an hour had passed. She had hinted at wanting to be shown the rest of the cabin, saying she had never been beyond the kitchen and that she had always wondered what the other rooms looked like. But knowing that she was only interested in his bedroom, he had told her gruffly that someday she should ask Raegan to take her through their home.

Liza hadn't liked the intimate sound of that, his referal to the cabin as his *and* Raegan's home, that his wife was mistress of the place and it wasn't up to him to take on her duties. There had been spite in her voice when she asked, "Where do you think your wife and the—Jamie have gotten off to?"

"They went to do some fishin'." The lie rolled off Chase's tongue. He wasn't about to tell this one he had no idea where the pair had gone. To begin with, Liza was a gossip, and in this particular instance she'd take great pleasure in spreading around the hills that Jamie Hart was making up to Chase Donlin's wife.

"But damn him, isn't he doin' exactly that?" Chase muttered as he rode along. It didn't help any to know that there wasn't a thing he could do about it. He had no papers that bound Raegan to him.

Deep in miserable thought, Chase rode past the fork that led to the Indian village without being aware of it. Although everything within him wanted to know if Raegan and Jamie had returned home yet, he didn't want them to find him waiting for them. Waiting like a jealous husband. For he knew that was exactly how he'd act. He would say things that he had no right to say, words that he would be sorry for later on.

When he came to another fork in the trail, Chase turned Sampson onto it. He would ride into the village, he decided, and pass some time with the other trappers, who would be at loose ends now that the trapping season was over and would congregate each day at the tavern. He'd play poker with them until sundown, show Raegan that he wasn't sitting at home fretting about her taking off with Jamie. As if she'd even notice his absence.

Chase glanced briefly at the sky as he dismounted in front of the long building that was both a store and a tavern. Dark clouds were gathering in the north, rolling and tumbling, promising rain. We need it, he thought, jumping up on the porch and entering the tavern half of the building.

"Hey, look who's here," someone called from the end of the bar. "Our newly wedded man."

"Yeah, we've been wonderin' when you'd pull yourself away from that purty little wife." Skinny Ike Stevens called from a corner table where he sat with three others, playing poker. "I reckon I win the bet." he added. "I told em' there wasn't a woman in the world that could pussy-whip Chase Donlin. "I said he'd be around before the week was out."

A frown darkened Chase's brow, alerting everyone that no more was to be said about his wife. He strode over to the table, pulled out a chair, and growled, "Deal me in."

The day lengthened. Chase lost a few hands, won a few. His mind was was only partially on the game. Mostly it was back at the cabin. Had Raegan and Jamie returned home yet? If not, where were they? What were they doing? A picture of Raegan in his friend's arms made him barely withhold a groan.

The first time Chase was aware that it was raining was when the tavern door banged open and a tall, bone-thin, soaked-through man stood in its entrance. Several groans went up throughout the room.

The cadaverous-looking man, hellfire blazing in his eyes, was a traveling Calvinistic preacher. His was the most strict of all doctrines, characterized by an austere moral code. He showed up at Big Pine a few days before the last Sunday of every month to hold prayer meetings. The man was never happier than when preaching, emphasizing the depravity of man.

He shook the water from his tall frame in much the same manner a dog would do, and started right in, roaring his hell and brimstone threats as the patrons expected. As also expected, no one paid any attention to him. Come Sunday, women from miles around would bring their children and attend the services he held beneath a large cottonwood tree when weather permitted, but for now their men could ignore him.

In the winter, when the snow sometimes came up past a man's knees, the people of Big Pine went without spiritual guidance. Many opinions were aired on where the preacher holed up in cold weather. Some said he had an Indian woman hidden away, others claimed that he went down to San Francisco, checking out the whorehouses. One man had jokingly said that he thought the preacher hibernated with the bears. "Look how thin he is when he shows up here in the spring."

"Damn!" Ike Stevens suddenly grated, tossing his cards on the table. "I just remembered it's me and Aggie's turn to put the old goat up. I'd better sneak out the back way and head for home. Aggie will scalp me if she has to put up with him alone.

"And you wanna know somethin' else," Ike said in an undertone, "I don't trust him around my two girls. I've seen him lookin' at them with lust in his eyes when he didn't think anyone was watchin'."

"It don't surprise me," a big, bearded man agreed. "Them preachin' men are sometimes more woman-hungry than anyone else. I think they work themselves up with all that preachin' and carryin' on, make themselves real randy."

"Yeah." Ike stood up, more anxious than ever to get home to Aggie and his daughters. Stevens was a lazy, carefree man, but he did take seriously the job of watching over the females in his household.

The bearded man shook his head as Ike slipped through the back door of the tavern. "He's gonna be half drowned by the time he gets home. It's comin' down in buckets out there."

The man to the right of Chase muttered, "I don't know which would be worse, drownin' or listenin' to that old coot preach to us until the rain quits."

Chase wondered the same thing. He too was becoming a little uneasy. It was dark outside now; he'd been gone from the cabin for several hours. That hadn't been his intention. He had only wanted to prove something to Raegan, not leave her alone with Jamie all this time—time that Jamie would likly take advantage of.

"No," he told himself. His friend would never make advances to the woman he thought was his friend's wife. Chase frowned. What if Raegan was drawn to Jamie's handsome looks, the smooth way he had with women? Would she make advances to *him*? And if she did, would Jamie be strong enough not to take her up on them?

He stood up. It was a little too late to worry about that. It was senseless to ride home through this downpour, but at least he could try to find shelter for Sampson.

When he made known where he was going, the man across from him said, "It's been taken care of, Donlin. I tied him along with mine in that stand of pine back of the buildin' "

"Much obliged, Rafferty." Chase sat back down, angry with himself. If he hadn't been so full of Raegan, he'd have known when it started raining and would have taken care of Sampson right off.

Drat her and her green cat eyes. He couldn't even think straight anymore, Muttering to himself, Chase picked up his cards as another hand was dealt.

Another couple of hours passed before the rain slowed to a drizzle and the family men left for home. On his way out of the tavern, Chase glanced at the clock over the bar and swore softly. It had gone past ten.

He kept Sampson at an easy gait and arrived at the cabin in less than half an hour. He dismounted at the barn and led the stallion inside its dry warmth. He picked up a burlap bag and started wiping the animal down, but he had given the shiny black hide only a couple swipes when suddenly Chase's shoulder was grabbed and he was spun around. Before he could catch his balance, a rock-hard fist caught him on the point of the chin.

Chase lay sprawled on his back in a pile of hay, staring up at Jamie in bewilderment. "What in the hell was that for?" He sat up.

"For wallerin' around in that whore's bed all these hours, that's what for." Jamie glared down at him. "I don't know what in the hell is wrong with your mind, man. You've got a wife that most men would sell their souls to have and you go off and lie with the likes of Liza Jenkins."

"Is that what Raegan thinks too?" Chase asked in stunned tones. It hadn't entered his mind that she might think that. He had stayed away only to prove to her that it didn't bother him that she had ridden away with Jamie without a word to him.

"Of course Raegan thinks it," Jamie thundered at him. "What woman wouldn't if she heard over and over how things were, or are, between you and the lusty widow. She's innocent in many ways, but she's not stupid."

"Well, she's wrong." Chase stood up and shook his head to clear it. Jamie's fist had had an impact like the kick of a mule. "I've been at the village playin' poker. I waited out the rain. As for Liza, I left her at her cabin and rode straight to the tavern.

"And nothin' went on between us either," he added when Jamie opened his mouth to speak again.

"All right, I believe you. Now go convince your wife." Jamie wheeled and splashed through the mud and water to the cabin.

If it were only that simple. Chase stared after the slender, wiry body of his friend. Raegan would think him soft in the head if he came to her and said, "Look, Raegan, I didn't sleep with Liza Jenkins tonight, nor will I ever again."

He shook his head. Jamie was mistaken, too. It wouldn't even enter Raegan's head to wonder, much less care, how many women he bedded. And besides, as far as explaining went, she had a little of that to do also. What about her ridin' off with Jamie without a by-your-leave? And how long had she been gone from the cabin? How did he know what she'd been up to with Jamie? No, by God, Chase Donlin wasn't the only culprit here, he told himself with building anger.

As Chase splashed through unseen puddles of water in the darkness, his ire grew. The cabin was in darkness. Raegan had gone to bed without leaving a lamp lit to guide his way. That showed just how upset she was at his absence, he thought with a scornful grunt.

But Raegan had been upset, was still upset when she went to bed and half an hour later was in no better frame of mind. She gave the pillow a whack in her helplessness to do anything about Chase's staying with Liza. He would look at her as if she'd gone mad should she go to him and say, "Look, I don't want you seeing that woman ever again."

A tear slipped down her cheek. He'd been seeing the widow long before she came into his life. Why should he stop now? To him Raegan O'Keefe was his niece and as such shouldn't give a thought to his love life.

She sighed raggedly. She might as well get used to the idea that he would continue to see the woman. She knuckled the tears from her eyes. Why couldn't she fall in love with Jamie? He was so kind, so sweet and thoughtful. Although he hadn't said anything as she made supper, she knew from the firm line his lips had taken that he was furious with Chase.

She had toyed with the idea of explaining to Jamie that she and Chase were not really married, that Chase had put that word out so she wouldn't be bothered by the trappers at Johnson's fur post. She hadn't told him, though. It was up to Chase whether or not the truth be told.

The wind blew a sheet of rain across Raegan's bedroom window, making her scoot deeper beneath the blanket. She had been washing the few dishes she and Jamie had used for supper when she had heard the first patter of rain on the roof. Aggie Stevens will be glad to hear that noise, she'd thought with a smile. She remembered then that if it rained too long, her own garden would be set back. She had turned around to say as much to Jamie, but he was leaving the kitchen, slamming the outside door behind him.

"Oh dear," she murmured, picking up a plate and wiping the dish towel around its surface. "He's really angry with Chase. I hope he doesn't say anything to him."

Wondering if things would ever straighten themselves out, she had then begun to slice several pieces of salt pork off a long slab. She yawned as she placed the thin slices of meat in a crock of water to soak overnight, to rid them of the salt. Tomorrow morning she would drain them, coat them with flour, and fry them for breakfast.

"I might as well go to bed, Lobo," she said, patting the wolf's rough head and yawning again. The animal stood up, whined and trotted over to the door. As she let him out and he dashed off through the darkness, she peered down the muddy trail that was barely visible through the slash of rain that dimmed the light from the lamp on the kitchen table. There was no sign of a big man astride a big stallion.

With a deep sigh, she closed the door and glanced around the kitchen. Everything was in order. There was nothing more she could occupy herself with, no excuse for her to stay up longer, waiting for Chase to return. Her shoulders drooped, He probably wouldn't come home all night anyway. She blew out the light and walked down the hall to her bedroom. As she undressed and crawled into bed, the rain hissed against the window as if it were trying to get inside.

And now it was two hours later, the rain was still pouring down, and she still lay awake. She turned over on her side and gave her pillow an impatient whack, telling herself that she was touched in the head for giving Chase Donlin a second thought, and she was damned if she'd continue to do so.

Her last waking thought, however, was of Chase and Liza lying cozily in bed, the rain a background to their love-making.

Chapter Eight

The rain had stopped and the sun rose, turning the hills red. Raegan stirred, turned on her side, and snuggled her cheek into the pillow. But her long hair had caught beneath her shoulder and the pulling of it was bringing her awake.

She stared at the wall opposite her, at one of her mother's samplers she'd hung there. Her thoughts went immediately to Chase then. Had he come home last night or was he still with Liza?

A warm breeze wafted through the open window, carrying with it bird song and a wet, woodsy odor. She frowned. Who had opened her window? Which of the two men had been in here while she slept? And why?

Raegan raised her head suddenly and sniffed the air. Did she smell salt pork frying? She sniffed again and definitely caught the distinctive odor of the briny meat. Someone was making breakfast. Jamie?

"Oh, let it be Chase," she prayed, scooting out of bed, her slender feet feeling for her slippers.

She padded across the floor, emptied half the pitcher of water into the basin, and dropped the bar of scented soap into it. She pulled her nightgown over her head and took the fastest sponge bath she'd ever had in her life. Ten minutes later she was dressed in a sprigged muslin the color of her eyes, her hair brushed and tied up high on her head, showing to perfection the delicate curve of her jaw and her slender white throat.

She closed the bedroom door behind her and walked down the hall. When she stepped into the kitchen, her heart leapt joyfully. As she stood just inside the door, Chase looked up from the skillet he was tending and could only stare at her. How beautiful she was, he thought. So innocent and fresh looking.

He swallowed, trying to speak, to say something. He must look like a simpleton, standing here, gawking at her like a green teenager. But nothing would come. It was as if his tongue were frozen, his jaws locked.

When Chase didn't speak, Raegan's happy smile faded away. Full of confusion, she smothered a sigh. Why had he changed so toward her? Changed so much he wouldn't even greet her in the morning? What had she done to change his smiling, caring manner to one of silent, brooding displeasure?

She could only think that he had already grown

tired of having her underfoot all the time, that she hampered his involvement with the widow. If she hadn't been here yesterday, masquerading as his wife, Liza would probably have stayed overnight with him, maybe even several days.

When Chase finally tore his gaze away from her, Raegan approached the stove and asked timidly, "Shall I finish making breakfast?"

The heady woman scent of her drifted to Chase as she stood close beside him. From the corners of his eyes, his gaze was drawn down her slender body, then back up to fasten on her proudly thrusting breasts. His voice was gruff when he answered.

"I've got it under control. You can pour the coffee if you want to."

Tears smarted Raegan's eyes at his harsh tone. She blindly picked up a hot-pad, and when she reached for the coffee pot, her arm brushed against his. The contact of her bare flesh with his set fire to Chase's blood. He jerked away his arm so fast that she looked up at him, startled.

A wounded look came into her eyes. Was even her touch distasteful to him? Her lips trembled and she fought back the tears that now hung on her lashes. Swallowing hard, she filled the three cups placed next to three plates, then asked stiffly as she set the pot back on the stove, being careful not to touch Chase, "Shall I call Jamie, or is he still sleeping?"

"He's down at the corral," Chase answered just as stiffly. He choked back the other words he wanted to say to her—no, yell at her. He wanted to demand where she and Jamie had gone yesterday. Had she let Jamie make love to her?

His back stiffened when Jamie said from the doorway, "Wrong, Chase, I'm right here,"

Chase grunted, but Raegan smiled at the freshly scrubbed face and slicked back hair. "Good morning, Jamie." There was a fondness as well as relief in her tone, making Chase grind his teeth together.

"Mornin' to you, sunshine." Jamie touched Raegan's shoulder affectionatly, aware of the dark frown on Chase's face as he saw the action. "Did you have a good night's sleep?" He let his hand slide down Raegan's arm and waited for Chase to knock him to the floor. Chase's fists only clenched.

"Yes, surprisingly I did sleep well," Raegan answered, "considering how the rain was lashing against the window."

Chase gave a barely audible snort of self-derision. It hadn't bothered her in the least that he'd been gone for hours, hadn't been home when she went to bed. And why should she care about him when there was such a handsome man to keep her company, flatter her, give her the sweet talk he couldn't give her?

"What about you?" Raegan smiled at Jamie as she took a seat across from him. "Were your dreams pleasant ones?"

"Indeed they were. I hated waking up this morning." His voice was warm, insinuating that a woman had been in his dreams.

Had Chase looked at his friend, he'd have seen

the mischief in his eyes, would have discovered that he was being baited. But he was too angry to look at Jamie, and his anger grew.

To hell with them both, he ground out silently. And to hell with his plans for trying to get back to the easy relationship he and Raegan had known when they first met. He had planned on telling her about the church services the preacher was going to hold Sunday, and that if she wanted to attend he would take her. But seeing as she and Jamie were so cozy-like, she probably wouldn't want to leave him that long.

Raegan sipped at her coffee, hardly realizing she was doing so as Chase banged around the stove, his actions showing clearly that he was displeased about something. When he pratically slammed the meat and eggs on the table, she looked at him in silent query, asking why he acted so.

But Chase refused eye contact with her as he filled his plate from the big platter and began to eat. She looked at Jamie and her eyes widened. By the devilish gleam in his eyes, he was enjoying Chase's boorish behavior. When he gave her a wide wink, she was hard put not to giggle.

"What're your plans for today, Chase?" Jamie asked lazily, helping himself to an egg. "It would be a fine time to go squirrel huntin'. With the forest floor rain-soaked, we'd have no trouble slippin' up on the little devils."

Chase didn't raise his eyes from his plate as he answered stiffly, "I've made other plans."

"Oh? Can't change them, huh?"

Chase didn't bother to answer and Raegan

ventured, "I suppose it's too wet to get started on the garden."

She had directed her remark to Chase, but when it became apparent he wasn't going to respond, Jamie said, "The ground will have to dry out for a couple of days, Raegan. But it's a fine time to get the rest of the weeds out of the flower beds. They'll come up real easy."

Raegan's eyes brightened. "That's true. Maybe we can pull some of the bigger ones out of the yard."

"I don't know why not," Jamie agreed, then slid a sly look at Chase. "We could get them all if a certain party was to pitch in and help."

Chase ignored the hint and lifted his cup to drain the last of the coffee from it. Fascinated, Raegan watched his throat work as the liquid slid down it. She had a strong urge to reach across the table and stroke her fingers down the muscular column.

She blushed furiously when Chase, lowering his cup, looked into her eyes. She dropped her lids, praying he hadn't read her thoughts.

And Chase, misreading the cause of the quickly hidden eyes, set his cup down with a hard thump. He rose and stalked out of the kitchen, muttering under his breath. What the hell did he care if she didn't want to look at him? Let her gaze into Jamie's eyes.

As he stamped off the porch, wondering how he was going to pass the day, for there was no way under the sun he'd hang around those two, Raegan looked at Jamie with troubled eyes.

"Is he always so—so cold and grouchy? He was

quite nice when he came to Minersville, and even up until . . ." She paused, enlightment growing in her eyes.

"Until I came along?" Jamie lifted an eyebrow.

"Well yes, I guess so." Raegan rose and refilled their cups with coffee. "But I can't imagine why." She returned the pot to the stove, then sat back down at the table. "You're his best friend. He said so."

The corners of Jamie's eyes crinkled with his tickled smile. "Ole Chase is jealous, for the first time in his life. He's so jealous he's almost blind with it."

Raegan idly stirred sugar into her coffee, looking thoughtfully out the window. "I think you're mistaken, Jamie," she said finally. "After thinking it over, I don't think you have anything to do with it. I think his ornery manner has to do with Liza Jenkins and his interrupted freedom. I should have never come here."

"Now what kind of talk is that?" Jamie scolded. "Of course you should have come here. You're his wife. This is where you belong.

"Besides"—he covered her clenched fist with his hand—"you're badly mistaken about his feelins' for the widow. I told you he doesn't give a snap of his fingers about her."

But he likes to sleep with her, Raegan reminded herself silently. He likes to go to the tavern and drink with the other trappers, play poker with them. She remembered the night they spent at Sid Johnson's fur post, where Chase had sat up all night playing cards.

She rose and went to stare out the window.

"No, Jamie, I'm a hindrance to him. I think he's sorry I'm here."

"Come on, Raegan, don't talk crazy. If it came down to it, Chase would rather lose an arm than lose you. He just don't know how to handle these new feelins' he's got." Jamie stood up. "Do whatever you have to do in the cabin, then come on outside. We'll give them weeds hell."

A long sigh escaped Raegan as she turned from the window. Jamie wouldn't be so sure of his words if he knew the true situation, she thought as she began clearing the table. He doesn't know the lie we're living.

Chase rode along the Platte, the reins held loosely in his hands. It wasn't a river to trust today, he thought, studying the muddy flow, thick after last night's downpour, swirling, chafing at its banks. But nevertheless it was majestic as it gleamed under the late April sky, swinging its way toward a wilder wilderness, a place yet unhabitated by white man.

The beauty and grandeur of the Platte faded from Chase's mind as he let Sampson wander aimlessly along, not knowing or caring much where they went. He was deep in thoughts of Raegan. Once he slammed a fist down on the saddle in his helpless frustration, making the stallion snort his displeasure. What in the hell was he going to do about her? he asked himself for the sixth time since leaving the barn.

Deep down, he didn't believe that Jamie had crossed that line, taking who he thought was his best friend's wife to bed. But if the attraction he was sure the pair shared should grow into love, Raegan only need make it known that she was free to marry anyone she wanted to.

His stomach knotted. He didn't think he could bear it if that came to pass.

The stallion came to a full stop, bending his head to crop at a stand of lush grass. Chase lounged in the saddle, his mind still on Raegan, wondering what she and Jamie were doing back at the cabin. He was swiftly brought out of his preoccupation, however, when Sampson raised his head, his ears twitching as if listening.

Tightening his grip on the reins, Chase kneed the stallion off the deeply trodden animal path and into the encroaching forest of pine and spruce. After a few yards he reined him beneath a thick-trunked pine, straining his ears and eyes.

Nothing stirred; there was no sound. He told himself that because of the sodden condition of the forest, he would hear no footsteps. But there should be birdsong, the chirping bark of squirrels. Something, or somebody, had frightened the wild inhabitants of these woods.

His ears alert for any alien sound, his eyes searching among the trees constantly, Chase was suddenly rewarded by a despairing cry of agony. He knew the sound could have only came from a female throat, and he immediately thought of the Tillamook woman. Had Roscoe dared to bring her back to the neighorhood?

He swung to the ground and looped the reins over a branch, then moved cautiously in the direction of the cry. His moccasined feet made no sound on the wet leaves and pine needles as he moved forward, his hand on his gun butt. He came to a large boulder standing in his way. When he started edging around it, he all at once jerked back, shaking his head. He must be dreaming.

But Chase knew that he wasn't, and he took another careful look, then smiled mirthlessly. He had no need to take special care of being quiet. The pair on the ground wouldn't have known if an army was marching up on them.

The Indian girl stretched helplessly on her back, her hands held over her head, was petrified with fright, blind and dumb to anything but the long, bony body thrusting cruelly into her. And the man, driving his sharp hips against hers, was oblivious to everything but the release he worked at achieving.

Chase walked up to the coupling bodies, a savage mischief in his eyes. He stood over them, his eyes narrowed speculatively, gauging the rhythm of the narrow buttocks moving up and down. Finally what he waited for began to occur. The thrusting body had picked up its pace, on the verge of reaching a climax.

With unholy glee, he lifted a foot and slammed it into the bare rear end.

All action stopped, the long body going stiff. "Well, preacher"—Chase sneered the word contemptously—"is this how you convert the people you call heathens?"

The preacher's alarm and dismay were palpable as he rolled off the girl and scrambled to his feet, tugging up his trousers.

"Look, Donlin," he whined, "I'm a man, just

like you. I need release too. When she begged me to lie with her, I became weak and sinned."

"Yeah, I could see she was really enjoyin' herself," Chase jeered. "You bastard." He took a threatening step toward the cowering man. "You were rapin' that girl, and if you say anything different, I'll smash your lyin' mouth."

He reached a hand down to the still fearful girl, recognizing her as one of Chief Wise Owl's tribe. "Are you all right?" he asked gently when she stood beside him. When she nodded that she was, he said, "Go on home. This one won't bother you again."

"I'm so ashamed," the young woman sobbed, tears running down her cheeks. "What will I tell my new husband?"

Chase brushed the dirt off her doeskin shift and carefully picked the leaves and needles out of her long braid. "Must you tell him anything?" he asked softly when she quieted down. "I arrived in time to keep the bastard's seed from entering your body. There will be no child from his attack."

The girl chewed thoughtfully on her bottom lip, staring down at the ground. Then looking up at Chase and wiping her eyes, she said, "I guess that would be the wise thing to do. Your people and mine have lived together in harmony for a long time. It would be a shame for discord to come between us."

Chase nodded solemly. "My thoughts too. And be assured that this varmint who calls himself a man will pay for what he did to you. Maybe not today, or tomorrow, but justice will catch up with him one day."

The girl nodded, then took off through the forest at a run. Chase watched her out of sight, then turned back to the man. "What are you goin' to do?" the preacher asked sullenly, his aborted release throbbing painfully in his loins. "I'll deny it if you spread the story around."

"You long piece of buffalo dung, do you think anyone in these hills would believe you?" Chase snarled. "You've got the hungry look of a skirt-chaser, and the men around here know it.

"I don't know yet what I'm gonna do about you. In the meantime, go ahead and hold services tomorrow. I wouldn't want the good women of Big Pine to miss hearin' the gospel read. They won't know that the man preachin' to them isn't fit to touch the Bible."

His hand shot out and grasped the front of the man's shirt. "But if you say one word about the sin of fornicatin', I'll have an Indian cut out your tongue." He gave the glowering man a hard shove. "Now get out of my sight before I change my mind and beat the hell out of you."

Raegan moved about the kitchen, preparing the evening meal, her sore muscles protesting. Except to stop for a quick lunch of cold beef sandwiches and a cup of coffee, she and Jamie had pulled and dug up weeds all day.

But it's worth every ache and pain, she thought with a smile as she glanced out the kitchen window. She could now see lush, green grass. All the weeds were gone, carried to the barn and stacked against the wall in a pile that was higher than herself. And more satisfying was the discovery of flowers trying to push their way through the matted growth that had for years tried to choke the life from them. They had somehow lived on, and later in the season when they burst into bloom, it would be a beautiful sight to feast her eyes on.

Her eyes grew misty. If only Mama was here to see it happen, she thought, then told herself not to look back. She stirred the pot of beans that had been cooking slowly all day, a large chunk of ham giving them flavoring. She lifted the lid from a pot of simmering potatoes and stabbed them with a fork for doneness. She nodded. Another fifteen minutes, and they'd be ready to be mashed.

As Raegan prepared to set the table, she stood in front of the china cabinet a moment, debating how many plates to put out. Would Chase be home for supper? He had been gone all day, and if he was with Liza, he might be gone all night.

She finally took down three plates. It would rile Chase no end if he should come in while she and Jamie were eating and there was no place set for him. She continued to glance out the window every few minutes, hoping to see Sampson come loping toward the cabin. But the tree shadows had lengthened and twilight was about to set in before she heard the rhythmic thud of galloping hooves. Her heart raced. There would be three for supper!

Keeping an eye on the open door, she saw Chase ride by, heading for the corral. A few minutes later, she heard his and Jamie's voices as they came toward the cabin. While they washed up on the back porch, she lit the lamp and put supper on the table.

"Sure smells good in here," said Jamie, who had evidently used the wash basin first, as he entered the kitchen. "I'm starvin'."

He took his place at the table, and when Chase's large frame filled the doorway, he grinned and asked, "What about you, friend? Anybody give you lunch today?"

Although she listened intently, Raegan wasn't able to make out Chase's muttered reply. She looked at him to see if he was going to speak to her, then bit back a sigh. All his attention was on the bowl of beans from which he was filling his plate.

Days of pain and bitterness boiled inside her. She'd be damned if she'd speak first. She had done nothing to make him act like a sore-horn buffalo, and she didn't care if he never spoke to her again—or looked at her. She scraped her chair back and sat down at the table.

Raegan had no idea what she was eating. It could have been some of the weeds her blistered fingers had tugged from the ground. She still shook with anger inside.

A couple of times, Jamie, attuned to her upheavel, gave her a sympathetic smile, the curve of his lips telling her at the same time not to mind the sour-faced man sitting across from her.

Several times he also tried to lighten the atmosphere, keep a conversation going. But when Raegan didn't join in at all and Chase only grunted occasionally, he gave up and tended to filling his empty stomach.

It was probably the fastest meal the old kitchen had ever witnessed. Jamie rose and thanked Raegan for a tasty supper, then walked outside. Without a word, Chase quickly drained his cup of coffee and stamped out behind him.

Raegan sat on, her slim shoulders shaking with the sobs she'd held back for several days. How much more could she take? How long could a person go along all tensed up and not break?

She smelled cigarette smoke and choked off her tears. She hadn't known the men had remained on the porch. She wiped her eyes and finished eating the food that had grown cold on her plate, paying no attention to the conversation going on between Chase and Jamie. Her ears perked up, however, when she heard Chase mention Sid Johnson's name.

" . . . there's been reports of Indians seen skulking around. Tillamooks lookin' for their woman. He said the women folk were becomin' nervous and upset."

"They've got reason to be," Jamie said, staring off into the darkness.

"Yeah. We've got to make sure Raegan doesn't wander too far away from the cabin. They're probably lookin' for a lone woman to capture to hold hostage for the one Roscoe took."

"And then torture her to death when no one brings their woman to them," Jamie observed.

Raegan suddenly felt ashamed of her tears. She had been crying because she was being treated coldly by a man, and at the same moment there was a woman out there somewhere clinging to life.

Or was the Tillamook still fighting to stay alive? Maybe she had given up the fight, no longer wanted to live. Raegan tried to convince herself that the woman lived, that if she didn't, Roscoe would have returned to the neighborhood.

She rose stiffly from the table, saying a prayer for the Indian woman as she filled the dishpan with water from the big black tea kettle. After she had dropped the bar of yellow soap into it, she scraped the plates and slid them into the sudsy water.

By rote alone, she brought the kitchen to order, her mind on the glum man outside. She knew now that she loved Chase Donlin with a deep and abiding love and that things could not go on as they were. It was evident she couldn't stay on here. She must think of another place to go, another way to get on with her life.

But where and how? The question drummed at her mind. How did a lone female with only a horse and rifle to her name go out into a world she knew nothing about and survive? She knew another way of life existed outside the wilderness; Mama had told her of the big cities, paved streets with big fancy stores where one could buy dresses of silk, taffatas, sheer muslins. She had spoken of the milliners with beautifully created bonnets of fine straw, satin or fur, gaily decorated with ribbons and flowers.

Raegan looked down at her faded calico dress. The question was, did she want the finery Mama had described so glowingly? She didn't really think so. She had never known such, and consequently had never hungered for it.

She dried the last pot and hung the dish towel on its peg, then walked through the parlor and out to the big front porch. She would stay there until the men went to bed: then she'd fill the wooden tub with water on the back porch and take a leisurely bath.

Raegan sat down on the top step and propped her elbows on her bent knees. Resting her chin on her palm, she gazed out into the darkness. In the thick and lonely silence there came the mournful howling of wolves, the hoot of an owl, and the weird, wild scream of a panther—all familar sounds to her now. She sighed softly. She loved this vast and silent wilderness, and she was loath to leave it.

But leave it she must, Raegan reminded herself. There was only heartache for her here.

Her mind kept returning to the only plausible solution to the problem of where to go. She would return to Minersville, stay at the shack, and resume doing the miners' laundry. She would live frugally, save her money, and eventually move on to the kind of large city her mother had talked about, even though the thought didn't appeal to her.

"And do what when I get there?" she asked herself. Since she could remember, she had lived in mining camps. That kind of life hadn't equipped her with the knowledge of how to earn a living. It was true she could cook—plain basic meals, but nothing fancy unless she followed the recipes in Grandmother Molly's cookbook.

She was a crack shot with a rifle or gun and could ride like an Indian, but what call would there be for such talents in a big city?

She did have a good education. Her mother had been very strict about the four hours set aside every day for lessons. And she was well read, thanks to the books Anne O'Keefe had brought from home as a young bride, hauling them from one mining camp to another. Maybe she could find a position as a schoolteacher.

Raegan turned her head slightly when she heard Jamie and Chase enter the kitchen. She listened until she heard their footsteps go down the hall and enter their respective rooms. When she heard the sound of two doors closing, she stood up and made her way to the kitchen, where the lamp still burned.

It took several minutes to carry water to the tub and then bring a gown, towel, soap, and washcloth from her room. But finally her preparations were done and she stepped into the warm bath. With a big sigh, she sat down in the water, then grinned ruefully. She had used up most of her energy preparing everything. When it grew a little warmer, she would use the river as Chase and Jamie did.

The soreness went out of Raegan's muscles as she lathered her body with the rose-scented soap. But soon the warmth of the day faded as true night came on, and goose bumps stood up on her flesh. She hurriedly rinsed off and stepped out of the tub. After a brisk rubbing with the towel, she slipped the nightgown over her head.

Still hurrying, she tossed her soiled clothing

into the bathwater to soak overnight, then added Chase's and Jamie's clothes, which had been crammed in a wooden box at the end of the porch. She had started the men doing that the second day she was there.

Minutes later, she was crawling into bed. Annoyingly, although she was relaxed, she was wide awake. Still niggling at her brain was the question of why Chase had changed so. One thing she knew for sure—before she left here, she was going to find out. She would tackle him about it tomorrow, then she would leave.

No, by God! She suddenly sat up in bed. Enough was enough! They would talk about it tonight. She would never get to sleep until the air was cleared between them.

Raegan swung her feet to the floor, and holding tightly to her courage, she slipped quietly down the hall and silently entered Chase's room.

The full moon, riding in a cloudless sky, shone through the open window and bathed Chase's face in soft shadows. He lay on his back, and she stood for long moments feasting her eyes on the firm mouth relaxed now in sleep, the dark lashes that were almost as long as her own and cast dark crescents on his high cheekbones.

A lock of his curling brown hair lay against his forehead and she had to stop herself from smoothing it back on his head. *Stop it!* she commanded herself. What was wrong with her, standing there with her mouth watering over him like a child gazing at a candy stick? *Get on with what you came here for.*

Raegan swallowed, then timidly laid a hand on

Chase's wrist, not to startle him but to wake him slowly. She gave a start when suddenly she was looking into his slumberous dark eyes.

And while she stood over him, her outstretched hand arrested in midair, he silently reached for her.

With a little sigh, she went down on the bed and into his arms. She gave a soft gasp as she came up against his bare chest and realized that he was bare beneath the sheet. He groaned her name, then his hot, hungry lips were taking command of hers.

Raegan was unprepared for the hot, liquid desire that flooded through her veins. She wrapped her arms around Chase's broad shoulders, breathing his name, instinctively arching her body into his. She felt the pressure of his virility press against her stomach, and hunger for the unknown raced through her in waves.

She murmured a protest when he drew away from her, afraid that he would order her from his bed. She relaxed when, settling back on his heels, Chase grasped the hem of her gown and began sliding it up her body. When the garment was past her hips, she raised up so he could lift it over her head.

He tossed it on the floor and they knelt, facing each other. Raegan shivered convulsively when Chase leaned forward and caressed his tongue across her sensitive, passion-swollen nipples. When she gave a soft moan, his mouth opened over one breast and drew it into his mouth. Her fingers stroked through his hair as he suckled her, moving from one breast to the other until both were hard peaks of desire.

Chase straighted up then and gently pushed her back onto the bed. He stretched out beside her and, propping his head on his palm, he let his eyes drift over her body, which glistened silvery in the moonlight.

"You are so beautiful," he whispered and slid his palm up and down the silken texture of her stomach.

Raegan lay perfectly still, afraid that if she moved she would break the spell Chase seemed to be under. Lately his moods had been like quicksilver; moving up and down, keeping her in a state of unrest and confusion. She didn't think she could bear it if he drew away from her now.

A sigh of relief fluttered through her lips when he lay down and drew her into his arms. Her eyes closed as his fingers stroked her face, her throat, then moved to her breasts. She squirmed in delight as he gently pulled and teased her nipples, not stopping until they were hard and extended. A soft little moan filtered through her lips when he bent his head and opened his mouth over the breast that wasn't crushed against him. As his tongue laved, his teeth nibbled, he took her hand and slid it down his flat muscular stomach to the long, thick length of him that pulsated like something alive.

He lifted his head and whispered huskily, "Hold me, honey. Stroke me the way you have in so many of my dreams."

Shy, but eager, Raegan's slim fingers closed

round him, marveling at his size. She wondered fleetingly if she would be able to accept all that power inside her.

She forgot everything as Chase's own hand slid down to the apex of her thighs, massaged a moment, then slid a finger between the lips nestled in silken, curly hair. He began to suckle her again, at the same time moving his finger deeper inside her, sliding it back and forth in rhythm with his drawing lips.

Raegan caught the slow pace and slid her cupped palm up and down his hard manhood rhythmically. The rasp of their larbored breathing filled the room as each came dangerously close to climaxing.

When Chase lifted his head and removed his hand, Raegan looked questioningly at him from desire-glazed eyes. "What's wrong?" she whispered, coming up on her elbows.

"Nothin', sweetheart." He gently spread her thighs wider. "I just can't wait any longer to get inside you. You want me there, don't you?" he whispered as he climbed between her legs and hung over her.

Raegan could only nod eagerly as she laid her head back on the pillow.

She felt Chase's controlled hunger as his hands gripped her hips, lifting them up against his. "It's gonna hurt at first, love," he murmured huskily, "but only for a moment."

Covering her lips with his, he raised his body away from her far enough to reach his hand between them and take his painfully throbbing arousal in his hand. He slid it slowly inside her narrow opening, then with one firm shove of his hips, pushed through the thin membrane, burying his length inside her. He caught her expected cry in his mouth, at the same time stroking her quivering body. When he felt the tenseness leaving her, he raised his head and smiled gently at her.

"Are you all right now?" he whispered, stroking his fingers down her cheek.

Raegan nodded and returned his caress. He dropped a kiss on her lips, the slid his hands beneath her narrow hips. And though he wondered at the delicacy of her body—could she really bear his largeness moving inside her?—he was powerless to withdraw from her. He held still a moment, sheathed inside her like a well-fitting leather glove, then mentally asked her forgiveness as he began to move slowly, keeping his eyes on her face, looking for any pain that might change her expression.

She wore only a look of sensual delight, and when her slenderness reached for him, wanting more of his man's strength, he breathed his deep relief. He began a rhythmic thrusting of his hips, sliding his arousal in and out of her, making the bed squeak, making his friend in the next room grin in the darkness.

When Chase felt Raegan's quivering response, knew she was fast reaching that crest of the little death, he gathered her close and bucked his hips furiously.

They clung to each other's lips drowning their ecstatic cries as wave after wave of release washed over them.

Chase slumped against Raegan with a groan, his hands clutching the sheet, his breathing fast and harsh. Never had he felt so whole, so complete.

Then, as gradually he was depleted of all passion, it seeped into his mind what he had done. He had lost control in his half-sleeping state and had made love to Anne's daughter. Not only had he possessed Raegan, he had taken her virginity. He had ruined her chance of someday marrying a decent man who would expect her to be chaste on their wedding night.

Filled with an anger of self-contempt, he rolled off Raegan and sat on the edge of the bed, staring at, but not seeing, his fists clenched on his knees. What if he had gotten Raegan with child? In his earth-shattering release, it hadn't entered his mind to withdraw, to spill his seed onto the bed.

And Raegan, her mind whirling in confusion at Chase's abrupt action, lay in troubled silence. Was he reverting to his old coolness? Surely not—not after what they had just shared. She sat up and touched him shyly on the shoulder. "What's wrong, Chase?" she whispered.

"Everything is wrong." He shrugged her hand away and left the bed to go stare out the window. "This should have never happened," he said coldly, "and it won't happen again."

"But why not?" Raegan's voice trembled. "It was beautiful, our love-making. How can you say it was wrong?"

Chase whirled away from the window and stalked over to the bed. "You're my sister's daughter. I'm supposed to take care of you, not use you."

Pain, and a stirring of anger, gripped Raegan. Mama hadn't been his blood sister and he knew it. So why was he acting like their coming together had been incestuous?

Because he isn't attracted to me that way, Raegan answered her own question. I just happened to be here when his body needed release.

She looked up at Chase and asked quietly, "Is that what happened, Chase? You used me? Like you use the whores at the village tavern?" She did not put Liza Jenkins in the same category. He cared for the widow.

Chase stared down at the delicate, lovely face, the pain-shadowed eyes, and clenched his fists. Of course he hadn't used her. He had made love to her with all the completeness that the word implied. This act had been a first for him. But that still didn't make it right, and if Raegan had any romantic notions about him, he must kill them right now.

He swallowed hard a couple of times, then answered cruelly, "Yes, I used you."

A shattered look spread over Raegan's face. Unable to watch her anguish, Chase turned away and started to walk back to the window. He took one step, and a bundle of fury stood in his path. As he stared in surprise, Raegan's hand flashed through the air, staggering him with a slap across the face. As he gaped at her, his hand going to the white imprint of her fingers, she grabbed her gown and ran from the room.

His cheek smarting, Chase stared at the empty doorway, repressing the desire to go after Raegan. For though he knew she was hurting, there was nothing he could say that would ease her pain—nor his feeling of guilt. With a ragged sigh, he lay back down on the rumpled bed, catching Raegan's scent as he pulled the sheet up over him.

"Oh, Anne," he whispered, "why couldn't your only child have been a boy?"

Chapter Nine

The eastern sky was just flushing pink when Chase came awake. Although his body was still languorously relaxed from the extraordinary love-making a few hours back, his inertia did not extend to his brain. Upon opening his eyes, the niggling question that had kept him awake half the night returned in full force.

What in the hell was he going to do about Raegan?

He had to do something, he knew, and do it fast. Even now, just thinking about her brought a stirring in his loins. He flung an arm across his eyes. Should he take her to some large city and enroll her in one of those fancy boarding schools where she would be taught all the social graces he'd heard of, be prepared to meet an affluent husband? A city-bred man would be more apt to overlook the fact that he wasn't the first with her.

And certainly she'd have no problem attracting a man. She had the beauty, the natural well-bred quality that would draw the gentry to her. Even in her faded old dresses and usually bare feet, she looked like a queen as she moved about the cabin doing the things that occupied a woman's time.

Chase suddenly found himself thinking of reasons why Raegan shouldn't go away. She would be miserably unhappy, taken away from an environment she knew and loved. It would be like caging a wild animal, settling her in a place where the houses were crammed together, where streets teemed with carriages and noises, people coming and going, jostling each other. The sparkling light would leave her beautiful eyes, leaving them dull with unhappiness.

He sat up in bed and swung his feet to the floor, reaching for his clothes. There must be a solution to this dilemma he found himself in and he intended to search it out.

Raegan awakened in the first gray dawn after a restless night filled with unanswered questions. She rose, washed her face, then sponged away Chase's scent from her body. She walked quietly down the hall, grimacing at the tenderness between her legs.

She was still in a grip of sick anger as she entered the kitchen, and her whole body burned with shame. In her surrender to Chase's lovemaking, she had allowed herself to become like all the other women he had lain with. As she laid a fire in the range and put on a pot of coffee, she was careful not to make any noise. She didn't want to awaken Chase and Jamie. She wasn't ready to face either of them yet.

When the coffee began to simmer and fill the kitchen with its aroma, Raegan pulled it to the back of the stove and walked out onto the back porch. As she gazed down the valley, where stands of tall spruce stood dimly in the night-like shadows, her thoughts were still on Chase. She had been so sure last night that he returned her love. The gentle way he had held her, the whispered endearments. True, he hadn't spoken the word love, but his every action had said it . . . and she had believed it then.

Recalling the pleasure he had given her, the lower half of her body tingled. She blinked back sudden tears. Their love-making hadn't affected Chase as it had her. To him it had been just another release of his loins, all passion for her forgotten once it was over.

The sky continued to lighten as Raegan stood on, only vaguely aware of Lobo bounding through the thick gray fog, coming to throw himself at feet.

She finally became aware of the cool morning air, and shivering, she turned and walked back into the kitchen.

Raegan came to an abrupt stop in the doorway. Chase stood at the stove, pouring himself a cup of coffee. He brought the steaming cup to the table and sat down. When he reached for the sugar bowl sitting in the center of the table, he saw her standing there.

He gazed at her for a long moment, no emotion showing in his eyes. He stood up after a moment as she made no move to enter the kitchen and walked to the stove and picked up the coffee pot. Pouring another cup of coffee, he placed it on the table and sat back down. "Come sit down, Raegan," he said, "we must talk."

Raegan reluctantly took a seat across from him, an angry defiance in her eyes. "I don't know what we could talk about. You made yourself perfectly clear last night. I got your message clear enough, and you can bet I'll never come near your bed again."

"I wish you wouldn't take that attitude about what I said last night," Chase said in a low, regretful voice. "Surely you can see it wasn't right, you bein'—"

With a dark, scathing look Raegan finished his sentence. "Anne's daughter! That's a damn poor excuse and you know it. Why don't you be honest and admit that you found me lacking as your bed partner, that I fell short of what you're used to."

Her voice had risen with her anger, her last charge almost yelled at him. Chase looked nervously toward the hall. Had Jamie heard? He turned back to face the green eyes that shot sparks at him. "Look, Raegan." He lowered his voice to a near whisper, hoping she would do the same, "that's not true. I have never before found such complete satisfaction as I did with you last night. But—"

"But nothing, Chase Donlin," Raegan cried. "Why don't you just take your lying words and get the hell away from me. I'm sick to death of hearing them."

"Fine," Chase snapped, slamming down his cup and surging to his feet. "I wouldn't dream of makin' you sick." As he banged out the door, he didn't see the tears that sprang to Raegan's eyes.

Anger hastened his movements, and it took but a few minutes for Chase to toss the saddle on Sampson, then swing onto his back. He dug in his heels, sending the stallion into a gallop. As he headed in a northerly direction, the sun had burned off the morning mists except for the lingering, loosely twisted ropes of fog that hung over the Platte.

He saw nothing of this, though, as his mount moved farther and farther into the remote, unsettled wilderness. His thoughts were on Raegan and the quarrel they'd had. Which one of them was wrong in their thinking?

Surprisingly, as he spent more time with Raegan, the less she reminded him of Anne. It was still true that every time he looked at Raegan, it was like looking at her mother. But where Anne's demeanor had been gentle and serene, Raegan was high-spirited, bursting with the lust for life. She had evidently inherited her fiery spirit from her father. He could not visualize his stepsister making the same wild, uninhibited love that her daughter had last night.

And another thing Chase remembered with surprise, although he hadn't noticed it at the time, was that he hadn't felt all that guilty about sleeping with Raegan. Her response to him in bed, the complete giving of herself to him, had driven everything else from his mind.

He squirmed uncomfortably in the saddle. Just remembering those lusty hours spent with her caused him to get a very painful arousal. He gave a short, harsh laugh. Was he to go around in an erected state from now on?

"You don't have to," his inner conscience nudged him. "You can marry the girl. You've already taken her virginity, spoiled her for a marriage with a good man. Does she deserve to be married to a brute because of you, brutalized by him, given a baby every year?

"No!" Chase exclaimed out loud; the very thought of that happening twisted his gut into knots. Truthfully, he couldn't bear to think of even a good, decent man making love to Raegan.

"So?" He prodded himself, "What are you going to about it?"

Without thinking about it, Chase answered promptly, "I'm going to marry her myself."

"But will she have you? She was awfully riled with you this morning."

"She'll have me. All I have to do is point out to her that I might have planted my seed inside her."

"What if she says that you should wait and see?"

Chase smiled a self-satisfied grin. He knew how to handle that. Raegan was very receptive to his kisses and caresses. She'd come into his arms, surrender her body to him again, and he'd make such lingering love to her that she'd be unable to live without him. She would need his hard strength the way she needed food and water.

"Don't feel so smug," the little voice jeered. "You can get caught in the same trap. She can become an unbreakable habit with you too."

Chase's face became sober and thoughtful. Was the word *become* the right word? Wasn't she already a very vital necessity to his being? A realization, like a hard fist to the stomach, came to Chase. He loved Reagan O'Keefe, and more then anything else in the world he wanted her for his wife. Suddenly he couldn't wait to get home and make that lovely girl his for all time.

Glancing westward, he noted that the sun would set in less than half an hour. He might as well make camp here and head for home tomorrow morning, he decided, steering Sampson beneath a large hardwood tree. He had dismounted and started to unsaddle, when his fingers froze on the belly cinch. A thin, reedy voice ordered, "Freeze, stranger."

Chase dropped his hands to his side and carefully turned his head. Standing a few feet away was an old man with a rifle pointed at his back. His face was brown and wrinkled like a piece of old leather, and he wore a drooping mustache.

The mustache stirred. "What'er you doin' up here in my neck of the woods?" the old man growled.

Chase started to turn around, then stopped at the sound of a trigger being cocked. "Look," he said impatiently, angered at himself for letting a man old enough to be his grandfather get the drop on him. "I didn't know anybody *owned* this region. I started out this mornin' lookin' for new territory to lay a new trapline and ended up here." It was none of the old man's business that his mind had been so occupied with a young, green-eyed woman he hadn't known where he was going.

"So you're a trapper, huh?" The voice wasn't quite as hostile now. "I kinda thought you was, but I wanted to make sure. Livin' up here alone, a man can't be too careful. You can turn around now."

Chase faced around carefully and stood quietly under the old man's close scrunity. When he seemed satisfied that no harm would be dealt him, he narrowed the space between them and stuck out a knobby hand.

"Will Daniels is my handle."

"Chase Donlin." Their hands met in a firm grip.

"I was gettin' ready to make camp," Chase said, "that is if you don't mind. I'll be leavin' first light in the mornin'."

"No need for you to sleep on the ground. I got a tolerable soft bed you can use."

When Chase looked undecided, the old man added, with an anxious note in his voice, "I'd be right pleased to talk to a white man for a change. I get mighty tired of palaverin' with Indians and listenin' to the youngin' chatterin'."

"You got a youngin'?" Chase couldn't keep the surprise out of his voice.

"Yeah, my grandchild. Orneriest little critter you'd ever come across."

Chase hid his grin. There was pride and love in old Daniels's complaint, despite the words he described the boy with. "I guess most young boys have a wild streak in them."

"Yes, that's true, but in this case we're talkin' bout a girl." His eyes took on a faraway look. "Can't blame her, though. I raised her like she was a boy. Poor youngin', ain't never owned a dress or anything fancy. I don't know anything about wimmen's frippery." After a moment, he added, "I figure it's just as well no one but the Indians knows she's a girl."

"How come they know her sex?"

"She's related to a bunch of them. Her mama was an Indian woman. A good decent woman. My son married her seventeen years ago and we all lived together in a sturdy little cabin near here." The faded brown eyes clouded over. "Star was three months old when a couple men stopped at the cabin. I know there was two, cause I counted two sets of hoof prints when I returned home. They shot and killed my son, raped his wife, then slit her throat." His voice trembled. "That wasn't enough for the bastards, though. They set fire to the cabin, the baby inside it. I was out huntin' at the time, but thank God I arrived back in time to carry Star out.

"It's been me and her ever since."

Chase didn't know what to say to the sad-eyed man. Consoling words seemed so inadequate. "Were the men ever caught?" he asked instead.

"No, they got clean away, may they burn in hell someday."

Daniels gave his boney shoulders a shake, as though throwing off the sad memories. "It's gonna be dark before long. We'd better get goin', see what Star has cooked for supper."

Leading Sampson, Chase followed along behind the old hill man who moved as silently as any Indian, and just as warily. He thought of the pain and frustration the old fellow must have suffered at losing his family and his home within a few minutes.

Would Jamie hang around the cabin to watch out for Raegan? he worried for the first time, visualizing the same thing happening to her as had happened to Daniels's daughter-in-law. The pain of such an event formed a knot in his stomach.

Of course Jamie wouldn't go off and leave her. He would enjoy having her to himself too much to do that. Besides, he knew the danger of the Tillamooks skulking around.

Nevertheless, he couldn't wait to get home. He had been a damn fool taking off the way he had without a word to Raegan. He mused on how his action had affected her. At first she had probably been hurt, but by now he knew she would be angry as hell. His lips curved ruefully. He most likely would find the door barred against him when he got back.

The path he and the old man were traveling was suddenly narrow and rock-filled, calling all of Chase's attention to where he stepped and to making sure Sampson didn't step on his heels. It was but a short time later that Daniels halted before the dark opening of a cave. It was so well camouflaged by brush and boulders that a person could walk past it a hundred times and never spot it.

"Wait here a minute," the old man said, then moved into the dark interior. A moment later, there came the scraping sound of something heavy being dragged against stone, then the flare of a struck match. A few seconds later, Daniels's shadow danced before him as he walked toward Chase, a lantern swinging from his hand.

"Bring your mount on in, Donlin," he said.

Chase gave Sampson's reins a tug, noting as they moved forward the heavy split-log gate pulled to one side. He realized that it had been the gate that made the grating sound. The lantern gave a feeble light and he jumped when he bumped into the rear end of an animal. An old mule, he discovered when he lifted the lantern, throwing its light on the animal.

"That's Mabel. Watch out for her hind legs," Will advised. "She's a mean bitch. Would just as soon kick your teeth out as look at you. Me and her have been fightin' for fifteen years."

"How come you to keep such a dangerous animal, especially round a youngin' growin' up?"

"It's a strange thing, but she's never been any danger to Star. She's always been good around the girl." He gave a dry laugh. "Star has a way with animals. I guess like knows like. Star is as stubborn as a mule, and just as mean sometimes."

Daniels pointed to a wide alcove off to one side. "That's Star's mount. Her pride and joy. She trapped one whole winter to get enough money together to buy the animal."

"And well she should be proud of this fellow." Chase studied the muscular stallion as well as he could by the dim light. The sorrel had great speed and endurance, he'd bet. Sampson would probably be hard put to out-run the big brute. Will's granddaughter must be big and strong to handle him.

"Tie your mount to one of the rings I've pounded into the wall," Will broke in on Chase's musing. "Put him a good distance from the sorrel. It'd would be an awful fight if them two started battlin' each other."

When Chase had snubbed Sampson to one of the rings pointed out to him and lifted the saddle off the broad back, Will started walking deeper into the cave. "Come on through to the livin' quarters," he called over his shoulder.

"You live in a cave?" Chase's lips curved in a half smile, not really surprised that this rough, grizzled hill man *would* live in a cave.

"Yep, sixteen years now." He stopped and stepped aside so that Chase could walk past him. "I only meant it to be temporary when I chased a bear out of here and moved in with my infant granddaughter," the old man grunted as he dragged another heavy gate across an opening where the cave narrowed to a width of no more than four feet, but where the tall ceiling remained the same. "There was a freezing rain comin' down, and I had to get her somewhere where it was dry.

"But as the days and months dragged by, I was so durned-busted busy takin' care of the youngin', runnin' a trap line with her strapped to my back, I never seemed to find the time or energy to build a cabin. By the time she was eight or nine and I had more time on my hands, me and her liked it just fine in the cave. It was home."

Chase walked behind the old man, down a stone tunnel with several twists to it. "When you stop and think about it," Will picked up his story, "it's better than a cabin. It's wind free, which you gotta appreciate in the winter. As you can imagine, it gets mighty cold up here. And in the summer, when we get them fierce storms, there ain't no safer place from the lightnin' than inside a cave.

"Star, she's mighty fond of settin' in the entrance, watchin' the lightnin' zig-zag among the trees, bringin' some of them down, her knowin' she ain't gonna be touched. 'Course, in the winter we get snowed in often. I always keep a sturdy shovel handy."

Will came to a halt and turned to Chase. "Well, what do you think?"

Chase gazed around the large, almost perfectly square room with appreciation. The setting sun flooded the room, showing in relief the coziness of the floor covered with bear and panther skins, the walls hung with colorful woven Indian tapestry.

In the center of the room, the old man had built a large, circular stone wall about two feet tall, topped off by a foot-and-a-half wide ledge. Inside the round fireplace, red coals glowed; smoke drifted up and disappeared through a crack about an inch wide and nine inches long. A black pot sat to one side in the warm ashes.

On either side of the fire-pit was a handmade rocker of pine poles held together with strips of animal hide. Both chairs were well padded with bright Indian blankets. Chase's eyes drifted to the north wall, where there was a long narrow table, a bench flanking each side. These were also made in the same fashion as the rockers. A bowl of wildflowers had been placed in the table's center. He looked at grizzled old Will and knew that the feminine touch came from his granddaughter. He could not visualize the old man picking flowers.

When Chase discovered the two beds along the south wall, his eyes widened. What ingenuity Will Daniels had used in fashioning them! He had built two regular-sized bedframes, then with a heavy rope had suspended them from the ceiling, coming within a foot and a half of the floor. Again, colorful Indian blankets had been put to use, covering thick mattresses of some sort.

Will saw his stunned look and gave his cackling laugh. "Star calls them swingin' beds. I got the idea from a cradle I fashioned for her right after we moved in here. I was afraid to let her sleep with me for fear I'd roll over on her and squash her little body. I couldn't let her sleep on the floor because of bugs." He smiled his toothless grin. "Also I could give it a push and it would swing her back to sleep if she happened to wake up durin' the night."

Fond reminiscence softened the old man's eyes. "She was a good baby. Never a cry out of her unless she was hungry."

"How in the world did you feed a three-month-old baby?"

A huge grin spread across Will's face. "That's a story in itself. Set down and I'll tell you about it."

Chase took one of the rockers and waited, sure that he'd be entertained. Will took the one across from him and began. "I first took Star to the Indian village a couple miles from here to see if there was a new mother who would wet-nurse her. There wasn't a baby in that whole tribe under a year old. But a young brave, Star's cousin, told me to go back to the cave, that he'd soon have my problem solved."

Will shook his head. "That baby was screamin' her head off by the time that young man arrived with a nanny goat. He had run five miles to a nester's place and stolen the animal. She had freshened recently and her teats and udder was full of good rich milk. Well, neither one of us had ever milked a cow, much less a goat. But Red Fox had watched the farmer milk his goats several times and knew that they had to stand on somethin' in order to be milked. He managed to get the nanny up on a flat boulder, then he held the bleatin' beast by the rope around her neck and looked at me. 'You milk now,' he ordered me."

The old man scratched his head as though he still couldn't believe that late afternoon. "I didn't even have a bucket, only a peach can I had emptied for lunch. I rushed inside to get it, and by then Star's face was beet red from anger and cryin'. I knew that somehow I had to get the milk out of that goat.

"I squatted down beside her and began tryin' to coax the milk from her. 'Damn pale-face fool,' Red Fox growled at me when nothin' came out of the teat, 'do not use thumb and finger. Squeeze with palm.' Back in the cave Star was screamin' louder and louder and I was gettin' nervouser and nervouser, and real mad at that arrogant brave. I slammed the can down and yelled, 'If you know so damn much about it, you get the milk out of this beast.

"My answer was a high-toned 'Brave don't do women's work.' I felt like grabbin' his tomahawk and scalpin' him with it. But of course I didn't. I was too thankful to have the blasted animal. So I got down to business, curled my hand around the full teat and squeezed. That brave smiled as wide as I did when a stream of milk hit the tin can with a ringin' sound.

"Then, with a can of rich, warm milk there rose the question, how was I gonna get it into that empty little belly. About that time Red Fox grunted and pulled an empty whiskey bottle from under his breechclout. He took the milk from me and emptied it into the bottle. And while I was wonderin' was he gonna pour it down the baby's throat, he reached into his breechclout again and brought out a piece of soft doeskin shaped like a woman's nipple. He fastened it on the bottle's neck then handed it to me. 'Indian women use this when they have no milk of their own,' he grunted.

"At any rate, Star grabbed onto that homemade tit and emptied that bottle in no time flat."

Chase looked at the old man in wonder. "Just goes to show that a man can do most anything when he has to," he said, mostly to himself.

"If he sets him mind to it," Will agreed. "Some give up too easy, though that kind don't last long here on the frontier." He stood up. "I'll just set this pot of stew on the coals to heat up a little more, then we'll have a swig or two of whiskey. Star will be comin' home soon and we'll eat."

"Where'd you get this likker?" Chase asked a few minutes later after sampling the fiery whiskey. "It's not bad."

"There's a fur post on the back side of the hill a mile or so away. I get my supplies there." Will sat back down. "I mostly keep it for medicinal purposes. I can't take a chance drinkin' too much and gettin' my brain all muddled. Got to be always on the alert for Star's sake."

He set his half-empty glass on the floor beside the chair. Then, at the end of a long sigh, he said, "I'm gettin' along in years and bothered a little by my heart. Sometimes the old ticker just seems to stop for a while, like it's tired and wants to rest a spell. While I hold my breath, willin' it to start up again, it scares me half to death, thinkin' of leavin' Star up here all alone."

Will lapsed into silence, staring into the fire, while Chase sipped at his glass of whiskey. He gave a startled jerk when the old man asked abruptly, "You married, Donlin?"

Chase's face softened. "I will be, just as soon as I get home."

"Got no more desire for other women, then?" Daniels watched him closely.

"No, my Raegan has spoiled me for any other woman."

The old man stood up and walked to the mouth of the cave. He stood there several seconds, turning his head, looking to his left and right, then walked back to the fire and sat back down. "I see Star comin' 'bout a half mile away. There's somethin' I want to ask you before she gets here."

"Ask away." Chase put his empty glass on the floor.

"I'm askin' you to take Star with you when you leave tomorrow mornin'."

Chase sat forward as if he'd been shot. "Are you serious, man?"

"Dead serious. I told you about my heart. What would happen to that girl if I dropped dead? As wild and independent as she is, Star couldn't handle that. That's bothered me for the past year. I worry about how she could take care of herself. I don't want her livin' with her Indian relatives and she knowin' nothin' about civilization. She'd be like a frightened little animal, suddenly shoved amongst a bunch of people she don't know. But if she stays up here, some man will get to her, ruin her."

It dawned on Chase why Daniels had questioned him about his married state. He wanted to make sure that his granddaughter wouldn't be jumped on as soon as she was out of his sight. Well, he thought, the old fellow didn't have to worry about that, because Chase wasn't taking her home with him.

He shook his head, prepared to answer that it was out of the question, but Will pressed on. "You'd take in an orphaned fawn, a wolf cub, wouldn't you? Tend them until they were able to be on their own? Would you turn your back on a young girl who is just as helpless in many ways?"

Raegan's face swam before Chase. If not for him, what would have happened to her? The answer came quickly. The same thing that had Will worried about his Star.

"How do you know that I'll treat her right?" Chase looked squarely at the old man, hoping to discourage him. "For all you know I may be the meanest bastard in these Oregon hills."

"No." Will shook his head. "I watched you with your stallion. You've got a gentleness in you. You'd not harm my girl—nor let anyone else, either." His eyes entreated Chase. "Will you do it?"

Chase threw up his hands in defeat. "Hell, how can I say no to the kind of argument you put up."

A wide, relieved smile split Will's face as he rose to his feet. Reaching a hand across the fire, he said, "Shake on it, friend."

Wondering what he had gotten himself into, Chase leaned forward and gripped the gnarled hand. The old man sat back down then with a long sigh of relief. "The old reaper can come for me any time he wants to now."

The girl's moccasined feet ran nimbly over the carpet of pine needles, following the old dog bounding toward the river she could see through patches of the trees. All day she'd had a hunger for fish. If she hurried, she'd catch enough for her and Paw's supper before sundown.

She arrived at the spot where she kept her canoe hidden in a stand of thick, tall reeds. "Get in, Scrounge," she ordered the dog. When the animal jumped in and was settled, she pushed the bark vessel into the water, then hopped in herself. As she knelt in its center, the boat circled a moment, then as though an unseen hand had grabbed it, started gliding downstream.

Star Daniels applied the paddle with long, powerful sweeps through the water. Half a mile away was her favorite fishing hole. She seldom left it without a string of six or so bass.

The canoe skimmed along and within fifteen minutes Star was turning its nose toward the river bank, bordered with tall grass. She stopped suddenly, then back-paddled a short distance. She quietly lifted the paddle from the water and let the canoe drift to the thick vegetation. She had spotted a flock of wild duck, a chance to get fresh meat without wasting a shot.

The canoe nosed silently into the foot-high bank as the girl held her breath. She prepared to step into the water, then swore angrily. The dog had barked and the startled ducks had scattered in all directions, squawking and flaying the water with wildly flapping wings.

In their confusion, however, some scutted into the grass instead of swiming for the open river. The girl's eyes shone with satisfaction. She'd be able to nab one after all. She swung herself out of the canoe and stepped into knee-high water.

But the ducks, experts at concealment, had glided away like snakes, leaving no rustle to mark their passage. It took her at least fifteen minutes to detect a faint stirring in the grass and to grab a good-sized fowl by the neck.

"Come on, Scrounge," she said with a big grin, "Let's get home. We'll fish tomorrow. Paw will be worryin' by now."

* * *

Will, still wearing a relaxed expression, tamped tobacco into a clay pipe. Chase's face, however, wore a harrassed look. Why had he agreed to saddle himself with a girl he did not know? And worse, what would Raegan think when he came riding in with her? Nothing good, he knew. She had probably consigned him to hell more than once already.

Daniels suddenly paused in lighting his pipe and cocked his head to listen. "She's here," he said in a low, nervous voice, and threw the unused flaming twig back into the fire.

A girl, the like of which Chase had never seen before, bounded into the cave, her narrow face lit with excitement. "Guess what, Paw," she exclaimed, then grew silent, a wariness jumping into her eyes when she noted the stranger sitting in her chair.

In the seconds before Will introduced his granddaughter, she and Chase stared at each other. Chase saw brown eyes that seemed too large in the small, deeply tanned face, and if the black, tangled mass of hair had ever known the pull of a brush, it had been a long time ago.

She was not tall, but her lithe slenderness in the close-fitting buckskins gave her that appearance. His eyes dropped to the knife stuck in her belt, a rifle in one hand, and a limp duck in the other. What kind of wild creature had Will Daniels stuck him with? he wondered, almost in a panic.

"We got company, Star," Will said with a cheerfulness that to a keen ear would sound a little forced. "Meet Chase Donlin. He's spendin' the night with us."

The brown eyes narrowed suspiciously on Chase for several seconds. Finally, barely nodding her head in his direction, the girl walked into a dark recess of the cave and there came the sound of splashing water. She came out a moment later, drying her hands on a coarse towel.

As she rattled tin plates and flatware, setting the table, Will looked at Chase apologetically and said in low tones, "Don't pay any attention to her churlish manner. She don't see many strangers and she's leary of them. She'll loosen up when she gets to know you."

Chase merely nodding, wondering again what he had gotten himself into.

When the Wild Child, as Chase privately called her, lifted the pot off the fire and placed it on the table with a dull thud, Will stood up. "Come on, Donlin, time to eat."

Chase would have liked to wash his hands, but one look at Star's scowling face made him give up the wish. He sat down on the bench next to Will, and when the old man shoved the pot in front of him, he filled his plate with the fragrant stew. Star slapped a half loaf of sourdough bread on the table then, drawing her knife, sliced it into thick slabs. As he helped himself to a piece, Chase hoped the knife hadn't skinned an animal recently.

He hadn't expected Star to eat with them—it was clear she had taken an instant dislike to him—but she sat down on the opposite bench and heaped her plate high with the meat, potatoes, and wild onions.

As was the custom with back hill-people, there was no conversation as the meal was eaten.

And even after Chase and Will left the table later, Will lighting the pipe he'd already prepared and Chase rolling a cigarette, the talk between them was of little importance. Chase knew the old man's mind was on how to tell his granddaughter his plans for her. He wasn't surprised when the old fellow sighed raggedly when Star finished washing the few utensils used and came to sit on the raised hearth on his side.

The girl hadn't spoken except for the few words on entering the cave. She now looked at her grandfather and asked, "What's botherin' you, Paw? You're lookin' hang-dog like Scrounge does when he's been up to mischief." She scratched the old dog's ears.

Will passed a gnarled hand over his chin, then, his scarred and grizzled face grave and avoiding the girl's eyes, he said, "In a couple weeks, I'll be leavin' to rendezvous with the other trappers to swap and sell our winter catch. I'll be gone for a spell, and I want you to go home with Donlin here, and stay at his place for a while."

Star stared at Will as though he had lost his mind. Several tense seconds passed, then, her eyes challenging, Star demanded, "Why can't I come with you? I always have before."

Will nodded. "I know that, and the last time I almost come to blows with a couple trappers who had their eyes on you." He laid a hand on her knee. "In the past couple years, honey, you've blossomed into a woman and the men ain't missed that fact." He looked at her earnestly. "I'm too old, child, to involve myself in a rough-and-tumble knife fight. I'd be killed for sure. What would become of you then?"

"But, Paw!" the two words came out on a wail. "You wouldn't have to fight. I can take care of myself. I'm as good as any man with a knife."

"I'll grant you that's the truth, but, Star, you're half those men's size and don't have half their strength. What would you do if three of them come at you at once? You know as well as I do that they're a rough bunch, and usually drunk at these meetins'. A man with his brain muddled by drink ain't his usual self. Where ordinarily he'd be too shy to even look at you, drink would give him the courage to rape you, given the chance."

"Then I'll stay at the Indian village until you get back," Star said after Will's long catalogue of the dangers she would face if she accompanied him to the yearly rendezvous had come to an end.

"No, you'll not do that! I won't have you comin' home with your hair full of lice, filled with their slovenly ways."

"Then I'll stay here with—"

"You'll go with Donlin, and that's the end of it!" Daniels glared at at the girl, a look that she had learned to respect.

Suddenly, tears were leaving dirty streaks down Star's face. With a sigh, Will stood up and went to her. He pressed her head against his chest and stroked her hair, his face as compassionate as it had been fierce moments ago.

"You'll be just fine with Donlin and his woman. You'll be havin' such a good time, you won't give me and Scrounge a second thought."

Star wiped a fist across her wet eyes. "I'll be takin' Scrounge with me."

Chase spoke for the first time since the argument began. "That would be out of the question, Star," he said gently. "My Raegan has a pet wolf. He'd kill your old dog the minute he laid eyes on him."

Interest sparked the girl's tear-red eyes. "A wolf for a pet?" she asked, her tone saying she was inclined to doubt it. "You mean a dog with some wolf in him, don't you?"

Chase grinned. "I know it's hard to believe, but Lobo is all wolf. Raegan raised him from a very young cub after his mother was killed."

Star studied Chase's face a minute, then blurted out, "Is your Raegan old like you?"

Chase's lips twisted in amusement as he ran a hand over his whiskered face. To a sixteen-year-old, he probably looked ancient. "Raegan is only two years older than you, Star," he answered.

"There, you see." Will sat back down. "You'll have that female friend you're always yammerin' about."

The girl's shoulders sagged and her head bent. "I reckon."

Chase looked at the old man and saw his Adam's apple bobbling up and down as he swallowed back the tears in his throat. He knew intuitively that Will was saying good-bye to his beloved granddaughter, that he wouldn't be here in the morning when Chase and Star rose.

Blinking rapidly, Will stood up and said gruffly, "Time we got to bed. You sleep with me, Star, and give Donlin your bed." As Star obediently walked across the floor to one of the beds, Will moved to the mouth of the cave and dragged a heavy gate across the opening. After he fastened it with a heavy chain, he blew out two of the lanterns, leaving a third one lit. He slid off his moccasins, said good night to Chase, and climbed into the swing-bed.

"Move over, Star," he grouched as he stretched his old bones. "You're hoggin' my side of the bed."

The mattress rustled a minute as the girl gave her bed partner more room, then it grew quiet in the cave except for Will's rumbling snores—and what sounded suspiciously like feminine sobs.

Chase stood and stretched, ready to test the unusual bed. Unlike the old man and the girl, he shucked down to his underwear before carefully easing onto the mattress of sweet-smelling hay.

Surprisingly, he found the unique bed very comfortable as it swung gently back and forth. Within minutes his eyes closed in sleep.

The next morning when he awakened, he found, as he had expected, that the old man and the dog were missing from the cave. Star had lit another lantern, and by its light she tended a skillet of salt pork. She looked over at the bed when she heard the ropes squeak as he sat up. Noting his searching, she said quietly, "He's gone. Paw hates good-byes."

When she moved across the floor to set the table, Chase hurriedly slipped into his buckskins, anxious to get started. He wanted to catch the preacher before he left the area.

The meat and bread and coffee were quickly consumed and they were ready to leave. Star gave the big room a lingering look, then, picking up her rifle, she walked down the narrow stone tunnel to where the horses were penned.

"If it's all right with you, Star, we'll move along smartly," Chase said, tightening Sampson's belly cinch. "We have at least twenty miles to travel, and I want to cover it as quickly as possible."

Star nodded and swung onto the sorrel's back. When they rode out of the cave, Chase leading the way, Star left the gate open. "You forgot to close the gate," Chase reminded her.

"It's all right," she answered. "Don't look, but Paw is on the next hill watchin' us. He'll come down and close it as soon as we are out of sight."

The girl was probably right, Chase thought. He could almost feel the old man's eyes boring into his back, wondering belatedly if he had made a mistake sending his granddaughter off with a stranger.

He nudged Sampson with his heel and led off at a fast clip, Star's stallion easily keeping up with him.

Raegan came to a long row of prepared soil and dropped two beans into the shallow trench Jamie had marked off. One chop of the hoe covered the seeds with the rich soil. She lightly stepped on the spot as Jamie had taught her.

"There should be no air pockets around the seeds," he'd explained, "otherwise they'll never sprout and push through the ground."

She paused and leaned on the hoe handle, wiping an arm across her sweating forehead. She was getting quite proficient at gardening, and well she should, she thought half angrily. She and Jamie had been out here working for a day and a half now, ever since Chase rode away without a word.

Raegan looked down the long row of turned-over sod, resting her eyes on Jamie as he turned at the end of the row and began preparing another long stretch in which he'd said they'd plant corn. He was so sweet, so considerate, she thought, remembering how he had tried to console her yesterday morning after Chase stormed out of the cabin. He had insisted that Chase cared for her, cared deeply. "I know the man," he'd added. "He might not realize it yet, but it will come to him, and when it does you're gonna see a changed man."

Raegan dropped the hoe and sat down beneath the big cottonwood shading one end of the garden. She dragged the old hat Jamie had found for her off her head and ran her fingers through her sweaty hair. As the tree-cooled air wafted over her face, Lobo flopped down beside her. She dropped a hand on his finely shaped head, her lips twisting in a mirthless smile. She had seen no evidence of Chase's caring for her. To her it seemed just the opposite. Last night, after they had made love, it had sounded like hate in his voice as he let her know how wrong they had acted. He hadn't said so, but she knew he put all the blame on her. If she hadn't come into his room, he would have never made love to her.

"Oh, Lobo," she dropped her chin on her bent knees, "what am I going to do?" Her whispered wail had barely drifted away when Jamie came hurrying toward her.

"You'd better go in and wash your hands. I hear company comin'."

She scrambled to her feet, her heart racing. Was Chase finally coming home?

"It's young Johnny, Henry Jones's stepson," Jamie hurried to tell her when he saw the hopeful look on her face. "And he's in an all-fired hurry. I didn't think that old mule of theirs could move that fast."

The aged animal slid to a stop in the yard, its sides heaving as Johnny, his face ashen, slid from its back. The teenager stood before Raegan and Jamie, nervously twisting an old felt hat between his fingers. When he didn't speak, only trying to swallow his Adam's apple, Jamie took pity on the gangly youth.

"What brings you here, son?" he asked. "You look a little pale. Is everything all right at your place?"

Johnny shook his shaggy head. "No, they ain't, Jamie." He swallowed a couple times then blurted out, "The Tillamooks done killed my stepfather."

Raegan gasped and dread jumped into Jamie's eyes. The Tillamooks had started their war of revenge.

"You're sure it was Tillamooks, Johnny?" Jamie asked after a moment, for Henry Jones was hated and despised by half the men in the area. He had cheated and stolen from just about all his neighbors. Any one of them, in a fit of anger, could have done him in. "It could have been some enemy of Henry's that killed him," Jamie suggested.

" 'Twas Tillamooks," Johnny declared vehemently, looking at Jamie but avoiding his eyes. "I saw two of them runnin' off through the woods right after I heard Henry yell."

"Scalped him, did they?" Jamie studied the young man's face, wondering about the red bruise on his cheekbone. Whatever its cause, it had been done recently, sometime this morning.

Hank shook his head. "They just stabbed him in the back . . . twice."

"That's strange." Jamie continued to watch the teenager. "Tillamooks always scalp their victims."

"I guess I scared them away before they could do it," Johnny muttered, still refusing to meet Jamie's eyes.

Jamie didn't say it, but he thought it highly unlikly that this thin teenager would scare away two strong braves on the warpath. If anything, they'd have killed him too. Something wasn't quite right with his story.

He reached down and pulled Raegan to her feet. "I'm goin' to go with the boy to take a look at Henry. You take Lobo and go into the cabin and bolt the door. I won't be gone too long."

When he reached for his gun and holster hanging from a tree branch, Raegan said, a worried frown on her forehead, "Be careful, Jamie, those two Indians may still be lurking around the Jones cabin."

"Somehow I doubt that," Jamie answered, preoccupied.

Jamie mounted and pulled the boy up behind him. Together, they rode through the woods to Jones's cabin.

With no word spoken between them, Johnny directed Jamie to where fat, bald Henry Jones lay sprawled on his stomach in a small clearing. His arms were outstretched, leaves and pine needles clutched in his fists.

The man was dead, Jamie could tell from the saddle. The body lay too still. He felt the nervous shudder that passed through the thin frame sitting behind him, and the suspicion that had taken hold of him back at the cabin grew.

Before dismounting, Jamie carefully scanned the area around the dead man. He didn't see one moccasin track. There was only the heavy imprint of Henry's big boots and two sets of bare feet. The larger ones belonged to Johnny, he judged, but the other set were those of a child. Strange.

As he swung out of the saddle, Johnny slid down beside him. When he knelt beside the body, Johnny moved to stand at his stepfather's head. There was no expression on his face when Jamie looked up at him, but he caught the hate that flickered in the boy's eyes.

He didn't bother to lift up the blood-soaked shirt to look at the wound that had killed the man. He knew what he would find. Stab wounds from a broad-bladed Bowie. A white man's weapon.

Jamie rose slowly to his feet and looked soberly at Johnny. "You did it, didn't you, son?" he asked gently.

Johnny began shaking his head in violent denial. But as Jamie continued to look at him, his eyes denying the boy's denial, the young man's face suddenly crumbled. He dropped to his knees, his bony shoulders shaking as he sobbed out what had happened.

"I was out huntin' when I heard my little sister cryin', 'You're hurtin' me, Henry. Please stop.' I knew right off what was happenin'. The bastard was tryin' to use her."

He looked up at Johnny, tears making dirty streaks down his thin face. "For God's sake, Jamie, Vera is only nine years old. Little and scrawny besides. He would have killed her, or at least ruined her.

"I started poundin' on his back, tryin' to drag him off her. He just laughed and hit me in the face with his fist." He gingerly touched the angry-looking mark on his cheek. He scrubbed at his eyes with the heels of his hands, then whispered hoarsely, "It was like someone else drew their knife and stabbed him in the back."

When sobs continued to shake the thin body, Jamie drew the boy into his arms and said quietly, "You did what you had to do, Johnny. There's not a man or woman in these hills would blame you for what you've done."

When Johnny grew quiet and his body stopped shaking, Jamie released him and stood up. "However, kid," he said, "we'll just let the folks around here think that the Tillamooks done it. You can tell your Maw the truth if you want to." Jamie asked, "Can you trust your little sister not to tell the truth of it?"

Johnny nodded eagerly. "Vera would die before she'd tell."

"All right then, let's get him on your mule and take him home."

Three dirty, ragged children burst from the dilapidated shack, young Vera bringing up the rear. They came to an abrupt stop, bumping into each other as they caught sight of Henry's limp body dangling across the mule's back. Within seconds, Meg Jones and her two older daughters, Nellie and Fanny, stepped through the door. Meg, who was somewhere in her thirties but looked more like fifty, stepped off the rotting porch. She walked over to her husband and, grasping a handful of his hair, lifted his head to stare into his sightless eyes. "What happened to him, Johnny?" she asked tonelessly.

"The Tillamooks got him, Ma," Johnny answered, putting an arm around his little sister Vera, who had sidled up to him. A thin line of dried blood ran down the inside of her skinny leg.

"Is that so?" Meg said with no more emotion than if her son had informed her that he had killed a snake. She didn't lower her husband's head gently back to the horse, but dropped it as though ridding herself of some insignficant object.

She stepped back from the horse and Jamie wondered at the transformation that came over her thin face. The deadness in her eyes had lightened, and a glimmer of hope entered them. As he watched, her narrow shoulders straightened, and the children gaped at her as, in a strong voice, she began issuing orders. Never before had they heard her use that commanding tone.

"You children stand back out of the way and stop your gawkin'." She roughly shoved them to one side. "Jamie"—she turned to him—"if you'll give Johnny hand, we'll get Henry into the cabin."

When Henry's heavy body had been struggled into the shack and placed on a sagging bed, Jamie asked, "Should I send Granny Pearson over to help you lay him out?"

"Thank you, Jamie, but there's no need. I'll do it."

"When will you have the burial?"

Jamie saw the struggle going on in the woman's eyes and guessed correctly that Meg Jones would rather not have a burial at all. If custom didn't demand it, she'd dig a hole and dump her husband into it before the sun went down.

She spoke finally. "Tomorrow mornin', early." When Jamie looked his surprise, she added, "No use to have a wake. Nobody would come. The sooner we get him in the ground, the faster we can get on with our lives. Me and Johnny and the older ones have to get a crop in the ground and get the garden planted."

There was an enthusiasm in her voice that Jamie knew hadn't been there for years. "You're probably right, Meg," he agreed, then said, "I'll get Ike Stevens to help me dig the grave."

Surprise flickered over Meg's face. "Thank you, Jamie, that's right neighborly of you."

As Jamie rode away, he could swear ten years had dropped off Meg Jones's face.

He was about a mile from the Donlin cabin when he met Aggie and her daughters. He pulled in the roan, smiled at the mother, and gave Mary and Angeline a flirtatious grin. Aggie gave the giggling girls a dark look, then said, "We just come from visitin' Raegan. Is it true? Has Henry Jones been been killed by the Tillamooks?"

"Ole fat Henry has been done in," Jamie answered, not correcting Aggie's belief that the Indians from across the river had killed the man.

"I don't reckon Meg and the children cried much."

"Nary a tear." Jamie grinned. "She's gonna plant him early tomorrow mornin'."

"I don't blame her," Aggie's eyes snapped. "I'd get that one under ground as soon as possible."

"Do you think Ike would mind givin' me a hand diggin' the grave?"

"Yes, he'll help you, but only because of Meg and the children. As for Henry Jones himself, Ike wouldn't care if he laid in the woods and rotted."

She fastened curious eyes on Jamie. "What about Chase? Couldn't he give you a hand? Where's he got off to anyway? Raegan mumbled somethin' about him lookin' for new trappin' areas."

Damn you, Chase, Jamie thought. He'd better get home pretty damn quick. His absence was makin' it damned awkward for Raegan. He met the sharp eyes that watched him intently. "Yeah, he is," he answered Aggie. "He might be back today, but in case he doesn't show up until tomorrow, I thought I'd go ahead and ask Ike to help me."

Aggie seemed satisfied with his response and lifted the reins that lay loosely on her mount's neck. "I'll tell Ike," she said as she nudged the horse into motion. Mary and Angeline looked coyly at Jamie before following her and giggled at the slow wink he gave them.

Raegan waved good-bye to Aggie and the girls, then hurried back inside, pausing to bar the door behind her. As she cleared the table of used cups and spoons, she glanced often out the window. She was still upset over what had happened to the Jones man. There was not another living soul in the vicinity of the cabin—unless of course there were Tillamooks lurking around behind buildings and trees, waiting to pounce upon an unwary person.

Had the war with the Tillamooks started? she wondered as she prepared a basin of warm sudsy water. Had they tired of searching for the woman and decided to seek revenge on any white person they come upon? "Damn that Roscoe to hell!" she muttered, wiping the table free of cookie crumbs she and her guests had spilled. How many would lose their lives because of his heinous act? she wondered.

She thought of Aggie and the girls hurrying home and prayed that they would make it safely to their cabin. She had been surprised when they knocked on the door shortly after Jamie and Johnny had left. It just wasn't safe for women to ride alone these days. Aggie had made light of her alarm until Raegan told her about Henry Jones. Her face had gone white, and she and the girls had eaten one cookie apiece, gulped down a cup of coffee, then headed for home.

Raegan moved to the side of the window and peered in the direction Jamie and Johnny had taken. Jamie had been gone at least an hour. Shouldn't he have returned by now? Her nerves tightening at an alarming rate, she poured herself a cup of coffee in the hope that the brew would help calm her.

"And where is that worthless Chase Donlin?" she muttered as she sat down at the table and reached for the sugar bowl. If he was so fond of his sister Anne, as he insisted on calling her, why wasn't he here to look after her daughter?

As Raegan stirred the spoon round and round in the cup, unaware of the action, her fretful thoughts flew out of her mind as Lobo crawled from beneath the table and sniffed at the door. Alarm shivering up and down her spine, she rose and hurried to the door, resting an ear against it.

She heard the faint beat of loping hooves. Whomever the rider was, he was in no hurry. And it was a white man, because as the hoofbeats came closer, she could hear the occasional ring of a horseshoe striking gravel. An unshod Indian pony made a thudding sound with its hooves.

When Jamie rode into view, she was so weak with relief that her trembling fingers had a hard time unbarring the door. She stepped out on the porch as Jamie swung from the saddle. "Is the Jones man dead?" she asked right away.

"As dead as he'll ever be." Jamie snubbed the roan to an apple tree Raegan was trying to coax back to life. "I just stopped by long enough to let you know I'm goin' over to the Stevens place to ask Ike . . ." He paused to look over his shoulder. "Riders comin'," he said, and stepped up on the porch, his hand on his colt.

Raegan's heart fluttered, then beat so rapidly she feared it would escape her body. "Shouldn't we go inside?" She tugged at Jamie's arm. "What if they are Tillamooks?"

Jamie shook his head, grinning crookedly. "It's your wanderin' husband finally comin' home."

The sun was straight overhead when Chase and Star came to a cross trail and took the one that led to the village of Green Valley. Chase wondered how far along the preacher was in his sermon. Was he almost finished shouting his hellfire and brimstone to the women? His sermon should be much shorter since he'd had his orders not to preach about man and woman lying together without benefit of the marriage vows. He had previously raged on for hours on that topic, waving his arms and shouting that fornicators were headed straight for hell. Tears would come into the eyes of many wives, suspecting that at this very minute their husbands could very well be pumping away at a whore while they waited for the services to be over.

He tightened his grip on the reins and urged Sampson to a faster gait, but his eyes still scanned the hills and valleys as they thundered on. He hadn't ridden easy in the saddle since the day Roscoe stole the Tillamook woman. As for that, neither had any of the other men. They had given up the pratice of hunting alone and now went out in pairs, one man watching their backs.

The stallion lunged up a hill, and the village lay below. Chase grunted his relief. The preacher was still in Green Valley. Even from this distance he could hear the high-pitched warning of a fiery hell. The man of the cloth was still going strong. He pulled the stallion up, motioning Star to do the same with her sorrel. She looked at him questioningly.

"Look, Star, I need to talk to the preacher a minute. Would you mind waiting here for me? It'll only take me a minute."

Star looked down at all the women gathered around the shouting man and readily agreed. She was mostly a stranger to white women, having seen only a few whores when she went with Paw to the rendezvous. And Paw never let her get near them.

"You go ahead." She swung to the ground. "I'll just give Champ a little rest while I'm waitin'."

Chase nodded and nudged Sampson into motion. Nearing the village, his gaze went to the cottonwood tree, where several women and children sat on the ground, listening intently to the words being hurled at them like bullets from a gun. When he stepped out of the saddle a minute later and tethered the stallion to a tree, the worshipers rose to their feet and burst into song.

"Looks like we arrived just in time, boy." He gave Sampson an affectionate pat, then leaned against the tree and waited until the last words of "Shall We Gather at the River" rose above the tree tops. He waited until the preacher was throwing a saddle on his bony mule, preparing to ride out, then straightened from his lounging stance.

He smiled and spoke genially to the women who milled about, catching up on gossip or calling to their children, as he made his way to the tall raw-boned man. He ignored the venomous dislike in the yellow-brown eyes when he stood in front of the Calvinist.

"I'd like a few words with you, preachin' man," he said, laying a restraining hand on the mule's back.

"Now look here, Donlin." Chase received a dark look. "I didn't say nary a word about fornicatin.'"

"I took note of that." Chase nodded. "I want to speak to you on another matter. Finish saddlin' up, then we'll talk."

The man of the cloth gave him a suspicious look, but tended to tightening the cinch and flipping the stirrups into place. "Well," he said, looking at Chase, "what do you want to talk about? I can't stand around here all day. I have to travel fifteen miles to the next village."

"I want you to perform a marriage ceremony."

"Has that half-breed friend of yours finally found a woman willin' to take him on as a husband?" the preacher sneered.

Chase ground his teeth together, tempted to back-hand the man across the mouth. He contented himself by answering, "No it's not Jamie Hart wantin' to get hitched. With the exception of one woman in these hills, there's not a female worthy of bein' his wife."

He received a dry snort, followed by, "Who wants to get married then that they have to send you to do the askin'?"

"Me."

"You?" The sunken eyes stared at Chase. "I heard you was already married."

"Well I'm not, and I don't want to hear any preachin' about it. All you have to do is show my intended respect and marry us. If you satisfy me with your behavior, I'll not tell a soul about you and the Indian girl—also providin', of course, you don't tell anyone about the marriage you're gonna perform today."

When he received only a black scowl, he took a menacing step toward the preacher. "Answer me, damn you. Is it a deal?"

The man tried to out-glare him, but in a few seconds he looked away, mumbling, "It's a deal."

"I figured you'd see it my way," Chase said sardonically. "Show up at my cabin an hour from now."

Now, Chase thought, as he untied the stallion and climbed onto his back, all I have to do is convince Raegan.

He found Star waiting where he had left her and gave her a wide smile. "Mount up and we'll get on home."

Chapter Ten

Raegan shielded her eyes with her hand, blocking out the sun's rays. So, at last he remembers he has a home, she thought, anger darkening her eyes. She transfered her gaze to Chase's companion and wondered who the Indian lad was as she took in the buckskins and long black hair.

But as the pair rode into the yard and swung down from the saddles, Raegan's face paled and her heart felt squeezed to death. It was no boy who stood beside Chase, but a young girl. *Damn the man!* she raged inside. How dare he bring his whore into their home, sleep with her practically under the nose of his supposed wife. What would Jamie think and do about that?

Chase gazed at Raegan, thinking how beautiful she was, how deeply he loved her. The westward-moving sun stroked its beams over her as though glorifying her as she stood regal as a queen. Her curls were piled on top her head and tied with a green ribbon, exposing the delicate lines of her features. Her green gingham dress lovingly followed the outline of her full breasts and tiny waist before the full skirt fell to her ankles. Chase wanted to grin at the sight of her bare toes peeping out beneath the hem.

Meanwhile, her face stony, Raegan kept her eyes on the girl. The tight buckskins on the slender body magnified every curve and swell as though she wore nothing at all. When she heard Jamie catch his breath, then breathe so heavily she thought his lungs would collapse, she wanted to turn around and slap his face. She stared at the girl's deeply tanned face, wondering what it looked like beneath all the dirt as large brown eyes stared back at her guardedly. She shifted her gaze to Chase and was surprised to see uncertainty in his eyes also.

Surely she was mistaken about that. Chase Donlin couldn't care less how she felt about him bringing home his woman. She didn't allow her face to show any of the furious anger that was building inside her as she said calmly, "So, you've returned home, Chase."

Chase flinched at her cold tone. He surely wasn't receiving a very warm welcome. He shifted his feet, then asked awkwardly, "Have you been all right while I was away?"

Raegan ignored his query. A lot he cared how she had fared in his absence. For all he knew, the Tillamooks could have raped and scalped her. She was about to ask Chase who his friend was when Jamie drawled sarcastically, "What's that you've drug home with you, Chase?"

"Hey now, Jamie," Chase began, a disapproving frown on his face, "that's uncalled for. This is—" He stopped short. Star was scowling ferociously, and her hand had whipped to the broad-bladed knife strapped to her waist.

"Whew!" Jamie took a step back in pretended alarm, his eyes sparkling devilishly. "Chase, you've done gone and brought us home a wildcat."

"Maybe I have at that." Chase grinned. "Do you think you could tame her?"

A slumberous look came into Jamie's gray eyes as he ran his gaze over the slender figure. "Maybe," he said softly. "I'd sure as hell like to try."

"Lay a hand on me and you'll draw back a stub," Star threatened. "I have no time for half-breeds," she sniffed contemptously.

Jamie threw back his head and roared with laughter. "Aren't you callin' the kettle black, you sharp-tongued little witch?" he came back at her. "Where do you think you got that dark skin and that black mess you call hair?"

Star tossed her head and, after giving Jamie an icy look, turned her back on him. He opened his mouth to prod her further, but Chase cut him off by turning to Raegan and saying, "Raegan, this is Star Daniels. She'll be staying with us while her grandfather goes to a rendezvous with the trappers in his territory."

He put a hand on Star's shoulder. "Star, this is my wife, Raegan. I'm sure the two of you will get along just fine—be company for each other." And while Raegan barely restrained an affronted gasp, Chase went on, "And this brash fellow is Jamie Hart, my friend. Beware of him. He's a devil with the weaker sex."

Star smiled shyly at Raegan, but Jamie received only a sneering curl of her lip. It startled her when she received the same grimace from him. To avoid further arguing between Jamie and Star and to escape Raegan's frigid manner, Chase said, "Raegan, shall we show Star to the room she'll be using?"

"And where is that, Chase?" Jamie asked coldly. "Your room?"

It dawned on Chase why he was receiving the dirty looks. Jamie and Raegan thought he had brought Star home to sleep with him. He was hard-pressed not to let loose the laughter that was almost choking him. At the same time, he realized that it was plausible they would think that, especially Raegan. His refusing to sleep with *her*, make love to her, would naturally make her think that he would look elsewhere for his pleasuring.

Well, he'd have to set them straight. Pinning Jamie with cool eyes, he said, "That's right. My *old* room. The one I used before . . . Raegan came into my life."

What he'd hoped for didn't materialize. Raegan and Jamie still looked at him coldly. "They'll just have to wait and see," he muttered to himself. Taking Star by the arm, he stepped up on the porch.

For a moment it looked as if Jamie wasn't going to step aside to let Chase and Star pass into the kitchen. He was wondering if he'd have to come to blows with his friend when Raegan wheeled and led the way inside. He could feel Jamie's eyes stabbing at his back as he followed Raegan down the hall to the bedrooms. His lips firmed. He was going to talk to that young man and straighten out his thinking.

Star stepped on Chase's heel once in her preoccupation with everything that was so strange to her. Poor wild little creature, he thought, this was probably the first she had ever been inside a real house, seen proper furniture. He tried to catch Raegan's eye as they reached his door and she stepped aside, waiting for him and Star to pass inside. But she stared ahead, her face still cold and stony.

Raegan was about to turn and walk back to the kitchen when she happened to glance at Star. The girl was looking at the bed in bewilderment. Raegan looked at the bed also, wondering what was wrong with it.

Behind her, Chase chuckled. "I'm afraid we don't have swingin' beds like you do, Star. You'll have to get used to a regular one."

Raegan was musing on what a swinging bed was, when Chase asked, "Will you help me carry my clothes across the hall, Raegan?"

Momentary bewilderment flickered in Raegan's eyes. Had Chase been sincere about not sharing his room with the girl after all? Her source of hope, her desire that it was so, died when her inner voice pointed out, "What's to prevent him from visiting Star before he comes to your bed?"

She nodded stiffly and grabbed an armful of soft buckskins that Chase was transfering from his chest of drawers to the bed. "Star, you can put your things in the drawers now." Chase smiled at the still bewildered girl. Then, his arms clamped over the balance of his clothes and his razor, shaving mug, comb and brush in his hand, he followed Raegan out of the room.

They were no sooner in her room, and the door closed, when Raegan tossed the clothes on the bed and turned on him. "How could you? She's only a child!"

Her condemnation brought Chase swinging around. "How could I *what*, Raegan? Bring an orphan girl into our home? Although she doesn't know it, she is gonna lose the grandfather who raised her. Should I have left her to live in a cave alone, prey to any man who came along? Would you rather I'd have done that?"

Chase had advanced on Raegan as his words whipped at her, shamed her. "What sort of man do you think I am, Raegan?" He jerked her slenderness up against his hard body.

"Do you put me in the same category as fat Roscoe or Henry Jones?" He glared down at her pale face. "For God's sake, the girl is only sixteen years old. I'm almost old enough to be her father."

Although Raegan knew that sixteen wasn't considered too young to be bedded—a lot of girls were married and mothers younger than that—she knew that Chase wasn't lying. He had brought Star home with him for the reason he had stated.

Her green eyes asking for forgiveness, she whispered, "I'm sorry, Chase."

The cold glint in Chase's eyes warmed. He sat down on the edge of the bed and patted the space beside him. "Come here, Raegan, I want to talk to you."

Raegan's heart beat slowed almost to a standstill, her mind reverting against her better instincts to what she had first believed. Chase did intend to visit Star at night, and this sharing of her room was only a front to deceive Jamie.

In dumb misery, she moved to the bed and sat down, bracing herself for what was to come. When Chase took her hand and held it, her heartbeat stepped up, thundering in her chest. "What do you want to talk about?" her dread-stiffened voice managed to ask.

"I want you to marry me." Chase's words hit her with the impact of a rifle shot.

"What?" The single word left Raegan's lips with the same explosive power. "What reason would you have for marrying me?"

Chase wanted to say, "Because I love you beyond all reasoning. Because if you don't share my life for the rest of my life, I would merely exist until the day I die."

But he knew she wouldn't believe him, and with good reason. He had no doubt it was still fresh in her mind how only two days ago he had declared how wrong it was for them to sleep together. He would have to make his actions convince her as time went by.

"I have a very good reason to marry you, Raegan," he said softly.

"Well I'd like to hear what it is." Raegan gave him a dark look. "Considering what you said after we . . . previously . . . it makes no sense at all."

"Has it occured to you that you might be pregnant?"

Raegan stared at Chase, her eyes widening, showing that the possibility had never entered her mind. After a moment, she threw back her head in a gesture of denial.

"Oh yes," Chase insisted. "You very well could be. To my shame I didn't take any percautions to protect you."

Raegan's face paled to absolute whiteness. She wanted to be married to Chase more than anything else in the world, but not this way—not a sham marriage, a mockery of the vows that should mean so much.

"Well." Chase squeezed her hand. "What's your answer?"

Raegan wanted to laugh hysterically. What answer could she give him except yes. Certainly she didn't want to bring a fatherless baby into the world. But what if she wasn't expecting? Chase would have married her for nothing. Had he thought about that?

"Shouldn't we wait and see if I am with child? It was only that one night."

"But how many times that one night?" Chase smilingly teased.

Raegan blushed, remembering that night of love-making. Chase's seed could very well be growing beneath her heart. She sighed, coming to a decision.

"All right," she agreed, "but we won't—you know, do anything in bed in case there hasn't been a baby started. If I get my flow at the end of the month, you won't have to feel guilty and you can have the marriage set aside."

Chase turned her hand over and stroked a finger back and forth on the soft inner side of her wrist. He bit his tongue not to smile when her pulse leapt and throbbed against his caressing action. With just a few kisses and the stroking of his hands in certain places, she would surrender herself to him within minutes. There was no doubt in his mind that he would make love to his wife tonight, no matter what agreement they might come to now.

He released her hand and stood up, drawing her up with him. "The preacher will be here before long and I've got to get Jamie and Star out of the house." He kissed her on her straight, slightly freckled nose. "While I take care of that, you can get ready."

Chase found Jamie out on the back porch, staring off into space, a dark frown on his face. He didn't turn around when Chase cleared his voice, preparatory to speaking. However, his head jerked around, his expression clearing, when Chase spoke.

"Jamie," he began, "I've got to have some time alone with Raegan. I've got a lot to make up to her, a lot of explain' to do. Would you take Star for a walk or a ride, stay away from the cabin for an hour or so?"

Jamie grinned. "That's askin' a lot of me, friend. That wildcat might decide to scalp me. Anyhow, I doubt that she'd go anywhere with me."

Chase frowned thoughtfully. That bothered him too. Unlike all the other young women and girls in the neighborhood, Jamie's good looks hadn't impressed Star in the least. He remembered then the girl's love of wild animals. "She'll go with you if you tell her you're takin' her to see the herd of wild horses that graze in that valley over by the Jones place."

"Oh, speaking of the Joneses." Jamie straightened up from his lazy stance. "Henry Jones is dead."

"The hell you say? How'd he die?"

"Well accordin' to young Johnny . . ." Jamie proceeded to tell Chase the whole story. "I was goin' to ask Ike Stevens to help me dig Henry's grave, but now that you're home you can help me."

Chase nodded absently, his mind on getting Jamie and Star from under foot. The preacher would be here in a little over half an hour. "I'll go get Star," he said.

Star was sitting in the straight-backed chair when Chase rapped on the door, then entered her room. Her shoulders were slumped and she wore a poignant look on her small face. Pity for the girl stirred inside him. She must be bewildered by all the changes taking place in her life.

"Have you settled in then, Star?" he asked gently.

"I reckon. I put my duds in that thing over there like Raegan said to do." She pointed at Chase's dresser.

What Star didn't add, and what had shocked her to the core of her being, was that for the first time in her life she had viewed all of herself at one time in the big mirror. Although she had a small framed piece of shiny tin to look into back at the cave, it only dimly reflected back pieces of her face at a time—her lips, her eyes, but never both at the same time. It had never revealed the deplorable condition of her hair. The clear still water of a shaded pool had always softened her image when she gazed into it, had shadowed her hair. Had she known the word appalling, she would have used it to describe herself. She recalled Raegan's luxuriant locks and wanted to bury her own head in her arms.

"That's fine," Chase said, although inattentively, anxious to get at what he had come here for. "How do you like my friend Jamie?" He set the opening for his next question.

Star lifted her head from the contemplation of her grubby hands and almost spat, "I don't like him at all. He's the hatefulest man I ever laid eyes on."

"He's not, not really," Chase tried to defend Jamie. "He just likes to tease. He sent me in here to ask you if you wanted to go for a ride with him."

"I wouldn't go with him to a spring of water if I was dyin' of thirst."

"I'm right sorry you feel that way, Star. You see, Jamie loves all animals and he wanted to show you a secret place of his. A valley of wild horses."

"Wild horses?" Star's small face brightened with interest. "I guess I might be able to put up with him to see that."

"Sure you could." Chase took her by the arm and practically lifted her from the chair. "You won't be sorry," he added, hurrying her to the door, then glancing at the clock as they passed through the kitchen. Star gave him a perplexed look when she was unceremoniously shoved out onto the porch.

She took her bafflement out on Jamie by saying ungraciously, "Well, come on, let's go look at those horses you're so fond of."

Inside the kitchen, Chase held his breath, afraid that Jamie's quick temper would make him refuse to take the sharp-tongued Star anywhere. But thankfully, Jamie contented himself with giving her a contemptuous look, then led the way to the barn to saddle up their mounts.

During Chase's finagling, Raegan had washed her face and taken a quick sponge bath. As she pulled her least faded dress over her head, she wished she had a new one for this special occasion. Every woman deserved a new dress when she was getting married.

She picked up her brush and began pulling it through her mahogany red curls, thinking that the event about to take place was hardly special to Chase. To him it was a punishment for losing control one night.

"I don't know if I can go through with it, Lobo," she said to the wolf, who had been watching her every move. She finished with her hair and laid the brush back down on the dresser. What a hellish life stretched ahead of her—living out the years with a man who didn't love her.

To Chase it wouldn't make all that much difference. He'd go along as usual, doing as he pleased, using the tavern women when he had the urge, visit Liza on a regular basis.

Actually, she thought angrily, he'd benefit from marrying her. While he was out carousing, being entertained by whores, she'd be in the background cooking, cleaning, and washing his dirty clothes.

"It's not fair," she cried. "I should have something to say about it."

"But you do," her inner voice spoke. "You can refuse to marry him. He won't hold a gun to your head, demand that you marry him."

"Oh, shut up," Raegan answered the voice crossly. "What do you know."

She gave a nervous jerk when Chase rapped on the door, announcing that the preacher was here. Her knees almost knocking together, her legs shaking, Raegan left the bedroom, closing the door behind her and shutting the wolf inside. She never knew how Lobo might react to strangers.

She heard voices in the parlor and directed her steps that way. Chase and a tall, gaunt man stood in front of the unlit fireplace. "Raegan," Chase said, "I want you to meet—" He turned his head toward the preacher and didn't know whether to laugh or grow angry at the way the man was gaping at Raegan. There was no lechery in the man's eyes, so he asked quite civilly, "What is your name, preacher? I've never heard it spoken."

"Samuel Brown," the tall man answered, never taking his eyes off Raegan.

"Well, Samuel Brown, meet my intended, Raegan. Now let's get to what you're here for."

Her features strained, Raegan nodded her head in acknowledgment of the preacher, deciding that she didn't like him. He was too stern-looking and had cold eyes. I don't have to like him, she reminded herself, then started when Chase walked over and stood beside her. Reverend Brown opened up a frayed bible and began joining them in holy wedlock.

As Chase spoke his marriage vows, Raegan wished with all her heart that he meant the words that came out of his mouth so sincerely. How wonderful it would be, she thought, as she repeated her own vows, if they could live together as a loving couple, have children, build a future together.

She left off wishing as the preacher said, "I now pronounce you man and wife," and with a soft look Chase slipped Molly Donlin's wedding ring on her finger. She looked down at the gold band on her third left finger. It felt heavy and alien to her. Jewelry of any kind was unknown to her. She continued to look at the ring, worn thin from years of wear, some of its luster gone. Grandmother Donlin had known much happiness wearing this symbol of permanency between a man and a woman. Maybe if she prayed hard enough, became the best wife she knew how, Chase would in time learn to love her. If only she could bring that about, the ring would once again adorn the finger of a very happy woman.

About to walk away, Raegan blinked her surprise when Chase lifted her chin and asked huskily, "Aren't you goin' to kiss your new husband, Mrs. Donlin?"

"I . . . I" she began in confusion at his unexpected question, but never got to finish as his warm mouth came down on her slightly parted lips, his tongue slipping between them. And what she had imagined would be a quick meeting of their lips went on and on, deepening, growing hungry and demanding.

When Samuel Brown said gruffly, "I'll need your signatures on the marriage certificate," and Chase released her mouth, Raegan had to catch at his arm to keep from falling. Only the preacher saw his satisfied smile as Chase bent over the table and signed his name where the preacher indicated. He stepped back and handed the pen to the preacher, who dipped it into a bottle of ink and handed it to Raegan. As she wrote her name in fine script beneath Chase's sprawling letters, she wondered how long she'd keep the title of wife.

She was wondering if she shouldn't invite the preacher to have cake and coffee, when without a word, the stern-faced man tucked the bible under his arm and stalked out of the room. She opened her mouth to call him back, then saw Chase shaking his head at her.

"Let him go," he said softly, pulling her into his arms. "I'd like some time alone with my new wife before Jamie and the wild child return."

When Raegan looked up at him in total surrprise, Chase dipped his head and took her lips hungrily. Raegan's hands came up to press against his chest, her mind crying out, "Stop him this instant. You know you have no will-power when he kisses you like this."

But as Chase's arms tightened and his kiss deepened, her body determined to function independently of her brain. When he thrust his tongue into her mouth, she gave up the battle. Her arms came up around his neck, and her body melted into his. When he felt her answering desire rippling through her in spasams, he rubbed himself against her.

Finally Chase tore his lips away from the ripe mouth he'd been ravishing and held Raegan away from him. She gazed up at him, her passion-ridden eyes reading the silent query in his. She nodded and he swept her up in his arms and started down the hall, her head nestled in his shoulder, only one thought in her mind. Chase was going to make love to her.

Then Chase almost dropped her as from outside came the sound of hard-ridden horses and Star yelling Chase's name.

Chapter Eleven

Jamie took the river trail when he and Star started off. It was cool and shady, and the sound of moving water always soothed him. Farther along the Platte, miles away, was his mother's village and it was to this river that he first began to take his hurts. He told the flowing stream of the ache in his heart, demanding of it why there was no place in his universe where he could fit in, be wholly accepted.

As Star rode silently behind him, his thoughts were uninterrupted and he continued to remember those hurts. It was true his mother's people accepted him to a degree; he was never physically abused by anyone, yet he wasn't treated like the other boys his age either. He was never allowed to participate in the important things the other boys might be involved in, such as when he reached the important age of thirteen.

At that momentous time, boys were sent out into the forest to bring down their first big game—usually a deer—with a bow an arrow. Much praise would be heaped upon the boy when he proudly returned with his kill. The chief would tell him that now he was a man, a young brave.

And so had began Jamie's lonely existence in the Indian village. As every other boy achieved his manhood, he shunned the half-breed. Finally, there was no one with whom he could roam the forest, fish the river, discuss such things as why the sun rose in the east and what kept the moon from falling out of the sky.

He had never known his father—only that he was an Irish trapper and had deserted his mother five months before her son was born. She had returned to her people in shame. Until she died, when he was ten years old, she was treated much as a slave, working from dawn until twilight. But she had toiled uncomplainingly, thankful to have a tepee and food for herself and her son.

Jamie remembered with a scowl how, at sixteen, he had entered the white world of his father, hoping that he could find a niche for himself there. It hadn't happened. It was far worse than in the Indian village. He had stayed on, though, out of stubbornness.

As the years passed, doing odd jobs to keep body and soul together, he had become proficient with the knife shoved into his knee-length moccasins and the gun strapped around his waist. He had called no man friend until Chase Donlin entered his life. He had found unconditional acceptance from the white trapper and the secure knowledge that this man would never let him down.

Jamie was brought back to the present when Star rode up beside him, her eyes gleaming with excitement as she silently pointed toward the river. He looked in that direction, and though his heart leapt in excitement at seeing two deer standing in a stretch of shallow water, he was angry that the rag-tail girl had spotted them before he had.

He pulled the roan in, brought the rifle from its sheath, and braced the butt against his shoulder. Taking aim, he gently squeezed the trigger, shooting the yearling. It dropped instantly, shot through the heart.

A pleased smile curving his lips, Jamie swung from the saddle, stepping onto the damp, gravelly bank as the young deer's companion splashed across the river to the opposite shore. Tillamook land. As he prepared to wade out to the fallen animal, Star cried out:

"Behind you, Jamie!" He whirled around, his eyes taking in two things—Star with her rifle to her shoulder and an Indian, around his age, springing at him with a blood-curdling yell. Jamie barely had time to side-step the hurtling body to avoid the slashing knife. He dropped his empty rifle and snatched his own knife from his belt, then crouched, the sharp blade held ready to meet the next charge.

As Star yelled, "Stand clear of him, you stupid breed! Let me get a shot at him," they came together like two furious wolves, snarling, teeth bared, knives slashing at each other. Jamie managed to catch the brave's wrist and twist it until his knife fell to the ground. But quick as lightning, his opponent had a tomahawk in his hand, delivering him a blow alongside his head. All the time Star continued to yell, calling him a stupid breed, that he was going to be killed if he didn't get out of the way and let her shoot the bastard.

Stunned, Jamie dropped to his knees, shaking his head to clear it, wishing that the infernal girl would shut up. When the Indian's feet came in sight, ready to finish him off, Star's rifle sang out at the same time he grasped the man around the knees. Startled by the rifle shot, and taken by surprise that Jamie wasn't out of the fight as he had imagined, the brave hit the ground with a heavy thud.

Jamie was astride him in a flash, his knife raised to deliver a fatal blow to the red man's racing heart. The knife poised in the air, he hesitated. As he looked into the Tillamook's eyes, so like his own, he understood why this man wanted to kill him—to kill any hill person he came across. Some man on this side of the river had broken the unspoken treaty between the two races, had stolen one of their women. In the brave's place, Jamie would have done the same thing.

Ignoring Star's "Kill him, kill him," he dropped his arm and stood up. The Tillamook stared up at him a moment then, agile as a cat, swept to his feet, picked up his knife, and loped off into the forest.

Jamie watched the brave until he disappeared among the trees, wondering if he had made a mistake. He became aware then of a warm trickle moving down the side of his face and a throbbing in his head. He gingerly touched the spot above his right ear, and when he brought his hand down his fingers were smeared with blood. In his fight for life, he hadn't realized that the tomahawk had cut him.

He vaguely sensed that Star had come to stand beside him, but he could clearly hear her contemptous, "I have never seen a more stupid man. Why in the hell did you let him go?"

Beginning to feel dizzy from the loss of blood, and fed up with Star's screeching, he turned baleful eyes on her and gritted painfully, "Listen, you *matethi-i-thi equiwa*, if you call me stupid one more time, I'm gonna give you the thrashing someone should have given you a long time ago."

What Star answered to that he didn't know, for the words had barely left his lips when the ground came up to meet him.

With a little cry of alarm, Star knelt beside Jamie. She lifted his face from the leaves and pine needles and gave a soft gasp at the sight of the blood pouring from his head wound. And though she was spitting mad at him for calling her an ugly squaw, she knew she didn't want this man to die. And if it was possible to save his life, she must get him back to the Donlin cabin.

Lowering his head gently to the ground, she ran into the forest and scraped some moss from the north side of a hardwood tree. When she had a handful, she ran back to Jamie and carefully pressed the green wad to the red, running wound.

"Now to get him onto Champ's back," she muttered, studying Jamie's lean, though heavy body. She patted his cheek, calling his name at the same time. When she got no response, she panicked and slapped him quite hard. He flinched and opened his eyes, then glared at her.

"I'm sorry," Star snapped, "but I've got to get you home, and you have to help me if I'm to get you mounted. Do you think you can stand up?"

Jamie nodded, but only managed to lean up on one elbow, sweat popping out on his forehead. Star thrust her shoulder between his side and his other arm and, giving a heave, raised him into a sitting position. "Now put your arms around my neck and I'll pull you to your feet."

"No," Jamie muttered, "I'm too heavy for you. And don't you dare call me stupid."

Star grinned impishly. "All right, *psai-wi-nenothtu*, I won't call you stupid. But I am very strong, so put your arms around my neck."

Jamie knew he was about to lose consciousness again so, with an effort, he clasped his arms around Star's neck as she hunched her sturdy little body and pulled him upright. As in a dream, he followed her instructions. "Put your foot in the stirrup, then I'll boost you into the saddle." It was the strident command in her voice that made him hang on, do as she ordered.

He did not know when she climbed up behind him, pulled him back against her chest, and they started out, Star keeping him steady with one hand, the other keeping the moss in place as she guided the mount with her knees. Nor did he come to when the Donlin cabin came in view and Star started yelling for Chase.

As Star brought the sorrel to a plunging halt, Jamie's mount trailing behind them, Chase came barreling out the door, Raegan at his heels. "Oh my God!" Raegan exclaimed, staring at the blood streaking Jamie's white face, the stain of it on the shoulder of his shirt. "What happened, Star?"

"A Tillamook whammed him with a tomahawk—the idiot let him go free when he could have put his knife through his rotten heart."

"Hurry, Chase, get him inside," Raegan said anxiously. "We've got to attend to his wound."

Star removed her arm from around Jamie's waist, and as he fell forward, Chase took his weight over his shoulder and carried him into the cabin and on into his bedroom. When he had laid Jamie on the bed, he said to Raegan, "Bring me a basin of water and that bottle of boric acid in the cupboard with the supplies."

Raegan hurried from the room, and within a minute she was back with what Chase wanted. He and the two girls released long sighs of relief when the moss was removed and the wound bathed. The tomahawk had landed only a glancing blow, but it had nicked a blood vessel in Jamie's temple, which was why he had bled so profusely.

"Do you think he'll need stitches?" Raegan asked.

"I don't think so," Chase answered, pouring the boric acid over the gash, then grinning when Jamie flinched and moaned. "It will leave only a thin white scar, and his hair will cover it. Our only concern now is to build back the blood he lost."

"I know just the thing for that," Star said eagerly. "Squirrel broth. Paw claims there ain't anything better for strengthenin' the blood. I'll go shoot a couple of the little critters right now."

She was already at the door when Chase called after her. "You can't go huntin', Star. The forest could be full of Tillamooks. I have to go dig Henry Jones's grave. I'll bag a couple on my way home. In the meantime, if he comes to, give him some tea with a lot of sugar in it."

Raegan followed Chase out onto the porch and looked up at the sun. "The sun is going to set in an hour or so—do you think you'll be able to finish digging the grave before dark?"

"Sure." Chase smiled down at her. "You've got yourself a very strong husband." Before she could make a snappy retort, he gave her a quick, hard kiss and loped off toward the barn.

"Oh, do be careful," Raegan whispered as the stallion galloped away, her fingers on her throbbing lips.

Chase rode up to the dangerously canting cabin, and the Jones brood came piling out the door, led by Meg and Johnny. "Afternoon, Meg," he said, swinging to the ground. "Jamie had a tussel with a Tillamook and has himself a crack on the head. If you'll show me where you want the grave dug, I'll get to it."

With a nod of her head, Meg stepped off the rotting porch and struck off through a small pasture that held the bony mule and a cow that looked half starved. They had walked about a quarter of a mile when Meg stopped and said, "We'll plant the old bastard here."

An uglier spot could not be found in all of Oregon, Chase thought as he looked at the small strip of land. It was treeless, with deep, weed-choked gullies on three sides. The soil was mostly gravel, without a blade of grass on it. "Hell," he said to himself, "when it rains and them gullies fill up, Jones is gonna be washed right out of his grave."

He took the spade Meg handed him and started digging. As the woman turned and walked back toward her cabin, he grinned wryly. "Maybe that's what she had in mind. Let the buzzards pick his brains."

With one last worried look up the hill where Chase had disappeared, Raegan went back inside and found Star at the stove, making a pot of tea. The girl blushed and muttered, "I thought I'd have the tea ready against when he comes to."

Their heads jerked around when, from down the hall, Chase's name was called crossly. Star grimaced. "It sounds like the big *muga* has done that now."

"Sounds that way, doesn't it. And his voice sounds quite strong too."

Raegan had glimpsed the relief in Star's eyes before she could hide it. She hid her smile when the girl jeered, "It would take more than a whack on the head to keep that one knocked out very long. I wouldn't be surprised if his hard head broke the handle on that Tillamook's tomahawk."

Raegan made no response to Star's unflattering remarks about Jamie, but as she went to answer his call, she mused that perhaps Star was hiding her real feelings about Jamie.

Jamie was sitting up in bed when she entered his room. "Jamie, you should be lying down. How are you feeling?" She sat down on the edge of the bed and raised the edge of the bandage Chase had tied around his head.

"I feel like that Tillamook is inside my head hitting it with a hammer," Jamie groused.

"Well, he gave you one good whack. You've lost a lot of blood."

"How'd I get home, anyhow? Did Chase come lookin' for us?"

"No, Star brought you in."

"She did?" Jamie's eyes widened in surprise. "I'll be damned. She must be a strong little critter."

"Yes she is, and strong-minded too., She'd made up her mind that she was going to get you home, and she did. By the way, what does *muga* mean in Indian?"

"She's still callin' me that, is she? It means bear, usually black bear. The one that does the most—and the loudest—growlin'."

"Were you growling at her?"

"Some, I reckon. She kept callin' me stupid."

Raegan managed to hide her tickled grin. "I do wish you two would get along. She's going to be here all summer, maybe longer. Maybe even permanently."

"Why in the hell would she stay here permanent?" Jamie scowled.

"Chase says her grandfather is dying and she has no one to go to. That's why he brought her home with him. She doesn't know anything about her grandfather's health, so don't say anything to her about it."

"That's a shame," Jamie said, pity for the young girl in his voice.

"She's made you some horehound tea. Would you like a cup of it?"

"Only if you or Chase brings it to me."

"Why not Star? She made it."

"Because we always get into a fight, and my head hurts enough already."

"All right, I'll bring it. Chase has gone to dig Henry Jones's grave."

The sun was ready to set, and Raegan was placing the plates on the table for supper when Chase rode in, a brace of squirrels lying across his saddle. Star, sitting on the porch, offered to stable the stallion and clean the game. He gladly agreed, for it had been hard work digging through rocks and hard clay.

He stepped up on the back porch, removed his soiled and sweat-stained shirt, then filled the basin kept there for washing up with water from a full pail. He lathered his face, neck, and arms, promising himself that after supper he would take a bath in the stream back of the cabin, a tributary of the Platte.

He walked into the kitchen and Raegan turned to look at him. She felt as though her heart would jump from her chest as her eyes immediately fastened on his broad, bare chest, his wide muscular shoulders and arms. There leapt into her mind the other time she had seen his magnificent body, had felt its bareness against her nakedness, her nipples buried in the soft curly hair that liberally covered his chest.

Chase pretended not to see the flaring of passion in Raegan's eyes, but after greeting her with a smile, he made sure that his bare arm grazed hers as he reached past her to take the coffee pot from the stove. "If you don't mind, I'll have a cup of coffee while you finish making supper," he said, taking a seat from where he could watch her.

"Not at all," Raegan answered as calmly as she could, her fingers suddenly dropping flatware and knocking over cups.

Ah, my confused little bride, Chase thought with a stirring in his loins, *how you will come alive in my arms tonight.* If his seed hadn't taken yet, it surely would tonight.

But had he been able to read Raegan's mind, he would have known that she was building up a defense against the yearning of her body. If her new husband had plans to sleep with her tonight, he might as well get the thought out of his mind. She would not lay herself open for more hurt—have him make love to her for hours, then tell her the next morning that he shouldn't have. He could sleep on the floor in his bedroll.

After what seemed like hours to Raegan, but in truth was only about ten minutes, she had supper on the table. She called to Star to come eat just as Jamie walked slowly into the kitchen. "Hey, Hoss, do you think you're ready to be out of bed? I was goin' to bring your supper to you," Chase said.

Jamie eased down in the chair at his place at the table, and Raegan hurried to set a place for him. "My headache has eased up considerably," he answered Chase, "and I see no reason to stay in bed like I was a invalid."

"That makes sense," Chase answered, and smiled at Star as she came through the door, carrying the skinny carcasses of the two squirrels. She placed them in a crock of water and, avoiding looking at Jamie, took the chair Raegan motioned her toward.

Raegan and Star ate in silence as the two men discussed the Tillamook's attack on Jamie and the ugly site Meg had chosen for her husband's grave. "I told Meg that we'd all come to Henry's buryin'," Chase said. "Do you think you'll be up to goin'?"

"Yeah, I'll go. A good night's sleep and I'll be fine."

Finally everyone sat back with replete stomachs. Raegan poured coffee, then began to clear the table. She was aware that Chase's eyes followed her every move, and she wanted to yell, "Stop looking at me like a hungry wolf." She gave him a cold stare when he stood up and said, "I'm goin' down to the river and take a bath. You want to come with me, Raegan?"

Looking away from him, she answered coolly, "I had a bath this morning. Besides, I'm going to bed as soon as I straighten up the kitchen."

"Fine, I'll hurry up my dip into the river," Chase said smoothly, mischief in his tone. "I don't want you fallin' asleep before I get back."

Raegan gritted her teeth but made no response.

Chapter Twelve

Raegan lay curled in bed, her nerves as tense as an overwound clock. Chase would be coming through the door any minute, and she knew he had every intention of making love to her. She knew also that it would take all her will power to repulse him. But reject him she must. She had come to the conclusion that he *wanted* her to be with child, was in fact determined that she would be. It would be to his advantage to have a wife tucked away, a woman to look after his needs especially in his later years after he had whored himself out and had no more need of a woman in a sexual way.

She flopped over on her back, fighting tears. And damn him, it wouldn't even enter his mind about how she might feel about all those years married to a man who didn't love her. Well by God, she cared, and she would have nothing to do with such a marriage. God willing, his seed wasn't taking root inside her already. She would see to it that he had no further opportunity to get her with child.

Raegan stiffened when the door softly creaked open. In the room bathed in moonlight, she watched Chase enter the room, then close the door behind him. She had seen past him that all was dark in the cabin, that Star and Jamie had retired also. That fact, for some reason, made her body tense all the more.

She watched Chase come toward the bed, unlacing his buckskins as he came. When he slid the fringed trousers down his legs, her nipples peaked into hard little nubs at the sight of the arousal that sprang free. How could his manhood have hardened when he hadn't even touched her?

As he sat down on the bed to peel the leather over his bare feet, she hurriedly scooted to the other side of the bed, her fists clenched, ready to do battle. She heard his soft laugh as he slid beneath the sheet and reached for her.

"Take your hands off me, Chase Donlin!" she whispered fiercely. "We agreed that there would be nothing between us in case I'm not expecting.

"Oh no, my pretty little wife." Chase brought her closer up against him, his stiff maleness jabbing at her belly through the material of her gown. "Those were your words, not mine."

"But you—"

Chase's mouth claimed hers, silencing her protest, drinking from her lips with a hunger that sent passion flaring through her whole body. She tried to fight his demand for satisfaction, but knew even as she did that she would lose the battle. With a moan of reluctant surrender, her arms came up around his neck, her fingers curling in the hair at his nape.

As the kiss went on and on, Chase's trembling fingers undid the tiny buttons of her gown and pulled free a breast. Cupping its fullness in his hand, his mouth left her lips and closed over the nipple. As he suckled her greedily, the fire in her blood turned to molten silver. She tore her arms free of the sleeves and pushed the gown down to her waist. Chase eagerly accepted her silent invitation, and for long breathless minutes, he switched back and forth between her passion-swollen breasts. He nibbled and sucked until the nipples stood out, rosy pink and pebble hard. Mindlessly weak from his drawing lips, she made no objection when he pulled the gown down over her feet and tossed it to the floor.

Chase slid his hand down her smooth body, stopping at the soft curls between her thighs. His probing finger found her wet and ready for him. He clenched his jaws together, forcing back the need to enter her now, to ease the ache that had ridden him since the first time she had lain in his arms. Tonight he was going to make *her* ache with wanting *him*, stamp it on her mind and heart that he was a necessary part of her life, that she was his for as long as she lived.

Raegan moaned a low protest when he released her swollen nipple, then held her breath when his lips began trailing quick little kisses down her stomach, and on down to the hollow of her hips. When his tongue licked at the silky smoothness of an inner thigh, Raegan's heavy breathing grew to gasping pants.

Her breathing stopped altogether when he knelt at her feet and gently drew her legs apart, then buried his face between them. "Chase, what are you doing?" she whispered hoarsely, coming up on her elbows.

"Shhhh." Chase raised his head. "I'm payin' homage to my wife." He gave her a rakish grin. "I wouldn't object if you did the same for me, later on."

Raegan lay back down, mulling over Chase's words. Did he mean what she thought he did? That she should take him into her mouth, thus paying him homage?

When Chase's tongue started flicking inside her, building sensations she'd never experenced before, she knew what he meant about paying homage. She also knew she wanted to do the same for him—to give him that breathtaking pleasure that was making her body writhe uncontrollably.

When Raegan realized that she was about to go over the edge, plunge into that spiraling sphere called the little death, she cupped Chase's head in her hands and urged him up beside her. He took her in his arms, kissed her long and hard, then lay over on his back, waiting.

Without hesitation, Raegan got up on her knees and licked her way down his long body. When she reached her objective, she curled her fingers around it. Her palm lovingly stroked up and down, feeling it grow, feeling it expand and contract rhythmically. When Chase moaned low in his throat, her sharp little tongue darted teasingly over its throbbing head.

"Please, Raegan, you're killin' me," Chase groaned. He bucked his hips at her. "Come on, honey, don't tease, do it to me."

Raegan took another moment to glory in the power she held over her husband before opening her mouth wide and sliding it down over that part that would later sap all the strength from her.

As she slowly moved her mouth up and down, curling her tongue around the male stiffness, Chase fastened his hands in her hair, gently urging her on. "Ah, honey, it feels so good," he moaned. "Your mouth feels like velvet sliding over me. Like warm cream . . . oh, God."

Chase knew he was fast moving to that apex of no return. He gently removed Raegan's mouth and lifted her up to lay her on her back. He just as gently parted her legs and climbed between them. He hung over her a moment to bend his head and draw a nipple into his mouth. As he suckled it, Raegan put her hands on his hips, pulling him down to her. "Please, Chase," she whispered, "I hurt."

He grasped her narrow hips and lifted them up to nestle inside his. Then, slowly, he buried his long length inside her. He moaned as he felt her tightly sheathing his arousal. He held her there, not moving as he savored the feel of her.

"Lord, Raegan, I've needed you so." The words sounded torn from him.

"And I have needed you," Raegan whispered back, arching her body to meet the thrusting drives he had begun. She caught his rhythm and they moved together for a long time. Sweat began to film on their bodies as they strove to make the moment last.

But at last it became too much, too hard to hold back any longer. In the next second, Chase was jerking against Raegan, calling her name as his seed spilled inside her. And Raegan could only cling to Chase's shoulders, afraid of falling, afraid to speak in the overwhelming spread of release that caught her up, lifted her to heights she never wanted to leave.

It was several minutes before their shattering spasms subsided. Chase lifted his weight off Raegan, but kept his manhood snugly inside her. "You are so beautiful," he murmured, smoothing the sweat-damp hair off her forehead. "If I live to be a hundred, I'll never get enough of you." He lowered his head to suck a nipple into his mouth.

As he teased it with his tongue and teeth, Raegan became embarrassed that she wanted him again. What would he think of her? Would he think that she was Liza Jenkins, wanton like the women who plied their trade at the village tavern?

Chase felt the tightening of the walls around his maleness, and satisfaction curved his lips. His wife was a passionate little thing, thank God, for he was a very virile man who needed sex on a regular basis. But love had never entered into his liaisons with other women, and now that he had discovered that love made all the difference in the world when you took a woman, he'd need Raegan as often as he could get her.

His long length began to swell. When it grew to fill Raegan tightly, her eyes widened in pleased surprise. "Again?" she whispered hopefully.

"Yes, again, my beautiful little love-nymph. Again and again, until we've worn each other out."

As Chase resumed his rhythmic stroking, cradling Raegan's small buttocks in his hands, making sure she felt every long inch of him, she rose to meet his thrusts, glorying in the slip and slide of her husband's delightfully big manhood. For the moment she forgot that he didn't love her.

Raegan awakened at the first rosy pink of dawn. She couldn't have slept very long, she thought, snuggling closer into the curl of Chase's body. She remembered then what had kept her awake all those long hours and felt embarrassed shame move through her body. Even though she knew he didn't love her, she had given in to her body's urging and entered into wanton love-making with Chase. She had let him coax her into doing things she had never dreamed went on between a man and woman.

What must he think of her? Not only did he not love her, now he'd have no respect for her. How was she going to face him in the light of day? She began inching herself away from the arm lying across her waist. She wanted to get out of bed before he awakened and wanted to make love again. She had only moved a few slow inches when his arm tightened, drawing her back against him.

"Where do you think you're goin'?" he asked softly, nuzzling her throat and shoulder.

Raegan ordered her leaping pulses to behave, not to listen to the husky wanting in his voice. She would not carry the past night into the new day. She had control of her emotions now, and she intended to remain in control.

When Chase felt her body stiffen, he raised his head and looked into her cool eyes. The arousal that had begun to grow died. They were right back where they'd started. She would only come alive to him at night, in bed. He sighed inwardly. It wasn't going to be an easy task, convincing her that he loved her, that she could trust him and love him back.

He dropped a light kiss on her forehead as he removed his arm and pretended that he hadn't noticed her silent rejection of him by saying lightly, "I probably wore you out last night, so we'll forgo a little love-making this morning. Anyhow, we've got to hustle along if we're to go to Jones's buryin'. Meg said early, and to her that means as soon as the sun peeps over the treetops."

Raegan sat up in bed, clutching the sheet to her chin. "You'd better wake up Star. I don't want to go off and leave her alone."

Chase nodded and slid out of bed. His broad-shouldered body showed clearly in the semi-gloom as Raegan watched him pull the buckskins over his firm, long legs and on up over his narrow hips. Her breathing increased as she watched him lace the bucks over the powerful man part of him, that discernible bulge that drew her attention all too often. He pulled the matching shirt over his head, and at the door, he said, "After I wake Star up, I'll put on a pot of coffee."

The door closed and Raegan dropped her head onto her bent knees. Things could not go on this way. A thought came to her then that brightened her face a bit. At least he hadn't repulsed her this morning. It hadn't appeared that he had any regrets about making love to her. With the hope that everything might in time work out for them, she tossed back the sheet and hurried to take her sponge bath.

Star, sleepy-eyed, was pouring the coffee when Raegan entered the kitchen. She smiled shyly. "Mornin', Raegan."

"Good morning, Star." Raegan gave her arm an affectionate pat as she joined Chase and Jamie at the table. "Did you have a good night's sleep? Did you miss your swinging bed?"

Star blushed an angry red when Jamie demanded, "What in the hell is a swingin' bed?"

She slammed the coffee pot on the stove, her eyes spitting fire. "What do you think it is, breed? It's a bed that swings."

"Now listen, you little hellcat," Jamie blazed back, "you'd better watch that tongue of yours or this breed will cut a piece of it off."

"Try it!" Star's hand flew to the knife nestled at her waist. "I'll slice you into little pieces if you lay a hand on me."

"You wild Indian!" Jamie jumped to his feet, his chair going over backwards. "I ought to take that pig-sticker away from you and—" His face suddenly paled beneath his tan. He hadn't seen Star's hand move, but suddenly the knife was in her hand, poised at his heart.

"Come on, breed," she hissed, "take it away from me if you dare to try." She flipped the knife back and forth between her hands, feinting jabs at Jamie, all the time tormenting, "Come on big man, start slicin'."

"Star! Jamie! Stop it, right now!" Raegan pounded a fist on the table.

"I'm not gonna let that half-pint hellcat pull a knife on me and get away with it," Jamie gritted.

"You shouldn't have threatened her," Raegan came back.

"I didn't mean it and she knows it."

"I'm afraid she didn't, Jamie," Chase said quietly. "The part of the hills Star comes from, the people are a different breed. Threatening to slice a person up is taken literally. In the same circumstances, they would act the same way Star did."

Raegan tugged Star down in the chair beside her. "Jamie would never take his knife to you, Star, or to any other woman. But he is deadly when it comes to using it on a man." She looked earnestly into the small face. "Do you understand what I'm saying, Star?"

Star reluctantly nodded her head and muttered, "I reckon."

Raegan patted the small hand clenched in a fist. "It's good that you know how to handle a knife and are able to protect yourself. But be sure it's an enemy you draw it on. Jamie is not your enemy."

"The hell I'm not," Jamie growled, picking up his chair and plunking himself in it.

Raegan gave him a stern look and he said no more. The four of them drank their coffee in strained silence.

The sun was showing its first streaks of light when the Donlins, Jamie, and Star arrived at the spot where Meg had directed Chase to dig her husband's grave. Chase was shocked to see Meg and young Johnny already shoveling dirt into the hole he had dug.

"She sure is in a hurry to get Henry in the ground," Jamie observed, swinging from the saddle and falling in behind Chase and the girls as they walked up the the grave.

Raegan gasped as she stood beside Chase and felt his body give a start of surprise. Henry Jones had been tossed into the three-foot hole in the same clothes he'd been killed in. He lay half on his side, his eyes still staring as they had when he was carried into the shack. It was quite evident that no hand had been lifted to prepare him for a proper burial. The man had lived as an animal, and he would be buried as one.

Meg looked up and nodded a greeting to the only people who had come to her husband's funeral, then continued to shovel dirt on that husband's head. Raegan shivered at the surpreme satisfaction on Meg's gaunt face. How she must have hated the dead man.

When no more of Henry's face showed, Chase and Jamie took over to finish shoveling the dirt.

As Meg stood wiping her face with the hem of her faded dress, Raegan studied her and the children from under lowered lids. She did not see a glimmer of grief in any of their eyes. She noted, however, that there was an avid light in the two older girls' eyes as they watched the rippling muscles moving beneath Chase's and Jamie's shirts.

Would their mother be able to handle her two man-hungry daughters? she wondered, switching her gaze back to Meg. She knew from the woman's hard face that she could. It would be interesting to see how the Jones family fared from now on, Raegan thought.

When Chase gave the long mound a final pat with the shovel and handed it to Johnny, Meg said gruffly, "I'm obliged to you men. It was right neighborly of you to help us out." Then, not even sparing Raegan and Star a glance, she said, "We'll be gettin' on back to the shack now. We got a lot of work ahead of us." She motioned to the children who hadn't taken their eyes off Raegan and Star. "Come on, youngins', time's a wastin'."

The children rushed to do Meg's bidding, but Johnny and little Vera moved more slowly. Each took time to spit on Henry's grave before following after their mother.

Nobody was shocked at the action—nobody except Star who didn't know how vile Henry Jones had been. Puzzlement showed in her eyes. The people from her part of the woods weren't much for carrying-on at funerals, but they always showed respect for their dead.

"You know," Chase said as the four of them climbed back on their mounts, "I think we're gonna see some big changes at the Jones homestead. That boy Johnny doesn't have a lazy bone in his body, and between him and Meg, they're gonna make the rest of that tribe pitch in and work."

"I think you're right," Jamie agreed, "but Meg is gonna have her hands full with Nellie and Fanny. They're both hot, and it won't take the men around here long to discover it."

Star looked her confusion at Jamie's remark, but Raegan had grown used to his rather off-color vernacular and knew exactly what he meant. Seeing Star's bemusement, she hoped the girl didn't ask her what Jamie meant by his remark.

The girl didn't. She asked Jamie instead. Bringing her mount up beside his, she asked, "What did you mean, them two girls are hot? I don't find the weather hot at all. In fact, the air is on the chilly side."

Chase saw Jamie's face grow red and couldn't help teasing, "Yeah, Jamie, explain yourself. I'd like to know too what makes you think Nellie and Fanny were hot this mornin'. Like Star said, It's right cool. I didn't see them sweatin'."

"Nor did I," Raegan joined in, knowing that Chase was ragging his friend.

Jamie slid a look at Star and found her innocent eyes watching him, waiting for an explanation. Damn. He shook his head mentally. A man had to watch everything he said around this ignorant half-breed.

But his thought wasn't indignant, it was more amused than anything else. "Come on." He gave

Star a friendly smile as he jabbed a heel into the roan. "Let's get away from these two smart asses and I'll tell you how I knew."

As Star lifted her stallion into a loping run, easily keeping up with Jamie, Raegan looked at Chase, a frown worrying her forehead. "I'm not sure Jamie is the proper person to tell Star the facts of life."

"Don't worry about it, Raegan." Chase grinned as they followed the pair at a leisurely pace. "He'll spin her some big lyin' tale, like seein' smoke comin' out of the girl's ears, or some such foolishness."

Raegan smiled at Chase. "I expect so. Underneath his harsh manner with Star, I think he's a little smitten with her. At any rate, I'm sure he respects her innocence.

Chase agreed, but added, "I'm wonderin' if that respect might turn into somethin' else later on. I don't want that wild child hurt."

"Wild child?" Raegan laughed. "Is that what you call her?"

"Yeah, to myself. The first time I saw her, that's how she struck me. You've got to admit she's sometimes like a wild little animal, and though she's sixteen, she's still much like a child."

"I guess it comes from the strange way she was raised with that old man," Raegan said. "But if Jamie should try, he'll not find it easy to coax *her* into his bed. The girl may be naive, but she's not stupid."

A companionable silence settled between Raegan and Chase and wasn't broken until they came upon Star and Jamie waiting for them about a mile from the cabin.

"Well, Star, did you find out how Jamie knew the Jones girls were hot this morning?" Chase asked, shooting Jamie a devilish look.

"Yes I did. Nobody else noticed, but Jamie saw a fine film of sweat on the girl's upper lips."

"Well, do tell." Chase pretended to take the sober explanantion seriously, at the same time hard put not to roar with laughter. "It looks like Jamie has a fine eye for details that most people overlook."

"Yes." Star looked at Jamie with admiration. "I didn't notice them two girls sweatin' at all."

A strangled snort came from Jamie and Chase, and Raegan bit her lip. "Come on, Star," she croaked, "I'll race you to the cabin." The two stallions lunged away, leaving behind two men bent over with laughter.

"You've got to be careful what you say around Star, Jamie," Chase said when their mirth died away.

"I'm findin' that out," Jamie answered, amusement still tugging at his lips.

"For instance," Chase continued, "If you sweet-talk her, she's gonna believe you mean every word you say. Old Daniels gave her over to me for safe-keepin'." He gave Jamie a sharp look. "I intend to see that he wasn't mistaken in his faith in me. So if you get an itch, take it to some female who has a film of sweat on her lip."

An angry red flush swept over Jamie's face. "Now dammit, Chase, I wouldn't take advantage of that girl anymore than you would."

Chase studied his irate friend and knew the man firmly believed what he claimed. But, he wondered, how would Jamie feel a month from now, seeing those lush curves and pretty face every day? Would he still be able to look on her as a child?

Chase said no more, however, and the two rode on in a stiff silence.

Raegan and Star had breakfast ready by the time Chase and Jamie unsaddled all four mounts and turned them into the fenced-in pasture back of the cabin. The early fresh morning had given them all a hearty appetite, and a large quanity of pancakes were consumed. Coffee was lingered over, conversation flowing easily and warmly. When the men rolled their cigarettes and wandered out onto the porch, Raegan and Star set about putting order to the kitchen.

Half an hour later, after the beds had been made, Raegan looked at Star and said determindedly, "Star, I'm sure you'd like to have a bath and get into some clean clothes. I'll have Jamie bring in the tub and fill it with water."

Alarm jumped into Star's face. "Not him, Raegan! He makes me feel so uneasy."

Raegan's lips twitched at the corners. The girl probably didn't know it, but she was physically attracted to the handsome Jamie. No doubt she was experiencing these *uneasy* feelings for the first time in her young life. "I'll have Chase do it then, is that all right?"

Star nodded, and Raegan turned to go talk to Chase and met Jamie coming through the kitchen door. Ignoring Star's scowling face, he said, "Me and Chase are ridin' into the village to see what news there is about the Tillamooks. Do you need anything from the store?"

"I don't believe so, but before you go will you please lift the tub off the wall for us?"

A wicked smile spread over Jamie's face. "If the little breed is gonna take a bath, maybe I'll hang around and give you a hand scrubbin' her up."

Chase arrived in time to grab Star around the waist as she hurled herself at Jamie, her small face working with rage.

"That'll be enough out of you, Jamie." He frowned. "Get the tub down and let's get goin'."

"I was only tryin' to be helpful, Chase." Jamie smiled his rakish grin at Star. "I was just gonna hold the wildcat down while Raegan scrubbed off the dirt."

Raegan saw the tears that glimmered in Star's eyes, and her temper flared. "That is absolutely enough, Jamie Hart! Now take that sharp tongue and get out of here."

"Yes, ma'am." Jamie tried to look repentant but failed as his amusement sparked his eyes.

"Don't pay him any mind, Star," Chase released his hold on her waist as Jamie left the kitchen. "He's just a natural-born tease." He turned to Raegan before following Jamie and cautioned, "Keep Lobo with you and your rifle handy. We shouldn't be gone longer than an hour."

"Don't you like Chase?" Star asked seeing the unhappiness in Raegan's eyes as her gaze followed her husband.

Raegan started to playfully ruffle the black hair, then drew back her hand. She wasn't sure what might jump out at her. Instead she tweaked the pert nose. "What a question, Star. I married him, didn't I?"

"That don't always mean anythin' back where I come from." Star said, following Raegan onto the porch. "When a girl reaches twelve or thirteen, her family marries her off to the first man who asks for her. Usually a cousin. Paw says that's why there are so many feeble-brained people in our neck of the woods. He says it ain't right for cousins to marry cousins, that it thins out the blood."

"Yes, I've heard that said," Raegan answered. "How have you managed to stay single at the ripe age of sixteen? Hasn't any man asked for you?" she teased.

"Yes they have. Lots of them. All the shiftless varmints up there know that I'm a good hunter and trapper and figure that I could provide for them while they sit around swillin' whiskey.

"Paw said I could choose the man I marry, but that I'd mostly likely be better off if I didn't settle for any of them."

"I'd say he's right, if that's the only type of man you have to pick from." Raegan smiled at the serious little face. "Now then," she changed the subject, "while I fill the tub, why don't you go get your clean clothes."

When Star returned, fresh buckskins over her arm, Raegan was adding a pail of cold water to that which steamed in the bottom of the tub. "I think we'll wash your hair first," she said, dropping a bar of scented soap into the water.

"You can start while I go put more water on the stove to heat."

Star lifted a hand to the snarled tresses, her cheeks flushing. "I expect it could stand some cleanin' up."

It took close to half an hour *cleanin' up* Star's hair. But it was time well spent, in Raegan's opinion. After several latherings and as many rinsings, what previously had appeared a dull, matted tangle was now as bright and shiny as a crow's wing as it hung in a straight line to the small of Star's back.

"You have lovely, healthy hair, Star," Raegan said, pulling it on top her head and fastening it with pins she took from her own hair.

"Do you really mean it, Raegan?" Star gently patted the top-knot. "You're not funnin' me?"

"I wouldn't story to you about that, honey," Raegan said softly. "You have every right to be proud of it. But right now, you'd better jump in the tub and take your bath. The men will be returning any time now, and I must get supper started. You wouldn't want Jamie to catch you in your birthday suit, would you?"

The thought of those devilish eyes seeing her nakedness set Star's fingers flying. She was out of the dirty buckskins and into the tub almost before Raegan could turn around and enter the kitchen.

The venison steaks were nearly finished frying, and Raegan was setting the table when a shy voice asked, "Can I help you with anything, Raegan?"

Raegan looked up and stared at the transformation in Star. Washed clean of the grime that had covered her face, the girl was lovely. There was an exotic look about her, the black waterfall of hair framing the dark almond-shaped eyes in the fine-boned face.

Her eyes dropped to the slender body. The clean buckskins, like the dirty discarded ones, followed every curve lovingly. How will Jamie take to this version of Miss Star Daniels? she wondered with a tickled smile.

She saw Star stir nervously at her long scrutiny, and giving her a bright smile, she said, "Chase and Jamie aren't going to recognize you, you look so pretty. I saw them ride in a while back. I don't supose you'd want to call them in for supper?"

"Oh . . . I . . ."

A deep chuckle sounded from the open door. "We've saved you the trip, Star," Chase said, running approving eyes over the girl. He would have remarked on her changed appearance, but knew he would embarrass the wild child if he did.

He stepped into the kitchen, Jamie following close behind him. And Jamie, ready to scowl at Star as usual, could only stare at her instead. She was like a young doe, with those innocent, wary eyes, ready to bound away at any untoward word or movement. As though afraid he might startle her into flight if he spoke, he silently sat down at the table.

As Raegan set out the food and plates, then poured the coffee, she watched Jamie from the corners of her eyes and grinned to herself. She doubted that young man would continue to rag their guest. He was enthralled with her.

"So what did you learn regarding the Tillamooks?" Raegan asked, putting her fork to the venison steak.

"They've been seen," Chase answered, "always at a distance, slippin' along from tree to tree. I guess Jamie is the only one who's been attacked so far. Everybody is gettin' a mite anxious, especially the womenfolk."

"So am I," Raegan said, wondering if the Tillamook woman was still alive. "I hope they find that Roscoe soon. I hope we did the right thing, letting him take the woman away."

"That bothers me too, Raegan," Chase pushed his empty plate away. He stood up and walked out onto the porch. Jamie gulped down his coffee and followed him.

"I know you're mad at Chase, Raegan," Star said timidly. "You treat him so cold. Is it because he brought me home with him?"

"Oh no, Star! You musn't think that," Raegan said earnestly. I'm very happy that you're here. Like all husbands and wives, Chase and I sometimes have our differences," she lied. "Sometimes I feel like laying into him with my rolling pin."

Star laughed. She had no idea what a rolling pin was, but she imagined it was a stick of some kind. "I expect he'll soften up for you, Raegan," she said. "The way he looks at you, I don't think there's anything he wouldn't do for you."

"Hah!" Raegan snorted inwardly. "A lot you know about it, Star." She stood up and said out loud, "Let's get the table cleared."

Chapter Thirteen

July arrived, hot and humid. The air was still, with only an occasional breeze to stir the leaves on the trees. Raegan crawled along between two rows of vegetables in the summer heat. Dragging a haversack behind her, she snapped tender green beans off their stems and tossed them into the sack. It was growing quite heavy and Raegan was pleased. Aggie Stevens had taught her how to string the beans on a heavy thread, then hang them in the loft to dry. According to her plump little neighbor, when winter set in and the garden was dead beneath several feet of snow, all she'd have to do was climb to the loft and take down a long strip of the dried beans. After soaking them in water overnight, they'd plump up, and after being cooked would taste as good as the day they were picked.

Raegan stilled her hands to straighten her stiff

back and wipe her sweating brow. She glanced over her garden. It had produced abundantly, and she was proud of the nourishing food she had already put away for the winter months, thanks to Aggie's tutoring.

Up in the loft was a good-sized bag of corn kernels she had sliced off the cob and carefully spread out to dry before bagging them. They, too, would need to be soaked and plumped up before cooking. There was also a bag of peas treated in the same manner, as well as a five-gallon crock of shredded cabage, smelling to high heaven as it fermented into sauerkraut.

And later this fall, when their tops died down, there would be potatoes and yams to be dug and stored in the cellar. Also, she musn't forget how the apple and pear trees had responded to her care. They were loaded with fruit, ready to be picked in the fall.

Raegan moved her gaze to the yard. The climbing rose she had feared was dead now climbed the chimney in a blaze of red blossoms. Her eyes shifted to the flower beds she and Jamie had sweated over. They were a riot of color—yellows, pinks, whites, and purples.

A sadness clouded her eyes then. Life could be so good if she thought Chase loved her. Sometimes she almost believed that he did. He seldom went to the village without her, and never went away at night anymore. He always treated her lovingly, even though she was usually cool toward him during the day. But the words "I love you" hadn't passed his lips.

Raegan turned her head to look toward the

cabin, when she heard Star's clear laughter ring out. She and Jamie were working in the cabin, and he had probably just told her one of his wild tales. It was quite evident these days that the girl adored Jamie, even though he often got the sharp edge of her tongue—as when jealously gripped her when other young women came around.

Hardly a day passed that some young woman didn't come visiting, presumably to call on Raegan. They fooled no one, however. It was Jamie who drew them to the Donlin cabin. And to Star's chagrin, he flirted with them outrageously, leading them on. What Star didn't know was that, inside, Jamie despised all simpering, giggling females. He knew that not a one of them would stand up to their parents and be seen in public with a half-breed.

Once, in a fit of bitter anger, he had said to Raegan that sometimes he was tempted to seduce the whole lot and leave the silly things with full bellies when he left the territory. "Wouldn't that make the righteous, bigoted parents howl?" he'd ended with one of his devilish grins.

Raegan resumed gathering her beans, wondering when Jamie would realize that he was in love with Star. She suspected that he was afraid to let down his guard and love. And Star didn't give him any encouragement. The girl didn't understand the sensations Jamie stirred inside her, and this worried her or, alternatively, made her angry. Consequently, her sharp little tongue was always at the ready.

Raegan suddenly became aware that the sky was quite overcast. Even as she stood up and studied the dark clouds that rolled and tumbled above her, a streak of lightning zig-zagged across the sky. It was going to rain, and rain hard if the thickening darkness was any indication.

She brushed the dirt off the knees of her skirt, and as she picked up the bag of beans, her eyes worriedly searched the valley where Chase had ridden off in search of game. He'd better hurry home or he'd get soaked. As she headed for the cabin, she could hear Star's and Jamie's voices raised in an argument. Didn't they ever get tired of nipping at each other? she wondered, half aggravated with them.

Mid-way to the back porch, Raegan slowed her steps. She felt the presence of something, or someone. She immediately thought of the Tillamooks. Every day, someone reported seeing the Indians moving ghost-like through the dimness of the thick forests. The thought of warring Indians close at hand had barely entered her mind when she heard the thud of racing hooves. Her mouth dry with fear, she wheeled and sprinted toward the barn, trying to call out to Jamie from a paralyzed throat. Then gravel was flying over her from sliding hoofs as a hand grabbed her hair and jerked her to her knees.

With terror-filled eyes, Raegan stared up at the fierce-looking, breech clout-clad Indian who jumped from the ragged pony's back. *Dear God,* she thought, her blood running cold, *I'm going to die at the hands of this savage.*

When the fierce-eyed brave jerked her head back, exposing the fine line of her throat, and reached for the knife at his waist, the desire to live loosened her throat. Her mouth opened and a piercing scream split the air as with a strength born of her desperation she grasped the red wrist of the hand that held the knife.

The power in her gripping fingers startled the brave. As he looked at Raegan in surprise, black smoke bloomed from a rifle, and a big hole appeared in the side of his face.

Raegan let loose one long, trailing scream as the Tillamook fell across her, blood spilling from his wound. Then Jamie and Star were beside her, Jamie flinging the dead Indian aside and then cradling her in his arms.

"It's all right, Raegan," he soothed her, rocking her back and forth as he would a child scared out of its wits.

Star, her small face anxious, took Raegan's hands and gently stroked them. When raindrops began speckling their clothes in darkening spots, she said, "We'd better get inside. It's goin' to pour any minute."

Jamie glanced down the valley at the approaching line of rain. "Are you all right now, Raegan? Can you walk?"

Raegan nodded, and with his assistance she rose to her feet. Her arms held by Jamie and Star, she ran between them toward the cabin. A beating rain came just as they gained the porch. "You two go on in." Jamie released his hold. "I'll join you as soon as I get rid of the Indian's body."

"What will you do with it, Jamie?" Star asked. "The others will be lookin' for him. If he's found here, they'll burn the cabin down, with us in it."

"They won't find the varmint here," Jamie spoke with convicition. "I'm gonna drag him down to the river and let the Platte carry him away." He jumped off the porch and sprinted through the rain to where the still body lay.

Inside the kitchen, as the rain beat a tattoo on the cabin roof, Star poured Raegan a cup of coffee and added a good amount of whiskey to it. "Drink this." She handed her the cup. "It will help calm your nerves."

Tears stung Raegan's throat as she swallowed the strong drink, but as it warmed her stomach she did feel a lessening of the tension that tightened her body.

"I wish Chase would get home," she said fretfully. "He's going to be soaked."

"Don't worry about Chase." Star poured herself a cup of coffee. "He's taken shelter somewhere. He'll be along when the rain stops."

"I expect you're right." Raegan took another sip of coffee, reassured by Star's reasoning.

Half an hour later, when Lobo scratched at the door, a relieved smile curved Raegan's lips. Chase wouldn't be far behind.

But when fifteen or twenty minutes had passed and there was still no sign of Chase, Raegan's worries returned. Why had Lobo returned home alone? Something had surely happened to her husband.

Jamie, who had returned to the cabin some time back and changed into dry clothes, was also worried. He kept his fears well hidden, however, as he pointed out to Raegan that his friend had more sense than the wolf. "Chase will remain in whatever shelter he's found until the storm is over."

Although only half convinced, Raegan said no more. She rose to look through the rain-streaked window, peering down the muddy trail leading down the valley. She couldn't shake the niggling dread that everything was not well with Chase.

Things were not well with Chase. They hadn't been for some time—not since he'd been sitting on Sampson on a small rise overlooking Liza Jenkins place.

When he could not scare up any game in the vicinity of his own cabin, he remembered the small herd of deer he'd often seen when he used to visit Liza. From her bedroom window, he had watched them graze in a small meadow abutting the forest about half a mile away.

Touching a heel to Sampson, he was soon concealing himself behind a large pine near the deers' feeding place. As he waited for one to appear, he recalled the hours spent with the widow and wondered why he had thought she was so good in bed.

His lips stirred in a slow, lazy smile. He hadn't had Raegan then to compare her with. His young wife satiated him as no woman ever had. Just a certain look from her across a room sent more passion racing through his blood than another woman's hands on his body could.

Chase broke off thinking about Raegan when he heard the clip-clop of a horse coming down the trail that led from Calvin Long's decrepit shack. He backed the stallion farther into the branches only moments before the squaw-man came riding by.

"So he's still nosin' after Liza," he said to himself, and wondered just how long their liaison had been going on. As far as anyone knew, the pair could have been carrying on even before Liza became a widow. *He* knew that no one man could be sufficient for the woman.

A broad grin widened his lips when Calvin tethered his horse, and Liza came flying out the cabin door, naked as the day she was born. From this distance he couldn't hear what was being said between the pair as Liza took Long's hand and pulled him into the cabin. He didn't have to imagine what was going on behind the closed door. He knew from past experience. Liza would be all over the man.

As Chase sat on in the still, hot air, patiently waiting to spot a deer, he became aware of the sullen black clouds building up to the north. If his quarry didn't come along soon, he was going to head for home. There was a lot of water in those clouds.

He looked down at the panting Lobo lying at Sampson's feet. The wolf was probably the reason he hadn't flushed any game all morning. He hadn't wanted Raegan's pet to go with him, but he'd had no choice. Once the big brute made up his mind to do something, there was no turning him from his course without shooting him.

Just as Chase caught sight of a deer stepping daintily out of the forest, lightning flashed and a roll of thunder rumbled through the hills. He tightened his knees on the stallion's belly, signaling him not to move, and brought his rifle up to his shoulder.

Sighting down the long barrel, he heard a twig snap behind him and the deer darted back into the shelter of the forest. Lobo gave a deep warning growl just as something hard and sharp pierced Chase's shoulder, its force sending him sidewise out of the saddle. In a split second he rolled to his feet, his right hand pressed to his left shoulder. The haft of a knife protruded from between his fingers.

Through pain-blurred eyes, he watched the Tillamook coming toward him, a tomahawk clenched in his hand. He shook his head, cleared his mind of everything but meeting the attack. Ignoring the blood that spilled down his arm and dripped off his palm, the fingers of his good arm touched the cold metal of his gun. When the Indian lunged at him with a ringing war cry, he grasped its handle as they fell to the ground in a fierce struggle for life.

Chase's bloody fingers kept slipping on the Colt as they rolled over and over, each seeking a vulnerable spot to use his weapon on. Chase found himself growing weaker by the minute as his blood continued to flow freely from his body. Just as he thought he'd spent the last of his strength, he managed to press the gun against the Tillamook's side and pull the trigger.

With a surprised look on his face and a soft sigh, the Indian flopped over on his back, his eyes staring sightlessly at the sky.

Chase lay helpless beside the dead man. The exertion of the fight had sent the blood pumping from his wound. He knew that if someone didn't come along soon, he'd bleed to death.

His last conscious awareness was the hard patter of rain filling the forest stillness.

"You'd best be gettin' home, Calvin," the Widow Jenkins said, stretching lazily, contented for the time being. She had exhausted herself with the man lying beside her. She wanted to sleep now, and wished her lover gone.

And Calvin Long was ready to leave. Liza had drained him. But he knew he would return tomorrow—after he'd pleasured his Indian wife. He had to keep her from becoming suspicious. Old Chief Wise Owl was her father, and he had no wish to get on the wrong side of that old savage.

"I reckon I'd better;" he answered. "This rain ain't gonna let up soon."

As he climbed into his clothes Liza, looked up at him, a salacious smile on her heavy lips. "Will the rain keep you from comin' over tomorrow?"

Calvin paused in the doorway, running his gaze over the wanton sprawl of her body. "I'll be here," he said before dashing out into the downpour and sprinting to his horse.

He was approaching the spot where Chase had watched him ride past when, through the falling rain, he saw two horses in the fringe of the forest. He recognized Chase's stallion immediately and knew that the hackamored pinto belonged to an Indian. He pulled his mount in and peered through the rain. What did it mean, these two horses, apparently alone, their tails turned to the lash of the rain? Did he want to get involved? he asked himself.

Curiosity made him turn his horse off the beaten trail and cautiously approach the mounts. He was almost on top of them before he noted the two fallen men.

At a glance, he knew the Tillamook was dead. Releasing a relieved sound, he swung to the ground and hurried to kneel beside Chase. He's dead, too, he thought, gazing at the chalk-white face. Nevertheless, he placed his fingers on the limp wrist, feeling for a pulse.

Finally he felt it, weak and slow.

Long sat back on his heels, studing the handsome face. The man was near death. If that flow of blood wasn't staunched soon, Chase Donlin was a goner.

Liza's lover had no liking for the trapper. The man was everything he would like to be. Besides that, Liza was crazy about him, had wanted to marry him. But Donlin had married another woman, and according to what he heard, damn near worshiped his beautiful young wife.

The speck of honor remaining inside the squaw-man would not let him ride off and leave the wounded man to die. Besides, there was a deep friendship between this man and his father-in-law. If the old Chief should ever learn that he hadn't given help to the trapper, he would see to it that his son-in-law would also die.

Grunting and staggering under Chase's dead weight, Calvin managed to struggle him across the mount's back, then climb on behind him. He nudged the mount and it started back towards the widow's cabin.

Liza was sitting at her kitchen table, having a cup of coffee after changing the bed linens. When she saw Calvin returning, her eyes narrowed on the limp and hanging arms. "Chase!" she exclaimed and jumped to her feet to fling open the door.

"What's happened to him?" she cried as Calvin staggered into the cabin, bent over from the weight on his shoulder. She stared at the blood dripping down Chase's arm, then glared up at her lover and demanded suspiciously, "Did you do this?"

"Of course not!" Anger and jealously rang in Long's voice. "A Tillamook done it. And while you're standin' there makin' false accusations, he's gonna bleed to death. And dammit, he's heavy as a buffalo."

Liza's face turned white at the word death. "Hurry, get him in the bedroom. We must stop the bleeding." She led the way to her room and swept back the top sheet.

With a heave of relief, Long dropped Chase onto the bed and, panting from exertion, turned and headed for the door. "I'll be goin' for Granny Pearson now," he said.

"No you won't." Liza's words were an order. "I can handle this wound as good as that gabbin' old woman. All I need is a lot of bandages to pack the wound." She ran from the room, returning within seconds, tossing a clean sheet on the bed. "Tear this in strips," she said, "while I go fetch a basin of water and a bottle of whiskey."

The irate man did her bidding, and when Liza

returned with the items she'd need, he said sullenly, "I'll be goin' after his wife and the breed now."

"No!" Liza glared up at him. "I need you here to help me. You have to pull the knife out, hold him down while I doctor him."

"His wife has a right to know, Liza," Calvin insisted.

Liza gave him a heated glower. "I told you, no. Now get over here and help me."

Chapter Fourteen

Chase roused when Calvin pulled the knife out of his shoulder and groaned when Liza poured whiskey over the wound. His eyes focused on the widow's face, and he wondered where Raegan was. It should be his wife tending him.

He lost consciousness again when Liza began packing the knife wound with the strips of sheet. A short time later, fever gripped him, growing stronger every hour.

Once, as in a dream, he felt hands caressing his body, fondling his manhood. He thought fuzzily that he could respond to Raegan's hot, coaxing hands, make love to her, even now. But he wasn't up to it after all. She would have to understand.

Toward morning, Chase's fever broke and he slept a natural sleep until almost noon the next day. When he opened his eyes, an exclamation of disbelief hissed through his teeth. What in the hell was he doing in Liza Jenkins's bed? He started to sit up, then fell back with a groan, his hand going to his bandaged shoulder.

It all came back to him—his fight with the Tillamook, the knife the Indian had put in his flesh. Calvin Long must have found him and brought him here.

"Liza!" he shouted, "where in the hell are you?"

"Right here, honey." Liza left off her contemplation of the rain and rushed to the bed. "How are you feelin'?" She sat down on its edge.

"I'm weak as a new-born wolf cub, but I feel good enough. How did I get here?"

"Calvin came across you while he was out huntin' and brought you to me."

Chase gave a grunt of derision at her lie. Hadn't he seen Calvin follow her into her cabin? He let her falsehood pass and asked, "How long have I been here?"

"Since around this time yesterday."

"Good Lord, Raegan will be out of her mind with worry. Unless . . ." He narrowed his eyes at Liza, "Unless Calvin took word to her. Did he?"

"Well no, honey." Liza lingeringly brushed a strand of hair off his forehead. "It's pourin' rain out there. It hasn't stopped for a minute."

"Dammit, woman, that's a miserable excuse." He brushed her hand away. "When's Long comin' back here?"

"Why, I don't know when I'll see him again." Liza stood up and, avoiding his eyes, began to straighten the bed covers. "Sometimes I see him ridin' by on his way to the village."

A contemptuous snort burst through Chase's lips. "You're lyin' through your teeth. A day don't pass by that he's not sneakin' down here. Practically everybody in these hills knows it."

"That's not true!" Liza tried to hold Chase's gaze as she made her denial. But the steady look he returned made her own waver. She looked away in resignation. "So what if he does? We're not hurtin' anybody." She turned her gaze back to Chase and said reproachfully, "You never visit me anymore."

Chase sent her an impatient look. "No, I don't, Liza, and I won't be in the future either. I love my wife, and I'm contented with her."

When Liza flounced over to the window with an angry swish of her skirt, he said in a more gentle tone, "You have no future with Calvin Long, Liza. Find yourself an unattached male and get married again."

Liza spun around, her eyes snapping. "I don't need you to tell me what to do, Chase Donlin. I'll do—"

A rap on the kitchen door cut off the last of her sentence. When she made no move to answer the knock, Chase called, "Come in, Long."

There came the sound of the kitchen door being opened, then closed, and shortly Calvin stepped into the bedroom, shrugging out of his dripping slicker. When he would have hung it on a peg, Chase spoke. "Long, I owe you for savin' my life yesterday, but I'd like to ask you for another favor. Would you ride to my place and tell my wife what has happened to me, and to come get me?"

The squaw-man gave a short nod. He shot Liza

a glance, relief and satisfaction on his face. When she refused to turn her head and look at him, he pulled the long waterproof coat back on and left the cabin.

Raegan awakened at dawn and lay still for a moment, listening to the heavy monotone of the rain pounding on the roof. Would it never cease? She had prayed last night that it would stop, that she and Jamie and Star could search for Chase without the hinderance of the blinding rain. Yesterday they hadn't been able to see more than a few yards ahead of them as they hunted until darkness drove them home.

"Maybe when we get back, we'll find Chase waitin' for us," Jamie had said, trying to buoy up her flagging spirits.

She had smiled weakly and replied that maybe he was right. But deep down, she knew he was wrong. Something had happened to her husband. A raging downpour wouldn't keep him away from her this long.

She had been right, of course. The only thing that awaited them was the empty cabin . . . and Chase's stallion.

Jamie had minutely examined Sampson and could find no evidence of foul play. There were no marks on the animal, and the saddle was tightly chinched. The big horse was, however, more nervous than usual.

"It's the storm," Jamie had assured her. "Thunder and lightnin' make animals uneasy. This rascal probably broke loose from wherever Chase tied him."

Raegan hadn't bothered to answer Jamie's claim. What was the use? They both knew he didn't believe a word he was saying.

She slid off the bed, wincing from stiff and sore muscles as she stood up. The three of them had been soaked to the skin when they returned to the cabin last night, with Star sneezing. In her concern for Chase, Jamie's worried look at the girl had barely registered with her. She wondered now how her little friend was feeling.

Jamie had breakfast on the table when Reagan walked into the kitchen, Star not far behind her. He smiled them a greeting as he took the coffee pot from the stove. "You girls eat hearty of these ham and eggs," he ordered, filling their cups. "We're gonna search every inch of these hills again, and not come back until we find Chase."

Raegan gave Jamie a weak smile and sat down in her usual chair. Chase's empty place across from her brought tears glimmering into her eyes. As Star helped her to an egg and a piece of meat, she prayed silently that today they would find her husband—and that he would be alive.

Jamie nudged her elbow. "Eat, Raegan."

Raegan reined the mare in on top of a hill and swept her eyes over the panoramic view. The rain had slowed to a drizzle, and it looked as if the clouds might dissipate and the sun shine again. She was bone-tired and weary of spirit. So far there had been no sign of Chase.

From her lofty spot, she could see most of her neighbors' cabins, including her own. She turned Beauty around and looked down at the village on the other side of the hill. There wasn't much activity going on in Big Pine, she noted, no doubt due to the rain. The trappers who usually roamed the single dirt street were either holed up at home or playing cards in the tavern. If Chase wasn't found today, their help would be enlisted. Chase was well liked by his peers and none would refuse.

Raegan turned her head to the left and could vaguely make out a small cabin sitting at the end of a long valley. She knew intuitively that Liza Jenkins lived there. She had wanted to go to the widow's yesterday, but Jamie had insisted it would be a useless trip, that it was impossible that they would find Chase there. Still, the thought kept returning to her that the woman would know something.

As she continued to gaze down at the cabin, trying to decide whether or not to ride down and question Liza and satisfy herself that Jamie was right, the cabin door opened and a man stepped outside. Her pulses leapt, then settled down. The figure was too small to be Chase.

The man disappeared from sight for a moment, then reappeared astride a horse. Raegan's eyes followed the course the mount took, turning Beauty around to keep horse and rider in view. After a moment she said in a hushed whisper, "It looks like he's riding to our place." When the rider kept the trail to the Donlin cabin, she was convinced. The man might not necessarily have news of Chase, but there was the off chance that he might.

She jerked the colt from its holster and fired

a shot into the air, a prearranged signal should any one of them come across some sign of Chase. Lifting the reins, she started Beauty down the hill. At the bottom she met Jamie and Star.

"There's a rider going to the cabin," she called out, not slackening her pace.

Calvin Long was about to step up on the porch when the three of them came thundering up. "You're a ways from home, Long," Jamie said, swinging to the ground. "What brings you down this way?"

Long looked at Raegan, who now stood beside Jamie. "Your husband was attacked by a Tillamook yesterday," he said baldly. "I brought him to Liza's place."

Raegan's face went deathly white, and Jamie gripped her arm to keep her from falling. "How badly is he hurt?" He asked the question she couldn't get past her lips.

"Not bad. A knife wound in the shoulder," Long answered gruffly. He didn't like the breed any more than he did Donlin. "We was worried at first. He'd lost a lot of blood before I found him."

"What about the Tillamook—did he get away?"

"No, he's still layin' where Donlin killed him."

Jamie frowned. "We'd better get rid of the body before his kin find him. It'll be an all-out war if they do."

Jamie could see from the startled look on Long's face that this fact hadn't occurred to him. "I'll go bury him in the woods right now." Calvin licked his fear-dried lips.

"How is Chase now?" Raegan asked anxiously, stopping Long as he was about to step off the porch.

"He's all right—weak as to be expected. He wants you to come get him." The last sentence Calvin tacked on was his own opinion. Chase had only said to let his wife know where he was, but Calvin wanted the trapper out of Liza's bed.

"Of course. We'll go right away," Raegan said. "Just as soon as we can change out of these wet clothes." She and Star stepped up on the porch.

"Hold on a minute, Raegan," Jamie called. "Chase won't be able to sit his stallion. While you girls change, I'll ride over to Ike's place and borrow his wagon."

"Should we wait for you?"

"No, you and Star go on. I'll met you at Liza's." Jamie sprang onto the roan, and with a jab of his heel, the horse cantered off. It took but a few minutes for Raegan and Star to get into dry clothes. Raegan locked Lobo in the cabin, then they, too, were racing away.

The fine drizzle stopped as the stallion and mare galloped along. The sun came out and shone hot, sending steam rising from the water-soaked earth, and perspiration popped out on the girls' bodies.

Liza, having passed by the kitchen window, saw Raegan and Star approaching the cabin. She muttered angrily under her breath, "I should have known she'd come hot-footin' over here."

She went to her bedroom door and glanced at the sleeping Chase, a crafty light coming into her eyes. She turned back then to watch the racing mounts come nearer and nearer. When they came to a plunging halt in the yard, she hurried into into her room.

"Let me check your bandages, Chase." She leaned over the bed, speaking fast in a high, unnatural voice.

Before Chase was fully awake, she was sitting on the bed, her body leaning suggestively over him. Chase grabbed her upper arms to push her away, growling that the dressing on his shoulder was fine. But Liza's strength was almost equal to his, and she refused to budge. When boot heels rang across the kitchen floor, she fastened her lips on his, stopping any other words he might have uttered.

When Raegan stood in the doorway, she saw what Liza intended her to see. Her husband holding a woman in his arms, kissing her passionately.

Raegan grasped the door frame, pain filling her green eyes, her vocal chords paralyzed. But there was nothing wrong with Star's voice. It rang out furiously. "What in the hell is goin' on here, Chase Donlin, you sneakin' rattlesnake."

Chase's body went rigid. Liza had deliberately set him up to cause trouble between him and Raegan. He fastened a none-too-gentle hand in Liza's hair and tore her lips off him. And she, a sham look of guilt on her face, sat up, making sure her robe slipped off one shoulder, plainly showing that she wore nothing else.

She gave Star a contemptuous look and sneered, "I heard you'd taken in another breed, Chase."

"You fat buffalo cow!" Star squealed and lunged for Liza.

Raegan shot out a hand and gripped her arm, holding her back. "Don't lower yourself to her level, Star," she said quietly. When Star reluctantly nodded, Raegan walked over to the bed. Chase met her searching gaze without shame or guilt.

"Well, Chase," she said finally, "what I just walked in on—was it what it appeared to be?"

Chase leaned up on his good arm, pain inching across his face as the wounded shoulder was disturbed. "I swear on my dead father's grave that it wasn't, Raegan."

Raegan looked at him another moment, then said, "I didn't think so. She turned cold eyes on Liza. "Where are his clothes? I'm taking him home."

"You can't do that!" Liza screeched. "He's too weak to sit a horse."

"You think she doesn't know that, blubber ass." Star moved to stand protectively beside Raegan, her hand on the hilt of her knife. "Jamie will be here any minute with a wagon."

Pure hatred shone in the glare Liza turned on the young girl. "It's not gonna help him, jolting around in a bouncing wagon."

"He won't bounce. Raegan will hold him in lovin' arms," Star taunted the livid-faced woman.

Her eyes narrow slits, jealous anger spurred Liza on. She took a step toward Star, hissing, "Listen, you dirty half-breed, keep your nose out of somethin' that's none of your business."

Star was ready to fly at Liza with clenched fists

when Calvin, who had entered the room unnoticed, spoke sharply. "It's none of your business either, Liza, what Mrs. Donlin does with her husband."

Liza swung furious eyes on Calvin, opened her mouth, then snapped it shut. From outside came the sound of creaking wagon wheels. She did not want to tangle with Jamie Hart.

Raegan was never so glad to see Jamie as when he came walking into the bedroom. She was beginning to think that she would have to physically fight the wild-eyed woman in order to take her husband home.

Jamie sensed immediately the tense atmosphere. One look at Raegan's face, Star's furious one, and Liza's red one told him everything he needed to know. He grinned unpleasantly at his long-time enemy and drawled, "What's wrong, widder woman? Don't you want to give Raegan her man back?"

Liza glared at her tormentor a moment, then wheeled and ran outside. Jamie gave a harsh laugh, then picked up Chase's buckskins that had been thrown over the back of a chair.

"Go get in the wagon, girls. I'll get Chase dressed and we'll be on our way."

As Raegan climbed into the back of the wagon, its floor covered with several inches of hay, and Star clambered onto the high seat, a pair of hate-filled eyes watched them. "You may have him now, missy," Liza muttered to herself, "but not for long, you won't."

Long helped Jamie settle Chase into Raegan's arms, then Jamie muttered, "Thank you, Long," before climbing up beside Star and picking up the reins. As they slowly rolled out of Liza Jenkins's yard, Raegan gently pushed Chase's head down on her shoulder, and just as gently smoothed the hair back from his forehead.

"Ah, my love." Chase sighed. "there were times when I thought I'd never see your lovely face again."

The breath stopped in Raegan's lungs. Had she heard Chase right? Had he called her his love? She had to know. She took his chin and turned his head so that she could look into his face as she asked breathlessly, "Did you just now call me your love, Chase?"

"Of course I did." He looked deep into her eyes. "Surely you know that I'm eaten up with love for you—that you're my whole world."

"Oh, Chase." Glad tears sprang into Raegan's eyes and ran down her cheeks. "I didn't know, not for sure. You never said so."

"I didn't?" Chase looked surprised. "I thought sure you knew. Didn't my actions tell you how much I loved you?"

Raegan laughed softly. "Your actions told me how you enjoyed making love to me. How did know that it wasn't just lust that keeps you at me half the night?"

"I could have the same thought." Chase looked at her soberly. "You've been drivin' me crazy the way you see-saw back and forth. At night a passionate lover, by day a cool, reserved lady with hardly a kind word or smile at me. I was beginning to feel like a whore, like you were using me."

"Oh, Chase." Raegan's laugh trilled out. "A man can't be a whore."

"The hell he can't," Chase growled. "Maybe not for money, but when he's besotted with a woman, he'd give everything he owned to get her to love him."

"It's a shame you wasted all that love-making," Raegan said in pretended sympthay. "If you'd have asked, I would have told you that I've loved you from the day you rode up to my shack in Idaho." She trailed a finger around his firm lips. "Are you sorry now that you wasted all that energy making love to me?"

"Wait until I get you home, I'll show you waste," he said, his voice husky with desire as he pulled her head down and covered her lips in a hungry kiss.

Jamie winked at a red-faced Star and tightened his grip on the reins, making the team go all the more slowly. The longer his friend had to wait to enjoy his wife's charms, the better he'd like them.

Chapter Fifteen

July had come and gone, and it was the middle of August. A tense uneasiness hung over the residents of Big Pine. The Tillamooks had stepped up their search for their woman, adding violence to their hunt.

A husband and wife living a few miles on the other side of Calvin Long's run-down shack had been tomahawked to death and fire set to their cabin. Ike Stevens and his family returned home from the village one day to find six of their hogs killed and one of their chicken houses burning.

There had been meetings at the village tavern, the men debating what to do about the threatening presence of the hostile Indians. Older, wiser heads pointed out that if they retaliated, they would be inviting a full-blown war with the tribe from across the Platte. They argued that they were too few to win a battle that would be fierce and bloody; many lives would be lost.

They went on to suggest that it was time Roscoe was tracked down. He should be brought back and made to confess to the Indians that he alone was responsible for the woman's abduction, that no other white man had touched their woman. A big, bearded man named Rafferty was hired to bring Roscoe in, but as the people of Big Pine waited, the arguments continued.

"It's plain our first plan is not workin'," said Sid Johnson, who had come in from his fur post. "The Tillamook haven't gone away like we thought they would."

"That's true," one of the young trappers agreed, "And even providin' we do run down that worthless piece of buffalo dung, what if the squaw ain't with him? If he's killed her, which in all likelihood he has, who's to tell the Tillamooks he's the guilty one? Certainly Roscoe will deny it."

So it had gone, back and forth, the young men insisting that the only way to handle the heathens was to shoot and kill every Tillamook they saw. They bragged that it would be easy to fight the savages. Didn't they have guns and rifles, while the red man only had tomahawks and bows and arrows?

The family men countered that there were three times as many Indians across the river, and they would win by numbers alone.

The two factions still argued about what to do, with nothing being settled. The elders cautioned the young to be patient a little longer, while Rafferty tried to find Roscoe.

* * *

Raegan sat on her big front porch, trying to catch a cool breeze off the river. As she slowly rocked, she tried to remember how hot the Idaho summers had been.

Much hotter than here in the Oregon hills, she decided after some thought. The part of the territory she knew best had been dry and dusty, with no greenery to break the ugly monotony of squalid mining camps that had always been home to her.

"I won't think of those times," Raegan said, pushing Minersville out of her mind. She would think only of the present, of how happy she was now. Chase had fully recovered from the Indian attack and was once again a figure of raw physical power. Their nights were filled with sweet, sometimes wild, love-making. But however it was, it was beautiful, a blending of their souls as well as their bodies.

Raegan thought of bedtime, starting a flurry in the pit of her stomach. Before falling asleep, they would exhaust each other, drawing the last drop of desire and passion from each other. Her eyes grew smoky as she remembered how before Chase entered her they always paid homage to each other. That was a part of the magic in their love-making. They had known that magic in the daytime too, she remembered with a dreamy smile. Often a need of each other would arise when they were away from the cabin. Then, chance of being discovered only lent more excitement to the moment.

A horse whinnied down in the pasture, and

Raegan opened her eyes. She straightened up and smiled, seeing Star and Jamie down by the river. Two fishing poles were stuck into the bank, their lines dangling in the water while the two fishermen lay stretched out on the ground.

Were they sleeping? she wondered. The pair were much alike. They could work like the very devil when necessary, then laze away an entire day.

Raegan rose, stretched, then stepped off the porch and walked alongside the cabin to the back yard. She lazily picked a scattered weed from the flower beds, then her aimless steps took her to the corral. Her mare stood beneath a tree in the corner of the pen, listlessly swishing her long tail at the horseflies settling on her rump. Chase's big stallion had gotten to Beauty one night, and she would be dropping her foal any day now.

A wry smile twitched her lips. Strange that Chase's Sampson had sired a baby in one mating, while his master hadn't after countless couplings. She'd have to point that fact out to him when he returned from the village . . . tease him a bit.

At Raegan's call, Beauty approached her slowly, her belly big with her foal. Raegan scratched the smooth spot between her soft eyes, crooning to her in the way the animal liked. Beauty stretched her neck over the pole fence, nudging Raegan's shoulder. But when the caressing fingers reached to scratch the rough, pointed ears, the mare suddenly backed away, her eyes rolling uneasily.

"What's wrong, girl?" Raegan soothed gently. "No one is going to hurt you."

The words had barely left her mouth when Raegan heard the stealthy footsteps behind her. She wheeled around, the blood freezing in her veins. Was she to be attacked by another Tillamook?

But it was no Indian slipping up on her. "Roscoe!" she tried to gasp, but no sound came out of her mouth. Before she could move, dash for the cabin, the fat man was upon her. He grabbed her wrists and, slamming her against the corral, leered down at her stricken face. "I been waitin' a long time to get you alone, little purty, to show you what a real man is like."

"Take your hands off me, you dirty scum!" Raegan panted, kicking out at his shins, connecting with one.

"Ouch!" Anger flared in Roscoe's eyes. "If you want it rough, you'll get it rough, you little hellcat." He fastened a hand around both wrists, then fastened the free one in the neck of her bodice. There came the sound of ripping material, then the feel of hot air hitting the part of her breasts exposed by the low cut of her camisole.

Raegan began to struggle in earnest then, twisting her body, again kicking out at the man who clearly meant to rape her. Her puny strength was as nothing against his. He simply threw his great weight against her slender body, rendering her helpless. "I'm going to faint," she screamed inside herself as Roscoe ripped away the camisole and fastened his thick, wet lips on a shrinking breast.

"You musn't faint!" the inner voice that usually derided her now urged her to be strong. "If you faint, you'll be completely at his mercy. He can do as he likes with you then. Fight!"

Raegan didn't waste her strength on screaming. It was doubtful if Jamie could even hear her. She began to struggle with a strength bolstered by anger and terror. Roscoe's hand on her wrists loosened a bit as an arousal pushed at the front of his trousers. She grabbed the moment, jerking free and giving the obese man a hard push.

Caught by surprise and befuddled by the lust that gripped him, Roscoe sat down hard. Raegan darted away, heading for the barn. If she could get inside and bar the heavy door, she would be safe until Jamie eventually heard her screams.

After what seemed an interminable time, but could have only been seconds, the barn door stood in front of her. Panting her relief, she sprang through it and slammed it closed behind her. Her shaking fingers clutched the wooden bar to slide it home. Then it dropped to the ground, and she went flying backwards, landing on her back with a hard thump.

And while she fought to catch her breath, Roscoe was throwing himself on top of her. In the back of her mind she wondered how he could have gotten to her so quickly, but foremost in her thoughts was the certainty that she had to somehow fight off the animal muttering obscenities at her.

She managed to roll from under him, at the same time trying to scream. She could not utter a sound. The breath had been knocked from her lungs. As her horror-filled eyes watched Roscoe crawl toward her, she saw from the corners of her eyes a pitchfork standing in a pile of hay. Just as he stretched a grimy hand to grasp her ankle, she called on her remaining strength and jumped to her feet. In one leap, she grabbed the three-tined fork.

Roscoe had gotten to his knees when she lunged at him. The sharp prongs caught him on the side of the face, and blood spurted from the three punctures. He screamed with pain as his hands went to his wounds. Raegan stared at him for a split second, then dropped the fork and ran screaming from the barn. She headed for the river, yelling Jamie's name at the top of her voice.

"Raegan! What is it?" Jamie had swept to his feet and was running toward her, pulling off his shirt as he took in her near-naked condition.

She threw herself against him, sobbing hysterically, trying to talk at the same time. All Jamie could make out was "Roscoe."

"You're safe now, Raegan." He stroked her back. "Try to calm yourself and tell me what's happened."

Finally, realizing that she was indeed safe now, Raegan gained control of her emotions, and after a long shuddering breath managed to relate what had happened.

"The lousy bastard," Jamie ground out when she finished. He handed the pale-faced Star his shirt and motioned her to help Raegan into it. "I'm sure he's well away from here by now, but I'm gonna see if I can find him. Star, help Raegan to the cabin and lock the door behind you."

"Be careful, Jamie." Star looked anxiously at him as she guided Raegan's arms through the garment's sleeves.

"Yes, Jamie," Raegan added her caution. "Roscoe is a sneak. He'll hide behind a tree and shoot you in the back."

Jamie's lips firmed grimly. Patting the gun at his hip, he said, "That one will never get behind this breed." He took off running toward the corral. Before Raegan and Star were halfway to the cabin, he was streaking away, riding the roan bareback.

"Who is this Roscoe?" Star asked, pouring a good amount of whiskey into a glass and handing it to Raegan.

Raegan took a long swallow of the amber-colored liquid. Roscoe had frightened her more than the Tillamook had. Maybe she was strange, but given the choice she would opt for death at the Indian's hand rather than be violated by the loathesome fat man.

After a second, smaller sip of the whiskey, Raegan was able to tell Star everything she knew about the man who had attacked her.

"Oh," Star exclaimed, her small face furious. "I hope Jamie finds him and cuts off his—"

"Exactly," Raegan cut off the rest of her heated exclamation.

Raegan was nearly back to normal when Star answered the door to Chase's knock. Raegan caught the teetering chair as she jumped to her feet and threw herself at him with a little wailing cry.

Chase's arms automatically opened to receive her, his surprised gaze taking in her tear-stained face. Holding her tight, he lifted a questioning look to Star. Where the irate girl related what had happened, an Indian word slipping in here and there, Chase's big body stiffened. "Jamie has gone after him," Star added.

"He'll not find the bastard," Chase grated. "I'll bet he's already beat it from these parts." he tilted Raegan's chin up so he could look into her eyes, "Did he . . . ?"

"No, Chase. I got away from him in time."

"Thank God." Chase hugged Raegan to him. The thought of the fat Roscoe violating his wife's delicate body brought bile rising to his throat.

"He hurt her breasts, though," Star announced tightly. "I saw the scratches on one when I put Jamie's shirt on her."

Chase's jaws clenched and a small tic beat in his cheek. Keeping an arm around Raegan's shoulder, he walked her toward the bedroom hall, saying over his shoulder, "I'm goin' to put Raegan to bed, Star. She needs to relax and sleep."

"Yes, you do that." A mischievous grin quirked the corners of Star's lips. She didn't know if Raegan would get any sleep, but she knew exactly how the big trapper would relax his wife. She was still much an innocent, but the noises coming from the Donlin bedroom every night gave her a good idea what went on within the four walls.

She thought of Jamie, and blushing a bright red, quickly pushed him out of her mind.

Chase led Raegan to the bed and began disrobing her. When she stood bare before him, he picked her up and laid her on the bed. She watched him move to the washstand and fill the china bowl with water. He picked up a washcloth and her bar of scented soap and carried everything to the bed.

He smiled down at her as he placed the soap and water on her nightstand, then sat down on the edge of the bed. Picking up the piece of soft flannel, he lathered it with the soap; then, squeezing out the excess water, he began to move the cloth over her breasts.

He bit out an oath when he saw the two long scratches on one white mound. He dropped the cloth into the water and took up the soap to roll it back and forth in his palms until they were liberally covered with lather. Raegan watched him as slowly, caressingly, he began to massage her breasts, his soap-slick hands sliding over and under them. When her nipples hardened and jutted out in peaks, he gently squeezed each one, then wrung out the washcloth and wiped away the suds.

"You are so lovely," he murmured, lowering his head to her breasts, hunger for her in his eyes.

With a half sigh, half groan, Raegan stroked his head as his lips drew a pebble-hard nipple into his mouth. She felt clean again as he moved his head to nurse the other breast—not only from the bathing he had given her, but from the cleansing of his mouth. He had taken away the profanity of Roscoe's slobbering lips.

When Chase lifted his head and looked deep into her eyes, she read the question in them. She wound her arms around his shoulders and whispered, "I'm fine . . . now."

He dropped a tender kiss on her lips, then stood up and got out of his own clothes. Raegan hungrily eyed the long, hard arousal standing up against his flat stomach. She gave him a sultry look, and when she opened her arms and legs, he came to her.

Out in the kitchen, Star grinned when there came the familar sound of rhythmic protests coming from the big fourposter. Knowing from experience that she would hear that particular sound off and on for no telling how long, she decided that she might as well get the stew going for supper.

Jamie arrived home a couple of hours later, just as an exhausted, though contented-looking Chase walked down the hall from the bedroom. "How's Raegan?" Jamie drawled with amused eyes as his friend dropped into a chair.

"She's sleepin'," Chase answered shortly, knowing that both young people were aware that he had been making love to his wife the better part of the afternoon. "I don't suppose you caught up with that bastard," he said, cutting short any more teasing.

Jamie shook his head. "I rode all over the hills and several miles down the valley. Didn't see hide nor hell of him."

"I figured as much. Roscoe knows these hills too well. It would be no trick for him to give anybody the slip. It would take an Indian to find his trail." Chase scratched Lobo's ears when the wolf came and sat on his haunches at his feet. "It's too bad I had this fellow with me today. He'd have torn that buzzard's throat out."

"Do you reckon the woman is dead and that's why he ventured back this way?" Jamie asked.

"It's likely," Chase answered. "His ever-ridin' lust would bring him out of hiding, lookin' for another unfortunate woman to abuse."

Star glanced out the window. The sky was dimming rapidly, and evening was almost upon them. She interrupted Chase and Jamie's conversation. "If you two want to wash up, I'll put supper on the table."

"Did you cook it all by yourself?" Jamie asked, a pretended misgiving in his voice.

"Yes I did." Star wheeled on him, her hands on her hips. Staring at him belligerently, she stated sharply, "I've been cookin' since I was ten years old."

"Cookin' what? Mud pies?" Jamie taunted, then adroitly dodged the soup ladle she flung at his head as he went through the door.

"That little girl is gonna really get her Indian up one of these days and scalp you if you keep on raggin' her that way," Chase warned the tickled Jamie as he joined him at the wash bench.

"Ain't she somethin'?" Jamie answered, a proud note in his voice. "Nobody's ever gonna put anything over on her."

"No," Chase agreed gravely, "not unless she loves that somebody. She'd be very vulnerable to the man she gives her heart to."

Jamie wondered if Chase was throwing him

a hint, warning him away from Star again. If he was, he was talking for nothing. That little spitfire wasn't about to give her heart to him. Hell, she backed away like a scared rabbit if he so much as touched her hand.

Supper was a quiet meal without Raegan's presence. When Star had inquired of Chase if she should call Reagan to supper, he had answered that right now, sleep was more important to this wife than food. "Her nerves are pretty raw right now," he'd added.

That remark led to the discussion of Roscoe. Where was he hiding? Was the Tillamook woman still alive? And that topic led to the Tillamook men. How safe were they to sleep at night with the warring braves prowling around? Their favorite cruelty to the white man was setting fire to his cabin, burning to death anyone inside it.

By the time the meal was eaten and the coffee drunk, it was decided that from now on when they retired at night, Chase and Jamie would take turns watching the cabin.

Chase and Jamie smoked their after-supper cigarette at the table, Jamie watching Star through narrowed lids as she cleared the table and washed the dishes. The swish of her shapely little rear end and the bounce of her perfectly shaped breasts brought his maleness to full attention.

"Forget it, feller," he told himself, crossing his legs to hide his condition from Chase.

The clock struck nine and Chase stood up. "I'll take the first watch, Jamie," he said. "I'll wake you up around midnight."

"Where will you be?" Jamie rose to his feet.

"Out in the barn, I guess," Chase answered after a thoughtful pause.

"Do you think that's a good idea?" Star frowned at Chase. "When Paw is huntin' deer in the early mornin' hours, he looks for the most uncomfortable spot he can find. He claims if a man gets himself all cozy settled, he might fall asleep."

Jamie looked at Star's serious little face and couldn't resist teasing her. "Would you advise us to climb a tree, then? The fear of fallin' and breakin' our necks should keep us awake."

Star heard the amusement in Jamie's voice but didn't rise to it as she usually did. She only answered, "And keep you alert, too."

"It's not a bad idea, you know," Chase said after Jamie stopped laughing, "and I'm gonna try it. That big old pine back of the barn will be easy to climb, and I remember as a kid I could see for miles around if I climbed high enough."

He picked up his rifle leaning against the wall next to the door. "I suggest you go to bed now, Jamie. Midnight will be here before you know it."

Jamie was leaning on a supporting post staring out into the darkness when Star stepped onto the porch for a breath of cool air. It was stiffling in the kitchen. And not much better out here, she realized, walking over to stand beside Jamie.

"Shouldn't you be in bed?" she asked. "Midnight is gonna be here before you know it."

"Yeah, pretty soon. I thought I'd walk along the river for a while. It's usually cool there." He slid Star a look from the corners of his eyes. "You care to go with me?"

Star looked over her shoulder to the lamp-lit kitchen. "I guess it'll be all right to leave Raegan alone for a while. Chase said she was sleepin'."

"She'll be fine." Jamie took her hand and led her down the porch steps. He grinned and remarked as they headed toward the river, "Chase is roostin' up there with the birds. He'll know if anyone comes around."

"I still say it's a good idea that he's up in a tree." Star gave Jamie's arm a whack with her hard little fist. "Paw knows about such things. He learned them from the Indians."

"Do you believe everything *Paw* tells you?"

"Yes I do. He's a wise old man."

"Did he tell you to beware of men?" Jamie's eyes teased her.

"You mean men like you?" Star bantered back.

"Yeah, I guess. Men like me."

"He said to be especially careful of breeds," Star teased now.

"You little devil." Jamie grabbed at her and missed as she swiftly eluded his hand. "He said that breeds are womanizers." Star ran down the path that was brightly lit by the full moon. "He says that they are only—" The rest of the sentence died in her throat as her foot slid on a hidden tree root. She flung out a hand, grabbing Jamie's arm as he laughingly overtook her.

Jamie's mirth died away, and Star stared up at the erratic pulse in his jawline. He gazed down at her a second, then with a groan and blind urgency he pulled her into his arms. He felt the tensing of her young body and whispered, "Please don't fight me now, my *match-squa-thi peshewa*."

For a moment Star leaned into Jamie, losing herself in the heat and hardness of his body. She pulled back then and asked in a trembling voice, "Are you playin' games with me, Jamie?"

Jamie gazed into the lovely little face raised to him. It was no game he played. He wanted her, had wanted her from the first time she called him breed. He hadn't realized it then, but he knew it now. He loved the wildness in her, the way her eyes could spit fire one minute, then become gentle when she looked at a baby animal or stroked Lobo's head with her small hand. She was everything he had ever wanted in a woman.

He forgot about Chase's warning, because it didn't signify. He would never dishonor Star Daniels. If she would have him, he'd marry her tomorrow.

His voice husky, his desire for her making it almost impossible to speak, he answered Star softly. "I'm not playin' at any game, Star. I want you so desperately that I hurt to the very depth of my soul."

"You will not love me, then leave me?"

"Never would I leave you. Only *Moneto* could ever make me go away from you."

"I am yours then," Star whispered and raised a slender hand to lay against his cheek, "for I feel the same way about you."

"You'll never be sorry, Star, I swear it to you," Jamie said huskily, his arms tightening about her. His mouth opened over hers in famished need, and when his hand cupped a small, perfect breast he could feel the wild beat of her heart.

In the warm, soft night they disrobed, Jamie spreading his shirt on the ground for Star to lie on. He came down beside her and took her exquisite little body into his arms. He felt her tremble and he asked softly, "Are you afraid of what is about to happen?"

"A little," her voice broke weakly. "It is somethin' I have never done before."

Jamie smiled at her innocent words, his chest tightening with his love for her. "Don't be frightened," he whispered, "It's going to be the grandest experience you've ever had."

He dropped his head between her breasts and gently drew a passion-hardened nipple into his mouth. Star gasped her pleasure as he suckled her and held his head close to her chest. Her body seemed to vibrate as he stroked a hand over her, moving ever closer to the dark triangle of hair that protected her virginity.

His probbing finger found her hot and moist, and he lifted his head to whisper as he slid a leg between hers, "I'm going to make you mine now, Star, for all time."

"Yes," she breathed, and covering her lips with his, her little cry of pain was captured in his mouth as he thrust inside her, breaking the barrier that had been there for sixteen years.

Later, when they lay in each other's arms, their hearts pounding, their breathing a harsh sound in the quiet air, Jamie leaned up and looked into Star's eyes. He saw neither embarrassment nor contrition in them. He gave her a hard kiss and said gently, "I expect we should get dressed and head back to the cabin."

"Yes," Star answered, sitting up. "Soon it will be time for you to relieve Chase."

Jamie helped her into her clothes, then, as he picked the pine needles out of her hair, he said huskily, "Tomorrow we will make our plans."

"Plans?" Star looked up at him uncertainly.

"Plans for our life together after we're married," Jamie answered, drawing on his buckskins. "We must decide which world we're going to live in. The white man's or the Indian's."

"Oh," Star said, then grew quiet. She knew where they would live. They would live with Paw. She smiled. There would be time enough to talk about such arrangements later. Right now, her heart was too full of happiness.

Chapter Sixteen

Two weeks passed with Chase and Jamie taking turns watching the cabin at night. They had seen no Indians and no sign of Roscoe, but the women were never left alone. It appeared that the same precautions were being practiced in other homes. Few men, and no women, were seen in the village these days. Big Pine was becoming a ghost town and the people asked each other when the stubborn Tillamooks were going to give in to the fact that no one there had their woman.

They waited eagerly for Rafferty to bring Roscoe in.

Meanwhile, Rafferty was closing in on Roscoe, although he didn't know it. But Roscoe knew. He had seen the burly, bearded man from the cave where he and the woman were holed up. He could see him now, off in the forest, moving slowly along, his eyes on the ground searching for signs. It would be but a matter of time before he found the cave.

Roscoe moved back into the dim interior, his gimlet eyes glittering like those of a trapped animal. He was hungry; he hadn't eaten in two days. He hadn't dared leave his place of concealment to hunt for game. Luckily, a spring ran across the back of the cave, and he at least had water. The woman moaned, and he sprang at her, delivering a sharp kick to her leg.

"Shut your yap, you red bitch," he growled, "or I'll cut your damn tongue out." He looked anxiously over his shoulder, afraid that Rafferty had heard the woman. But it remained quiet outside, and when he crept to the cave's opening and peered outside, he saw Rafferty walking away from the vicinity of his hiding place.

But the fat man knew that he was safe only for the time being. It was known in the village that their best tracker never gave up on whatever prey he was after. "I've got to get the hell away from here," he muttered. He would leave Oregon altogether. He would find a boat or a canoe and paddle down the Platte as far as he could go.

"And I hope the Tillamooks swarm over the village and kill every bastard there." Without a glance at the moaning woman, knowing that she would soon die without food, he left the cave on foot. His horse had wandered away the day after he had visited the Donlin place.

The woman, having picked up some English from her captor, knew that Roscoe wouldn't return. She began a slow crawl toward the narrow opening, praying that she would find someone who would help her.

It was an evening in the last days of August when Chase prepared to climb the big pine and take up his watch. He grabbed a tree branch, started to pull himself up among the branches, then paused. He had heard a low moan coming from the barn. He froze, his head cocked, listening intently. Had the sound of pain come from a woman? It had sounded feminine, but what if it had really been that of a man pretending—a Tillamook trying to lure him out in the open where a well-aimed tomahawk could split his skull.

While he hesitated, trying to make up his mind, the moan came again. This time it was stronger, and definitely that of a woman in distress. His first thought was that Roscoe had the Indian woman in the barn and was abusing her in some manner.

His hopes high of capturing the man to take him across the river and make him admit his crime to the Tillamooks, Chase crouched low and moved from beneath the pine. Then, as quickly as he could in his stooped position, he ran across the moonlit stretch of land to the dark bulk of the barn. He leaned his ear against the wall, alert for any sound inside.

For several seconds, he heard nothing. Then a long, drawn-out moan of intense pain drifted through the crack where his cheek rested. He straightened up. There was a woman in there, and as far as he could tell, she was alone. A neighbor woman? Maybe one who had been taken prisoner by some Tillamooks and had managed to escape them?

His hand on his Colt, just in case the woman wasn't alone, Chase ran alongside the building until he came to the door that stood open. He darted in and stood to one side so he would not be silhouetted in the open doorway, accustoming his eyes to the deeper darkness. He had no way of knowing what awaited him in the shadows.

A rustling of hay and a keening wail brought his eyes swerving to the stall at the end of the barn. He moved on silent feet until, standing on his toes, he could stare down into the enclosed space.

Chase recognized the Tillamook woman immediately. She lay on her side, her knees drawn up, making little mewling noises. After a careful look to see if Roscoe might be hiding somewhere, he swung open the stall door and knelt down beside the woman. When he laid a hand on her shoulder, a frightened cry escaped her. When he left his hand where it was, she rolled over on her back, staring up at him out of wild eyes.

"Good Lord!" Chase's eyes looked a little wild too as he stared at the woman's swollen stomach. "I'll not hurt you," he said gently. "I'm just gonna carry you to my cabin. This is no place to have your baby."

The woman's pain-filled eyes searched his face, and Chase thought he saw recognition in them. At any rate, she nodded her assent. He carefully scooped her up in his arms, thinking that she was nothing but skin and bones, that she weighed less than a hundred pounds, baby and all.

He reached the cabin with his feather-weight burden and kicked the heavy door. When he heard chairs scraping and Star give a startled yelp, he called out, "It's me. Hurry, let me in."

There came the scrape of the inside bar being lifted, then Jamie stood staring at the poor creature in Chase's arms. "What the hell?" he exclaimed as Chase brushed past him, the woman's face contorted in pain.

Raegan's hands flew to her mouth. "It's the Tillamook woman!"

"And about to give birth any minute," Chase said grimly. "Where shall I put her?"

"Put her in my room." Star ran down the hall and flung open her door.

Chase lay the laboring woman on the bed, then turned to the others crowded in behind him. "Do either of you girls know anything about birthin' a baby?"

Raegan and Star shook their heads helplessly. Neither had ever been around a baby, much less helped one into the world.

Three pairs of startled eyes jumped to Jamie when he said in businesslike tones, "I know how to go about it. I watched my grandmother deliver a few when I was a youngster."

"You were allowed to watch?" Chase looked at Jamie, doubt in his eyes.

An embarrassed red spread over the young man's face. "No one knew I was watchin'. My grandmother would have skinned the hide off me, had she known."

"What an ornery teenager you were," Raegan rebuked him, "But thank God that in this instance you were."

Jamie grinned at Raegan, then became very serious. "Boil me a big pot of water, find some strong thread, and I'll need a lot of clean rags—white ones if you have them."

As Raegan and Star hurried from the room, he called after them. "And Raegan, I may need your help. I think it would comfort her to have a female around."

Raegan nodded, and as she and Star left the room, she said to Star, "You go heat the water while I find the thread and tear up a sheet."

At first Raegan was embarrassed when Jamie pulled the suffering woman's dirty doeskin shift up past her waist, exposing her thin, bruised legs, bony hips, and contorted stomach. Her face became as red as the beets she had dug out of her garden yesterday when Jamie, after scrubbing his hands with soap and hot water, made a through examination of the expectant woman.

But when she saw the worried seriousness on his face as he gently pressed the woman's stomach, then just as gently probbed her private parts with a finger, she knew he was doing what a doctor or a mid-wife would do. She thanked God that Jamie Hart was there.

Raegan, doing what she could to ease the woman's suffering, bathed her face and several times lifted her head to sip at a glass of cool water. She had also brought in a bowl of clear chicken broth, and the woman had swallowed it so fast that tears had sprung to Raegan's eyes.

"God knows the last time she had anything to eat." Jamie said, his own eyes damp.

When the woman began moaning in one long continuing sound, Jamie made a second examination. When he straightened up, he said, "She'll deliver any time now. The baby is small, and thankfully it's comin' out head-first."

He brushed the sweat-damp hair off the soon-to-be mother. "Poor soul," he murmured. "She's hemorrhaging and she's half starved." His tone said it didn't look good for the woman.

Five minutes later, Jamie said in hushed tones, "Here it comes. It's about over."

Raegan watched with hypnotic fascination as a small head covered with short black hair appeared between its mother's thin, bruised legs. She held her breath when narrow shoulders followed, then stopped.

Jamie darted a look at the woman's face and saw that she was too weak to bear down, to push the baby out. He very gently supported the tiny head and shoulders and eased the baby from her body. "A boy!" he whispered, almost in awe as he looked into Raegan's sparkling eyes.

He looked back down at the infant when it made its first weak mewling cry and exclaimed softly, "Good Lord, he's pure Indian. She must have been with child when Roscoe took her."

Jamie busied himself with tying off the cord, and Raegan knelt at the new mother's head. Holding her thin hands, she said gently, "You have a boy."

A leap of joy shone in the black eyes a moment before they began to glaze over. "Promise." She tried to squeeze Raegan's hands for emphasis, "take Papoose . . . to father . . . He chief . . . of . . . tribe."

Raegan's startled eyes jumped to Jamie's worried face. "No wonder the Tillamooks are so determined to find her."

Jamie gazed down at the mother and child. "And here we stand with that Chief's prince . . . and his dead wife," Jamie said, his face grim.

"Oh, Jamie, are you sure?" Raegan cried.

"I'm sure." He gently closed the staring eyes. "She died with her last breath telling you to take her son to Tillamook land." When tears surged to Raegan's eyes, he squeezed her shoulder in sympathy. "It's hellish, I know, but we've got to think of the baby now. He's got to be cleaned off and wrapped up in something. And fed as soon as possible. He's awfully weak and may not make it either."

Raegan jumped to her feet just as the door opened and Chase and Star entered the room. "We heard the baby cry and figured it was all over," Chase said.

"It's over for good as far as the woman is concerned. She bled to death," Jamie said tiredly.

Star let out a small cry, and Chase asked, "What about the baby? Is it gonna make it?"

"I don't know." Jamie stretched his stiff back. "He's awfully weak, but I'm hoping he's got the same determination to live that his mother had." He watched Raegan bathing the infant. "I don't know how in the hell we're gonna feed him, though."

Chase remembered old Daniel's story about

how he had given nourishment to Star when she was a baby. "Try to spoon some weak sugar water into him until I get back," he said on his way to the door. "I'll return within the hour."

As Chase rode toward Chief Wise Owl's village, he wondered what excuse he could give the old chief for wanting a woman's false nipple. No one else must know about what had just happened in his cabin.

He couldn't believe his good fortune when, at the edge of the village of wigwams, Sampson almost trod on the young woman Chase had saved from the lusty preacher. She recognized him as he climbed out of the saddle. After asking after her health, he explained his reason for the late-night visit.

She listened somberly and nodded when he finished speaking. "I'll be right back," she said, and darted away.

Chase watched her disappear into a wigwam, then within minutes she was back, thrusting a small, soft object in his hand. "It belongs to my aunt," she whispered. "She'll not miss it. She has others. My poor relative never has enough milk for her babes."

"I deeply appreciate this," Chase said, "but I would ask another favor of you."

"And what is that, friend?"

"That you not tell of my visit tonight, that we will share another secret."

"The favor is given, Chase Donlin," the young woman said quietly and walked away from him.

Chase swung onto the stallion's back again, satisfied that none of tonight's events would ever pass the woman's lips. Seldom did an Indian break a promise, and never to a friend.

Twenty minutes later, Chase raced up to his cabin. He hurried inside the kitchen and smiled at the three people sitting around the table. "Ever see one of these?" he asked, tossing the doeskin nipple on the table before Jamie.

A slow grin spread across Jamie's face as he picked up the cone-shaped object. "Hell, yes," he said. "I don't know why I didn't think of it. Where did you get it?"

"From a friend," was all Chase said.

"What is it?" Raegan asked, looking curiously at what Jamie held in his hand.

"It's a make-believe woman's nipple," Star exclaimed. "Paw fed me my milk through one of them when I was a baby."

"Well then, wildcat, you know what to do with it, don't you?" Jamie teased.

Before Star could give him a rude rejoinder, Raegan said, "Well I don't know what to do with it."

Star explained its use and Jamie added, "Water the canned milk down some. If he gets diarrhea, he'll never make it."

As Raegan and Star prepared the milk in an empty whiskey bottle, much like the one that had held Star's goat milk, Jamie looked at Chase and said soberly, "We're in deep trouble, Chase. The father of the baby is a Tillamook chief."

"Are you sure?" Chase gaped at him. "It's not Roscoe's?"

"As sure as sure can be. The little fellow is pure Indian." And while Chase was digesting that piece of news, Jamie added, "The woman asked Raegan to take the baby to his father."

"Well, she sure as hell isn't going to," Chase said vehemently. "She'd never get away from that village alive."

Jamie dropped the subject, having the same sentiments. A short time later, Chase, Jamie, and Star watched Raegan put the leather nipple to the baby's mouth. Instinct and hunger parted the almost blue lips. Great sighs of relief left four throats as the small lips moved eagerly, drawing in the infant's first nourishment.

Raegan felt as though she was holding a bundle of rags, so light was the baby as she set the rocker into motion. Jamie had said he'd be surprised if the baby weighed four pounds. As Chase and Jamie discussed what to do with its mother, Raegan cuddled the little one to her breast, crooning to him softly.

"My grandmother once told me that the Tillamooks believe that the land of the dead is located somewhere to the west," Jamie said. "When a person died he was put into a plank box, then placed in a canoe. Then another canoe is inverted over the first, and they're wrapped together with wide strips of rawhide."

"I hate to give up our canoes." Chase frowned. "Mine is only a year old."

"Don't worry about it." Jamie grinned. "Old Wise Owl has them hidden all up and down the Platte. Later on tonight, I'll just help myself to a couple. He'll never miss them." After a brief pause, he asked, "Where will we take the body?"

As Chase looked thoughtful, gazing at the

dead woman, Raegan said, "Somewhere pretty, Chase." She was remembering the ugly spot Meg Jones had chosen for her husband. "She deserves a peaceful place."

"Yes she does, and I've thought of the perfect place. There's a small valley about five miles due west past Chief Wise Owl's village. She can lie in peace there."

He rose and walked over to Raegan to look down on the sleeping baby. The small lips had lost their bluish tint and were now a pale pink. It looked as if the little one would make it. He touched the silky head, then smiled at Raegan. "You look real good with a baby in your arms, wife."

Raegan heard the yearning in his voice. She, too, would like to have a baby; she dreamed of it often and felt sure in her heart that some day she would conceive. And that was why, she told herself, she must be careful not to become too attached to the little mite in her arms. There was also the fact that the child was a full-blooded Tillamook and must somehow be handed over to his father.

Jamie approached her and Chase. "Raegan," he said, "Do you think you and Star could bathe the woman, maybe put a pair of Star's buckskins on her?"

"Yes of course, Jamie." Raegan stood up. "I'll put the little brave on our bed and get right to it."

"You'd better put Chase's slicker under him if you don't want to sleep on a wet bed tonight." Jamie grinned at her.

"That reminds me," Raegan said, "One of you will have to go to the village tomorrow and buy some white flannel yardage. Five yards should do it. I have to make this little fellow some clothes."

"I'll go," Chase said, "right after Jamie and I take the woman's body away."

Raegan and Star bathed the bruised and battered body of the Tillamook woman, tears running down their cheeks. As Star towel-dried the long black hair, she wondered out loud why some men were so cruel. What made them beat defenseless women?

"I don't know, Star." Raegan slid the buckskin trousers up over the thin hips. "That awful Roscoe is the first one of his kind I've ever encountered."

"I've never met any like him," Star said, relief in her voice. "I'm not sayin' that Paw's friends ain't rough. Some of them might get drunk and slap their woman if she nags him, but I've never heard of any treatin' their womenfolk like this one has been treated."

"Could be your grandfather never let you know about such men," Raegan pointed out. "I've a feeling he sheltered you from the harsher aspects of life."

"That could be," Star answered thoughtfully. "He's always very careful about who comes around me."

"There, now." Raegan straightened up from bending over the woman. "What do you think, Star?"

"I think she looks real nice, Raegan," Star answered.

"And peaceful," Raegan said. She laid her hand over the cold, crossed ones and whispered, "Somehow I'll see that your son gets to his father."

Chapter Seventeen

The near-dawn sky was overcast as Chase and Jamie rode away from the cabin, the canoes holding the Indian woman's remains resting on a travois. Jamie's roan dragged the contrivance behind him, for Sampson would have no part of the two poles that occasionally nudged at his heels.

As they moved deeper and deeper into the thick forest, moving around trees, both men cast nervous glances around them. Both were hopeful that the woman's relatives weren't up and around yet. It they should be caught with her body, there would be no escaping death. It would be painful to the extreme, and slow in coming.

"Let's step up our pace a little," Jamie said. "Daylight will be here in another hour."

After ascending and descending another hill, the men came upon a small, tree-studded valley.

It was beautiful and serene, the gray of approaching dawn emphasizing the green of pine, the pale brown of pine needles. As Chase and Jamie placed the canoe-coffin between two trees, hidden beneath the interwoven branches, the sun rose.

Chase laid a palm on the top canoe. "Rest in peace, Tillamook woman," he said softly, then climbed back onto his stallion.

Jamie mounted his roan, and as they rode away from the lonesome little valley, he said, "She'll rest in peace when Roscoe receives Indian justice."

The sun was a couple of hours high when, tired and bleary-eyed from lack of sleep, they rode up to the cabin. Star came running out to put the horses in the barn and tend to them, and Raegan had a pot of coffee waiting.

"Did everything go well?" she asked as they dropped into chairs and watched her fill their coffee cups.

Chase nodded. "I don't think anyone saw us. It was quiet in Wise Owl's village, and we didn't see any sign of Tillamooks." He yawned widely, then took a long swallow of his coffee. "I'm gonna catch a couple hours sleep, then I'm goin' over to Granny Pearson's cabin and bring her here to stay with us until this Indian scare is over."

"But you tried to talk her into that before, and she'd have none of it," Raegan reminded him. "She said there wasn't an Indian alive she couldn't handle."

"She's a stubborn old bit," Jamie said, affection for the fiesty old woman in his voice. "What makes you think she'll be willin' to come home with you now?"

"She won't be willin', but she'll come, even if I have to hog-tie her and throw her across that broken-down mule of hers. It's too dangerous for her be livin' alone away out there by herself."

Chase finished his coffee and stood up. He curved his hand around the back of Raegan's neck. "I'm gonna go to bed now," he said, then gave his wife a wicked look. "You gonna come tuck me in?"

Raegan blushed a deep red, sensing that Jamie and Star, who had just returned from the barn, were watching her with amusement. Blast Chase, he wasn't at all discreet about wanting to make love to her. She should be used to it by now. Avoiding the knowing looks from the two young people, she rose and walked ahead of her randy husband, leading the way to their bedroom.

When Chase closed the door behind them and pulled her into his arms, the scolding words on her lips died away. She said instead, "Are you sure you want me to go to bed with you? You must be awfully tired."

He bucked a full arousal against her pelvis. "Does that feel like it?" he whispered against the corner of her lips.

"Well, I don't know," she teased. "Seeing is believing, and I haven't seen anything yet."

With a rougish look in his eyes, Chase unlaced his buckskins and freed his rigid maleness. "There now, take a look."

"Oh yes, quite handsome." Raegan stroked a finger down the stiffness jutting out at her.

Chase shivered, then said in a husky voice, "Now that you've mentioned it, I am a little tired. If you don't mind, you can do all the work this time."

It took but a minute for them to get out of their clothes and fall into the yet unmade bed. They had already aroused each other to fever pitch with their touching and innuendos, and when Chase moved onto on his back, Raegan climbed astride his hips. His long shaft throbbed against her belly and she bent over, and taking its head in her mouth, she drew on it a minute before sliding it inside her hot moistness. She leaned forward then until her breasts hung over Chase's mouth. When, with a deep groan, he drew a nipple between his lips, she began to move on him, lifting and driving in rhythm with his drawing lips.

In the kitchen, Star and Jamie looked at each other when the tell-tale noises floated down the hall. And though their lips curved in an amused smile, there was a longing in their eyes. "Damn that Chase," Jamie said, a slight resentment in his voice, "In there gettin' pleasured by his woman while I have to go to bed, leavin' my woman sittin' in the kitchen."

He stood up and drew Star into his arms. "We'll go down by the river this afternoon," she soothed him when he released her lips from a long kiss.

True to his word, Chase brought Granny Pearson home with him. He hadn't had to hog-tie her, nor did she come kicking and screaming. But there had been a belligerent look in her bird-like eyes, and in the two weeks she'd been at the Donlin cabin that look hadn't quite left them. She let Chase know that there was a rift in their friendship by not talking to him unless she forgot for a moment that she was mad at him. With Jamie, she was her usual herself—affectionately cross.

Much to everyone's relief, she and Star took to each other right off. Raegan and Chase had had some reservations there. If the old woman snipped at Star, she would receive the same treatment. When the two got along like sugar and cream, Jamie laughingly remarked that it was obvious they were two of a kind, ornery little critters.

Granny had taken to the baby also. "Where did you get this skinny little papoose?" she asked, stroking the baby's cheek with a gentle, crooked finger.

An uneasy silence fell over the room. No one had remembered that they would have to explain the baby's presence. It was Star's agile mind that came up with an answer.

"He belongs to Jamie's cousin. There is sickness in their village, and the little one's father brought him to Jamie until it is safe to bring him home."

And while everyone held their breath, waiting to see if the shrewd old woman would believe the explanation, she studied the baby's face and remarked, "I can see the resemblance. He looks a lot like you, Jamie."

Everyone managed not to laugh out loud, but if Granny had looked at them, she would have seen the suppressed mirth in their eyes.

"But I wish she'd stay out of my kitchen," Raegan muttered as she moved about her dying garden. She was so tired of hearing, "I think you need a pinch more salt on the meat. The stew tastes a little bland, why don't you add more onions? You make your corn bread too thick. I like to spread it thin in the pan. Are you sure them potatoes are cooked enough to mash?"

She bent over to cut the dried stem of a pumpkin, then carried it to the growing pile of the yellow vegetables. Later Chase and Jamie would carry them to the barn and bury them in the hay up in the loft. *I know it's unchristian of me at such a time,* Raegan thought, *but I wish it were only Chase and I living together.* There was always someone under foot, and the cabin was beginning to bulge at the seams from so many of them. Already Jamie had been banished to the barn so that Granny could have his bed. Sometimes Raegan wished that she and Chase had taken over the hay. Granny had even put a damper over Chase's love-making. Because of the threat of the old woman's caustic tongue should she overhear them, he held back, taking away a lot of the pleasure the previous abandonment of his body used to bring her.

"Well," her inner voice pointed out, "there's nothing you can do about the situation now, so put it out of your mind. Think about something else."

She'd just do that, Raegan thought and let her gaze wander over the surrounding hills. Each day she fell more and more in love with them. Her eyes left the distant grandeur then and lighted on the back yard. Chase and Jamie had cut cord after cord of wood and stacked them between the trees that grew close to the cabin.

She smiled wryly. Much of their labor was already being put to use in the big fireplace. The nights were chilly now, for September was coming to an end, October only a week away. In the early mornings, frost shone on the grass, and Chase had predicted that before long the Platte would be skimmed with ice. "Winter will be upon us before we know it," he had added.

Let it come whenever it's ready, Raegan thought contentedly. The Donlins were ready. She smoothed a palm over her flat stomach. She was almost certain she was in the family way. She had missed her monthly, an unusual occurrence. She had always been regular, almost to the day.

She whispered a little prayer that it was so. For despite the strict orders she gave herself, she was becoming attached to Boy, the name they had all settled on until the father could name the little one himself. She gave a deep sigh and walked toward the cabin. Somehow, some day, the child must be taken across the river. And soon, before the snows came.

But how to get the little one to his father, she did not know. The Tillamooks still roamed the forest and were still a danger to one and all. Rafferty had returned with the news that he had been unable to find any trace of the fat man. "But I haven't given up on the bastard yet," he had growled, much put out that Roscoe had managed to elude him and that his perfect tracking record would have a strike against it. "I'm gonna pack myself some grub and search a different area."

Raegan prayed that the big man would be successful in finding his prey, for the young trappers could not be held back much longer. Trapping season was fast approaching, and they had no intention of giving up up their source of livelihood or having to watch their backs as they ran their lines. The evil Roscoe's ears must have rung with the threats made on his life, the dire things that would be visited on him before he died.

Raegan turned her head in the direction from which Star's laughter trilled from along the river. "Thank you, God, for small mercies," she murmured. Evidently the girl had gotten over her quarrel with Jamie.

Star had ignored Jamie as if he didn't exist ever since the four of them had gone to the Jones place day before yesterday to help Meg and young Johnny winterize their cabin. Sitting down on the porch, Raegan recalled that day.

She hadn't wanted to go, and had said so the night Chase remarked that he and Jamie had made plans to give their neighbor a hand tightening up their decrepit dwelling and that she and Star should come along too.

"Aw, come on, honey," he had coaxed. "It will do you good to get away from the cabin for a day. Granny can stay with Boy, and we'll leave Lobo with her. Between him and her sharp tongue, she'll come to no harm." When she had still demurred, he had pointed out, "You won't be able to go anywhere when the snows come." She had finally given in only to please him.

The next morning, shortly after breakfast, the four of them had ridden off, Chase leading and Jamie bringing up the rear. Each man kept a hand on his thigh, only inches from Colt or rifle should the occasion arise where they had to reach a weapon in a hurry.

It was a beautiful sunny day, and Raegan wondered if there was a more beautiful spot in the world than this remote, sparsely settled wilderness. She left off her musing as, on the underside of a hill, the Jones home stood a short distance away. When they pulled reins in the debris-filled yard, Meg stepped out of the cabin and stood surveying them suspiciously. When Chase called a genial greeting, she merely nodded her head and muttered, "Howdy."

When they weren't invited to dismount, Raegan whispered, "We should leave. The woman doesn't want us here." She remembered how rude and unfriendly Meg had been to her and Star the day her husband had been buried. She had only talked to Chase and Jamie, and that mostly to refuse any help from them.

But Chase paid no attention to the woman's displeasure at their appearance. He swung to the ground and flipped the reins over an old hitching post that was ready to fall to the ground. With a no-nonsense look on his face, he said, "Meg, winter will be here soon, and Jamie and I have come over to give you a hand tighten' up the cabin and layin' in a supply of wood."

When Meg began gruffly denying that she and her family needed any help in that department,

Chase dismissed her words with a wave of his hand. "We all need help at some time in our lives. If one day I should come to you for assistance, would you turn me down?"

"Well, of course not." Meg frowned at him. "But I don't know how the likes of me could help Chase Donlin."

"You never know, Meg. There are many ways in which a person can help another. And so, you stubborn woman, deep down you know that one lone woman and a teenage boy need a helpin' hand occasionally. Why don't you be a friendly neighbor and let us help you?"

"He's right, Meg." Jamie swung to the ground and stood beside Chase. "why are you bein' so all fired stand-offish? I know that I take any help that comes along. I'm not proud."

"Well, I ain't proud either." Meg gave him a hard look. "I just think that me and the youngins' can handle it."

Young Johnny stepped out on the stoop, his two older sisters slouching along behind him. "We could use a little help, Maw," he said tentatively. "We've been so busy with the crops, everything else has piled up on us. I don't know as we've got time to fix up proper for the winter."

"And we dang near froze to death last winter," Fanny, the oldest daughter, added to Johnny's argument, her eyes hungry on Chase. "If you think back, you'll remember that the snow blowed through the cracks, coverin' the bed and floor."

"Hush up!" Meg turned on her daughter, her face beet-red from embarrassment. "Get back in the house and finish feedin' the youngins' their breakfast." Raegan realized suddenly that cantankerous Meg Jones was a proud woman and that her living conditions were cutting that pride to pieces. There had been a time, she suspected, when this woman had led an entirely different existence, a life where she had been carefree, loved, and protected by loving parents. Then, over the years, she had married two different brutal men who had turned her into a bitter, broken woman.

But a bit of spirit had lived on in her, Raegan's eyes saw as they moved over Meg's angular body. Her patched dress was clean, and her gray-streaked hair had been neatly brushed into a bun at her nape. No longer brow-beaten by Henry Jones, she was slowly pulling herself up out of the black pit of hopelessness he had dug for her.

"Well, Meg said crossly, "If you insist, I'm obliged."

Chase poked Jamie in the ribs, taking his grinning attention away from Fanny, who stared openly at his crotch. "Stop oglin' Fanny and let's get started."

Jamie, always ready to tease, gave Fanny one of his wicked winks before turning to follow Chase. As he walked past Star, still seated on her horse, she gave him a hard kick in the rear.

"What was that for?" he demanded, rubbing the spot where her foot had connected.

"Figure it out for yourself," Star retorted, and to Raegan's surprise and Jamie's disbelief, she leaned down and gave him such a swat on the back of his head that his hat fell over his eyes.

"You little brat, I'm gonna whale the daylights out of you." Jamie reached to haul her out of the saddle, but Chase's roar brought his hands reluctantly to his sides.

"Can't you two be together for ten minutes without goin' for each other's throat?" Chase stamped over to them. Star dropped her head and Jamie stalked away after giving Star a look of retribution. Chase shook his head in disgust as he turned to Raegan. "I thought they'd been gettin' along better," he said.

"They have," Raegan answered. "Star started this fight because she's jealous. She didn't realize that Jamie was just having sport with Fanny. She believes he was flirting with her."

"Do you think the wild child is fallin' for Jamie?" he grinned as he lifted his arms to help Raegan to dismount.

"Shhh, I don't want her to hear, but yes, I think so."

Chase's grin turned into a wide, tickled smile. "Can you imagine those two married to each other? They'd make a perfect pair if they didn't kill each other with their hair-trigger tempers."

When Raegan was standing beside Chase, she said with a frown, "I don't know why Star and I are even here. There's nothing for us to do, and I know we aren't welcome."

"Don't let Meg's attitude fool you. She's as proud as she can be to have neighbor women callin' on her. It's probably the first time she's had a woman visit her since she's lived here. Give her a little time to get used to it."

And Chase had been proven right later on, as much activity went on for the next few hours. Chase put Nelly and Fanny to work, mixing clay and dried grass and water to a thick compound that would dry rock hard after being spread in the gaping cracks between the logs of the cabin. Then, while Jamie and Johnny pulled a cross-cut saw through good-sized logs that had at some time been dragged in from the forest, Chase set about with hammer and nails, tightening the sagging door and loose windowframes. And during all this bustling about, Meg shyly walked over to where Raegan and Star sat beneath a tree. She sat down beside them, and the smile that parted her lips was stiff, as if her mouth hadn't tilted upward for a long time.

"That Jamie, he's a nice young man," she said, watching Jamie, who energetically pulled and pushed his side of the saw. "He'll make some woman a fine husband once he settles down. He's kinda wild right now."

Raegan agreed to every sentiment Meg expressed, but Star only gave a grunt. Nellie had settled herself a few feet from the men, her eyes and body sending silent messages to Jamie. And the knowing smile Jamie sent back to the girl was meant to rile Star, to pay her back for having slapped him on the head. Raegan felt her little friend's slender body growing stiffer by the minute and hoped that she could control the anger Raegan was sure was seething inside her.

A short time later, however, Raegan's own ire began to build. Fanny was helping Chase cord the wood that Jamie and Johnny had cut. Every time Chase bent over to load his arms, Fanny was close beside him, doing the same, making sure her body touched his somewhere. But Raegan's irritated frown faded when her husband said impatiently, "I'll do this, Fanny. Why don't you go set down and visit with the women, or find something else to do."

"That's right." Johnny glowered at his sister. "Get inside and clean the cabin, make up the beds and wash the dishes." He raised his voice to get Nellie's attention. "Go help Fanny in the cabin."

"You just shut up, Johnny." Nellie began, "I don't have to listen—" She snapped her mouth shut when she caught her mother's eye.

Meg said but one word. "Get."

When Nellie and Fanny flounced into the cabin, Meg muttered, "I wish them two girls would find husbands." She rose to her feet and brushed off the back of her dress. "I expect I'd better go keep an eye on them. They shirk their share of the work whenever they get the chance."

"I wish that Roscoe could get hold of that Nellie," Star grated. "He'd cool her off."

"You don't mean that, Star," Raegan gently chastised the younger girl. "He's an awful man."

Star studied the toe of her moccasined feet. "I guess I don't really mean it," she muttered. "I wouldn't want her hurt like the Tillamook, but I think a few slaps would do her good."

"You mean like the one you gave Jamie's head?"

"Yes! And I'd like to wallop him one again."

Amusement twinkled in Raegan's eyes, but she said no more. Another hour passed, and the men stopped working to drink the coffee Nellie brought out.

Except for Jamie. He had walked off into the woods. When, a moment later, Nellie followed him, Raegan darted a look at Star. Had she also seen Nellie follow Jamie? The black fury on the small face said that she had. Before Raegan could stop her, she was on her feet and striding toward her stallion. Raegan jumped to her feet, calling out to Chase.

"Star is leaving," she said anxiously, watching Champ thunder away, Star leaning over his neck, urging him on.

Chase swore, then yelled for Jamie, who was just coming out from among the trees, Nellie at his heels. Raegan saw the aggravation on his his face and wondered what had put it there. Had Chase interrupted something, or was it because Nellie had followed him? Maybe the poor fellow had needed to answer a call of nature, and she had kept him from doing it. At any rate, she felt sure that nothing else had happened between him and Nellie.

Jamie's eyes went straight to where Star had sat ever since they arrived. "Where is she?" he asked. "What has she done now?"

"The wildcat has taken off by herself," Chase answered, between anger and worry. He looked at Meg and Johnny apologetically. "I'm sorry, folks, but we've got to go after her."

No one heard what answer was given them as they hurried to mount up, then sent the horses racing away. All three prayed that the Star hadn't headed for her cave and her grandfather.

They were unable to overtake Star's stallion. Carrying her slight weight, his long, powerful legs had moved like the wind. They had been about ten minutes behind the furious girl when they came to a plunging stop in front of their own cabin, and Raegan had flung herself off her mare and hurried to Star's room. Raegan hadn't been surprised to find Star shoving her clothes into a haversack. It had taken a lot of talk to convince her to stay on, to obey her grandfather's wishes.

Now Star's laughter rang out again, and Raegan muttered, "I wish they'd stop fooling around and bring home some fish for a change. I've never seen anyone fish so much and catch so little."

Had Raegan been down by the river and seen through the ground-sweeping branches of a large willow tree growing on the stream's bank, she would have discovered why there was seldom fresh fish on the table at suppertime.

After the first day Jamie and Star made love, Jamie had hidden a rolled-up blanket among the branches of the willow. That blanket now lay on the ground, spread out to receive the two naked bodies stretched out on it.

The two young lovers were at at last satiated and lay curled in each other's arms, their pulses returning to normal, their hearts gradually beating at a normal rate. After a while Jamie leaned over Star and, smoothing the sweat-moist hair off her forehead, spoke what had been on his mind for some time.

"I'm tired of sneakin' around, makin' love to you on the ground. We must make serious plans, decide when we're goin' to get married, where we're goin' to make a life together."

Tracing his dark eyebrows with a slender finger as she looked lovingly into his eyes, Star said softly, but firmly, "We have only to decide when we'll marry. We will live with Paw, of course."

Jamie laid his head back down so that Star couldn't read his face and demand to know why that strange look had suddenly come over it. She did not know that her grandfather was dying, might very well be dead now. But she would have to know sooner or later, for come trapping season she would head for her grandfather's cave regardless of how strongly Chase and Raegan tried to talk her out of it.

Could he live in a cave? Jamie wondered. Chase had described it as being snug and comfortable. Still, it seemed unnatural to him for humans to live underground. But he knew he would try it for Star's sake. He'd live anywhere as long as she was with him. He repressed a heartfelt sigh. How he dreaded the time she had to learn about her beloved Paw.

He gathered Star protectively into his arms. He would be with her, supporting her with his love. That settled in his mind, Jamie said, "Since it's decided where we'll live, the next question is, who will marry us? Big Pine only has a visiting preacher who comes occasionally when the weather is good. With winter approaching, it's doubtful he'll come again until next spring."

Star was quiet for a minute, then hesitantly

began to speak. "Paw wouldn't like it, and maybe you won't either, but the chief of the Indian village not far from our cave is my uncle. We could have him marry us."

Jamie remembered the Indian village he'd grown up in, never quite accepted, and had his doubts that this chief would be any different toward Star. "Are you sure, honey, that he would do it?"

"Oh yes, I'm quite sure. He would feel honored to merge our souls together. He had a deep affection for my mother, his sister, and he passed that love on to me. When my mother was killed, he wanted to take me and raise me. Of course Paw wouldn't stand for it. Paw doesn't even like for me to visit my mother's people."

Jamie felt as if a weight he had carried for years had been lifted from him. Maybe at last he would find a people who would welcome him, let him be a part of their world. In his joyful excitement, he squeezed Star so hard, she squealed. "It's settled then," he said, his happiness in his voice. "As soon as this unrest with the Tillamooks is settled, we'll say good-bye to Chase and Raegan and take off for your cave."

He gave her small rear a playful slap. "Come on, you shameful hussy, get your clothes on. Do you want old Granny to come lookin' for us? Can you imagine what she'd have to say, findin' us both buck-naked?"

With much laughing and giggling, they gathered up the clothing that had been torn off in a hot flash of passion and helped each other to dress.

Chapter Eighteen

Raegan sat in the garden, soaking up the warmth of the sunshine, her face lifted to catch its full rays. Soon the days would grow shorter, the sun paler, giving little cheer and no warmth as it slanted through the trees.

Occasionally she glanced at the distant hill, hoping to see Chase returning from the village. Were the men reaching any decisions about the Tillamooks yet, or were they still arguing among themselves, the young and impetuous against the older, steadier minds?

Inside the cabin she heard the baby beginning to stir in the cradle Chase and Jamie had made for him. She smiled wryly. He'd start to fuss soon, working up to a full, loud hungry cry. She didn't stir, though, to go to the infant. Granny would be hovering over him right now.

But she should go in and start supper, she

thought, get to the stove before Granny did, otherwise who knew what concoction she'd cook up and place on the table. She bent over to remove her muddy work shoes, then lifted her head to listen. Faintly at first, then louder, sounded the awkward gallop of a horse. She stood up and peered at the hill to her right, then took an anxious step to the edge of the porch. It wasn't a horse approaching the cabin, but the Joneses' old mule. And astride its bare back, young Johnny was coaxing all the speed he could get from the animal.

"What's wrong, Johnny?" Raegan demanded when the pale-faced, wild-eyed teenager pulled the mule in at the foot of the porch. "Has something happened to one of the family?"

"No." Johnny slid to the ground. "Is Chase here, Miz Donlin'?"

"No, he's not, Johnny. I expect him any time though. Jamie's down by the river. Can he help you?"

Johnny nodded distractedly and started loping toward the sound of Jamie's and Star's laughter as the pair walked toward the cabin. Then, mid-way to the couple, Raegan called out, "Chase is riding in now."

Before Chase pulled the stallion in, Johnny was running alongside the mount. "Good Lord, boy, what's wrong?" Chase asked anxiously as he dismounted.

"Roscoe is back!" the words came between pants.

"What?" broke simultaneously from Chase's and Raegan's lips. "Are you sure?"

"I'm dead sure. I saw him plain as day, sneakin' along the river. Maw saw him too. She sent me over to tell you."

Chase swung back into the saddle. "I'm goin' back to the village to round up the men," he said just as Jamie and Star hurried up. He looked at his young friend and said, "Raegan will explain everything to you."

"You be careful, Chase," Raegan ordered in a trembling voice. "You know what a back-shooting snake Roscoe is."

Chase leaned down and kissed her hard on the mouth. "Don't worry, honey, the likes of that one won't get the best of me." As he turned the stallion back toward the hill he had just descended, he said to Johnny, "You go on back home, son, and keep an eye out for the Tillamooks. With luck, this means we're comin' to an end of our troubles with them. Once we get our hands on Roscoe, he's gonna tell them the truth."

Raegan remained on the porch until Chase disappeared over the other side of the hill. She whispered a prayer that he would be all right and that Roscoe would be taken. How wonderful it would be to go to bed at night without the fear of having their cabin burned around them!

His feet crunching on leaves was the only sound in the night as Roscoe nervously made his way through the forest. A moonlit evening had settled in a couple of hours ago, but he was cautious about where he would sleep. He finally came to what he had been searching for—a wind-fall. A large tree that some storm had felled, its bare branches resting on the forest floor, formed a shelter for man or beast.

Tired and hungry, he crawled beneath the heavy branches, scratching his face and neck on them as he squirmed around trying to make himself comfortable. When he was finally settled, he scooped a thick layer of leaves over his body. The night air was cold and he had no blankets.

Roscoe's luck had changed the day he went off and left the woman to die alone in the cave. His plans to reach the Platte, steal a boat, and row away had died within an hour of starting out. He had nearly walked into three Indians roasting strips of meat over a small fire. He had jumped behind a tree, his mouth gone dry with fear. When it appeared the men hadn't seen him, he carefully backed away until they were no longer in sight. He looked up at the sun, got his bearings, then started walking toward the Platte again.

But again Roscoe glimpsed the bronze, half-naked braves slipping through the forest and finally, in desperation, he'd laboriously climbed a tree and waited for darkness. And so it had gone for nearly three weeks; sometimes he hadn't covered more than a mile in one day. He lost weight from a diet of berries and roots, and his face was showing the strain of dodging the Tillamooks and thinking that he would never reach the river.

At last there came the day when he knew he wasn't too far from the Platte. Yesterday he had come upon the lesser branch of it, the one that flowed past the Donlin place before continuing on to the Indian village where he hoped to find a canoe.

As he closed his eyes in sleep now, Roscoe had a feeling that tomorrow would be a better day for him. Somehow he would elude the red heathens, find a means of traveling the river, and leave the Oregon hills behind for ever.

It was cold and still when Roscoe came awake, the sun just rising. He lay quietly for a few minutes, listening for the scuffing sound of moccasins. When he heard nothing but the skittering of small animals rustling the leaves, he crawled from under his shelter and struck out, his stomach growling from hunger.

His spirits became quite high as he stole through the forest and saw no sign of the Tillamooks or big Rafferty. He dreaded running into that one almost as much as he feared being taken by the Tillamooks.

Anxious sweat did bathe Roscoe's body once. The time he had to walk across a cleared patch of land only yards from the Jones cabin. He walked as fast as his weakened condition permitted, hoping that none of the Jones tribe would see him. He saw no one, heard no one cry out, and with a sigh of relief he re-entered the forest.

Finally he spotted smoke from several cooking fires lifting up among the trees. The Indian village was only yards away. It entered his mind to linger on the chance that a squaw might come his way. His carnal hunger almost equaled that of his belly. But common sense told him not to be a fool, that his biggest concern was to find a canoe and get the hell out of there.

It took Roscoe about five minutes to find a freshly made dugout sitting in the woods at the edge of the village. He lifted it lengthwise over his head and hurried away. Half an hour later, he reached the swiftly running Platte. The gravel grated as he pushed the canoe into the water, then heaved himself into it.

A satisfied look on his now skelton-like face, he picked up the paddle and dipped it into the water. Somewhere along the river he would find food—and a squaw.

The sun had disappeared, twilight had come and gone, and it was true night when Raegan, along with Jamie and Star, heard galloping hooves approaching the cabin. All three stood up from the seats where they had taken up a vigil right after supper. When Lobo didn't raise his ruff, they knew it was Chase coming in.

"Did you find the bastard?" Jamie asked as Chase climbed the two steps to the porch and dropped tiredly into the chair that Raegan had just vacated.

He shook his head. "The varmint got away. We never did see him, but we picked up his tracks by the Jones place. We followed them to Chief Wise Owl's village and saw where he had taken a canoe and gone on to the river."

"And there," Jamie grimly finished for him, "he launched the canoe and we don't know if he went downstream or up. A tried-and-true trick for someone on the run."

"That's about the size of it," Chase answered, then looked at Raegan. "I'm about starved, wife, did you save me any supper?"

Raegan took his hand and pulled him up. "You

know I did," she said softly. "It's keeping warm on the stove."

The four of them trooped into the kitchen, stepping quietly so as not to awaken Granny and Boy. While Raegan filled a plate from various pots on the stove, Jamie asked with a frown, "You're not givin' up on Roscoe, are you, Chase?"

"Not a chance. As soon as it's daylight tomorrow, we're startin' after him. We intend to break up into two groups, one bunch of us goin' downriver, the other upriver. Whichever one of us finds where he's landed to make camp will continue to track him. Time is runnin' out for the fat one."

When Chase picked up his fork and dug into the plate of stew, Jamie announced, "I'll tend to Sampson, Chase, you look beat."

Chase was tired, and more worried than he had let on. What if the Tillamooks attacked the cabin while he was gone? He could be away for days. Could Jamie and the two girls hold them off? All three were crack shots, but there could be twenty or more warring braves swooping down on them.

He didn't make love to Raegan when they went to bed a short time later. He only held her close in his arms, praying that no harm would come to her, that they would grow old together.

Roscoe nosed the canoe onto the river bank shortly before sunset. As soon as he had pulled the birch-bark vessel onto the bank and dragged it behind some brush, he struck off through the forest hunting his supper. He could fire his rifle now. He was on the white man's side of the river and far enough downstream to be safe from the Tillamooks who roamed the woods around Big Pine.

Half an hour later, he had shot two squirrels. He hurried back to where he had stashed the canoe and gathered wood to start a fire. While it crackled and burned, he skinned and cleaned the small animals. In a short time, his mouth watered as he watched the meat roasting on the spit he had fashioned from the green wood of a willow, its juices dripping, making a splattering noise as it hit the red coals below.

The wild game was only half cooked when Roscoe could no longer deny his hunger. He jabbed his knife into the hind quarter of one small carcass and lifted it to his mouth. And though it burned his fingers and his lips, he sank his rotten teeth into the meat, tearing it from the bone like an animal. Soon only a small pile of bones remained. Rubbing his full belly, Roscoe let loose a belch that startled the birds roosting in nearby trees. He shivered as he walked to the river and knelt down to drink. Darkness was coming on and with it a cool breeze.

After relieving his bladder, he turned the canoe over on its side and crawled beneath it. Feeling safe for the first time in weeks, it was but moments before his rumbling snores were issuing into the night.

Daylight was just arriving when Roscoe awakened. He crawled from under his shelter, then dragged the craft to the river and stepped inside it. Dipping and pulling the paddle through the water, he was miles down the river when the men from the village began arriving at the Donlin cabin.

Chase came awake when Raegan's warm body stirred in his arms. He had an immediate arousal, and in the dawn's semi-light he pushed the blanket down around their waists and gazed at the perfection of her breasts, one flattened against his chest. He had been too tired last night to make love to her, but he was fully rested now and and looked forward to sliding between the silky smoothness of her legs and burying his aching stiffness deep inside her.

Bending his head, he took the free nipple into his mouth and slowly suckled it as his hand smoothed down her flat stomach, coming to rest on the curly triangle of hair nestled between her legs. Although still half asleep, Raegan instantly raised her hips to press against the finger that rubbed erotically on the small nub of her femininity. At the same time, her hand moved down to curl its fingers around the hard thickness that jabbed at her belly. A sound, almost like the purr of a cat, fluttered through her lips as she stroked that part of her husband that she knew would soon work its magic inside her.

After indulging in the sweet torture a few minutes, Chase raised his head from Raegan's breast, and she released his throbbing maleness as he sat up and reversed his position. As his mouth replaced the spot where his finger had previously teased, her mouth closed over that which she had just left off fondling.

This foreplay that always proceeded the coupling of their bodies was of short endurance. Both were too eager for release. When Chase climbed between Raegan's thighs, grasped her hips, and raised them to receive that first long thrust, she whispered. "Hurry, love, hurry." Her impassioned words made Chase swell all the more, and with a low groan he buried every long inch of himself inside her.

And as he rose and thrust, pumping inside her, she bucked her hips to meet his drives, thrashing her head back and forth from the pure pleasure of his smoothly sliding staff.

But both were holding back, wanting this joining of their bodies to last as long as they could restrain themselves. It could be days, possibly weeks, before they would know this mindless pleasure again.

However, the time came when Raegan could no longer bear the bliss, and Chase was sweating from the stress of keeping control of the juices that fought for release. When Raegan began to whimper, to beg softly, "Now, Chase," he braced his hands on either side of her head, and his elbows straight, he bucked furiously inside her.

When they reached the crest and soared off into space, their ecstatic cries awakened Granny in the room next to theirs. She opened one eye, grumbled, "It's a wonder that randy pair ain't killed each other yet," then turned over and went back to sleep.

Raegan had made Chase breakfast, and they were drinking their coffee when the men began to arrive. As they milled around outside, eager to get going, to find Roscoe and hand him over to the Tillamooks, Raegan laid a hand on Chase's.

"You will be careful, Chase." Her eyes were dark with worry. "I don't know what I'd do if you were taken away from me."

Chase stood up and pulled her into his arms. "Don't fret about me," he whispered in her hair. "It's you I'm worried about. Don't leave this cabin unless Jamie is with you, and then only if it's really necessary. I know what I would do if I should lose you. I'd go stark raving mad." With a long, hard kiss, he released her and left the cabin to join the waiting men. Raegan hurried to the window to watch them ride away, choking back a sob when, just before disappearing over a hill, Chase looked back and waved to her.

Raegan remained at the window, wondering how it would all end. Would the men find the man who had started it all? And what if they didn't? Would the Tillamooks wage an all-out war on the whites? She thought of her neighbors, who had become such good friends—Aggie and Ike and their two silly daughters; Granny Pearson; Sid and Ruthie; Rafferty; even the Jones tribe. And what about dear little Star, whom she loved like a sister? Should she be taken back to her cave until the unrest came to an end one way or the other?

All these thoughts were running through Raegan's mind when Star walked into the kitchen. "Boy is windin' up, Raegan," she said with a grin. "I think the little chief is hungry."

"And soaked besides," Raegan said ruefully.

She turned from the window and went into the parlor where the baby's cradle was placed each evening. It was quiet in there, and close enough to Raegan and Chase's bedroom so that they could hear him should he cry in the night. She bent over the fist-waving infant and lifted him from his warm coccoon of blankets. She carried him into the kitchen and laid him down on one side of the table. As she had prophesied, Boy was wet through. By the time she had changed him, his lusty cries had rung throughout the cabin. "If chiefs are chosen by the strength of their voices, it's a sure thing that you'll be one when you grow up," she muttered, wrapping the baby brave in a clean, dry blanket. "Star, would you . . ." She was talking to an empty room. No one stayed around if they didn't have to when Boy let it be known he was hungry. Even Granny took to her room.

Sitting down in the rocker that had been brought into the kitchen for the sole purpose of feeding the baby, Raegan picked up the bottle Star had prepared and left sitting on the table. Boy's little mouth opened eagerly to receive the doeskin nipple. With a tender smile curving her lips, Raegan watched the little cheeks go in and out, the tiny mouth working to draw the milk in. "Wouldn't your father be proud if he knew about you?" She stroked a fat little cheek.

Raegan suddenly stopped rocking. Why hadn't she thought of it before? Right here in her lap might lie the solution to all their troubles. If she took Boy across the river, to his father, and told the man how Roscoe was responsible for the stealing of his wife and how she had died giving birth to his son in Raegan Donlin's cabin, wouldn't that man be grateful? That at least he had a son, and that she had brought that son to him? Wouldn't that prove to the chief that the people of Big Pine were peaceful people, wishing no harm to the red man. Surely they had a Roscoe among them too and would understand.

"It will work, I know it will," she whispered confidently.

But how was she to get away from Jamie? She chewed thoughtfully on her lower lip. He would never allow her to leave the cabin alone, and he was seldom out of the cabin and only for a few minutes at that. Star would loudly object to her plan, too, but she could handle her. Besides, someone should know where she was going in case her plan didn't work. "But it will," she told herself, then set to wondering if she could convince Jamie that she needed something badly from the village store.

Her mind ran down a list of items that might send Jamie to Big Pine. Everything she thought of she had to reject. It seemed there wasn't a thing that they couldn't do without. The bottle grew light in her hand, and looking down, she found the baby fast asleep, the bottle empty. It struck her then that the one thing that would send Jamie to the village was canned milk for Boy's bottle.

She leaned her head back and laid her plans. She must go to the cellar and hide all but one can of the four sitting on a shelf there. She would need to fill a bottle to take with her. Next she would gather up Boy's clothes and stuff them into a pillowcase and hide it under the bed until she was ready to leave.

Having thought it all through, Raegan forced herself to calm down, to hide her excitement. She must carry on with her usual routine, and that began with her making the beds while Star cleaned the kitchen. She stopped the rocker with a drag of her foot, rose, and carried the sleeping infant into the bedroom. Before she made up the bed, she gathered up his clothes and put them in a pillowcase, telling herself it was lucky she had washed all his things the day before. She wanted the baby's father to see that she had been taking very good care of his son.

Raegan had finished with the three bedrooms and was dusting the last piece of furniture in the parlor, a chair-side table, when she heard Jamie enter the kitchen. The palms of her hands grew damp with nervous sweat. Could she convincingly tell him her lie? She must. The lives of the people in Big Pine might hinge on what she planned to do today.

Jamie and Star paid no attention to her as she entered the kitchen and walked across the floor to open the trap door. She went down the steps and made her way through the dimness to where the cans of milk sat beside a pail of gourds. For a moment she wondered where to hide the tins, then decided that a good place would be behind the big flat rock where she kept her butter and eggs.

After making sure they were well out of sight, she picked up a ham hock. Balancing it on her arm, with the can of milk she intended to take with her in her hand, she climbed the cellar steps. Lowering the trap door, she forced herself to say calmly, "I'm afraid you'll have to make a trip to the village, Jamie. We're out of Boy's milk."

"Are you sure, Raegan?" Star looked up at her. "I'd have sworn there were at least four cans left when I brought up one yesterday."

"Well, I guess you were mistaken." Raegan set the can on the table and added, "This is it," then waited with held breath for Jamie's response.

Finally, after several tense moments, he expelled his breath on a frustrated sigh, and with a note of misgiving in his voice, said, "I guess there's nothin' to do but go get the little scutter some milk. I'll be glad when he can chew on a piece of meat."

As Raegan let her pent-up breath escape softly through her lips, he ordered, "Keep the cabin locked and don't open it to anybody until I get back. And keep the rifles loaded and next to the door. I won't waste any time goin' to the village and should be back in an hour or so."

As Star locked the door behind Jamie, Raegan hurried to the bedroom. She didn't have much time. She must be well away from here before Jamie returned, or he might catch up with her and bring her back. She worked swiftly, slipping the sleeping baby into the heavy sweater and leggings she had finished knitting only last week. She swung her shawl around her shoulders, tied it under her chin, and with the pillowcase in one hand and Boy in her arms, she walked into the kitchen.

Star stood at the table, preparing the baby's next bottle. She looked up at Raegan's entrance and gaped. "You're dressed to go outside, Raegan, and takin' Boy with you. You shouldn't do that. You heard what Jamie said."

"Shhh, keep your voice down before you wake Granny. And yes, I heard what Jamie said. He said keep the door locked and the rifles loaded. He said nothing about us going outside." She took the sling Jamie had made for Boy off the wall. She would carry the infant on her back, Indian style, leaving her hands free to grip Beauty's reins.

"Raegan." Star frowned at her. "You know as well as I do that Jamie doesn't want you leavin' the cabin even if he didn't say so."

Raegan sighed. "I know that, Star, but I'm going to try something that I hope will bring an end to this worrisome upheaval we've been living in. I'm taking Boy to his father."

Star's mouth dropped open. "Raegan, you're crazy. Chase is gonna have a ragin' fit, you know that. And what if you never make it to the baby's father? What if a Tillamook kills you before you get to the Indian village?"

"Boy will be my safe passage," Raegan answered, praying that it was so. There was the possibility that she wouldn't get the chance to explain why she was on Tillamook land, carrying an Indian child. But she had to take that chance, she told herself. She eased the sleeping baby into the sling and lowered him over her back. She fastened the ties under her breasts, then picked up his bottle and slid it into the pocket of her dress.

She walked to the door, and picking up her rifle leaning on the wall there, she smiled at Star. "Come give me a hand saddling Beauty."

"Oh, Raegan, I wish you wouldn't." Star wrung her hands. "I have bad feelins' about this."

"Don't, honey. It's going to be all right. I'll be back before you know it, and all will be well."

Ten minutes later, Raegan was waving goodbye to a pale-faced, Star. "Be sure to lock the door," she called back as the mare entered the forest, traveling in the opposite direction from the way Jamie had taken.

Chapter Nineteen

The autumn morning was clear and cold, the sun shining frostily on the trees, as Raegan kept the mare at a lope. Boy's little body was limp with sleep, cuddled against her back.

She was going to miss him dreadfully, Raegan thought, then laid a gentle hand on her belly. Her own baby would fill the gap left by the little Indian prince.

She had been riding for two hours when she spotted Sid and Ruthie Johnson's fur post in the distance. She steered Beauty off the trail and pushed farther into the pine forest. Sid had gone with Chase and the others to find Roscoe, but Ruthie was no Star. If she thought it necessary, the Indian woman was capable of physically detaining Raegan from her errand.

When she felt she was safely past the post, she guided the mare back onto the trail. If she remembered correctly, another half mile would bring her to the Platte.

It grew so quiet that even the mare's hooves made no noise on the needle-strewn ground. Raegan shivered. It felt as though the trees were pressing in on her, smothering her. She wished suddenly that Lobo was with her. He hadn't been around the cabin when she left.

She forgot the wolf as all at once the Platte lay before her, murmuring, slapping at its banks. Her nerves twisted into knots as she gazed across the river to where the foothills trooped down to the stream. Somewhere in that seemingly impenetrable forest lay the Tillamook village.

Doubts began to assail her. Would it be that simple? Would she be able to just hand Boy over, explain about him and his mother, and then leave? For the first time, she wondered at the wisdom of her big plan. Jamie had said once that nothing was ever that simple, that cut-and-dried with the Indian. Every event that happened in his life had to be weighed, thought out, debated.

Perhaps it would be different this time, she hoped. After all, wasn't she bringing the chief a son? She nudged Beauty with a heel, steering her into the river. It was shallow at this point, and Beauty had no trouble picking her way across. When she stepped onto the gravelly bank, Raegan reined her in.

Now, which way should she go? Somehow she had expected to find a trail leading off through the forest, one that would lead her to the Tillamook village. But the narrow width of land that lay between the forest and the river was smooth and untrampled.

Where *did* I get the idea that the village lay within sight of the river? she asked herself, wondering whether to turn Beauty left or right. It could be miles into the forest and she might not ever find it. What if she became lost, and she and the baby starved to death—or worse, were eaten by wild animals? The woods were full of wolves, panthers, and bears.

Her courage began to fail her. It had been a foolish notion she'd had. As much as she hated to abandon her plan, for she still thought her idea was a good one, the sensible thing to do was return home.

With a resigned expression, she started to turn Beauty around, back into the river. Then something made her pause. There were eyes watching her. She knew it—she could feel them boring into her, hostile and vengeful. It had to be an Indian. No white man would be on this side of the river.

Tension tied her stomach in knots. Should she make a run for it? No, she shouldn't. What if Boy got an arrow in his little back? After all, the Tillamooks wouldn't know that it was one of their own slung over a white woman's back. It's too late to do anything now, she thought, hearing the thud of unshod hooves approaching her.

When a wiry little mustang moved out from among the trees, the blood drained from Raegan's face. On the pony's back sat a fierce-eyed Indian. She yelped in alarm when he rode up beside her and grabbed Beauty's bit.

"Why has white woman traveled into Tillamook land?" His guttural voice made the hairs stand up on Raegan's arms, but at least he spoke English.

For a moment her terrified mind went blank. She could only stare at the dark, scowling visage only a few feet from her own. Then Boy whimpered, and though she was trembling inside, she forced herself to face the brave unflinchingly. She had heard that Indians respected courage.

"I have come to speak to your chief about something very important—to both the red man and the white."

"Are the pale-face men so cowardly they send a woman to fight for them?"

Raegan frowned and her chin came up. "They're not aware that I am here. Most of the men are away, tracking down a man who has brought great trouble to our people."

The Indian studied her pale face, his expression giving no hint of what was in his mind. "This man they seek, what is his crime that makes your people hunt him?"

Raegan licked her dry lips. "I would rather tell the chief. There are other things I would tell him . . . and show him."

She was subjected to another penetrating stare, then the Indian spoke. "I am the chief of our people. Speak."

Raegan's eyes widened a fraction. He didn't look like what she imagined a chief would. In the first place, he seemed too young—probably only in his mid-thirties. And where was the long, feathered headdress and colorful robe she'd seen in pictures? This man wore simple buckskins.

"How do I know you speak the truth?" she demanded.

"I have said so." His hand shot out and grabbed her wrist. Giving it a cruel twist, he repeated, "Speak."

"All right!" Raegan's eyes shot anger at him as she wondered if the bones in her wrist were crushed. When he released her, she continued, "Last March, a fat man, known only as Roscoe, stole one of your women—your wife, I learned later. The people of Big Pine were very angry at what he'd done and chased him out of the area, hoping to avoid trouble with your people."

She sighed. "As you know, it didn't work."

The chief ignored her almost accusing remark. "How did you learn that Shy One is my wife?"

Raegan looked down at her white knuckles gripping the reins. What would this stern-faced man do to her when he learned that his wife was dead? Would he immediately cut her throat with that wicked-looking knife tucked in the top of his fringed trousers?

She swallowed, then lifted her head and explained as gently as she could how on that August night she had found his wife in her barn, how she had later delivered her of a son. She didn't think it would be wise to let this proud man know that a man had brought his flesh into the world.

His big body jerked when she told how his wife had died after giving birth, but his face remained stolid. And only a flicker of relief shone in his black eyes when she related how she and a friend had entombed Shy One's body in two canoes, pointing their prows west. "I will take you to the place if you like."

As though he hadn't heard her offer, he asked, "This son Shy One birthed, is he a half-breed?"

Raegan's lips tilted softly as she untied the strings that held Boy's sling. She carefully pulled the infant around to lie in her lap. Folding back the blanket that protected his face from the cold air, she looked up at his father.

"Meet your son."

Fierce pride and elation flooded the chief's face as he looked at the pure Indian child. "Mine," he said, touching a gentle finger to its soft cheek.

"What you name my son?" He frowned at her.

"I have given him no name, knowing that you would want to do that. In the meantime, I have been calling him Boy."

That pleased the chief; she could tell by the softening of his lips. "What papoose see the first time he open eyes?" he asked.

Raegan thought a minute, trying to remember what the baby might have seen when his black eyes opened for the first time. She had been sitting in front of the fireplace bathing him right after Jamie took him from his mother's womb. Her face had to be the first thing his son's eyes looked upon. The chief is not going to like that, she thought nervously and wondered if she should lie to him, tell him something else. She knew that Indian babies were sometimes named in this manner and certainly he wouldn't want to call his son by her name.

But she couldn't bring herself to lie to the man. She looked up at him and said as bravely as she could, "I'm afraid it was me your son first looked upon."

He was startled, she knew, but after staring thoughtfully at the ground for a moment, he said, "Then his name shall be *Kesathwa* after your hair."

Raegan smiled her pleasure. "I am greatly honored," she said and held the baby out to him. "I must be getting back home, before dark, I hope."

The chief made no move to take the infant. "I can not let you go, white woman. You must come with me to my village. You will stay there while I take some braves and track down this man who took my wife."

When Raegan began to protest, angrily and fearfully, he shook his head at her. "Do not act like the spoiled white woman who gives her husband arguments. If the braves and I find that what you say is truth, then I will take you home. Besides, it will give *Kesathwa* time to know his grandmother and get used to her tending him."

Raegan stared at him, blinking rapidly. It wasn't suppose to happen this way. She shook her head. "I've brought you your son, kept my promise to his mother. Now I must return home."

Before she finished protesting, the chief again grabbed Beauty's bit and Raegan was following the mustang off through the forest. "Didn't you hear me?" she yelled at the broad back. "I want to return home."

The tall Indian jerked the two mounts to a halt. Turning around on the mustang's bare back, he pinned Raegan with a black, threatening stare. "Did you not hear *me*? I said that you will stay with my son until I return. Only then will you return to your people—if you have not lied to me."

Raegan stiffened, divining the promise of violence if she continued her argument. "You, insufferable, unreasonable man," she muttered to herself, but said no more to the chief when Beauty was tugged into motion again.

They left the river and moved through the forest. No word was spoken between them as they traveled wilderness no white man had ever set foot on. The air grew colder, and despite her heavy shawl, Raegan's teeth chattered.

Was Boy warm enough? she wondered. Evidently he was, or he would be making his discomfort known in a very loud voice.

As Beauty followed the other mount for what seemed hours to Raegan, the tree shadows lengthened and twilight approached. Stars were twinkling coldly when she saw through the trees ahead the light of scattered campfires. Her nerves tightened. They had reached the end of their journey.

A few minutes later, her companion sawed on the two reins. As the spent horses blew and snorted, Raegan sent her gaze ranging over the Indian village.

Scattered through the trees were many long, rectangular, pine-plank houses with slanted roofs. Several families could live in one, she thought, and found out later that this was the case. A blue haze of smoke hung over the village, created by the cooking fire in front of each abode.

The chief slid off his mount and lifted his arms to receive his son. When Boy had been handed down to him, he said shortly, "Follow me."

Raegan stiffly dismounted and, stumbling drunkenly in her exhaustion, walked behind him.

Men, women, children, and barking dogs converged upon them when the chief stopped in front of a building larger than the others. Curious, sullen looks were turned on Raegan momentarily, but mostly their interest was focused on the baby in their leader's arms.

The chief raised a hand to silence the many questions posed to him. He spoke in his native tongue at some length, and Raegan watched a succession of expressions race across the listeners' faces—anger, sadness, then finally, joy. By reading the emotion on his people's countenance, she easily followed the chief's story.

He said something to his people then that sent the men to a large communal campfire and the women to gather under a tree, where they began a wailing lament for the chief's dead wife. As Raegan stared at them, gooseflesh rising on her arms, the chief nudged her and motioned her to step inside what she assumed was his home.

She was sure of it when she saw the soft furs on the floor and on the walls. There would be no drafts in this building when winter arrived.

In the center of the room was a large fire-pit, in which burned a cheery fire, its smoke rising to the roof and escaping through a hole cut for that purpose. Along one wall were several neatly stacked furs, which she assumed was the Indian's bed. Boy began to fuss, and she carried him to one of the piled furs and laid him down.

By the time Raegan had changed the baby from the clothes that were soaked from head to toe, his hungry cries were becoming deafening. She had just cradled him in her arms and was offering him his bottle when the door opened and an Indian woman stepped through it.

She watched the middle-aged woman walk toward her, admiring the regally held head, her stately walk. There were only a few threads of gray in the black hair pulled back from the broad forehead of the attractive face. There was warmth in her dark eyes when she sat down next to Raegan. Pantomiming with her hands, she made it known that she was Boy's grandmother.

With a smile, Raegan held the baby out to her, then moved to another pile of furs. A gentle look replaced the stoic one on the proud features as the woman gazed down at the tiny face of her grandson. She gave Raegan a look of approval after slipping the nipple from the baby's mouth and examining it.

The two women sat in silence, the only sound Boy's greeding sucking of his milk. There was sadness on the woman's face as she gazed at her grandson, and Raegan knew she was thinking of his dead mother.

Raegan turned her head to the door when it opened again. A young Indian woman stepped inside, bearing a tray on which was a bowl that sent out a steaming aroma of meat and spice. Raegan's stomach growled in hungry response. She looked up at the newcomer as the wooden tray was placed before her, her smile of thanks dying on her lips.

Never had she seen such hate on another person's face. The black eyes pierced with their hostility. *She hates me for the death of her chief's wife,* Raegan thought, then changed her mind after seeing the same look bent on Boy.

My God, she's jealous. Raegan wanted to laugh hysterically at the woman's foolish notion. The woman was in love with her chief and had plans to replace his dead wife. Raegan hoped she would not be successful, for she would not be kind to Boy.

Evidently, the older woman had caught the heated glower that had been turned on Raegan and the baby, for after a few sharp words from her, the young, sullen-faced woman turned on her heel and stalked out the door.

She is an enemy, Raegan thought, but after only a slight hesitation she dipped her fingers into the bowl of stew. Jamie had mentioned once that Indians used no flatware when they ate.

The bowl was empty and Raegan's stomach full when the chief came into the big room, bringing the odor of fresh air and pine with him. He squatted down in front of Raegan, his black eyes going over her face, lingering on her hair, which looked pure gold from the firelight shining on it. He picked up a thick strand of it, and as he let it slide through his fingers, he spoke.

"I am taking three of my best trackers to your village of Big Pine, where we'll pick up the fat one's trail. My mother will stay here with you and little brave. You will be safe as long as you stay at her side. Do not be foolish and try to leave the village. It would sadden me to return and find that my braves had thought it necessary to put a knife through your heart."

And while Raegan stared at him, her heart hammering like a mad thing, he rose and walked to where his mother sat, holding his now sleeping son. He gently swept his fingers across the baby's smooth brow while conversing with his mother for a short time. He stood up then, and without another glance at the white woman, the tall, handsome chief walked out into the darkness.

The older woman removed her moccasins and leggings. Then, giving Raegan a smile, burrowed beneath the top fur and snuggled her grandson to her side.

Raegan stared into the blazing fire, uneasy about the chief's behavior, his intent look at her face, his playing with her hair. Did the red man want her, in the bibical sense? Would Chase have to fight him and his people in order to take her away from here? Would one problem be solved, only to be faced with another?

When the fire had died down to a bed of red coals, Raegan sighed as she too crawled between the furs.

Chapter Twenty

A heavy twilight was deepening when Chase and his group of seven men, tired and hungry, drew rein for the night.

It was young Johnny's job to start the fire when they made camp, while the others, except for Chase and Sid, took turns gathering wood to keep the fire going all night. Chase and Sid did the cooking.

Soon, smoke curled upward from Johnny's crackling fire and the savory odors of brewing coffee and roasting meat hung in the air. Tonight Sid was cooking since Chase had provided the meat. He had shot the heads off seven squirrels as they had ridden along.

Cigarette smoke wreathed Chase's head as he sat staring into the leaping flames, seeing only vaguely the dissolving trail of steam lifting from the blackened coffee pot. He was thinking of

Raegan and how much he missed her, and wondered if she was all right. He had thought that by now they would have caught up with Roscoe and would be on their way home. They had been following his course down the river for four days now. But Chase and the other men hadn't reckoned that along the river they would come upon stretches of underbrush so thick and wide that they would waste hours hacking a path through it. Consquently Roscoe was always a day ahead of them.

When the men had separated four days back, Sid Johnson's hound had picked up Roscoe's scent the following morning. Sid had insisted on bringing along the old dog. The men had teased the fur post owner, declaring that he'd have to let the dog ride with him every once in a while to rest up. And Sid had indeed taken the old fellow up on the horse occasionally to give his legs a rest.

But old Sounder, as Sid called him, was much praised when it was he who discovered where Roscoe had slept the night before, letting them know they were on the right track.

"He's picked up Roscoe's trail," Sid had yelled, pointing to the hound, who sniffed the river bank, the hair on his neck bristling. Some doubted that was the case as they headed their mounts toward the hound, and one man mused out loud that he was smelling a wolf track, while another laughingly said he was smelling his own tracks. It turned out they were both wrong, for there were Roscoe's tracks and the scuff marks where he had dragged the canoe into the water. With wild whoops, the chase was on.

By now the other group of men were back home, Chase thought with some envy.

A shrill burst of feminine laughter brought Chase back to the present. The trappers had insisted that the skinny whore from the tavern accompany them. When Chase had demurred, they had argued that at the end of a hard day, a man needed his pleasuring. They pointed out that he, a married man, should surely understand that.

He had argued back that her presence would cause trouble among the men, but when the men promised faithfully not to fight over her and to draw cards for their turn in her blanket, he had agreed. Half the men were married anyhow and shouldn't be interested in the whore, he had told himself. He soon discovered that to some of the men, their married state didn't make any difference.

A wry smile tugged at the corners of his lips. As it turned out, only he, Sid, and one other man hadn't visited the woman he had previously spent a lot of time with. Even young Johnny had been introduced to the pleasure of a woman's body, the trappers donating the money for the young man's first sexual experience.

Chase stood up when Sid called out that the meat was done and they should get their plates and line up. There followed a few minutes of clattering tin plates and cups as the men dug into saddlebags for their own personal tins.

There was little conversation as the men hungrily consumed the roasted squirrel and drank the coffee. There was one small roasted squirrel leftover from the meal, and stripping the meat from the bones, Sid fed it to the old Sounder. "You sure do pamper that old hound," one of the men ragged Sid.

"He ain't got many teeth left." Sid defended his old friend.

"Yeah, I reckon." The man looked a little shame-faced and pulled a deck of cards from his vest pocket. "Come on, gents." He grinned. "Time to draw for the first crack at our fair lady."

The man who drew the high card gave a whoop and, grabbing the giggling whore by the hand, rushed her to the blanket spread under a pine, not too far away from the fire. The nights were chilly this time of year, and there was always the danger of curious wolves coming around camp.

The fire burned down to coals, and as cards were drawn again, Sid piled more wood on the fire, then sat down beside Chase. As the coals hissed, smoked voluminously, then leaped into flames, he groused, "Do you think we'll ever catch up with that bastard?"

"We will, Sid. Sooner or later he's bound to light somewhere. Probably at the first village or town he comes to. He'll be needin' a woman by now."

"He ain't the only one." Sid half laughed. "I need Ruthie real bad. This is the first time I've gone longer than two days without her pleasurin' me."

"I sympathize with you, friend," Chase said, grinning.

"Does Roscoe have a last name?" Sid asked after a few minutes of silence as one man left the whore's blanket and another took his place.

"I'm sure he does," Chase answered with amusement. "Most men do. We'll probably never know his, though."

Sid nodded agreement. "There's a good many men who have left their names behind them for some reason or other. There's no tellin' what made that bastard run from his."

After a while Sid said good night and rolled up in his blanket. All the men but one had sought their blankets as soon as they finished their turn with the whore. Finally, her last customer rolled off the skinny woman and unrolled his sleeping gear.

But Chase sat on, staring into the ruddy glow of the campfire, thinking of Raegan. It grew quiet, the only sound in the night an occasional stamp of a horse's hoof and the snores coming from most of the blankets spread around the fire. Suddenly, Chase cocked his head and listened intently. He had heard an alien sound in the forest. At length, he caught a swishing sound, like that of a body moving carefully against brush. Indian? he asked himself.

Keeping the movement of his hand hidden, he drew his gun from its holster, slowly twirled the cylinder, found it full of cartridges, then replaced it, making sure the holster flap was out of the way so that it wouldn't catch or drag at the weapon in case he had to use it.

He rose slowly, in a casual way, and walked over to the horses, pretending that he was checking to see if all were securely tied. All the time, his eyes were sweeping the area. He moved on to a tree opposite the campfire and, seemingly at ease, answered nature's call, the act of a man about to retire. His eyes roamed over that area too. He saw nothing but the thick growth of trees.

Relacing his buckskins, Chase returned to the fire. Whoever had been out there in the darkness was gone now. Nevertheless, when he crawled into his bedroll, he kept the Colt handy to his touch.

All day a thick mist had hung over the river, and the sun hadn't once broken through the clouds that hovered like a gray cloak. Roscoe, lifting and dipping the paddle, sending the canoe skimming downstream, looked up at the angry clouds and knew that he would be rained on before the day was over.

An hour later, heavy rain was pouring down on him and there was no chance of leaving the river. Trees were a dense barricade right up to the edge of the water. And to worsen matters, the canoe was beginning to fill up with water and there wasn't a thing he could do about it except swear and sweat. If it should sink, he'd be a goner. He couldn't swim.

The vessel was nearly ready to capsize when Roscoe paddled around a bend in the river and sighted a rude log building about thirty yards away. "A fur post, by God," he exclaimed and nosed the water-swamped vessel toward the long, low-to-the-ground structure. At that moment, the rain that had slowed down a bit renewed itself and came down so fiercely that Roscoe couldn't see a foot ahead of him. He didn't see the huge log floating downstream, but he felt it when it rammed the canoe, breaking it in two.

As the craft broke apart, one half sinking immediately, Roscoe grabbed onto the part that still floated, yelling for help at the top of his lungs as he stared death in the face. His strength was giving out when a pair of hands grabbed him under the arms and dragged him into a boat. More dead than alive, he was rowed to the fur post and flung into a chair before a burning fireplace.

On their fifth day of tracking Roscoe, bitterly cold wind beat against Chase and the men. Dark clouds had run before its onslaught, tumbling and rolling like a turbulent sea.

Sid rode up alongside Chase. "We're gonna get rained on before dark."

"I'm afraid so." Chase bent his head against a blast of wind. "As cold as it is, we'll be lucky if we don't get snowed on."

Sid dropped back behind him, and the single file of mounts clomped along. The wind grew to a howl, and the pine branches overhead waved and creaked. Then, half an hour later, the wind died away and the rain came, shooting straight down. The men were soaked before they could dig the slickers out of their gear and shrug into them.

It grew dark early, brought on by the rain clouds, and Chase peered ahead, searching for some kind of shelter. Finally he saw a stand of spruce, so thick he doubted the sun ever managed to pierce through the interwoven branches.

He smiled his relief. He had thought that tonight's supper would be strips of dried beef, but under that thick shelter, a fire could be built. "This way, men," he called and turned Sampson toward the trees.

As Chase had surmised, the forest floor was barely damp as he swung out of the saddle. He tied the stallion to a tree, then called to Johnny, and the two of them went searching for dry wood. They found that the supply was plentiful, and within minutes each had gathered an armful of dry sticks and good-sized limbs. While Chase went to get the tarpaulin tied behind his saddle, Johnny got a fire going. Chase spread the large piece of canvas alongside the campfire, then emptied the grubsack onto it.

As sparks rose from the crackling fire and disappeared into the shadows, the men and the whore came and stood around its warmth, rubbing their cold hands together as their wet clothes steamed.

"You men are gonna have to step back if you want any supper tonight." Sid pushed his way between them, a brace of young pheasants he had shot that day swinging from his hand, green slender sticks in the other.

The men moved back a few steps, leaving the cook barely enough room to spear the plucked fowl with the wooden spits, then rig them over the fire. Sid shot them dark looks, mumbling sarcastically that they were fine trappers if they couldn't stand a little wet and cold.

The trappers only grinned, confident of their ability to withstand most anything Mother

Nature saw fit to visit on them. But if there was a warm fire nearby, they were as eager as the next man to feel its warmth.

Sid didn't object, however, when the skinny little whore edged closer and closer to the heat. He even folded a blanket quite close to the fire and motioned her to sit on it. The big man had a softness for children and the weaker sex. It didn't matter to him if the female was his wife, a neighbor woman, or a worn-out whore. The woman smiled her thanks and held her hands out to the heat radiating off the flames. Evidently, there was another man in the group who shared Sid's sentiments, for one of them had given up his slicker to the woman.

Solid darkness came quickly to the sodden forest, but as the weary men and one woman fell upon the roasted meat, the roaring fire pushed the gloom back. The meal was quickly eaten and wet clothes hung around the fire to dry; then the men sought their blankets, none interested in drawing cards tonight. The skinny whore sighed in relief and scooted into her blanket before one of them changed his mind.

The next morning, Chase rolled out of his blankets and stood up, feeling cramped and sore. It had stopped raining sometime during the night, but the air was damp and bitterly cold. He looked at young Johnny's thin body hunched up in his bedding and didn't have the heart to awaken him. The boy had been dead beat last night when they made camp, but hadn't uttered one word of complaint. This morning he would make the fire and let the kid sleep a little longer.

He hunkered down and began raking together the remains of last night's fire. There were some live coals among the ashes, and the small pieces of wood he laid on them caught readily. When it flamed to his satisfaction, he picked up the coffee pot and walked down to the river to fill it. Heavy clouds still hung overhead, and white mists curled along the river as he dipped the vessel into the water.

Chase returned to the fire, piled on more wood, then started the coffee to brewing. Soon the heat he had created reached the men, and they began to stir. They sniffed the aroma of the coffee and within minutes, buck naked, they were crowding each other for a spot before the fire.

"Your clothes are dry, men," Chase informed with a frown, "so get them on and drink your coffee."

A few minutes later, dry and comfortable, their bellies warm from the black brew, some of the men began to eye the refreshed woman with an interest they'd lacked the night before. Chase caught their looks and shook his head at them. "There'll be no card drawin' now. Saddle up and let's get goin'."

There was some grumbling, but ten minutes later, the men were mounting up and following after Chase.

The early chill of the morning struck Raegan's uncovered shoulders, bringing her slowly awake. As she pulled the soft fur covering up to her chin, Boy's grandmother rose from her bed beside him and kindled the red coals in the fire pit into leaping flames.

As Raegan gazed into the glow of the fire, her first thought as usual on awakening was, what would the new day bring? She was no longer afraid for her safety in the Indian village. Although she received many hostile looks, no one had bothered or approached her. She had even made two friends—Boy's grandmother for one. Because of the love they both shared for the baby, a close bond had grown between them. It saddened her, though, that she no longer had the care of the little fellow. His grandmother had taken over that duty with great tenderness.

However, for an hour each day she was allowed to hold and play with the baby, whose first weak cry had sounded in her cabin. But she could only watch as he was bathed and given his bottle, the two things she had most enjoyed doing. But as the chief had said, the little one had to be weaned away from her.

Boy, as she continued to call him, now drank goat's milk. Where the animal had come from she didn't know, but she suspected that its previous home had been in some white man's pen. At any rate, the baby was thriving on his new milk.

Raegan looked across the fire pit to a small figure huddled in a bed of furs. She smiled. The chief's ten-year-old son was her other friend. The youngster had learned quite a bit of English from his father and he was her interpreter when she wanted to converse with his grandmother.

From their first meeting, the solemn-eyed boy had been drawn to her. When they were alone together, he let her cuddle him a bit, for he grieved for his mother. Sensing that the white woman would sympathize with him, he had let fall the tears that would be ridiculed had his people seen them. Always the Indian male, from five years on, must be stoic and show no weakness.

She had learned many things from her young friend—that his name was White Feather, that his father was called Lone Wolf, and his grandmother was Grey Dove. He had always lived in this village, he'd said, but there were numerous tiny villages scattered along the Platte, each with its own chief. These chiefs were chosen according to their wealth.

White Feather also told her that each village had a man called a shaman. He explained that this man was like the white man's preacher or priest. The shamon also interpreted dreams, performed ceremonies and cured the sick.

Raegan remembered with a smile that it had been through White Feather and Grey Dove's help that the chief had agreed that she could go to a nearby stream every day and bathe.

It had come about on the second day after her arrival at the village, when she and White Feather were alone in the plank house. He sat close to her, his head leaning on her shoulder. He looked up at her and said, "All the time you smell like flowers. Do you not put bear grease in your hair?"

She had laughed and given him a quick hug. "No, White Feather, that is not a custom of the whites. However, if I don't get to bathe soon, I'll begin to smell like the bear itself."

White Feather giggled. "I would not like for you to smell like the grizzly. I will go speak to my grandmother."

So it had been decided that each noon, when the sun was at its warmest, Grey Dove and White Feather would accompany her to a small pool formed by a waterfall a short distance from the village. When she had voiced her pleasure, White Feather had teased, "Grandmother say white people have strange customs, but that it is already known by our people that the pale-faces are strange to begin with."

"Oh they are, are they?" She had pulled him to the floor and tickled his ribs, sending him into gales of laughter.

Raegan remembered how their hilarity had come to an abrupt end when the haughty-faced woman who served her meals entered the house. She shot them both a black look, then slammed the wooden bowl of stew onto the floor before stalking outside.

White Feather had stared after the woman, a brooding look in his eyes. "I do not like that one," he sighed. "She thinks to replace my mother with my father. I worry that he will only see the beautiful face that hides her true ugliness."

"Your father is a very wise man, White Feather." She put an arm around the narrow, sagging shoulders. "When the time comes for him to choose a wife again, I'm sure he'll choose one who is gentle and will be kind to his two sons."

"I hope that you are right, Raegan," he'd answered, but there was doubt in his voice and a worried frown on his forehead.

From outside came the sounds of the village coming awake. Dogs barked, children laughed or cried, and smoke from cook fires wafted under the door. Raegan turned over on her back, wondering where Chase was waking up this morning. "Please, God," Raegan whispered, "send Chase to bring me home."

Chapter Twenty-One

A thick fog continued to envelop Chase and the men for the second day, sometimes blotting out their view of the river. Young Johnny rode up alongside Chase, his narrow shoulders hunched in his thin jacket.

Chase knew the lad was cold and tired. No one had dreamed it would take so long to run Roscoe down. When Johnny sneezed three times in rapid succession, Chase looked at him, a worried frown on his face. He didn't want the boy to catch pneumonia. "Why don't you go back home, son?" he said gently. "We'll get Roscoe eventually and bring him in."

"No," Johnny said shortly, straightening his shoulders. "I represent the Jones family and I'll stay on. It's my duty." Chase nodded and said no more about his returning home. He would only hurt the boy's pride if he insisted.

Chase was bringing up the rear today, and ever since moving out this morning he'd felt that they were being followed. But every time he looked behind him, he saw nothing except maybe a squirrel or a bird or a fox—never any sign of a hostile Indian or a fat man. Still, the feeling persisted.

It was early in the afternoon when Sid, riding in front, spotted the rude building tucked alongside the Platte. He reined his mount in and held up a hand for the others to do the same. Chase rode up beside him, and together their eyes scanned the area around what they recognized as a fur post.

Their slow study showed half a dozen boats and two canoes pulled up on the river bank. Hope flared in Chase's heart. Did one of the vessels belong to Roscoe? Were they finally coming to the end of their hunt?

From inside the building came the laughter of women, the raucous guffawing of men. Chase kneed the stallion into motion, waving to the others to follow him. They quietly approached the building and swung from their saddles.

Just as quietly, three fierce-eyed Indians slipped through the forest only feet behind them. When Chase pushed open the post's door and he and the trappers stepped inside, the braves noiselessly leapt up on the porch and flattened themselves along the wall. Revenge burned in Lone Wolf's black eyes.

Inside, suspicious-looking faces were turned on the strangers who had invaded a territory not their own. Then quickly it was noted that these weren't ordinary men. Not one was under six feet tall, and all had the shoulder span of a buffalo as they stood spread-legged, their eyes inviting a confrontation.

The anger grew to sullenness on the men's faces, but a path was made for Chase and the trappers to approach the rough plank bar. "I'd like some information," Chase said quietly.

"Go to hell," the bearded bartender growled.

Chase drew his Colt and laid it on the bar. "I'll take you with me, mister."

When some of the men growled a protest and started moving in on Chase, there came the clicking of eight triggers being cocked. The would-be defenders stepped back, and the bearded man growled, "What's the information you're seekin' "

"I'm lookin' for a fat, bearded man who came down the river, on the run for killin' the wife of a Tillamook Chief."

There was a stunned silence as the customers in the post stared at Chase in disbelief, as if asking what damn fool would lay a hand on a Tillamook woman, much less kill her. Then alarm spread over their features. What if the man dragged out of the river had led the revenging tribe to their door?

As one, all heads turned to the man asleep in a chair, half hidden in a shadowed corner. Chase pushed away from the bar, and with the trappers following him, he crossed the sawdust-covered floor and looked down on the man who was no longer fat. He reached down and grasped

Roscoe's shoulder in a painful grip, startling him awake. When his eyes flew open, Chase jerked him to his feet.

A path was made for Chase as he hustled the whimpering Roscoe out the door. "What are you gonna do with me, Chase?" Roscoe suddenly hung back.

"I'm not goin' to do anything to you, Roscoe. I'm goin' to let the Tillamooks take care of you. We're goin' to take you to their village, which we should have done in the first place, and you're gonna tell their chief that you, alone, stole his woman."

Roscoe's eyes widened in terror. "You can't do that! They'll kill me!"

"Of course they will," Chase answered coldly, pushing him to walk off the porch. "Do you think they'll hand you a bunch of flowers for killin' one of their women?"

"I ain't goin'," Roscoe yelled, and with a hard jerk he was free of Chase's grip. But as he staggered backwards, he came up against a hard, bronzed body. While everyone gaped at the sudden appearance of three Indian men, Roscoe stared wildly into a pair of black eyes that promised death. His mouth opened and closed like a fish taken from a line and tossed onto a river bank, making no sound. The two braves with the tall Indian laughed loudly and pointed at his feet. Roscoe had wet himself, the urine puddling around his boots.

When Roscoe looked pleadingly at Chase, the tall Indian ordered, "Do not look at them for help. Nothing and nobody will save you. I am

Lone Wolf, chief of my tribe. Before many more sunsets, I will avenge my wife's death."

"It wasn't me who took your wife," Roscoe wailed like a woman. "It was Rafferty there." Roscoe pointed at the stunned man. "He's fat like I used to be."

Angry muttering rose among the trappers, and three started toward the lying man. Chase stepped in front of them when the chief began to speak again. "Twice I have heard that you stole my woman, caused her death. Now I want to hear you say it."

When Roscoe clamped his mouth shut and shook his head, Chase gave him an impatient look and ordered, "Tell him, Roscoe. Tell him the truth and you'll be dealt with fast. Lie to him and you'll be days dyin'."

With the trapped look of a fox cornered by a back of yelping hounds, Roscoe's eyes darted around, seeking a way to escape his looming death. There was nowhere to run, and his face suddenly crumpled in defeat. "I done it," he whispered hoarsely.

After a sharp intake of breath, Lone Wolf's lips twisted in a cruel, mirthless smile. Chase had advised Roscoe badly. There would be no fast death for the fear-crazed Roscoe.

And Chase was also wrong in thinking that all he had to do now was climb on his stallion and head for home and Raegan. Cold apprehension fluttered along his spine when Lone Wolf looked at him and said, "White man, are you not curious about who told me first about this man?"

Stark pain stared out of Chase's eyes. This savage had somehow gotten his hands on Raegan.

The chief slipped a noose around Roscoe's neck, then turned to Chase. "I can see from your expression you know of whom I speak. Your wife is a brave woman."

Chase lost all reasoning, was unable to listen to common sense telling him not to anger the arrogant chief or he risked never seeing Raegan again. He lunged for the chief's throat, but Sid and two others caught and held him.

When he stood quietly, only his fists opening and closing, Lone Wolf nodded approval and spoke again. "Your wife brought me my son and related how he came into her possession. She also told me about this man." He gave the rope a tug, choking off Roscoe's breathing for a moment.

Chase gritted his teeth and waited for the handsome Indian to finish toying with him. "I hated detaining one so fair," the Tillamook chief said with mock regret. "She is like the rising sun, a fresh breeze off the hills. But you must understand that I had to make sure of her story."

"All right! You've found out she spoke the truth." Chase shook himself loose from his friends. "I'll be goin' after her now."

Lone Wolf gave him a mocking smile. "Perhaps I want to keep her. Her beauty and soft voice are restful to me." He pinned Chase with glittering black eyes. "Will you fight me for the fair one?"

"You're damned right I'll fight you!" Chase's whole body vibrated with blind anger. "I'll fight your whole damn village for her!" he shouted. "I'll tear your village apart."

All traces of amusement and teasing left the chief's face. "You talk foolishly from anger and a deep fear of losing your wife. This pleases me, for now you know what I have suffered."

"I knew all along, man." Chase quietened down. "And now I ask you, husband to husband, don't make *my* wife pay for *your* wife's death."

Lone Wolf stared down at the ground for what seemed like ages to Chase. When he could stand it no longer, Chase demanded harshly, "Well, what's it to be?"

Black eyes were lifted to him. "I must think on it. You go home and wait for my decision." When Chase gave an angry start, a cautioning hand was lifted. "And do not think that you and your men can slip into my village and steal the fair one away. I would gather all the tribes along the Platte, and within an hour every man, woman, and child around your village would be dead."

"Come on, Chase," Sid said quietly, taking him by the arm and stepping off the porch. "There's nothin' you can do. You can't sacrifice the whole village, no matter how you hurt. Besides, I feel that everything is goin' to turn out all right. The chief strikes me as bein' an honorable man."

Chase allowed himself to be led to his mount, every fiber in his being wanting to pull his Colt and put a bullet in the Indian's heart. But he knew he was whipped, and he climbed into the saddle weary in body and aching in his heart. As they rode away, Sid looked back and watched Roscoe being led away, the rope tight around his neck. A shudder shook his big frame. He wouldn't want to be in his shoes.

It was early dawn when Raegan was shaken awake. She peered up at White Feather as he exclaimed, "My father has returned home, Raegan!" He held up a heavy blanket. "Come, put this around you. We will go see if his journey was sucessful,"

Raegan sat up, blinking the sleep from her eyes as she realized what this might mean. If they had found Roscoe, made him talk, she could go home. She was ready to leave her bed of furs when Lone Wolf walked into the house. She eased back down and watched the tall man affectionately clasp his eldest son's shoulder, then stride to the pile of furs where his mother and infant son slept. He gently awakened the grandmother and conversed with her in their native tongue as he carefully uncovered the baby, then gazed down at him tenderly.

Raegan knew when the conversation turned to her, for both mother and son turned their gaze on her. Grey Dove smiled as she answered a question put to her, and Lone Wolf nodded his head in satisfaction at her answer. What had been his question? she asked herself as he rose and came to her bed.

She was becoming uneasy as Lone Wolf silently regarded her. What was he thinking? What were his plans for her? She drew a breath of relief when White Feather spoke, breaking his father's concentration on her.

"Father, did you find the man you sought?"

"Yes, my son. After several days' ride we found the man."

A hard light shone in the boy's eyes. "And is he the one who caused my mother's death?"

"Yes." Lone Wolf squatted down and reached a hand to Raegan's hair. "The fair one did not lie to me." He slowly stroked the silky tresses.

"And will he suffer before he dies?"

"He will suffer as no man has ever suffered before." The answer came in a hard voice. "My only worry is that he will die fast. He is a coward and has little endurance."

He ran a finger down Raegan's cheek. "Unlike the fair one's man."

"You saw Chase?" Hope and dread mingled in Raegan's voice. "Please don't tell me that you killed my husband!" She had risen to her knees, her hands clasped together as though in prayer.

A bleak look flickered in the handsome brave's eyes as he continued to stroke Raegan's cheek. "Your man is unharmed," he said finally. "I would say that he and his companions have been home three days now."

In her relief that Chase was alive, Raegan became aware of the caressing hand on her face. She moved her head and the hand dropped. She smiled happily. "Now that your wife will be revenged, I'll make ready to return to my home." She threw the coverings aside and gathered herself to rise. In another hour it would be daylight, and she would be on Beauty's back, racing toward home and Chase.

"I have not said that you may leave." A hand on her shoulder pushed her back to the furs.

"Of course I can leave." Raegan's eyes snapped angrily. "It is only fair that I should."

She received a humorous smile at her imperious tone. "What a fierce brave you would be, fair one, had you been born a man." With a graceful lift of his body, Lone Wolf stood up. "I will reach a decision after the buzzards have eaten the flesh from the bones of the killer of my wife. When the sun reaches the timberline, his torture will begin with the running of the gauntlet. I want you to watch it. White Feather knows where to bring you."

Raegan rose to her knees, opened her mouth to shout angrily that she didn't want to watch the torturing of Roscoe, that she wanted to go home. But Lone Wolf was gone, closing the door behind him. Again she sank back down, frustrated tears running down her cheeks.

"Don't cry, Raegan." White Feather patted her back. "Come, you must wash your face and brush your hair. The sun is almost at the tree tops. I can hear the braves and women gathering at the council house."

Raegan washed her face, but White Feather had to pull the brush through her hair and settle a blanket over her shoulders before leading her outside. It had finally hit her that she might never leave this village—that Lone Wolf might decide to keep her.

She moved woodenly beside the boy and made no objections when he directed her to the front of the crowd so that they wouldn't miss any of the torture that was about to be visited on Roscoe.

A double line of Indians stretched before the assembled men and women, about fifty yards away from the council house. All those lined up carried either thick willow switches, rawhide strips, or lengths of bush bristling with thorns. With widened eyes, Raegan realized what it meant—running the gauntlet. Roscoe would have to run down that wide aisle, feeling the taste of lashes on his back. Actually, that didn't seem all that horrible, she thought, considering his crime. In the end, the trappers would have done much worse to him.

Her eyes were drawn to a struggle going on in front of the council house. Roscoe was trying to break free of the two men tearing off his clothes. When he stood naked, taunts and jeers sounded down the lines. Again he made a break for freedom, and again he was caught and held fast. Then the chief barked an order and he was dragged down to the opposite end of the lines. He would begin his run from there, ending at the council house—if he made it.

All was quiet until Roscoe received a hard push to his back, propelling him forward. When the first stinging lash cut into his buttocks, he started a wobbling run, with yelps of pain as blow after blow struck his bare flesh, stinging, cutting, ripping the flesh off his back, buttocks and thighs. He stumbled once but caught himself and ran on, knowing that if he stopped he was a dead man. Through a haze of pain he saw the council house looming up, and with the last of his strength he flung himself before its door.

As Roscoe knelt in the dirt, his back bloody and his sides heaving, a young brave stepped forward and clubbed him alongside the head. He raised his shaggy head, surprise on his face. He had thought that now he would be free to go, that running the gauntlet was the extent of his punishment. He soon learned, however, that it had just began as he was led away and tied to a tree. When three braves advanced on him with sharp hunting knives drawn, he began to scream even before they started peeling strips of skin off his chest.

A roiling began in Raegan's stomach as she watched with horror-filled eyes what was happening to Roscoe. Never would the trappers have done that to him. "White Feather," she gasped, "I am going to be sick."

The boy took one look at her white face and helped her to her feet. He led her behind a tree, where she lost what remained of last night's supper. "I think you should go back to the plank house now, Raegan," he said, taking the cloth band from his forehead and gently wiping her mouth. "Come, I will take you."

She nodded numbly and leaned on his young body as he led her away from the screaming Indians who felt not a bit queasy at what was happening to Roscoe.

Chapter Twenty-Two

Chase paced the front porch in long, angry strides, pausing occasionally to look in the direction of the Tillamook village. He had been home two days, and still there was no sign of Raegan returning to him.

A grimace of pain etched his forehead. He couldn't bear it much longer, not knowing what was happening to her, whether he would ever see her again. That haughty chief had taken pains to let him know that he was much taken with Raegan, that he debated keeping her for himself. He had no wife now—what if he did decide that Raegan would replace the dead woman?

The fear of that happening tied his stomach in knots. He had to force himself not to think of such an event happening. He had to make himself believe that Raegan would be sent back to him. For otherwise, the thought of her beautiful white ody clasped in Lone Wolf's arms would drive n out of his mind.

'he door opened behind Chase, and he turned ıead to smile at Star as she came and stood e him. The young girl suffered also, he knew. mall face was pinched from worry and sleepless nights. And Jamie was like a wild man, making the same threats against the Tillamooks that Chase himself had made at one time. Over and over, he'd had to point out to the angry young man how useless it would be to go after Raegan, that such an action would endanger them all. And he musn't forget Granny. That poor old soul was so upset that she hadn't spoken one cross word since his return.

"What are we gonna do, Chase?" Star spoke, a tremble in her voice. "How are we gonna bear it if we never see her again?"

"Don't say never, Star," Chase's voice was as hard as granite. "I'm givin' that bastard to the end of the day to release her. If she's not home by nightfall, I'm gonna have Rafferty head for Fort Laramie. That Indian will let her go when a troop of soldiers rides into his village."

Star did not speak the thoughts running through her mind. In the time it would take Rafferty to ride across half of Oregon, all of Idaho, then half of Wyoming, alert the Captain there of what was going on, then return to Big Pine, there would be snow up to their butts. It would be an impossible feat. Poor Chase was so upset he wasn't thinking straight. When she walked away from Chase, he wasn't even aware that she'd gone.

Chase lingered on the porch until nightfall. A million stars sparkled in a moonless sky, and still no Raegan. The long pacing had, however, brought him a sort of peace. He had arrived at the firm conviction that if he did slip into Lone Wolf's village and steal Raegan away, the Chief would not carry out his threat of killing every man, woman, and child in the area. The man had played on his fear of losing Raegan. Tomorrow, as soon as he could slip away from Jamie, he was going after his wife.

White Feather helped Raegan to lie down on the furs, then hurried to awaken his grandmother. They conversed a moment in their language, then the elderly woman rose and walked to Raegan's bed.

Raegan opened her eyes when she felt Grey Dove's palm on her forehead. The hand lingered there a moment, then moved to feel behind her ears, then pressed lightly on each side of her throat. The warm hand then moved down to her stomach and probbed gently just above her pelvis. A moment later, with an amused grin, Grey Dove say back on her heels and said something to White Feather that made him smile widely.

"What tickles you so, White Feather?" Raegan grunted, feeling that she might vomit again.

"You are going to have little one, Raegan!"

Raegan nodded her head weakly. "I know that, my little friend."

The boy jumped to his feet. "I must go tell father."

Raegan had been dozing when White Feather returned with his father, but came fully awake to a hand stroking her hair. Her eyes popped open to gaze into black ones that somehow seemed wistful.

"Why did you not say that you are with child?" Lone Wolf asked, "Why did your husband not tell me?"

Raegan gave a small shrug of her shoulders. "I did not think it would make any difference. And as for my husband, he does not know. I wanted to be sure first." She waited a minute, then asked with a mixture of hope and dread, "Will you let me go now?"

The chief was silent for so long that Raegan was sure he was going to say no. Helpless tears were forming in the back of her eyes when he lifted a questioning eyebrow at White Feather, who knelt anxiously on the other side of Raegan.

"Well, son, should I let the woman warrior return to her husband?"

"Yes, father," the boy answered at once. "Although it will sadden me to see her go, it is the honorable thing to do. If not for her, we would not have my little brother."

Regret leapt into the proud chief's eyes, and Raegan knew he was thinking of the wife who had given birth to that baby and had then died. In a split second, though, his eyes were wiped clean of all emotion. He rose, and gazing down at her, said, "Be ready to leave in an hour. First you will show me where my wife was taken so that I can bring her back to her village, and from there you can go home." He turned on his heel and quietly left the plank house.

When the door closed behind his father, White Feather moved to kneel beside Raegan. "I will feel bad when you leave me." There was a slight tremor in the boy's voice when he added, "I shall miss you."

"And I will miss you." Raegan sat up and took his small brown hands in hers. "Do you suppose your father will let you visit me occasionally?"

"No. Father would not want the habit broken of the Platte dividing our two races. It is wise not to break this unspoken truce. The fat man almost brought war between us."

"Yes," Raegan agreed sadly. "It's a shame, though, that it has to be this way."

The boy gently freed his hands and stood up. "You must get ready to leave now. My father does not like to be kept waiting."

"Yes." Raegan tried to keep her happiness from her voice. "I'll see you later," she said to his small back going through the door. She rose then and padded across the floor to where Boy lay sleeping in his grandmother's arms. When she knelt down, Grey Dove smiled at her and held out the baby.

Raegan cradled him against her chest, tears brimming in her eyes. She would never see the tiny mite again. She kissed his soft cheek, then handed him back to his grandmother. Grey Dove wrapped a blanket around him, then giving Raegan's shoulder an affecionate squeeze, she rose and also left the house.

It did not take Reagan long to prepare herself to leave. She washed her face in the basin of water that had been brought in the night before, brushed her hair, and straightened the furs on her bed. By the time she had smoothed out some of the wrinkles in her dress, Lone Wolf stalked into the house. "Are you ready?"

"Yes I am, but I would like to say good-bye to White Feather and Grey Dove. Do you know where I can find them?"

Lone Wolf shook his head. "Tillamooks do not say good-bye while alive. Only in death do we say those final words."

"Oh, but—"

"Come, we go now." The Chief interrupted her and stode toward the door. Raegan hurried after him.

Beauty stood saddled and waiting, a wild, shaggy Indian pony beside her. She gave a glad cry at seeing her pet and took the time to give the mare's shinny rump a pat before swinging onto her back. The air was brittle with cold as they headed out, and Roscoe's screams still rent the air.

Only once was there a short conversation between Raegan and Lone Wolf as they traveled a narrow path to the Platte. After several aborted attempts, Raegan said timidly, "Chief, I would like to speak of something that bothers me greatly, yet I hesitate to interfere in matters that shouldn't concern me."

A faint grin twitched the corner's of Lone Wolf's lips. "That is hard for me to believe, little warrior, but what is this matter that you will speak of anyway?"

She gave him a crooked smile, then began before she lost her nerve. "You know the attractive woman who served my meals?" When Lone

Wolf nodded, she went on, "It has come to my ears that she would like to be your second wife. I have observed her closely these days I've been in your village, and I've come to the conclusion that she is jealous of your children and would not be kind to them. She would neglect them, especially if the two of you should have children together."

The chief's face remained as stoic as usual as he answered, "Everything you have said, I have already thought. Do you think that as chief of my tribe I am not wise enough to choose the right woman to put in charge of my children, Fair One?"

"Oh no, of course not," Raegan hastened to assure the stiff back turned on her. "It's only that . . ."

"That my son has been mentioning his fears to you."

Raegan didn't answer yes or no, and a silence grew between them until they came to the river and crossed it. The Chief drew rein on the gravelly bank and waited for Beauty to splash up beside him. "Which way to my wife?" he wasted no time asking.

Raegan sat a minute getting her bearings and remembering Chase's words . . . a small valley about five miles west of Chief Wise Owl's village. She pointed in an easterly direction. "She was taken to a place about five miles west of an Indian village."

"Chief Wise Owl's village," Lone Wolf grunted. "I know its location." Without further words he turned his pony's head to the right, motioning Raegan to follow him.

It took about an hour for them to reach the pretty spot Chase had chosen. Raegan and the dead woman's husband drew rein beside the two canoes tied together, one inverted over over the other. Several minutes passed before Lone Wolf looked at Raegan, a pleased look in his eyes. "Your man has chosen well," he said softly. "I would leave her here if she was on the right side of the river."

"You will be unable to move her by yourself. Will you return later with help?"

"Yes. Tomorrow." He looked at Raegan and inquired lightly with teasing eyes, "Will we be safe from your big trapper, Fair One?"

Raegan knew that he was teasing her, for she knew that this stalwart Indian feared no man, and furthermore death held no fear for him either.

Her eyes twinkled up at him. "You are having fun at my expense, of course, but my husband will be so happy to have me home, he would help you take your wife back to your village."

His lids lowered to hide his expression, Lone Wolf leaned over and lifted a lock of her hair. Feeling its silkiness, squeezing it in his hand, he said softly, "Any man would be happy to have you in his home."

He let her hair slip through his fingers one more time, then turned his pony around and rode away, not looking back once. Raegan stared after him, knowing that she would think about the handsome Indian more than once. But there was a man waiting for her whom she would think of all the time. Her heart light, and her mind singing, she turned Beauty in the direction of the cabin, and Chase.

It was early in the afternoon before Chase could slip away from Jamie. Inside Sampson's stall, he slipped the bridle over the stallion's head, then lifted the saddle onto his back. He led him outside, glancing at the cabin to see if a face was peering out the window. Numerous trips had been made to that window by the four people who waited anxiously for Raegan's return.

He was tightening the saddle's cinches when something made him look up. On a distant hill, clear of trees, a horse and rider were silhoutted against the sky. He rubbed his eyes, afraid to believe what his mind told him. But when he caught a glint of red hair, his heart pounded so hard he thought it would burst.

"Raegan!" he breathed, "At last you're comin' home." He flung himself in the saddle, and clumps of soil flew as the stallion lunged away.

With glad cries, they met at the bottom of the hill, their mounts coming to rearing halts. Before the stallion's hooves returned to the ground Chase was off his back, sweeping Raegan out of her saddle.

For long moments they only held each other, giving heartfelt thanks to God for having reunited them. Then Chase held Raegan away and looked into her eyes with silent query.

"I'm fine, Chase." She cupped his whisker-stubbled face in her hands. "Outside of missing you and being frightened a few times, I am the same as when I left."

Chase squeezed her hard. "I was afraid Lone Wolf would . . ."

"No." Raegan placed a finger across his lips, shutting off the rest of his words. "Lone Wolf is a very honorable man. I know that he desired me, and had I been willing he would have made me his wife. But in the end he realized that could never be."

"Ah, but I've missed you," Chase said with a muffled groan as his lips came down on Raegan's with hungry urgency. When Raegan felt a persistent arousal jabbing at her stomach, she gave a throaty laugh. "I think it's time we got on home."

"Yes!" Chase agreed and lifted her onto Sampson's back and swung up behind her. Snuggled in his arms as they rode toward the cabin, Raegan told him about White Feather and Grey Dove, how they had befriended her and made life bearable while she was held captive.

"And what about Roscoe?" Chase asked. "Do you know how he was punished? Is he still alive?"

Raegan shuddered. "Let me tell you about that another time, Chase. Right now I can only say that he suffered as much as the Tillamook woman did at his hands."

"Indians are experts at exacting revenge," Chase said, then pulled Sampson to a halt in front of the cabin.

He was lifting Raegan to the ground when the door flew open and Star and Jamie burst through it. Star flew down the steps and threw herself into Raegan's arms, then gave a loud grunt as Jamie rushed up to wrap his arms around both of them, squeezing her between his body and Raegan's. Chase laughingly pulled Raegan free of the enthusiastic greeting, but Star clung to her arm as they stepped up on the porch and into the kitchen, where she was greeted by Granny.

"Well, girl, you finally made it back." Her thin lips were spread in wide snaggle-toothed smile as she gripped Raegan's hands. "And about time too. Chase ain't been fit to live with since you up took off with the little papoose . . . Are you all right, honey? Them heathens didn't beat you or nothin'?"

Raegan laughed softly. "No, I wasn't beaten, Granny, and I was treated very well."

"Good." Granny released her hands. "I can go home now with an easy mind. Jamie, stop that idiotic grinnin' and go saddle my mule."

"Yes, ma'am." Jamie saluted the old lady smartly, trying to hide his idiotic grin. As he walked toward the door, he was brought up short at her next words.

"And then I expect you and Star have somethin' to tell Raegan and Chase."

Raegan and Chase looked at him expectantly, but Jamie, after his slight pause, continued on out the door. When they transferred their gaze to Star, she only shrugged and changed the subject. "Are you hungry, Raegan?"

Granny let loose one of her cackling laughs. "I don't know about Raegan, but I ain't ever seen a hungier-lookin' man than Chase."

A dark red spread over Chase's face. "Granny," he said, "some day that tongue of yours is gonna cut your throat." He looked at Raegan, and his eyes grew smoky from what he read in hers. She was just as hungry as he was, and not for food either.

"Do you want to eat now?" he asked, his eyes saying he hoped she didn't.

Raegan smiled and shook her head. When he wrapped his arms around her shoulders and led her out of the kitchen, Granny snickered and said slyly, "Push that skillet to the back of the stove, Star. They won't be leavin' their room until suppertime."

Star nodded with a wide smile, and when Jamie returned shortly and asked where Chase and Raegan had got off to, she and Granny said at the same time, "Guess."

Jamie grinned, then said to Granny, "Come on, you old hag, your steed awaits to take you home."

Granny gave Star a hug, jabbed her elbow in Jamie's stomach, picked up the haversack holding her clothes, and marched outside, Jamie trailing along behind her.

When Chase led Raegan into their bedroom, she stood a minute, breathing in the familar smells, so unlike the odor of the Indian camp. "Oh, Chase." She turned in his arms. "I can't tell you how good it is to be home."

"You can't feel any better about it than I do," Chase whispered before closing his lips over hers. When he finally lifted his head, he said huskily, "I'm goin' to make love to you until we're too weak to get out of bed."

Raegan gazed up at him, her love shining in her eyes. Then, patting her stomach, she said softly,

"Don't get too rambunctious, love. You wouldn't want to hurt your little son or daughter."

"We're goin' to have a baby?" Chase asked in awed tones. When Raegan nodded happily, he said with a worried frown, "Maybe we shouldn't do anything."

"Oh yes, we're going to do something." Raegan looped her arms around his neck. "We're just not going to do anything fancy."

Chase scooped her up in his arms and laid her on the bed. He undressed her slowly, feasting his eyes on her loveliness. His eyes still on her, he hurried out of his own clothes and lay down beside her.

The hours passed, dusk came, and all the while Chase made tender love to his wife.

The next morning, Chase and Raegan stood on the back porch waving good-bye to Star and Jamie. "I still can't believe that they were able to keep their love for each other from us," Raegan said from within Chases's arms. "I knew there was a growing attraction between them, but I never dreamed they had fallen in love."

"I think it might have been my fault nothin' was ever said to us. After the first week I brought Star home with me, I warned Jamie off her. He was probably afraid to tell us."

"I wonder if they'll find her grandfather still alive?"

"I'm afraid not." Chase sighed. "But at least Star will have Jamie to console her."

Raegan tilted her head to look up at Chase. "Do you realize that for the first time we're going to have our home to ourselves?"

Chase nuzzled her throat and murmured thickly, "We can make love anytime, anywhere we want to. How about goin' back to bed?"

Raegan pulled his head down so that she could reach his lips. "You just spoke my mind."

* * *

Raegan's Light Bread

1 cake yeast	Two potatoes the size of Chase's fist
1½ tsp. sugar	2 tsp. salt
1½ pint warm water	Flour

While yeast is dissolving in warm water, cook the potatoes and mash them. Then add yeast water along with salt and sugar. Mix well and place in a crock and leave it on a warm hearth to rise. When the mixture has risen almost to top of crock, begin to add flour until you have a firm dough. Let it rise until double in size, then knead it real good before shaping it into loaves. Let it rise again, then bake in moderate oven until broom straw stuck in loaves comes out free of dough.

Chase loved to eat a slice of warm Light Bread spread with butter.